Praise for
Emily's House

"With lyrical prose and an irresistible narrative voice, Brown gives the reader a scrappy and little-known literary heroine to root for—the Irish maidservant who helped rescue Emily Dickinson's poems. The immigrant experience is lovingly rendered against the backdrop of family drama, the historical details are immersive, and Dickinson fans will love this novel!"

—Stephanie Dray, *New York Times* bestselling author of
The Women of Chateau Lafayette

"Amy Belding Brown brings us a warm, intimate, and rich portrayal of Irish immigrant Margaret Maher, maid and confidante to Emily Dickinson. Margaret's story gives us a fascinating glimpse into another time while placing us directly inside the Dickinson household. I was captivated by this story and I know you will be, too."

—Kathleen Grissom, *New York Times* bestselling author of
The Kitchen House

"What a joy it is to once again revel in Amy Belding Brown's incomparable voice. In *Emily's House*, Brown introduces us to the remarkable Irish maid who saved Emily Dickinson's unpublished oeuvre from certain destruction after her death. Margaret Maher's own disappointments mirrored her mistress's many, but the two women formed a bond so deep that if not for Maher's abiding determina[tion] . . . [b]een lost to us forever. D[o] . . . [tr]easure? I think we must, [a]

—R[o] . . . [Sh]e Is Mary Sutter

Other novels by Amy Belding Brown

Mr. Emerson's Wife
Flight of the Sparrow

Emily's House

Amy Belding Brown

Berkley

New York

BERKLEY
An imprint of Penguin Random House LLC
penguinrandomhouse.com

Library of Congress Cataloging-in-Publication Data

Names: Brown, Amy Belding, author.
Title: Emily's house / Amy Belding Brown.
Description: First edition. | New York : Berkley, 2021.
Identifiers: LCCN 2020050429 (print) | LCCN 2020050430 (ebook) |
ISBN 9780593199633 (trade paperback) | ISBN 9780593199640 (ebook)
Subjects: LCSH: Dickinson, Emily, 1830-1886—Fiction. |
Maher, Margaret, 1841-1924—Fiction. | GSAFD: Biographical fiction.
Classification: LCC PS3552.R6839 E45 2021 (print) | LCC PS3552.R6839 (ebook) |
DDC 813/.54—dc23
LC record available at https://lccn.loc.gov/2020050429
LC ebook record available at https://lccn.loc.gov/2020050430

First Edition: August 2021

Printed in the United States of America
1st Printing

Cover design by Emily Osborne
Cover images: dress by Crow's Eye Productions / Arcangel; hands and
house by Jasenka Arbanas / Arcangel
Book design by Nancy Resnick
Title page and part title art by Khosrov Hakobyan / Shutterstock.com

This book is dedicated to the memory of
Patricia Wyman Belding
1930–2018

beloved aunt, mentor, visionary, writer, and poet
whose cheerful curiosity and warm encouragement shaped
my early interest in writing and whose passion for
Emily Dickinson's work informed my own.

Part I

Thresholds

Chapter One

1916

More than once I've had the thought a life can be measured in doorways. Answering a knock or stepping over a sill ofttimes leads to what I'm not expecting. I've learned to be a bit curious when a threshold's being crossed. So you might think I'd be interested when Rosaleen Byrne comes banging into my kitchen with a new hat on her head and her mouth full of gossip. But I'm not in the mood for a chinwag this morning—up to my elbows in minced pork and bread mash. Yet here she is, all bustle and burn with the cold March air coming off her and her face red as the sausage I'm making.

"Margaret," she says, unbuttoning her coat like she's planning on staying, "I just heard the news and came straight here. Ran near all the way." Sure, she does look out of breath with her bosom heaving up and down. It's a bit concerning—she shouldn't be running anywhere at her age. Must be two or three years older than myself and I'm past seventy.

"What news is that?" I say. It's not likely she's heard anything interesting I don't already know. My boardinghouse in Kelley Square is the place everybody comes when they want to hear the latest. Rosaleen lives clear on the far side of Irish Hill. She's got a knack for digging up secrets—I'll give her that—though most of the time they're not secrets at all but tidbits common as spiders. I give the mix a few more squeezes and commence wiping my hands on my apron. One of my bad days, it is, the rheumatism pounding away in both thumbs, not to mention my knees.

"About the Dickinson property," Rosaleen says. "I'm guessing it's a shock to yourself."

I don't know what she's talking about, but I have a bad feeling. "Who was it told you?" I ask, still wiping my hands, choosing my words so as not to let on.

"The new maid that works for Mrs. Hills. The red-haired one. Ran into her in Cutler's Store and it's all she talked about." She already has her coat half off. Likely she's planning to dump it over the back of a chair instead of hanging it proper on a hook beside the door. "I expect half the town knows by now."

I nod as if I'm agreeing, but my temper's rising. I know she'll be revealing her gossip sooner or later, but it nettles me she's making such a show of it. God help me, I won't be giving her the satisfaction of asking.

I go to the sink to wash my hands and calm myself. Turn the tap and warm water splashes out. Sure, it still takes me by surprise after all those years yanking pump handles and filling buckets for heating. A daily miracle, it is—hot water conjured with just a flick of the wrist. I take my time, and when I turn around, Rosaleen's plunked herself down on a chair and is pulling a handkerchief out of her handbag.

"From what I hear that girl's head is always in a muddle," I say. "She's as likely to twist the truth as tell it."

"Aye, I've heard that too." Rosaleen snaps her bag shut and dabs her nose with the handkerchief. It's a fancy one, with deep lace at the hem. "But she says she got it word for word from Mrs. Hills herself. 'The big Dickinson house on Main Street is up for sale,' Mrs. Hills told her. And Dr. Bowen is thinking of buying it."

There's a snag in the middle of my chest. "Which house?" I hear the blade in my own voice. "She owns them both."

"Not the Evergreens, where she's living," Rosaleen says. "The big one next door they call the Homestead."

Miss Emily's house? I almost say it out loud. I have my answer, but God's truth, it rocks me. And in my head I'm thinking, *Emily won't like this*, as if she's still among the living.

Rosaleen says something else but the rumble of a train coming into the depot is drowning all sounds but itself. Takes a minute or two till the screaming of whistles and brakes passes, so I busy myself wiping the faucets. When the noise finally fades, she's still talking. "I hear it's been on the market two weeks but nobody here in Amherst knew a thing till today. Except Mattie D, of course. And maybe yourself—working for that family so many years and all?"

She's fishing, to be sure. But I won't have it spread all over Amherst I didn't know about the sale. Instead of answering, I scowl. Everybody in Amherst calls Emily's niece *Mattie D*, but hearing it come out of Rosaleen's mouth irks me. Feels like she's belittling my own family. "Her name is Madame Bianchi now," I say.

"Madame Bianchi." Rosaleen makes a snorting sound and opens her bag to put the handkerchief away. "What kind of name is that? Herself with her fortune and fancy ways, acting like a countess since she married that Russian. She's haughty as her mother before her."

"God keep her soul," I say quick to ward off the Faeries,

though I've sometimes had the same thought myself. But I don't like hearing any ill talk of the dead. Besides, I'd seen a different side of Sue Dickinson through Emily's eyes.

Rosaleen is casting a glance at the kettle on the cooker's back burner. I know she's hoping I'll be wetting the tea, but I've heard enough of her prattle and need to be alone to think my thoughts.

"Well," I say in a brisk way, "I promised my boarders sausages for supper. 'Tis sorry I am I can't be offering you a cup of tea, but it's getting on toward noon and my casings won't be stuffing themselves. And I expect you've got errands to be doing." I give her a kindly nod to gentle the sting.

She looks a bit startled but up she gets and fidgets herself into her coat, and soon enough I'm bundling her out the door. Sure, I'm glad to be seeing the back of her, though I know she'll likely be spending what's left of the morning noising it all over Amherst that Miss Margaret Maher's too full of herself to be sharing a cup of tea with a friend.

Soon as she's out the door, it strikes me I could have been right about the maid's story—it might not even be true. Wouldn't be the first time Rosaleen scattered fables amidst her gossip. From the window I watch her pass my brother-in-law's house and cross the yard to the train depot. Wonder how many other ears she'll be bending before she gets home today. Seems strange I didn't hear her news from my niece first. Nell's always stopping by to tell me what she hears around town. Makes it all the more unlikely there's reason to believe Rosaleen. The more I think on it, the less sense it makes. Why in Heaven's name would Mattie D be selling the Homestead? She loves the place as much as I do, surely. She's the last of the Dickinson line to own it, and she knows the big yellow house is a treasure, sitting so proud behind its handsome hedge and fence.

Taking care of the Homestead was my job for thirty years. When I left back in 1899 and walked down Main Street to my sister's place in Kelley Square, I thought I was shed of the Dickinsons for good. Felt like a blessing that sorry day, with Emily and Austin and Vinnie all gone to their graves and the house shut up like a tomb.

Now I can't pass the place without wanting to take another peek inside. I'm always glancing at the upstairs west windows, where Emily's bedroom was. More than once I've spied a white flutter there and wondered—was it a trick of the light, or maybe her ghost? The quare thing is I always walk on feeling more comfort than chill. As if the place is consecrated.

Mattie D inherited everything after Vinnie died. The houses and land and all her grandfather's money. Last time I saw her was at her mother's funeral. But I remember her best as a girl running along the path between the Homestead and the Evergreens. Carrying notes back and forth between her mother and Emily. Forty years ago, it must have been. She was lively and full of spark as Emily herself. The pair of them headstrong and fierce, full of secrets and schemes. Used to think they were clever as new-minted dollars. But Mattie D sometimes uses her cunning in heedless ways. Like running off to Europe and marrying a Russian. Like renting out the Homestead.

That unsettled me, to be sure, but I saw the need. A house needs people living inside or it goes to ruin. Needs curtains at the windows and lamplight glowing in the parlors at dusk. Needs the clinking of silverware on china and the creaking of stairs from time to time as folks go up and down. It's calmed me, knowing it still belongs to a Dickinson.

It's plain I need to find out what's true and what's not. Before it's too late.

And at the minute, smack in the midst of stuffing sausage casings, I resolve to pay a call to the Evergreens this very afternoon. I'll talk to Mattie D face-to-face and root out the truth. And if need be I'll give her a piece of my mind.

I finish up quick with the sausages and give the table and counters a good scrubbing. Scrub my hands too to get the sausage smell off them and then, for good measure, I rub them with a dollop of Hinds' Honey and Almond Cream from the bottle Nell gave me last Christmas.

In my bedroom I change into a clean skirt and blouse and—for good luck—pin my new hat to my head at a jaunty angle. It's when I'm regarding myself in the mirror I'm struck by a familiar jingly feeling—like I'm starting on a new adventure. Seems the Homestead still has the same uncanny pull on me it did back in 1869, when I first came under its spell.

Chapter Two

1869

It's said many a fateful change begins on a dreary day. And God's truth, there's none more dreary than a February afternoon with the snow coming down and the cold stabbing my bones. I'd been working as maid to Mrs. Talcott only four months—just temporary to tide me over. She didn't have many visitors, so when a knock came on her front door, I was curious who it was.

The man was tall and spindly, standing there tapping the porch floorboards with his fancy cane. Had a gold nob on top. Caught my eye, it did, even in that gray light. "I'm Mr. Dickinson," he said, and gave the cane another thump—made me look back to his face. It wasn't a pleasing face at all. Grim and hard with fierce brows and sharp little eyes.

Sure, I knew who he was. Everybody in Amherst knew of Edward Dickinson. His name was always turning up in the papers for one highfalutin thing or another. He was a lawyer and a landlord, treasurer of Amherst College, and a founder of the Agricultural College too. Called him the Squire, folks did, for his proud, swaggering ways. Many a time I spied him in the center of town, strutting along in his grand clothes, swinging that very cane.

I gave him a proper nod. "Come in, sir. If you'll wait in the parlor, I'll be fetching Mrs. Talcott."

He stamped the snow from his boots, took off his hat, and stepped over the sill. I waited for him to give me his coat, but he didn't take it off. Just laid his skinny hand on my arm and said, "You're Margaret Maher." He had the air of a man who thinks saying something makes it so.

"I am, sir," I said.

He gave me a tiny smile, with the corners of his mouth quirking up and the skin stretching stiff over the bones of his cheeks. It was plain he didn't do much smiling. "It's you I've come to see."

Sure, I couldn't think why. "Me, sir?" An evil thought prickled my mind. "Is it Tom Kelley?" My brother-in-law sometimes worked for the Squire inspecting railroad tracks and doing the odd job. Had he been struck by another accident—and himself still getting used to having only the one arm?

The Squire shook his head and a little bark came out of him. Might have been a laugh—I wasn't certain. "No, no," he said. "Tom's fine."

I felt a purity of relief, for Tom was a lovely man. Worked hard and brought his wages home to my sister and never took to the drink. Saved enough to buy a lot by the train depot and two square houses stood there now—one for himself and one for his brother James. Named the lot Kelley Square, like a country estate. Made me laugh, for what County Tipperary lad ever thought to be naming his house? Tom had ambitions, he did.

"In fact, it was Tom who suggested I come," the Squire said. "I'm here to hire you."

I frowned. Fourteen years I'd been living in America, and

working for the Boltwood family most of that time. Now I was done with all that and about to be making something of myself. Come Beltane, I'd be off to California where my brothers, Michael and Tommy, were already digging gold and silver out of the hills.

"Sure, I'm working for Mrs. Talcott now," I said.

"So I understand," he said. "But it's a temporary arrangement, is it not? I have it that her niece is coming from Baltimore next week and you won't be needed." It was plain he already knew my situation. He was a sly one, the Squire.

"I'm leaving town first of May, sir," I said, himself still standing there in his coat and scarf and holding his hat in his hand. "I won't be coming back. You'll be wanting to find somebody steady." I thought certain he'd turn around and go out the door. Who's so foolish to be hiring a maid when he knows she can only work a few weeks?

"I'm prepared to offer twice what Mrs. Talcott is paying," he said as if he'd not heard me. "I assume you'll be able to put the money to good use."

Twice the wages. My mind was calculating how much it would come to. Six weeks of work for double what I was getting could be earning me twenty dollars or more.

"We have an agreement, then," the Squire said, sticking out his hand for me to shake, though I'd said nothing. "I'm sure you know where we live. Just down Main Street. The yellow house on the left before the railroad tracks."

"I do, sir," I said, for didn't I walk past the very house every time I visited my sister?

He seemed not to notice I didn't shake his hand. "I shall expect you in a week, then." He popped his hat back on his head and went out the door.

"I'll think on it, sir," I called after him.

Down the steps he went and didn't look back. Left me standing in the doorway watching him go down Prospect Street till he turned the corner. Marching along like a fancy rooster, he was. Set me wondering if he believed I'd said yes, or if he thought himself so grand it didn't matter I had not.

I spied my friend Molly Ryan coming around the back of the Hollands' house with her market basket on her arm. Gave her a wave and went back inside. With luck I'd be chatting with her soon, and the Squire's offer would surely be a story worth telling.

In truth, though, his visit rattled me. If the Boltwoods got wind of it—and likely they would—they'd be tormented. It vexed them that the Dickinsons were thought more important than themselves and they wouldn't like me working for them. It's something I've noticed about gentry—for all their fancy manners, they don't admire one another. Mostly they just want to be grander than the rest.

Fanny Boltwood was the first one hired me when I came to Amherst and I was always grateful for her kindness. Not yet fifteen I was then, gawky as a foal and green to boot. But she lectured and scolded, and after a while, I was good as any maid in Amherst. Got so she even used to boast to her friends of my butter making.

Five years I worked in her big house, doing every kind of drudgery alongside her cook and housekeeper. Then her son married Clarinda Williams and Fanny sent me over to them. Clarinda, like Fanny, was overfond of correcting me, but I liked her well enough. I was her only servant and spent every waking minute keeping house and minding her little ones. When the family moved from Amherst to Washington, DC, and then to

Hartford in Connecticut, I was the one doing the planning and packing.

Sure, I'd still be in Hartford if not for my da dying. Got back to Amherst just two days before he took his last breath. Five days later, Tom fell off the Lamp Black Factory roof and crushed his bones to powder. Lost his arm and came so close to dying I heard the Banshee howling, and myself the only help poor Mary had for his nursing.

Clarinda got a temporary maid to take my place and begged me to return soon as Tom recovered. But it took all summer for him to heal—it was a blow to a big strong lad like himself. He had more than his share of pain, and the days so hot he had to lie on a cake of ice to keep from perishing of heatstroke. My sister couldn't have got along without me, not with six children and the littlest only four months old. But once Tom recovered and I was packing my trunk for Hartford, didn't I come down with the typhoid? Couldn't lift my head off the pillow for weeks and weeks.

Clarinda wrote me cheering letters and sent vials of tonic to cure me. In truth, I'd have gone back if my brother Tommy hadn't sat with me evenings reading out loud from *Four Months Among the Gold-Finders* and singing the praises of California. Before I was even able to get out of bed, the two of us were scheming to join Michael, who was already there working in the gold mines and sending letters about how grand the place was. Tommy and I agreed when we got there we'd put our money together to buy a house with room for taking in boarders. I'd run the place while Michael and Tommy were mining. I'd be making myself proud instead of drudging for rich folks. Helped cure me, those plans.

When Tommy left for California in October I wasn't yet

strong enough to go. But I promised to be following him come
May. Michael wrote he couldn't wait to see me again and he'd
already arranged to rent a room in San Francisco so I wouldn't
have to worry myself finding one. I bought my ticket and tucked
it in the bottom of my trunk. Every night I held the little
daguerreotype of himself and Michael in their California clothes
and said a prayer for the three of us. I took on temporary work,
putting up preserves for Mrs. Hill and cleaning the Lessey house
three times a week. Then Mrs. Talcott offered me a short-term
job. I saved every penny for the journey. It was to be my greatest
adventure.

Didn't have the courage to tell Clarinda, though. I thought it
best to wait till I got to California and write her a long explaining letter. I wanted to be far enough away there'd be no use trying to persuade me back.

The next morning I made quick work of my errand at the butcher's
and stopped by the Hollands' kitchen to have a chinwag with
Molly Ryan. Molly and myself had enjoyed many a chat. The
pair of us liked nothing better than putting our heads together
over a lady's magazine full of gowns and hats. But that day—with
Mrs. Talcott's veal fillet tucked in my basket at one end of the
table and the two of us having our tea at the other—we didn't
speak of fashion. I was too busy telling her about Squire Dickinson's offer.

Gawking, she was, with her brows raised and her eyes round
as dollars. "All that money—'tis a small fortune! Think what you
can be buying!"

She didn't have to tell me, for I'd already pictured soft wool
shawls on my shoulders and smart hats on my head. "'Tis tempt-

ing, surely," I said. "But I need to be saving the money for my boardinghouse in California."

"Your boardinghouse, is it?" Molly had a wicked twinkle in her eye. "Sure then, the Dickinsons are the folks to be working for, but you'll be earning every penny. From what I hear they're quare hawks, every one of them."

"Aye, I've heard so myself," I said, recalling a bit of tittle-tattle my sister had shared a few weeks back. "'Tis said they're hard folks, not friendly nor good-natured either. An ailing wife and two spinster daughters, the son living next door, disagreeable as his father and haughty besides."

Molly nodded. "And the older daughter—they say she's daft as a bedbug."

I took a look at the clock. "Lord have mercy! Mrs. Talcott will be wondering where I've got to!" I stood up quick and got my basket. I had no more time to be spending with Molly. Not when Mrs. Talcott's dinner was waiting to be made.

"He's worrying, Squire Dickinson is," I told Mary and Tom the next Sunday. "There's something dark and muddling about him. Like thunder itself, grumbling over the hills." Sunday was my day off and the three of us were sitting in the kitchen at Kelley Square after the washing up. Tom was having his third cup of tea and Mary was knitting a pair of gaiters while I rocked my youngest nephew in my arms. Jamie's teeth were coming in hard, giving him a fierce misery.

"Stern but fair is what he is," Tom said. "Are you taking the job, then? Did you give himself a yes?"

"Sure, he didn't give me the chance," I said. "Acted like he thought it was settled—without even a handshake."

Tom chuckled. "The Dickinsons have a way of getting what they want, surely."

"Like rich folks the world around," I said, thinking of Squire Cooke selling the farm in Tipperary and turning us Mahers into exiles from our own country.

Tom looked down into his cup. It was painted all over with green leaves, pretty as a picture. "That's as may be," he said. "But they're not mean-spirited. Pleasant enough once you get to know them."

"And how long does that take?" I asked, rocking Jamie. "I've not much time before I'm off to California."

Mary gave a long sigh. She'd made it plain she didn't like my going.

Tom looked up at me. "If the Squire's set on having you, you'll not be finding it too taxing. The rest live to please him."

Wasn't sure I liked the sound of that. Men used to being coddled are the troublesome ones.

"What of the older daughter?" I asked. "Is she cracked like they say?"

Tom shook his head. "Emily's not cracked. Peculiar, though, to be sure. I've seen her out weeding her garden, happy as the day is long. Then a buggy will turn into the drive and she'll disappear. Like she's made of the air itself."

Made me curious, what he was saying. "Is she bashful, then?"

He rubbed his shoulders back and forth along the chair rail. "I don't know what ails her and that's the truth. Most times she's like anyone else. Sharp with her tongue maybe. But all the family's that way."

"Mrs. Talcott calls her the Myth of Amherst," I said. "Says nobody's laid eyes on her in years."

Tom laughed. "Emily'd like that, I wager. Fond of making a

mystery, she is." He drank the last of his tea and clattered the cup down on its saucer. "A few years back she had trouble with her eyes. Went to Cambridge for treatment and stayed for months. Cured her mostly, though sometimes the light afflicts her. You'll not be seeing her, then."

There was the sound of running above us. Then a young one wailing. Mary shook her head. "Likely it's Katie," she said. "Woke up cranky and even Nell hasn't been able to make her happy to-day."

"I'll go have a word." Tom heaved himself out of his chair. The pin fixing his left sleeve to his shoulder came loose and the empty sleeve fluttered down.

Mary put down her knitting and got to her feet. "Come here, love, and I'll fix it." I watched her pin the sleeve and pat his chest. Sometimes she reminded me of Mam, with her tender ways and good common sense. In truth, she'd always been like a mother to my brothers and me. Fifteen years older than myself, she was, and I'd looked up to her all my life.

She turned to me. "Will you be wanting more tea?"

I moved Jamie to my other shoulder and rubbed his back, though he didn't need soothing, for he was fast asleep. "I'll burst if I have another drop, surely."

"Bless you for rocking the wee lad. And himself fretting all week." She held out her arms to take him.

"Go on with your knitting," I said. "He's grand where he is. Been missing the Boltwood children, I have, so Jamie's comforting my bones and mending my heart."

"There's naught wrong with your heart," Mary said. "'Tis your tongue wants mending."

I laughed. Rocking away with Jamie's little breaths tickling my neck, I was feeling too comfy to argue. Mary dropped back into her chair and took up her needles and we settled into a sisterly quiet.

After a time Mary said, "So you're still fixing on going, is it?"

"Aye, you know I am," I said. "Been wanting to see the place since before we left Tipperary." I thought of the thin little book about America I'd read as a schoolgirl. It belonged to the teacher and sat on a shelf by his desk. The story about California I read over and over. Seemed like it was the Garden of Eden. "Our brothers are prospering there, so why shouldn't I be prospering too?"

"I'll not be sparring with you," she said. "But I don't know what I would have done without you when Tom was hurt so."

My boldness melted on the spot and tears came into my throat. "It's not that I'm wanting to be away from you, Mary. I'm thinking you might persuade Tom to move out there too so we'll all be together again. Michael says it's sunny and warm the year round and there are more jobs than men."

She gave me a sad look. "We both know Tom won't be getting a regular job. He's lucky the Squire looks out for him. He's a good man, the Squire is."

Couldn't think of anything to say to that. I was quiet for a bit, listening to the click of Mary's needles and Jamie's sweet breathing. I heard Tom's feet on the stairs. "I'm guessing I'll soon be taking the measure of the man for myself," I said, "since I'm to be working in his house. Sounds like doing his bidding could be a kind of adventure itself."

Chapter Three

It was sleeting the morning I started at the Dickinson house. Had the look of a fortress as I drew near, bowing my head against bits of ice spinning in the frozen air. Like needles, they were, pricking my face and bouncing off my cape. I unlatched the carriage gate and followed the drive past a side porch around to the back of the house. Only family and guests were to be going in and out the front, Tom said.

Close behind the house was a barn. Sure, it was comforting as a milk cow, seeing it, putting me in mind of the farm in Tipperary and giving me a homesick tingle. Had a notion to step inside just to be smelling the hay and running my hand down a warm animal flank.

Instead, I pulled my hood tighter and gave the house a hard look. It was massive—two stories with an attic and a cupola, the porch on the west end and a long ell on the east. Close up I could see the walls were brick under the yellow paint. Shutters the same dark green as my calico dress framed the windows. A handsome house, surely, but something about the place made my skin prickle. Felt like sorrow was rising off it like steam from a kettle at the boil. I squeezed my eyes shut. Maybe a sad spirit was haunting the place, or a Faery was warning me off. I waited till the feeling eased before knocking on the ell door.

It was a few minutes till I heard footsteps and the door opened to a pretty, round-faced woman. She had a big orange cat draped over her arm. "Can I help you?" Her voice was crispy, but then she said, "Oh, you must be the new maid," in a kinder way. Before I could get out an answer, she waved me in and shut the door quick behind me. In a shed we were, with fresh-split wood stacked against the far wall and a narrow stairway on my right.

"Margaret, isn't it?" She didn't wait for my answer. "I'm Lavinia. Hang your cape on a peg there and I'll show you around." She gave me a smile—a little quirk at the corners of her cunning mouth. I still hadn't said a word—wasn't given a chance, for she didn't stop talking. "You must call me Vinnie. Emily and I don't stand on ceremony. But be sure to address our mother as *Mrs. Dickinson* or *ma'am*. She's dreadfully old-fashioned."

I was surprised at the careless way she spoke of her mother, but there was no time for pondering. I followed her through a passage cluttered with brooms and mops, and into a washroom. First thing caught my eye was the copper kettle set into a brick firebox. It was filled with water and steaming away. I'd never worked in a place with the luxury of having hot water close to hand all day. I just stood admiring the wondrous thing.

"I see you've noticed one of Father's improvements," Vinnie said. "He's quite proud of it—and our soapstone sink." She waved her hand at the east wall, where a stack of dirty pots was waiting to be scoured. "The very *best* soapstone, we've been told." She blinked her eyes in a comical way. "The well is under the kitchen, so you won't have to step outside to fetch water." She pointed to the pump mounted next to the sink and I smiled. It was welcome news, surely.

"Come along," she said, hurrying me into the kitchen. Sleet was ticking on the windowpanes and gray light leaked onto the walls and floor. But the room was warm and cheery with its yellow casings and walls green as a Tipperary meadow.

"Wait here and warm yourself by the stove while I fetch Mother." She bustled away through another doorway.

I stood where she'd left me, picturing myself working there. Looked like everything I'd be needing was at hand—a grand cooker, a long worktable, four stout chairs, and a stool. Tubs and basins, shelves and cupboards and a drying rack filled with dish towels and cloths. The oven was decorated with a pretty medallion and the warming doors had fancy scrolls. Sure, somebody in the house liked pretty things. A happy bubble grew in the pit of my stomach. It was not at all the feeling I was expecting.

Vinnie came back with a thin woman whose skin was gray as I'd ever seen. I thought surely she was at Death's door. "Mother, this is Margaret." The cat Vinnie was holding glared at me with wicked yellow eyes and swished its tail like a beast. Sure, I was never fond of cats—they're always up to one mischief or another.

"Margaret." Mrs. Dickinson nodded. She was twisting a little watch on a chain. A slow twisting, like the bones in her hand might be breaking if she moved too quick. "You're highly regarded in the village for your industry and skill." She gave me a little smile. "We are so pleased you could come to us. So very pleased."

For the first time since I stepped through the door, I spoke. "Thank you, ma'am." I knew I ought to be saying I was happy to be working for them, but my tongue wouldn't gather the words.

"You will find we live quite simply." Her tired eyes cast a wave of pity through me. "My daughters and I are used to doing a good deal of the housekeeping. But we need someone to keep us organized." There was something fluttery about her. Made me think of a trapped bird, she did. "To help us put our best face forward, if you will."

"I'll do my duty, ma'am," I said. "Best as I can."

"Very good," she said. "Have you made arrangements to have your things sent?"

"My nephew's bringing my trunk round directly," I said, hoping young Michael wouldn't forget. He was Mary's eldest boy, but only eleven and not overfond of keeping his promises.

"Excellent." The fluttery smile again, and then her lips thinned. "You may have Thursday afternoons and Sundays off," she said. "I believe that's standard. Mr. Dickinson comes home from his office every day at noon, and likes his dinner ready when he walks in the door." She fluttered her hand toward a tall cupboard. "There's a ham already in the safe for today. I brought it up from the cellar earlier."

I nodded. "Very good, ma'am."

"Lavinia will show you to your room so you can settle in before starting dinner. We eat promptly at noon." She turned and slipped away.

Vinnie gave me a wink and led me through a pantry, up narrow curving stairs, and along a hall. "You can use the back stairs if you want, but these are more direct. And don't let Mother alarm you. She means well. If you please Father, you'll please her."

Lucky I was behind her, or she'd have seen me rolling my eyes. Didn't matter if I pleased any of them. I'd be gone from this house by the end of April.

She opened a narrow door and stepped back. "Here you are," she said, and there she left me—in a gray room plain as a monk's cell. It had a quare shape, for it was wrapped around a chimney.

Sure, the warmth of it was welcome on this winter day. It had two little windows, a bed and chair, a little chest of drawers, and three pegs on the wall. I was glad to see there was room for my trunk—the same trunk that had crossed the water with us Maher children when we emigrated, with all our worldly goods packed in tight together. Da, it was, gave me the key to it the day we left, and I still wore it around my neck.

I peered out a window at the snowy yard and the long picket fence going down the street toward the railroad tracks. It was a comfort knowing my sister was a short walk away. I poked around the room, sat on the chair to try it, opened and closed the chest drawers, and tested the bed—it was lumpy and sagged in the middle. It would take some getting used to, but I could endure it. I'd slept on worse, surely. I crossed myself and said a quick prayer for patience, then looked out the window again. There was no sign of my nephew—only a stray dog trotting down the street, minding his own business.

Standing there, I felt the house folding itself around me. It was so quiet I had the feeling nobody but myself was in it, though such a thought was nonsense, surely. I'd seen Vinnie and Mrs. Dickinson with my own eyes—and surely Emily was somewhere in the place. I waited long as I could bear, then slipped into the hallway and crept down the stairs I'd come up, quiet as I could over the creaking risers. I heard no sound except myself. But when I stepped into the kitchen, there was a woman standing at the west windows, looking out. A woman with red hair tucked into a brown net at her neck and wearing a dress white as the snow in the yard.

To be sure, I didn't move forward nor back, just stood like a stone watching the woman everybody'd heard of but never saw—the Myth of Amherst herself. It was like standing in a dream waiting for what would happen next, everything misty and strange.

After a minute she turned. She didn't seem surprised to see me. "You're Margaret, aren't you?" Her voice reminded me of the low notes of a fiddle.

"I am," I said.

She wasn't as pretty as I expected—not half as fetching as her sister—though I couldn't for the life of me have told you what I *was* expecting. But she wasn't plain either. Uncommon-looking, with that thick hair curling around her pale face. And her eyes—they weren't brown nor gray but a quare mixing of hazel wood and maple together, and maybe a bit of darker oak. Don't know why trees came to my mind, but so they did.

"I'm Emily," she said, still looking at me. The little hairs rose on my neck. For sure as it was sleeting outside I knew I was being seen through and through. She was taking the whole of myself in at one glance. The feeling was so strong I looked away.

My eyes lit on the sink with its stack of pots. "Excuse me, miss," I said. "I was just coming down to see if my nephew has delivered my trunk yet." A lie, for I'd been watching and seen no sign of him. A double lie because it was the confinement, not the trunk, that drove me from the room. "Sure, I'll be doing the washing up now while I wait." I hurried into the washroom.

"Be off with you, then," she said, pronouncing her words in an Irish way. Her laugh followed and my back went tight. I don't like being mocked, not even if it's my betters doing the mocking. I pumped water into the sink and let the splash of it drown her voice. The soapstone was smooth and cold under my fingers.

～

Young Michael soon came knocking with my trunk in his arms and his mouth full of excuses for being late. I told him I didn't want to hear his blather and made him carry the trunk upstairs. "Mind you don't bump the walls," I warned.

"It's uncommon cold out," he said, following me into the room and plunking the trunk down. His chest was heaving—and no wonder. The trunk was packed full and not an easy thing to be carrying. But I had to smile—it was plain he was trying to prove how manly he was.

"It's an awful quiet house," he said.

I thought of Kelley Square with all its coming and going and happy family noise. In truth, he was saying what I thought myself. "'Tis how the gentry live," I said. "Quiet and proper."

"I'm glad I'm not rich, then," he said. "Would give me the spooks. Have you met her yet?" He was standing by the trunk, his hands on his bony hips and his elbows poking out like tree knots.

"Met who?" I said, pretending I didn't know who he was asking after.

"The quare one," he said. "Emily."

"'Tis no concern of yours," I said. "Now go on home before the mistress finds you sneaking around her house."

He dug in his pocket and pulled out an envelope. All wadded up and crumpled, it was. "It's for you," he said. "Came in today's mail."

It was from Clarinda Boltwood—another letter begging me to hurry back to Hartford and going on about how sad the house felt without me in it. She wrote a whole page about her boys. Missing me, they were, little Georgie driving her to distraction asking where I was. Felt a pang of guilt for not telling her my plans.

When I looked up Michael was snooping around the room, peering under the bed like he was hunting treasure. I slid the letter into my pocket. "Go along now, lad," I said. "And tell your mam I'll be seeing her on Sunday, same as always."

It was quick work putting my room to rights—in truth, there wasn't much to be done. The trunk was a grand fit under the window. I hung my brown calico and extra shift on the hooks and put the rest of the clothes in the chest. I made up the bed with the sheets and blankets folded at its foot and tried to fluff the pillow but the down inside was so old it wouldn't puff, so it just lay on the bed flat as a flounder. I propped my daguerreotype of Michael and Tommy on the little chest of drawers and slid my rosary under my pillow for safekeeping.

It was Mam gave me the rosary before the crossing from Ireland. Said it was given her by a kindly friar when she went on pilgrimage to Saint Patrick's Well in Clonmel. Made of goat's horn and she'd no idea how old it was—it could have been carved in the time of Saint Patrick himself, she said. A beautiful thing, it was. The wee little beads so pale they looked like pearls. The day she slipped it into my pocket, I promised myself it was the only one I'd ever use.

I went back downstairs to have another look around before starting dinner. I poked through the cupboards and shelves, finding all the necessaries for doing my job: bowls and pots and skillets, bread pans, ladles, and a big covered butter crock. A flour barrel stood in one corner of the pantry and a cone of sugar sat on a shelf beside a jug of molasses.

I was taking the ham out of the cupboard when I heard footsteps. I turned to look but no one was there. The house was too

quiet, to be sure. Tom had warned me the Dickinsons kept themselves to themselves even in their own house, but this was quare
strange. Michael was right—the place was spooky.

Working in that silent kitchen as the gray morning bled away
toward noon, I felt a wave of sorrow I couldn't account for. It was
so deep I wondered if a ghost had crossed the threshold. God's
truth, the only thing keeping me from leaving the Homestead
that minute was my own pride.

Chapter Four

What a fuss and flurry the Dickinson family made when the Squire came home for dinner. You'd think they'd not laid eyes on himself for weeks. I was in the kitchen spooning mint jelly into a glass bowl when I heard the front door open and shut. Then a great swishing of skirts and slippers as the family rushed to greet him. Next the Squire's voice rumbling through the wall and Mrs. Dickinson's chirpy responses.

My hands were buttery from nerves. But I picked up the serving tray with its platter of ham and bowls of potatoes and parsnips, took a deep breath, and went through the pantry into the dining room. It was jumbled with heavy furniture—a black sofa and a sideboard topped with a soup tureen stuffed with papers. The dining table was in the midst of it all, covered in the linen and blue china Vinnie had told me to use for setting.

The family was already sitting down, except for Emily. Her plate and silverware were waiting but she was nowhere to be seen. I set the platter in front of the Squire.

"Thank you, Margaret." He picked up his napkin and patted it over his knees.

I looked at the empty place. "Should I be taking a tray up to Miss Emily, then?"

The look Mrs. Dickinson gave Vinnie put me in mind of a scared rabbit, but Vinnie smiled and flickered her fingers. "Sometimes she's late. You go on and eat now, Margaret. If she doesn't come down, I'll bring a tray up to her later."

The Squire gave me a stiff nod, so I went back and ate my meal in the kitchen, listening for Mrs. Dickinson's call to clear things away and bring in the pudding. I wondered what was wrong with Emily. Maybe she was peevish or had a headache. Maybe her sister and herself had a spat.

I'd seen enough of the world to know rich folks are petty and small as anybody. They can squabble and storm over the littlest things, no matter how grand they are entertaining their friends. But usually they do things proper when it comes to dinner and socials and such. So it was curious the careless way they took Emily's not being there.

Her chair sat empty all through dinner and dessert, and by the time I cleared things away, Vinnie had made up a plate of food and carried it upstairs.

After I finished the washing up, Vinnie showed me through the rest of the house. It was an unsettling place that winter afternoon. From the dining room off the pantry, we went down a hall full of shadows and hard angles to the front part of the house. There were two parlors, front and back, fussed with chairs and tables and settees. A square piano stood in one corner, like a beast in the gloom waiting to be noticed. The walls were covered with portraits and landscapes and etchings in great gilt frames. Heavy green draperies covered the long windows.

The library was across the hall—a dark room with shelves of books stretching all the way to the ceiling. It near took my breath away, all those pages and pages of words to be reading. In the middle of the room was a great desk, so solid it looked like it might have been lodged in that spot before the house was built.

"Father's desk," Vinnie said when I ran my hand over the shiny top. "You must not touch anything on it. Mother's the only one allowed to dust here."

It surprised me, Mrs. Dickinson doing housework. It was a task neither Clarinda nor Fanny Boltwood would ever have stooped to. I followed Vinnie back into the hall and up the front stairs. Something made me stop when I reached the top—a quare pinched feeling as if the air had all been sucked out of the second floor.

"Margaret?" Vinnie's voice brought me back to myself. She was standing at the far end of the hall. "This is my bedroom," she said, opening a door so I could see. "Emily's is across the hall, but we won't go in. She can't bear interruptions."

Interruptions from what? I wanted to know, but all I did was nod.

"First thing in the morning you're to light the bedchamber fires," she said. "Except Emily's. If she leaves the door open a crack, that's her signal that she wants her fire lit too. But if the door's tight shut, you're not to go in."

"Not even if I knock, miss?" I couldn't fathom anyone wanting to lie in a cold room on a winter morning when a fire's easily laid by a maid.

"Never," she said firmly.

There was a guest room next to Emily's and the master bedchamber down a short hall. Vinnie showed me a linen closet and storage room and the narrow stairs up to the attic and cupola. "You're not to go up there unless you're told," she said. Sure, I didn't ask why, though it puzzled me. I was always running up to the attic to fetch something at the Boltwoods' and Mrs. Talcott's. "And use the back stairs to the servants' wing when your duties take you up and down."

I didn't tell her I'd be using whatever stairs were handy to my task. When a job is new, it's best to keep your mouth shut and your eyes open.

In truth, I think it was the house itself kept me quiet that first day. Holding my tongue doesn't come natural to me. It's a rare day I'm not speaking what's on my mind. But the place made my lips pinch tight over my teeth, till by the end of that day it was all I could do to whisper, "Yes, ma'am," when Mrs. Dickinson sent me off to bank the fires for the night.

Took me some time to go to sleep on that lumpy bed. The house felt too big around me. Too many empty rooms and too much shadowy air. Too much space for ghosts.

It took me a week to settle in at the Homestead. Like any place, it had its own peculiarities. Outside the kitchen door there was a flagstone patch the Dickinsons liked to call a *piazza*. And I quick learned the porch on the west side wasn't a porch at all, but a *veranda*. The house itself was full of hidden nooks and crannies. I once opened a cupboard to get some crockery and found a little door in the back stuffed with papers—laundry lists and medicine receipts and registers of expenses. In the room next to mine, there was a big crate of old frocks. Fancy, they were—made of velvets and fine wools—but long out of style. And one dreary afternoon when Vinnie and Mrs. Dickinson were out, I crept up to the third floor and poked round the attic.

The next day I climbed the twisting stairs all the way to the cupola, and stepped up into a room so small it could hold no more than two people. Nothing was in it besides an old chair, but God's truth, the place took my breath away. Four pairs of doubled windows washed the place in light and every inch of the room—walls, casings, even the floor—was painted pure white. I stood marveling, till I thought to wonder why I wasn't supposed to be up here. Who'd be caring if a maid took a few minutes for herself at the top of the house? It was a quiet, peaceful place, and the only room where I could be seeing Kelley Square.

For all the Homestead's mysteries, one thing was sure—being maid there was a sight easier than at the Boltwoods'. The wages were better, there were no little ones to be minding, and I wasn't the only one doing chores. Vinnie swept and dusted the dining room and parlors while Mrs. Dickinson aired the bedrooms. Emily mended clothes and did most of the baking. Vinnie told me the Squire favored Emily's bread so much he wouldn't eat any other. It lightened my work, surely, since I was the Dickinsons' only house servant.

One of the chores Vinnie set me was playing with her cats. A nuisance, to be sure, and foolish besides. She was forever taking in strays. She had near a dozen—most of them barn cats. But her favorites spent all their days indoors. Five of them there were, and she'd given them names. Tabby and Tootsie were good mousers, so I didn't mind them slinking about the pantry. But the rest didn't do a thing to earn their suppers and were always underfoot, mewling and rubbing against my skirts to trip me up. Made me grumble, petting them, for I surely could have been putting myself to better use. Later I learned Emily had no liking for them either.

Emily was as Tom said—there and not there. I never knew when I'd be seeing her. Some days she kept to her room from morning till night. Others she was already in the kitchen when I went down to kindle the fire. I'd find her measuring flour into a yellow mixing bowl or sitting by the west window, writing on scraps of paper, murmuring to herself.

Didn't say much to me. Saved her talking for others. Times I had the feeling she was listening to a far-off conversation in the air—or maybe just hearing whatever was in her own head.

Most afternoons she flitted about the house or worked in her conservatory—the narrow room off the library full of plants and windows. Vinnie said the Squire had it built for her, and I think it was a kind of hiding place, for nobody else went in or out without herself inviting them. Once I heard her singing little tunes in there—sounded like a bird in a forest.

Emily had a habit of coming into a room without making a sound. Many times I chanced to look up and she'd be standing a few feet away, just *watching* me, and myself having no idea how long she'd been looking. The first time it happened, she was mixing dough at one end of the big worktable while I was chopping meat at the other. I felt a prickle on my cheek, and when I turned, she was staring at me with those great eyes of hers.

"Are you needing me to be doing something for you now, miss?" I asked. But she shook her head and went back to her measuring and mixing.

Gave me the shivers, it did, but I got used to it after a while. Didn't startle every time, knowing it was just Emily's way. I began talking to her, for it eased the silence of the kitchen. When she didn't answer, I'd just rattle on. It wasn't like talking to the air, and it wasn't like a chat either, but I was glad she didn't seem to mind, because the truth of it was I liked the company.

One day I told her about the time I chased a rascally pig

across Da's potato field. She stopped her mixing and laughed. "You're a wild one, Maggie," she said. Her laughter was a pleasure to my ears. But I didn't care for her calling me *Maggie*.

"My name's Margaret, miss," I said.

She smiled. "But I've decided Maggie is what I shall call you. It's a fine name—one of my favorites, in fact. I've sometimes wished it were my own. Don't you like it?"

It was the most she'd said to me at one time and it didn't seem friendly, in spite of her smiling. I couldn't think why she'd favor a country name like Maggie. Margaret wasn't a hard name for Americans to be saying, like some. "Sure, I'd like it well enough if it was my own," I told her. "But I was born Margaret and have always been called Margaret."

She turned out the dough on the board and rolled up her sleeves. "We've had other Margarets," she said. She could have been talking to herself for all the notice she took of me. "But none of them were at all like you. So you must be Maggie."

And from that day on at the Homestead I was always *Maggie*.

It was *Maggie, can you help move this table?* Or *Maggie, come and see this bird!* Or a hundred other requests, but never *Margaret*, not even from the mouths of the Squire or Mrs. Dickinson. I got used to it, but I can't say I ever liked it. From the time I was a child, I knew names had meanings—Mam once told me the name Margaret means *pearl*. She said a pearl's the only jewel that needs no cutting or polishing. Comes perfect from the hand of God Himself. And I ought to be treasuring myself like one.

But the name Maggie meant nothing at all.

Chapter Five

The first time I came face-to-face with Sue Dickinson, I'd been chopping salt pork and stale bread to make a stuffing. I heard a thump and knew right off it was the door at the back end of the front hall—the one Vinnie was always using when she went out. I knew it wasn't herself, though, for she and her mother had already gone off to Northampton in the carriage.

I put down my knife, wiped my hands on my apron, and went to see who it was came in without knocking. Readying myself to be chasing them out. Hurried through the pantry and near bumped into a woman coming down the hall from the parlors. Wearing a cape with a fur collar, she was, and even in the gloom I could see she was handsome.

"Where's Emily?" she said. It was more order than question.

In truth, I wasn't sure. Likely in her room or the conservatory, since I hadn't heard her go outside. My brain was jumping—trying to figure who the woman was and what to do with her. Took me a minute to unstick my tongue.

"If you'll wait in the parlor, ma'am," I said, "I'll find out if Miss Emily is receiving visitors today."

She tipped her head back and raised her chin so she was looking down her nose at me. "Don't be absurd." She had a sharp, clear voice. "I'll find her myself. You can go back to wherever you came from."

She said it like she was sending me all the way back to Ireland. It was clear she had no use for me—just wanted me out of her way. I squared my shoulders and stepped to block her. I'd see to it she didn't disturb Emily, whoever she was.

And just that minute didn't I hear Emily's footsteps hurrying down the stairs? The woman pushed past me as Emily came into the hall and the two of them near threw themselves into each other's arms. "Oh, Sue—you came!" Emily's voice was full of feeling, as if they were long-lost sisters who hadn't seen each other in years. And without giving me a glance, Emily whisked her off to the conservatory. Wasn't till then my brain woke up and I comprehended the woman was Susan Dickinson, married to Austin, Emily's elder brother.

Should have known who she was the minute I laid eyes on her. I'd seen her before from a distance, riding along in her carriage and taking the air on the town common. I'd heard about her grand entertainments and how the gentry of Amherst clamored for her invitations. The queen of Amherst society, folks said.

Seemed quare she and Emily were so attached—they weren't a bit alike. Sue was elegant and sociable, while Emily was plain and kept to herself. Took me a few weeks before I saw the sense of it. They had the same way of talking about books. And near breathless, the pair of them, when it came to poems. They liked nothing better than whispering together in the shadowy corridor between the dining room and parlors. They even had a name for it—called it the Northwest Passage. Gave it an air of mystery and adventure.

Never knew what Emily and Sue said to each other, though. They kept their secrets close, those two.

Just when I settled in, there came a day set me back on my heels. It was the middle of March with a warm thread in the air, smelling of a thaw. Spent the morning ironing and I didn't begin my errands till after dinner. I was hurrying along North Pleasant Street when I spied Fanny Boltwood walking toward me. She was leaning on her husband's arm and looking weary and sad. I'd heard news her brother was taken sick and maybe dying, so my heart went out to her. I waved and called, "'Tis good to be seeing yourself, Mrs. Boltwood. I hope Mr. Shepard's better. I've been saying prayers for him."

But Fanny didn't say a word, didn't even look at me. Nor Mr. Boltwood either. At first I thought they hadn't heard me. But then they came closer and walked right past, looking straight ahead. My belly clenched like I'd been punched. It was plain as day they were *cutting* me.

My pity for Fanny turned to vinegar. I stood in front of the hat shop watching them walk on down the street. A little wind came up, scraping the skin on my face and rocking the shop sign so it creaked. Humiliation covered me like a cloak—I couldn't even move at first. Then, slow as an old woman, I headed back to the Homestead, though by the time I turned onto Main Street, I could hardly see, the tears were running from my eyes so.

For days I was filled with sorrow and shame. I wondered how to find out what was wrong. I tried to think what I'd do if I saw them again. But the Boltwoods were scarce as gold in a beggar's pocket.

Then one icy afternoon, Mrs. Dickinson bid me carry a basket of cake and jam to the Boltwood house, with a note for

Mr. Shepard. Didn't want to go, surely, and I fretted every step of the way.

The Boltwoods lived near the College. I went round to the back and found Ellen, their cook, doing the washing up. She was happy to see me—left the dirty dishes soaking, wet the tea, and set out a plate of biscuits to share while we chatted.

"'Tis a surprise seeing you turn up," she said. "I thought you were in California, likely married by now to a handsome lad with money in his pockets." Her eyes were sparking, and no wonder. Didn't every maid dream of finding money and love at the same time? "But here you are, still in Amherst and working for the Dickinsons."

"Not for long." I helped myself to a biscuit. "First of May I'll be boarding a ship for San Francisco."

"Sure, I'm not believing it!" she whispered.

"What's the chatter here?" The biscuit was tasty, but dry. Not like the sweet little cakes Emily made.

"Mr. Shepard's sinking," she told me. "The mistress is very low—and no wonder. But it makes her a bear to work for. Can't do a thing to please her these days."

I'd nodded and was about to ask if they'd hired a new house-keeper, when footsteps made her bolt out of her chair and busy herself at the cooker. I turned in my own chair to see Mr. Bolt-wood walking into the kitchen, big as life.

I knew he saw me. I watched his eyes slick across the room and stop. For just a flash I thought he was going to speak. But he turned his head away and went straight through to the dining room. Never said a word.

For a minute I didn't move—it was a shock to be passed over by a man whose house I'd cleaned for years. I got up quick and carried my cup to the sink. "I'd best be going." My voice had cracks in it. "We'll finish our chat another time."

Ellen nodded but we both knew I wouldn't be coming back. And when I saw her at the post office three days later, she said Mr. Boltwood told her I wasn't to step inside the house. "He said you care nothing about his family," she whispered. Her face was bright red. "Says you've betrayed them working for the Dickinsons. Told me I'd best keep my distance from you or they'll be turning me out."

I gave her a hug and told her not to fret. "They're cross because I have dreams of my own, is all," I said. "They can't think past what's best for themselves—like rich folk everywhere." But there was a cold stone in the back of my throat.

My troubles with the senior Boltwoods made Clarinda's letters all the harder to be reading. At the end of March came a flood of them. Letter after letter she wrote, so many Vinnie started noticing and got snippy. Told me I oughtn't to be getting so much mail—it wasn't seemly for maids, she said. It struck me maybe she thought they were love notes from a lad. One day, when we were polishing the dining room furniture, I told her there was nothing wicked about the letters—they were from my former mistress in Hartford.

Vinnie stopped her polishing and looked at me. "You're planning to leave Amherst," she said. "You're going back to Hartford, aren't you?"

"It's not Hartford I'll be going to," I said, thinking of Clarinda's latest note tucked in my pocket. "'Tis California. To be joining my brothers." I wondered if she heard the spark in my voice.

She stood with her rag hanging in midair. She had the look of a spooked rabbit. "Surely you're jesting."

"I amn't," I told her. "Mr. Dickinson already knows." I saw a smudge on the table and gave it a swipe. "I told him myself when he hired me."

Vinnie stood very straight, making herself taller. She looked like her mother, proper as Queen Victoria, with her pretty mouth turned down. "Father never mentioned it," she said. "And Emily won't like it." She dropped her rag and went out of the room, leaving me wondering what Emily had to do with it. The cloth lay where she'd left it, a dirty scrap of gray on the shining table, limp as a dying bird.

In truth, I felt a bit guilty leaving the Dickinsons. I knew good maids were hard to come by. The Squire paid good wages, Mrs. Dickinson was patient with my mistakes, and Emily and Vinnie never carped on my faults. I fretted for a week till I had the clever thought I'd find somebody to replace me. I began asking around. Did anyone know of a hard worker who cooked and cleaned and kept her mouth shut? I finally found a girl in Palmer who'd worked for the Dickinsons before and talked her into taking my place. Felt better after that. All I had to do was tell the Squire.

Before I got the chance, he sent for me. Vinnie, it was, told me he was waiting in the library.

"What's it about, then?" I asked.

"I've no idea," she said. "Father can be very secretive."

A feeling of doom came over me as I hurried down the hall. The door was open and there was himself sitting in his chair behind his grand desk with those lovely books all around.

"You were wanting to see me, sir?" I stepped into the room.

He gave me a little smile. A rare thing, that smile, so I thought maybe he'd be telling me some good news

"Close the door, Maggie, and sit down." He nodded at the leather chair by the window. Gave me a minute to collect myself before he said, "I've been informed that you have plans to relocate to California."

"I do, sir." Made me smile, thinking of it. "You'll remember I said I'd not be working past April."

Even in the dim light I could see his frown coming on. "Unfortunately," he said, "it seems your plans must be postponed. I received a letter from your brother Thomas today." He plucked an envelope from his desk and gave it a wave.

"Tommy?" I couldn't think why Tommy would be writing to the Squire.

"Yes, indeed," he said. "He asks me to tell you he no longer wants you to join him. The journey is risky and the camps are rife with crime and debauchery. He knows you have a good position here and hopes you will remain with us in Amherst."

I tried to follow what he was saying, but the words came to my ears like separate beads on a string, making no sense. I couldn't believe Tommy wouldn't be wanting me to go, or that he'd use words like *rife* or *debauchery*. I looked at the Squire to see if he was telling the truth. But his face was the same as always—a mask painted over bones.

"May I see it, sir?" I held out my hand and he leaned across the desk and gave it to me. It was Tommy's writing on the envelope, to be sure. Reading it, I saw right away the Squire had told me true. Tommy wanted me to stay where I was.

My insides plunged about as I handed back the letter. I felt feverish and frozen at the same time. God's truth, it seemed my own brother had betrayed me.

"Your brother's advice is sound," the Squire said, looking down as he folded the letter, pressing the creases with his thumbs. "I trust you'll take it."

"I'll think on it, sir," I said.

"We need you, Maggie." His voice was gentle. "Surely you know how much we value your work. My daughters sing your praises daily. You're not at all lazy like so many Irish girls."

Maybe he expected me to be proud or flattered by what he said. I searched in my mind for the right words to answer him, but all I found was a blister of hard feeling.

"'Tis not your decision, sir," I said, "my staying or going. I amn't a slave, surely." God's truth, I was cross.

He didn't even blink. He stood up and came around the desk toward me. "Maggie, even if you were to leave, I doubt we could replace you. Certainly not by May."

"There's no need, sir." It made me uncomfortable, him standing and myself still sitting. "I've already found a girl to take my place. One you know, for she's worked here before." I told him about the girl from Palmer, how she'd come as soon as she was needed.

He frowned and made a sound like a horse snorting. "She was here only a few months—two or three at most—and her work was unsatisfactory." He put his hands together behind his back. "No, she was not satisfactory at all. We won't hire her again. Mrs. Dickinson made that quite clear when she left."

My surprise must have been on my face, for he nodded. "It's to your credit that you looked for a replacement, but you simply must continue with us. Emily says you're a treasure."

"Miss Emily?" This was a surprise. Emily had never given any hint she was so admiring. I looked at my hands where they lay in my lap. They were red and cracked from the lye soap I'd used that morning to rid the kitchen towels of stains.

"Indeed, she insists we cannot do without you. And I agree." He smiled again—then his voice changed, so low and frightful the hairs on my arms stood up. "Perhaps you don't fully understand your situation, Maggie. Leaving us now would be a serious mistake on your part. I would not be able to bring myself to look kindly on you—or your family—ever again."

"My family?" I said.

"I daresay Tom Kelley values his job with the railroad," he said in the same terrible voice. It was like he was dropping stones into a well, each word falling down and down with awful speed.

I blinked. "You'd not get him sacked, would you, sir?" My ears felt hot.

"I can't say what I might do—if I were sufficiently angered." He turned slowly and went back to his desk and sat down. He set his wrists on the edge of the desk and opened his hands like a priest giving the blessing. "Think carefully, Maggie."

I wasn't sure if the Squire was expecting me to speak. But he seemed to be waiting for something, so I nodded. "I will, sir," I said.

"You may go now," he said, waving his hand and turning back to the papers on his desk.

I was already standing. I smoothed my apron and tried to keep my legs from shaking as I walked across the room and out the door. The stones he'd dropped were knocking together in the pit of my belly, and I thought I was going to be sick.

That night I gave the pots such a scrubbing they came shining out of the water without a spot on them. I was going over and over in my mind what the Squire had said, and thinking about corruption and wickedness and power. For months I'd dreamed about California every spare minute. My ticket was already paid for and my traveling clothes bought. I imagined telling himself I'd do what I liked. Made me smile, thinking of it—how his bushy eyebrows would crawl up his forehead and his hard little eyes would widen and the skin around his lips go white.

It wasn't till the small hours I climbed the back stairs to my room. God's truth, I was weary. I unbuttoned my calico and changed into a clean shift. I took my rosary from under my pillow and got down on my knees. And didn't I feel the Blessed Mother looking down on me with all the pity of the world on her dear face?

I wasn't planning to tell Mary my troubles, but Sunday evening at Kelley Square, it just came out. We'd finished the washing up after supper and were sitting at the table having another cup of tea. She asked how I was liking the Dickinsons, and before I could stop myself, I was telling her what the Squire said he'd do if I left them. Told her how raging and helpless it made me feel, how hateful it was to be trapped.

"I'm thinking I'll go mad if I stay," I said. "God's truth, I'd rather go back to the Boltwoods than bow to himself. We could have stayed in Tipperary if we were looking for a boot to lie under." I expected her to be as outraged as myself.

Instead, she put her hands to her head and smoothed her hair, something she did when she was agitated. "Oh, Margaret, for the love of Jesus, why must you torment me so?"

God's truth, I was surprised. "'Tis not myself tormenting you," I said. "'Tis the Squire. I'm after living my own life, is all."

"I don't know why you can't make your peace with staying in Amherst." Her voice was watery. "If the Squire turns on Tom, he'll make our lives a misery. He'll have no job nor any prospects and we'll all be starving out on the street."

"You won't be starving," I said. "Tom will find other work and I'll be sending you piles of money from California." But my voice wobbled. In truth, I didn't know what the Squire might do.

Mary sat shaking her head as the night came down all blue and black around us. "Don't you have any pity? Here I am with all these children to look after and a husband with only one arm. How would he be getting another job?"

Her words shook me. But I saw the sense of what she was saying. I was bound to my sister, and it wasn't right to risk her family's happiness for my own prideful dreams. My duty was plain. Mary needed me, so I'd be staying in Amherst.

But it was a great bog of sorrow I was mucking through that night as I walked back to the Homestead.

Chapter Six

At the end of May, the Squire raised my wages. Told me he was pleased I'd decided to stay on. He said I should feel free to take two-day-old bread to my sister's family because he wanted to be sure they'd not go hungry. He said as long as I was the Dickinsons' maid, my family and myself would be provided for.

Sure, I didn't like his charity, especially when the cost was my freedom. It wasn't my idea to stay and himself saying so made me cross, glad as I was for the extra money. But nobody can be a good maid when anger's at the boil. If I couldn't stop myself yearning for California, I could wait till a more promising year. So I saved my wages and bided my time and fixed on making the Homestead kitchen my own.

Mary was fond of saying my heart was too warm for my own good. Put me in a room with some poor beggar I never laid eyes on, and in five minutes, I'd be sighing and weeping like his dearest darling. Folks took advantage, she said. It was the easiest thing in the world to get me to-ing and fro-ing to satisfy some rich lady's whims.

She was right about my affections, to be sure. By summer I was starting to feel tender toward the Dickinson women. Even began speaking of the Squire's wife as *Mother Dickinson*. Soon enough I had the other Dickinsons sorted too.

Austin stopped by every day, with his loud voice and great pillow of red hair atop his head. It was plain he thought himself important. Tom said Austin was a squire in training, and that was God's own truth.

Sue came and went as if she lived at the Homestead. Sometimes I didn't even know she was in the house till I saw her coming down the front stairs with Emily. She and Austin had two children everybody doted on. Ned was eight, same as my niece Nell. Spindly and bookish, he looked solemn as a judge. Not a bit like other boys, nor like his father. Sensitive, he was, same as his aunt Emily.

Mattie was three, a little mite of a thing, but high-spirited as they come. Her parents and grandparents were forever chiding her for one thing or another, seemed to me. Even Vinnie was stern with the child. Only Emily admired her pluck. She'd slip her a sweet when nobody was looking, and take her into the conservatory for stories and pretend tea. Like conspirators those two were.

Same as all gentry, the Dickinsons had visitors. Sometimes professors from the College would come to talk with the Squire or pay a social call on the family. Friends and relatives came and stayed the night, like the newspaper man Samuel Bowles and Judge Otis Lord, a close friend to the Squire. Emily and Vinnie's kindly cousins Louisa and Frances came from Boston and their aunt Elizabeth visited from Worcester. She was a disagreeable woman if ever I saw one, with a sour face, the manners of a general, and a gift for meddling. Whenever she came she put on a pair of white gloves and went around the house inspecting every blessed thing for dust. If the tip of her finger came up gray after poking the back of a candlestick or running it along the rung of a chair, it was myself she scolded, though it was Vinnie mostly did the dusting.

Sometimes Aunt Elizabeth snooped around my kitchen, where she had no business being. Once I came in from sweeping the veranda and there she was big as life, moving things on the pantry shelves—putting spice tins on the wrong shelf and shifting dinner plates. I had to cross my arms tight over my chest to keep from pushing her away. "Is there something I can be getting for you?" I asked.

She put down the plate she was holding and looked at me like I was a spider she wanted to step on. "I'm frankly surprised my brother hired you. Look at this." She stabbed the plate rim with her pointy finger. "Two chips, plain as the nose on your face. *Two.* And both nearly as large as the tip of my finger. Truly, you must take more care in your washing." Her voice was sharp as her face.

"It wasn't myself chipped the plate, ma'am," I said.

Her eyebrows went up. "Are you suggesting it was someone else in this household?" She didn't wait for me to answer. "That's absurd. In any case, that doesn't excuse its presence in this pantry. Any maid worth her keep would have removed it long ago. It's good for nothing but pan drippings now."

Likely my face went bright red. She was waiting for me to speak, but I knew I'd say something wicked if I unloosed my tongue.

She made a ticking sound in the back of her throat and shook her head, making the silly little curls on her brow bounce. "I suggest you work on improving your competence and attitude immediately. My brother is a kind and generous man but his patience is not inexhaustible." And she left the room, muttering the word *Irish* clear enough for me to be hearing it.

I waited for the boil of my anger to settle to a simmer and managed to make a grand dinner. Everybody but Aunt Elizabeth praised my butter and the brown gravy. But that evening when I was lighting the lamps, I heard her in the library. Speaking to the Squire, she was, and it didn't take more than a minute to know I was the topic.

"You really ought to see about getting a good English maid," she said. "Or a German one. The Irish are notoriously shiftless."

I heard himself answer but couldn't make out the words, just his low voice rumbling along.

"Well, honestly, Edward," he said. "There's more here to concern yourself with than Emily's satisfaction."

His chair creaked. He must have stood up. Then her skirts hissed against the wall and I skittered into the parlor to hide myself as she left the room. It was a good reminder to keep my guard up. There were always folks bent on humbling the Irish.

The next day was Aunt Elizabeth's last—she was leaving right after breakfast. In truth, I was glad of it and didn't even mind herself ordering me to pack her bags. I was that eager to see the back of her. Even waved good-bye from the kitchen window.

Emily and Vinnie came into the kitchen after seeing her away, jolly as if they'd just come from a *ceilidh*. It unsettled me, so I busied myself in the pantry, putting things right while the two of them were talking and laughing away. Then Vinnie said, "It's time you assumed your social responsibilities in this community, Emily." And didn't her voice sound exactly like Aunt Elizabeth? Both of them burst out laughing as if it was the funniest thing in the world.

Sure, I wanted to laugh myself. But even a fool knows it's wicked to mock your elders. I didn't even think about it, just marched back into the kitchen.

"'Tis your father's sister you're mocking," I said as if I was talking to my own nieces and nephews. "You oughtn't disrespect your family." Soon as I spoke I was sorry—it was the sort of thing could get me sacked, to be sure. But instead of being cross, they blinked and laughed again. Emily said, "Don't be vexed with us, Maggie. We love Aunt Elizabeth, but she's a human corset, and a tight one at that. A person needs to breathe after a week of wearing her." Which set Vinnie giggling again. God's truth, I couldn't help chuckling myself.

It was after that day Emily started talking to me when we worked in the kitchen. Asking questions, mostly. They came out of the blue—not joined to anything I was doing. Maybe she was hungry for ordinary talk instead of the grand Dickinson conversations about politics and philosophy and poetry.

She asked what it was like where I came from. God's truth, recollections of the hard times growing up across the water were close to me as breathing. Seemed all I had to do was turn my head and I was back in Tipperary, grieving one thing or another. But I knew the misery wasn't what Emily wanted to be hearing, so instead I told her about the yellow gorse on the hill and the turtledoves nesting in the rowan tree behind our cottage, the dunnocks singing from the hedgerow and the flocks of swifts. She smiled and rocked back on her heels and closed her eyes like she was seeing it herself.

Sometimes Emily's questions made me tetchy—too personal to be asking. Like what my father was like and who my friends were and if I'd ever been in love. Felt she was probing too deep. But the truth is I was so grateful for a change from the long kitchen quiet, I always answered.

Once she asked me to talk about leaving Ireland. First thing came to my mind was the live wake our neighbors gave us the night before we left. Then she wanted to know what a live wake was, said she'd never heard of such a thing.

"'Twas a wake for folks leaving after the Great Hunger," I said. "We all knew it wasn't likely we'd be meeting again on this earth." Just answering her tumbled me back to that day, as if I was thirteen again, saying good-bye to most all the folk I ever knew. "All our friends and relations came to see us away," I went on. "We were stuffed into my uncle's cottage, more than thirty of us packed tight and making enough noise to frighten the Devil himself. Folks were keening and crying and saying farewell all the night long."

I didn't tell her more, but my remembering was fresh as the night it happened. Even as I worked I could still see Katy Hogan sitting in the corner with her shawl over her head, keening in her grandest voice. The air hot and sulky, as if all four of the Maher children had died in one stroke and even the wind wouldn't blow for the grief of it. Danny McClatchy bleating on about the English with his voice wobbling in his beard, so scuttered he kept falling off his stool. All of us singing "Éamonn an Chnoic," our voices so sweet they were near raising the thatch off the roof. The terrible lonesome feeling that came over me, till I found Mam and sat leaning against her while she put her hand atop my head like a warm cup.

Emily stopped her bread making. "What does it sound like—the keening?"

Took me a minute to figure out an answer, for there's no good way of describing keening to those who've not heard it. Finally, I said, "'Tis the loneliest sound in the world, surely. Like the cry of the Banshee. Makes your hair stand on end, it does."

Emily was turned in my direction, but it felt like she was looking past me instead. "I once heard wolves on a winter night," she said softly. "Their singing is unearthly."

"Aye," I said. "'Tis something like that. But more uncanny."

"It seems strange, grieving a death without anyone dying." Emily went back to her kneading, her arms pumping. "There's plenty of time for mourning—an eternity of time—is there not?"

I nodded, though I wasn't certain what she was meaning. Was she talking about Purgatory?

"On the other hand," she went on, "perhaps there's wisdom to be learned from the practice. After all, there's a certain exhilaration in the prospect of attending one's own funeral." She looked up at me and smiled. There was a mischief in her eye I'd seen before.

But I knew death isn't the sort of thing folks should be jesting about—it draws the notice of the Faery Folk. So I quick changed the subject.

To be sure, Emily was overfond of speaking about things nobody else did. And her sentences would ofttimes veer off in curious ways—she might start talking about the sea like it was a lad, or the hills having shawls as if they were women. I sometimes couldn't make hide nor hair of half of what she said, but it was nice to have the company.

I watched the way she bound herself to the house and yard. As if stepping past the front gate would cause her to plunge into some dark pit. More than once I spied her standing behind the hemlock hedge, peeking out at passersby. Like a ghost she was in her white dress, drifting through the garden and up and down the stairs. She had a way of stepping out of the shadows that made my hair stand up and more than once I yelped with the shock of it.

One night after I finished up in the kitchen late, and all the house was dark and quiet, I heard music on my way upstairs. I crept down the Northwest Passage to the parlor, and there was Emily playing the piano in the dark—a tune so lovely the Faeries could have made it. Sure, maybe it was a Faery Tune, for I couldn't move with the beauty of it. I stood enchanted, listening and watching the moonlight slide in under the drapes and lie in silver strips on the carpet.

From the doorway I could see her fingers stroking the keys the way Vinnie stroked her cats. The tune was lonesome and glad all at once, making me think of Ireland and my family and all the lads I ever loved. I must have sighed out loud, for Emily stopped playing. For a minute the only sounds were the house creaking around me and my own heart thumping in my chest.

"Maggie?" Emily said, and there she stood in the doorway, her white sleeves floating spooky in the air beside her. "What is it? Are you ill?"

Sure, I was feeling embarrassed to be caught. But even more I wanted to be hearing the tune again. "I amn't, miss," I said. "Listening to you, is all. 'Tis a lovely tune. Would you be playing it again?"

"Oh," she said. "I couldn't repeat it. It's just something I dreamed up."

I think it was that first beckoned me to her—knowing she made her own music, like a Tipperary fiddler or Mary crooning a lullaby to one of her young ones. After that night I found myself listening for her feet on the stairs and turning when she came into a room.

August came and the Dickinsons put on their Commencement Tea. It had been an annual event for as long as she could remember, Vinnie said. All the College lads and Amherst gentry came for nibbling and mingling—it was the grandest party of the year. The family fretted over preparations for weeks, and by the end of July, everyone was in a tizzy. And no wonder, for there was a mountain of work to be done. It didn't all fall on me, to be sure. Vinnie was a hurricane of cleaning and Emily baked pans and pans of black cake and gingerbread. The Squire hired young lads to beat the carpets and girls to polish the silver.

Eliza Thompson came—Vinnie told me she'd been running the Tea for years, knew how everything was to be done. Took over my kitchen, Eliza did, and I wasn't a bit happy about it. She was quiet and pretty, with skin the color of chestnuts and the manners of a lady. Sure, I never saw a servant more dignified. But when she was in a mood, she squinted her eyes and got a crafty look on her face, so I did what she said, no matter she was sometimes bossy and proud.

The day of the Tea the sun came up fiery red and the air was steamy. Emily whirled in and out of the kitchen, as lively as I'd ever seen her. Once I ventured to ask if she'd be attending the Tea. I figured she'd say no, since she made a habit of keeping to her room when visitors came.

"Oh, Father will never forgive me if I don't show myself," she said. "I've always poured wine for the young gentlemen." The way she was smiling as she left the room set me blushing with sinful thoughts.

Eliza chuckled. She was putting out cherries on a silver pedestal tray.

"I've never seen Miss Emily like this," I said. "Acts like a young lady at a frolic—not herself at all."

"Oh, she's no stranger to levees," Eliza said. "There's more than a few wild stories about her younger days. She and her sister, both."

"Sure, I'd like to be hearing them," I said. "Hard to credit Miss Emily was ever wild. Why did she change, then?"

Eliza shrugged. "The world's a noisy, tumbling place. I reckon a lady like Miss Emily needs to concentrate on her work."

"What work? Mending? Baking?" Made no sense to me. The housework Emily did wasn't the sort required much thinking.

"The work God gave her, I expect." Eliza was spreading a layer of grape leaves on the cherries. "What's inside her head. And she's still plenty wild in there." She looked up at me. "Have you taken a close look at her fingers? Seen the ink stains?"

"I have, to be sure," I said, feeling tetchy. Hadn't I been living at the Homestead six months? "I know she writes stacks of letters."

Eliza started dropping raspberries onto the grape leaves. She was making the most elegant fruit dish I ever saw. "That's not the half of it," she said. "Miss Emily's a poet. You can't spend your life on frivolities when the Good Lord's given you a talent. Says so right in the scriptures."

I didn't know what scripture she was meaning, but I believed her. One thing I'd learned—Protestants in America were fond of quoting the Bible. Even Emily—who never went to church—could pull a scripture verse out of her head at the blink of an eye.

I wondered if Eliza was right about Emily. I never heard of a woman writing poems. Didn't sound proper at all. I wanted to know more, but there was no time to ask, for the guests were starting to arrive.

By one o'clock the house and yard were swarming with people. It was a happy confusion, with Eliza making pitchers of lemonade and myself loading trays with squares of gingerbread and cake. My two eldest nieces—Mary and Meg—came up from Kelley Square to help serve.

At two the Squire and Mother Dickinson walked down the front stairs like royalty and commenced greeting folks in the parlor. Austin and Sue brought Ned and Mattie. Vinnie was a swirl of liveliness, bustling through all the rooms and outside too, her hair done up in ribbons and a new lavender gown showing off her shoulders. And Emily was wearing a new frock of white lawn embroidered with roses and floaty as goose down, her hair caught in a gold net. She looked a picture, standing behind the punch bowl in the dining room, pouring cups of wine from a decanter. She was laughing and flirting and her cheeks were glowing as if she'd got a fever. Truth to tell, I was gawking at her more than once, for I'd never seen her acting so. She was having as grand a time as anybody.

Late in the afternoon I saw herself and Sue out walking in the garden. They made a pretty picture, Sue in blue and Emily in white, arms around each other's waists and their two heads bent together like they were whispering the sweetest of secrets.

Chapter Seven

After what Eliza Thompson told me the day of the Tea, I started taking note of Emily's poem writing. God's truth, I've always admired a poet. I'm guessing it's the Tipperary in me—for there's no place on earth grows more noble poets. At first it was when I was tidying her room and saw some of the papers were poems written out in lines across the page. Then I started finding little verses salted with dashes around the house, scribbled on envelopes and the backs of recipes and other scraps. Sometimes she stored them in her pockets and they fluttered out when I was sorting laundry. I watched her in a new way after that.

Since I first came to the Homestead I'd been mailing letters from Emily to a *Mr. Higginson, Editor.* But it wasn't till after the Tea I thought to ask Vinnie what an editor was. She told me it was a man who decided what to print in a magazine or a book. Like stories or essays or poems, she said.

"Is Mr. Higginson printing Miss Emily's poems, then?" I asked.

Vinnie laughed. "Emily would be overjoyed if he were. We'd not be able to keep her in Amherst—she'd be off ascending Mount Olympus. But"—she tapped the silver-and-amethyst brooch at her neck—"I fear it's unlikely. Mr. Higginson has pointed out that her poems lack form and polish."

I didn't know where Mount Olympus was or why Emily would be climbing it. But I felt a kinship with anybody whose dreams had been crushed.

Then came a hot summer morning with both Emily and myself in the kitchen when a lad came rapping on the door. It was the delivery boy from the Amherst House handing me an envelope. "For Miss Dickinson," he said.

"Reward him with some gingerbread, Maggie." Emily was standing right behind me. Startled me, it did, because she usually whisked herself out of sight the minute she heard a knock. "And don't let him leave until I've composed a reply. Bar the door if you must." She plucked the envelope from my hand and off she went upstairs.

I gave the lad his gingerbread and went back to mincing kidneys for a pie. He chattered away, telling me he lived in the woods north of town and wanting to know if I'd seen the Independence Day fireworks at the fairgrounds. I was about to slice more gingerbread to quiet him, when Emily came back and pushed a folded paper into his hand.

"Now hurry on your way and be sure to give my note directly to the gentleman," she said, sliding a peppermint in his pocket as he went out the door. "It's of great importance."

She turned. "Mr. Higginson will be visiting this afternoon, Maggie," she said, her cheeks near pink as the peppermint. "And everything must be"—she paused a minute—"a perfect, paralyzing bliss."

Sure, I never saw a woman take more care getting ready. She wanted everything just so—fresh flowers in the parlor, the pillows plumped, and the drapes drawn to keep it cool. No one was to disturb Mr. Higginson and herself. Not even Vinnie or Mother Dickinson. I was not to offer refreshment—she'd be doing it herself. And once I showed himself into the parlor, I must stay out of sight in the kitchen till he left.

She sent me to the garden for flowers—cinnamon roses, lilies, sweet williams, and zinnias. I filled the garden basket till it was rioting with pink and orange and yellow. She arranged them in three vases and then chose two lilies the colors of sunset to carry up to her room.

When I heard the clunk of the front door knocker, I opened it to a pillar of a man. "I believe Miss Dickinson is expecting me," he said into his beard. He handed me his card and I took it straight up to Emily. She came out of her room wearing a blue net shawl over her white frock and tiptoed down the stairs. The two lilies were cradled like babbies in the crook of her left arm. I felt I was watching a dream.

It was a long afternoon, and quiet too. The house was empty of sound as an unrung bell, except for those murmuring voices in the parlor, which could have been mistook for the humming of bees. Vinnie and her mother had gone out to please Emily, so I made myself useful in the kitchen. At five I heard the front door close and then Emily's footsteps running up the stairs. She stayed in her room the rest of the day. Didn't know if that was a good or bad sign.

But when she came down the next morning, she was glowing. Her eyes danced and cheeks flushed so she almost looked pretty. She ate a hearty breakfast—which wasn't at all like her—and had two cups of coffee. She was pouring a third when Sue came in. Emily jumped up, her smile so wide I thought her face would split. The two of them scuttled off to Emily's room, whispering like schoolgirls.

"If I didn't know better, I'd be thinking Mr. Higginson's her beau," I said to Vinnie later. She was dusting the parlor chairs and I was polishing the piano. Had my eye on the sorry droop of a Damask rose looking ready to fall out of its vase.

She laughed and spun around so her skirt flipped its hem and I could see her neat black slippers with their perfect bows. "Emily's beau? Oh no, Maggie. Emily admires him exceedingly, but not as a suitor. Although"—she shrugged and smiled in a way that told me she was up to some Dickinson mischief, and pleased with herself for putting a fanciful idea in my head—"we never know with Emily, do we?" And her eyes twinkled at me as she came over and plucked the poor rose from its vase.

Sure, that was the truth of it—no one ever knew with Emily.

The very next afternoon, it was, I found six of my little apple butter tarts gone from the pie safe. I was certain there'd been an even dozen when I put them there to cool. But Mattie and Ned had been in and out of the kitchen all morning long. Mighty distracting they were too—Mattie was always asking questions and Ned poking about the pantry.

"Go on with you now," I'd told them more than once. "'Tis a grand day with the sun pouring down and you should be out in it."

And out they'd go—likely to pet the horses or plague Tim, the stableman, awhile—only to come running back in to pester me for milk and cake. Thing is, I couldn't remember if they were watching when I put the tarts away. I didn't think Ned would be stealing them, but in truth I didn't trust Mattie not to.

Had a mind to march myself over to the Evergreens and learn the truth of it. I was about to untie my apron when I heard children calling and laughing near the house. Vexed me, it did. The Squire had made plain one of my chief duties was keeping the place quiet so Emily wouldn't be disturbed. All week I'd been chasing neighborhood boys away, and when I went out the kitchen door, I followed the voices around to the front of the house. And wasn't there a flock of young ones—girls and boys both—giggling right under Emily's window?

"Whist!" I called, waving my arms. "Be gone with yourselves this minute! You're not to be coming inside the gate." Then I heard Mattie calling in her lisping voice, "Thank you, Aunt Emily!"

All the children were looking up. And there was Emily, leaning out her bedroom window and pulling up a basket on a rope. She was laughing away, merry as the children.

Mattie spied me then and ran up, cheerful as the sun itself. "Look what Aunt Emily gave us!" And didn't she hold up one of my apple butter tarts? I was cross, to be sure. Would have snatched it out of her hand if I didn't know it was Emily's doing.

Took me some time to quiet myself. Good thing I didn't see Emily till supper, or likely I'd have said something I'd be regretting. But the mischief was still in her eye when she sat at the table. It was clear she thought it all a grand jest, though I was out six tarts and feeling mortified besides.

It was the next spring when a change came in the way I saw Emily. Maginley's Circus was in town and Molly and myself had a grand frolic on my afternoon off, watching the clowns and acrobats dancing on the horses. The next day I had a mountain of ironing to be doing but I was still feeling the cheer of it. There I was, bent over the long board and humming a tune, when I heard a scream from the barn. I plunked my iron back on the stove and ran out the back door.

It was Emily sitting in a heap in front of the horse stall. One foot poked out from under her skirt and her face was puckered with pain. Soon as I knelt I saw she'd buried a nail in the bottom of her slipper. It was sunk into her foot near up to its head and blood was oozing out around the shaft. My stomach heaved.

"You'll be all right, miss," I said. "I'll have that out in a jiffy. My brother Tommy stepped on a clout nail once and I fixed him up good as new." Quick as a cricket, I ran back to the kitchen for a clean paring knife.

God's truth, I eased the wicked nail from Emily's foot in no time. Smooth as butter it came out, with only a flinch from herself. The only sound out of her had been that one awful scream.

I peeled off her slipper and wrapped her foot in my apron and tied it around her ankle. She was shaking all over and leaning against me as we hobbled to the kitchen. Like a child, she was, with her head resting on my shoulder, her hair smelling like sunlight and cherry blossoms and sadness all mixed together. I could feel the lonesomeness coming out of her, same as I knew myself when I first came to America. Sure, I didn't know what hers was made of but I could feel it deep as my own.

Not a whimper came from Emily when I washed her foot and wrapped it in a plaster of pork rind and oiled silk. She wrinkled her nose at the smell, but I said it worked for my brother, drew the corruption right out. "Tobacco works too, miss," I said. "But I amn't rummaging through Mr. Dickinson's library to find some."

Surprised me when she laughed. Felt like a tiny spark between us. Soon as I settled her on the dining room sofa, I ran to fetch the doctor.

Dr. Bigelow admired my plaster, and the pair of us carried Emily up the stairs and put her to bed. All the rest of the day, I was running up and down, bringing her tea and food and changing her dressing. Truth is, I didn't mind the extra fetching and carrying, for I've always liked helping the sick. But I was glad at the day's end to creep off to my room.

I'd just finished saying my prayers when Mother Dickinson knocked. She looked like a world of troubles had come down on her.

"Ma'am?" I was shivering in my shift with the night chill around me and my head swirling with weariness.

"Emily's asking for you," she said with her voice wobbling. "She says no one else will do." It wasn't her words compelled me, but her look, frayed and worn as a threadbare towel too old to soak up water.

"Sure, I'll just be taking a minute to grab my shawl," I said. "Now go on to bed and get your rest."

Emily was awake in her bed with the blankets drawn up to her neck and her face pale as the pillows. Her hair had escaped its braid and was spread around her head in dark red waves. I plumped her pillows and smoothed her blankets. "Is it pain you're having now?" I asked. I knew sick folk—no matter their age—were comforted when someone was taking charge, even a maid. I put my palm on her forehead to check for fever, but her skin was blessedly cool.

"You're as welcome as sun after a rainstorm." She smiled, a small curve of her lips like the Blessed Virgin contemplating Our Lord. "You've brightened my darkness," she said.

"Hush now," I said. "'Tis the laudanum talking, and you're making me blush besides. Is there something I can be doing for you?"

"Tell me an Irish tale," she said. "I want to hear you talk."

A sad vexation came into the pit of my stomach. I wondered if she was mocking me again. "Why would you be wanting an Irish tale?" I asked.

"Indulge me, Maggie," she said. "I need some enchantment tonight. And what better enchantment is there than lore from Ireland?"

Took a minute for my mind to roll back over stories I heard as a young lass. "Have you heard of Dagda and his harp?" I asked.

She shook her head. In the lamplight her eyes were shining like a child's.

I took the chair from her writing desk and drew it close to the bed and sat myself down. "It happened in the misty long-ago times," I said. "Before Saint Patrick came to Ireland and drove out all the snakes. Dagda came down from the north with his magical things—his magic club and his magic cauldron and his magic harp made of oak and inlaid all over with jewels. When he plucked the strings, he could order the seasons or fit his warriors for battle. Its music could soothe his soldiers' wounds and heal all their sorrows."

Emily sighed. Her eyes were closed but she was smiling. "Don't stop," she whispered. So I went on with the story, telling of Dagda's capture by his enemies and himself playing the harp to render all of them helpless with the Music of Tears and the Music of Mirth and the Music of Sleep. As the story unwound from my tongue, I fell into the enchantment myself. Took me back to Tipperary, it did, sitting with our family around a basket of potatoes at the end of the day, hearing Da's voice telling this very tale and feeling Mam's quick fingers combing my hair. The truth of it is I felt more content than I had in months, sitting there in the near dark with Emily.

Coming out of the story was like swimming up a long river against the current. I looked at the bed and there lay Emily, with the tears running down her face. I thought the pain was troubling her, but she said it was just the Music of Tears. "It snares my heart," she said then, and asked me to sing the harp's songs to her.

"I'll not be knowing them, miss," I told her. "And if I did, I daren't sing them, for they belong to the Faeries. Human folks should never play with magic. 'Tis awful whimsical. A charm can curse easy as it can cure."

She was watching me. "I should have known you wouldn't give up your secrets." She gave a little laugh. "But I thank you for the story."

I looked away. The moon was shining in the window, round as a dollar, its silver caught in the tops of trees.

"If you're looking for a song, there's one in that," I said.

She sat up to look, then sank back on her pillows. "There is, indeed," she said. "Or a poem at least." Her voice was dreamlike and slow. "It's a truth as old as God."

She dozed a bit and I fear I did so myself, till the sound of voices roused us both. She vowed she'd have a look. So I helped her up and together we made our way to the window. Below us, rolling along the street, came two horses pulling a cart piled high with crates. Then more horses hauling carriages, and after that three elephants, tail to tail, with a lad walking beside them. In the deepest part of the night, the circus was leaving town—all that bright color and happy music and quare animals stealing away. It was the most strange and beautiful thing.

Neither of us spoke till they were out of sight. Then Emily sighed. "There's something about it that puts red in your brain, isn't there? I could almost hear drums."

Quick as she said it, I saw the color red flashing in my own mind and fancied I heard a band. Made me think of all the grand parades after the War of the Rebellion.

Emily clutched my arm and I saw she was shivering. I guided her back to bed and checked her foot for signs of corruption. I was applying a fresh bandage when the first dawn bird started singing. Emily looked at me, and I looked at her, and the pair of us were smiling.

Later, Emily was fond of telling folks how she watched the circus stealing away in the dark. "Like thieves of happiness," she'd say, her eyes flashing mischief. "All those big strong men softly calling *hoy hoy* to hurry the horses." But she never told a soul I was with her. It was our secret.

That long strange night a bond formed between us, mistress and maid. Thin as a thread it was at first, loose as a ribbon in the wind. But over time it grew sturdy and limber and strong.

Part II

Shutters

Chapter Eight

1916

March is fickle as the Faeries. You never know from one hour to the next if it's winter or spring. Before I met Emily I thought it a sorry month, made of mud and melancholy. But she loved this time of year. Made her feel alive, she said—it was that full of promises. Sometimes she dragged me outside and set me sniffing till I smelled it too. There's no perfume more hopeful than mud, she'd be telling me. Maybe just to set me laughing and shaking my head.

The street is muddy from snowmelt and frost coming out of the ground, so I keep to the gravel path alongside the fence in front of the Dickinson properties. It takes me five minutes to walk from Kelley Square to the Evergreens. It's the kind of fanciful place you might be finding in a book. A jumble of towers and porches and balconies with a cupola like a crown and windows shining in all directions. Pretty as a Faery glade in May, it is, with the house hiding behind flowery shrubs and ornamental trees, but today it looks winter brown and witchety.

I open the gate and close it behind me. My heart's pounding a sight too fast. I'm not feeling bold as I was this morning.

Wondering what I'll have to say to convince Mattie D not to sell the Homestead. *If* she's selling it. Could be Rosaleen has her story all wrong. Wouldn't be the first time.

I start up the flagstone walk. Don't remember ever going to the Evergreens this way—I was always cutting along the path between the two houses. I can't stop myself from looking east, and there's the Homestead, flecked in sunshine. It tugs at my heart. I have half a mind to follow the path, though it's hard to make out now, overgrown with scraggly vines and brambles. But it would be a grand thing, letting myself in the back door and taking a peek in the kitchen.

Instead, I keep my feet on the stones and climb the steps to the fancy front door. I feel bold, but I've no mind to be slinking round to the back like a servant. I wonder who'll be answering and if I'll be let in. I've lost track of all the maids Sue and Mattie D have had over the years. Seems like half the domestics in Amherst worked at the Evergreens one time or another—even my own niece Meg.

I scold myself for fretting like I'm still a servant and need to worry about such things. I'm not a maid anymore. I own and run the best boardinghouse in Amherst. Paid for its building with my own money and never skimped on furnishings. I remember how scandalized Mary was when I bought real Belleek porcelain for the dining table. Said it was a shameful waste of money, for the boarders wouldn't care. A rough lot, she said they were.

"They're from Ireland, every last one," I'd snapped at her. "And why shouldn't they be having a bit of comfort and a clean place to live when they're far from home? 'Tis a lonesome thing living in a strange land and it's my own money I'm spending, after all."

Sure, she'd clapped her mouth shut after that and never said another word about my china. A rare thing for herself, not to be giving her opinion on everything under the sun.

I knock on the door and wait. After a bit I hear footsteps and the lock turning. But when the door opens, I step back—I'm that surprised. For it's Mattie D herself standing there. Tall and thin as a stick she is—there's more meat on a chicken's forehead than the woman has on her bones. She's done up in a drab gray suit with not a trace of ribbon or lace. Not even a bow at her throat. The Sisters of Mercy would be approving, but I'm not a nun nor ever wanted to be, no matter I've been Catholic all my life.

Looks like Mattie D's surprised as myself. She's giving me a confounded frown, and I can see she doesn't know who I am. Sure, it never crossed my mind she wouldn't recognize me.

"Margaret Maher," I say to help her remember.

Her face shifts. "Maggie?"

"Aye," I say. "It's been an abundance of years, but 'tis myself, surely."

"Whatever are you doing here?" Even in the shadows, her eyes look the way they did when she was a girl—wary and sad. There's something frayed about her, makes me want to smooth her cheek under my hand.

"I've come for a friendly chinwag," I say.

Her wide, down-turning mouth tightens. So like her father's mouth, it is. Not that I'd ever be telling herself so. I know she's still bitter about him, though he's been dead twenty years—but who could be blaming her after what he did to his family?

"A chinwag," she says. She's not moving from the doorway.

"Aye," I say. "Folks say you're selling the Homestead. I'm thinking that can't be true. So I came to find out."

Her face pinches up, just like that. All hard lines and sharp angles. "You're still the same Maggie, I see. Nosy as ever."

Feels like a slap across my face, her words. My temper comes up and I have to pinch myself to keep civil. "Sure now, there's no call to be taking that tone," I say. "I amn't a maid now, nor have I been one for seventeen years. You'd best invite me in like a proper guest."

She blinks—two, three times—and tightens her shoulders so she's taller, though I wouldn't have thought such a thing possible—she's a good head taller than myself already. "The Homestead is legally mine to dispose of, as you are well aware," she says. "Now please leave."

Seems I have my answer.

"I don't know how you can part with the dear old place," I say, and—no surprise—tears prickle my eyes. "It was Miss Emily's whole world. What would your mother say?" I watch her face, hoping to find the flicker of guilt I'm sure must be lurking. "You're betraying Miss Emily, you know. It was her home. Wouldn't surprise me if her spirit's still lingering."

She gives her head a shake, like a horse refusing the bridle. "Let me make it clear to you"—she's glaring at me now and speaking slow, like she's talking to a child—"this is not your concern. It has nothing to do with you."

I glare right back. Mary was fond of saying God mixed the mettle too strong in me and likely she was right—I've always been headstrong and willful, forever bedeviling Mam and herself when I was a girl. But being a servant, I learned to hide it from those who paid my wages. So maybe Mattie D doesn't know my true nature.

"'Tis plain somebody needs to be talking sense into you," I say in a voice hard as her own. "And since there's no one left but myself who's known you since you were a girl, I'm thinking it *is* my concern." Now I'm in a fury, and not disposed to hide it. "The

Homestead does have to do with me. And you know it's so. I'm the one lived there thirty years. God's truth, 'tis more my house than yours, no matter the name on the deed."

"I've asked you to leave," she says, and her voice sounds exactly like Sue's. "Now I'm ordering you."

Hard as stone the woman is. Just like her grandfather—and my memory of the Squire in his library holding Tommy's letter pops up behind my eyes. There's a heave in my belly, for the old feelings still cling like barnacles on a ship's keel.

"Suit yourself," I say. I turn and march back down the walk.

God's truth, I'm in a fury. It's been a long time since I was this stirred up. And I'll not be letting it go—the Homestead ought to be owned by somebody who knew Emily. And there's no call for Mattie D to be treating me like I'm nobody. I've known her since she was a child, and many a time looked after her when her mam and Emily were putting their heads together over poetry. How often did I praise the funny little stories she wrote when she was a girl or serve her the biggest slice of chocolate cake? How many times did I comfort her after one of Austin's scoldings? Lord, I practically helped raise her.

She's changed even more than I thought. Maybe Rosaleen's right and she's got too full of herself. All those grand airs and fancy trips to New York and Europe, not to mention marrying that foreign husband. It strikes me I've not seen Alexander Bianchi for a long time—years maybe. Nor even heard gossip of his coming and going like I used to. I wonder if he's still in Amherst.

Sure, I'll never understand what Mattie D sees in him. He always looks puffed up and proud—like an English duke. Smiling in a quare way makes me think he's hiding something under his great mustache. His eyes cold as stones in winter. There's something slippery about the man, to be sure.

It's sad the way a man can get a hold on a woman. How even a worldly, traveling woman gets her heart twisted around a man's smile. One of the quare mysteries of love, I reckon.

Heaven help me, I ought to know.

Chapter Nine

1874

Five years I'd been working at the Homestead when Patrick Quinn came knocking, right in the midst of my washing up after the noon meal. In truth, I wasn't inclined to open the back door to some stranger's foolishness. Most in Amherst knew better than to be stopping by the Homestead on my afternoon off. I shook the dishwater from my hands and wiped them dry with the rag tucked into my apron strings. Even so, they were soapy and sore and I had the devil of a time turning the doorknob.

The rain was coming down hard and made no sign of stopping anytime soon. I gave my hands another wipe and took a wary look at the lad on the back stoop. He was a man grown but untidy as a boy in his rumpled coat and crooked hat with little rivers of water running off his shoulders. Sure, I'd never laid eyes on him before. But I couldn't let him stand there with the rain filling his boots now, could I?

"Come in before the weather beats you to it," I said, pulling the door wide. Wasn't till he was inside did I see how tall he was. Near big as Tom Kelley, and handsome besides. The kind of looks to be making the blood rush to my face when I was younger. But I was over all that now. Already three years past thirty and seen enough of the world to know there's a wide ocean between good looks and good deeds.

He slid the hat off his head and gave me a proper nod. "I'm Patrick Quinn," he said, and didn't he have the music of Tipperary on his tongue? Gave me a quare little shiver, for it was a sorry place where I came from, and at that time, I didn't relish the remembering.

"And what might you be wanting?" I handed him the rag to dry himself.

"I'm looking to speak with Mr. Dickinson," he said. "James Gallagher sent me."

"Best be speaking to myself, then," I said, bold as a bucket. I wasn't of a mind to bow and scrape to a stranger, especially when I had no idea who James Gallagher was. "I'll give the Squire your message soon as he gets home."

"A squire is he?" said Patrick, holding his hat in one hand and wiping his forehead with the other.

"He's an important man." I scowled at the water dripping off his hat onto the clean floor.

"I know that surely," Patrick said. "He's in the Massachusetts legislature. And from what I hear, he's rich and miserly as Queen Victoria herself. But that don't make him a squire." His dark eyes were glistering and the corners of his mouth quirked up.

"*Whist!* Stop your tongue!" I was shocked at his boldness. Not that he was wrong about the Squire. But it wasn't right for some stray lad to be slandering the man in his own house. I saw Patrick's smile had disappeared, so maybe he was having second thoughts for acting the maggot. I snatched my rag out of his hand. "You'd best tell me your message and be on your way," I said. "I've work to do."

He shook his head. "My instructions are to give it direct to himself. So I need to know when he'll be home."

"'Tis no business of yours," I snapped.

"I'll wait till he comes, then," said Patrick. And didn't he commence undoing his coat buttons before my eyes? Sure, it surprised me. I wasn't used to having my words flouted in my own washroom.

"You can button that right back up," I said. "He won't be back till tomorrow's train from Boston."

His mouth quirked again and I saw I'd just told him what he was asking. Sure, I don't know why I did that. It just came out.

"Would you be knowing a place I can stay the night, then?" he asked.

Right off I thought of Tom's brother James and his wife, Ellen, living next to Tom and Mary. They took in boarders from time to time if somebody put in a good word. But I'd never heard of Patrick Quinn, had no idea where he came from or what business he was up to. And it nettled me he wasn't trusting myself with his message.

"There's the Amherst House just up the street," I said. "In the center of town, it is. And if that's too costly for you, there's lodgings over the river in Northampton. A bit of a walk never did anybody harm."

A gust of wind came up and the rain pelted down, rattling the windows. It couldn't have rained harder—it was coming down like Judgment Day. Sure, it was as if God Himself was scolding me for lacking charity. And Patrick wasn't smiling anymore.

I didn't like the lad and he was no friend of mine. But there he stood, looking so downcast the thought of turning him out into the weather made me gloomy myself. That's the way it is with me—I get cross but it won't last.

"Sure, never mind that," I said. "Best you be waiting here till the rain lets up. Give yourself a chance to dry out."

"'Tis tempting me, you are." He gave me a sweet, pleading look.

I pointed at the water dripping off his coat hem. "Take that thing off and hang it on a peg before you make a bog of my washroom."

He shed the coat, but said not a word of regret for the puddle I'd be wiping up. It was plain there was a bit of the rascal in him too, for wasn't he biting off a grin while he was obeying? Nettled me all over again. I turned back to the stack of dirty pots still waiting in the sink. I wasn't half done with the washing up and my afternoon off was wasting away.

"Now go on and sit in the kitchen," I said, pointing to the doorway. "There's a rocker by the stove. And don't be touching anything."

A dimple showed in his right cheek, but he gave me a nod and went through into the kitchen while I got busy with my work. His footsteps told me he wasn't sitting in the rocker but walking around the room, likely poking his nose where it didn't belong. And what lad's nose belonged in a kitchen anyway, unless he was a cook? Struck me he might be finding Emily's corner, where she kept her papers for writing ideas. I began fretting and hurried myself along so fast the pots didn't get their usual shine.

I was drying my hands when I came into the kitchen, ready to give him a good scolding. But there he was, sitting in the rocker like I told him, looking me up and down. Melted the words right on my tongue, that look. Hadn't been given one like it since George Garrett tried stealing kisses from me in Clarinda Boltwood's kitchen. It rattled me, remembering George's soft mustache tickling my neck, and didn't that same sugary feeling come into the pit of my stomach? Seemed a lifetime ago I was working for Clarinda and flirting with her boarder.

"You keep a lovely kitchen," Patrick said.

"'Tis a cheery enough place." I was still warm from thinking of George, so I blathered on a bit. "Bigger than most with plenty of light and this pretty yellow paint around the windows."

He nodded. "There are worse places to be working, surely." I smelled the damp on him, mixing with the whiff of burning wood.

"You're soggy to the bone," I said. "A cup of something hot will do you good. I'll wet the tea."

"Thank you kindly." He gave me that look again, making it clear he was liking what he saw. I put the kettle on, added wood to the firebox, and got cups and saucers from the pantry. "Go sit at the table," I said.

He rubbed his neck and got up slow. It was easy to tell his bones were aching. Took a few minutes but I was soon putting a cup of hot tea in front of the lad and sitting down with my own. I couldn't help noticing he stirred in three big lumps of sugar when I passed him the bowl. Took his tea sweet, he did. So I sweetened my own.

I watched him drink. I wasn't nettled anymore but I was still curious what his message was. "Maybe you can give your message to the Squire's son," I said. "He's a lawyer like the Squire and they share the same office. He'll likely come by in a bit. Most days he brings the mail and chats with his mother and sisters." I knew there was a chance Austin wouldn't come at all. Since the Squire had been elected, Austin was spending time dallying at the courthouse in Northampton or gadding about in his fancy new carriage. Rumor was he favored driving around the countryside with a friend by his side. Man or woman, didn't seem to matter. Though it was unlikely even Austin would be out in this downpour.

He shook his head. "'Twas Mr. Edward Dickinson inspected the Hoosac Tunnel for the legislature. So he's the one I'm needing to see."

Sure, I remembered the night two months past when the Squire returned from his trip to the tunnel, looking tired and troubled. Had two friends with him, both needing food and a place to sleep. While they sat in the front parlor, I had to scurry around, making up the guest beds and putting together a cold supper.

For a minute my head felt as full of bees as Emily's garden. "Did you come from North Adams yourself, then?" I asked. "'Tis a long way for walking."

He chuckled. "I took the train, to be sure."

Of course he did. I felt the fool but asked my next question anyway. "So you work on the tunnel, do you?"

Give me a long look, he did, solemn as the Pope. "That I do," he said after a minute. "It's a hellhole of a place. I've seen more than one strong Irish lad blown to smithereens before my eyes."

Sure, I couldn't think what to say. I knew there'd been some bad accidents digging that tunnel. It was all rock under the mountain, folks said. Just three months ago in the newspaper, there was a story of a man killed in a blast, leaving his children fatherless. Felt like a stone in the bottom of my belly when I read about those young ones. Eight of them there were, and the littlest still in her cradle. Sure, it wasn't the sort of chat I wanted to be having with anybody, let alone a stranger. I was sorry I asked.

So I turned to other things—how long was the ride from North Adams to Amherst? How did he come to Massachusetts? Did he still have family in Ireland?

He was spilling stories soon enough. It didn't take much to get Patrick Quinn talking. He talked about emigrating from Ireland and living in New York City. What a rank place it was but he liked the excitement of it. He said he'd signed up with the Union Army when the war came and marched all over creation to fight the rebels. He went back to New York when it was over but couldn't find a respectable job. So he worked his way north through Connecticut and Massachusetts and Vermont and finally hired on to the tunnel crew. Learned a lot more than he bargained for, he said, but wouldn't say what. It was a pleasant enough chat till he mentioned seeing a train full of strikebreakers roll into North Adams.

"Four years ago, it was," he said. "Gathered a great crowd, that train. The owners sent strikebreakers to take the place of union lads at the shoe factory, you see. The yelling and the raging was so bad police had to escort them to the factory."

I'd read in the papers about union strikes, and didn't like the sound of it. Nobody I knew did. The Squire sputtered about strikes at least once a week. Tom and Mary had no use for unions at all, said they were a greedy, complaining lot. If a body worked hard, he'd get the wages he deserved, Tom said. Made no sense to claw at the hand feeding you.

"You don't support trade unions, surely," I said.

"I do indeed," Patrick said. He was looking at me steady. "It's evil to my way of thinking, denying lads the right to organize for decent wages and working conditions. That train came all the way from California, stuffed with lads from China. Like cattle, they were."

"California, was it?" I said, and felt my heart knocking with the old longing I thought was behind me.

"Yes, California," Patrick said. "All that way. Just to break the strike."

"My brothers are in California," I said. "Been there for years, digging gold and silver out of the mines and getting rich."

"Are they, now?" said Patrick.

I liked the way he was looking at me, like he wanted me to say more. "I was after making plans to go too. But I got typhoid instead."

His brow folded into a frown. "'Tis a rough place, California, so they say. Not for women such as yourself. 'Twas good you didn't go." His eyes held me steady.

I felt a flush coming up on my cheeks. Patrick Quinn was a flirt. "I've always liked a bit of adventure," I told him. "And Michael and Tommy write about how lovely it is. With roads and hotels and churches too."

Patrick was shaking his head. "I think they're having fun with you, your brothers."

Didn't like the tone he was taking. "They never wrote about any China folks," I said. "Maybe you're the one having fun."

"Nay, they're all over the place out West," Patrick said. "Work for pennies and save most of it to send back to China."

Sure, it reminded me of myself when I first came to America, saving my wages till I had enough to pay for Mam and Da's crossing. "That's naught to be blaming a body for," I said. "Sending money home is the right thing to do, surely."

"It's not themselves I'm blaming," he said, sounding tetchy. "'Tis the bosses. Using themselves to break a strike when most of them can't speak a word of English. It harmed both the strikers and the strikebreakers too. I was there—I watched the police marching them straight from the depot to the factory and they never came out till the strike broke. Nasty piece of work, it was." He shook his head and finished his tea.

I tried to picture Chinese lads marching in a long line like a sad parade. Once I saw a cartoon of Chinese men in the paper but they looked more like dolls than people—wearing long robes and flat hats bigger than skillets. In truth, I didn't know what they really looked like.

"Would you like some pie?" I didn't wait for him to answer, just got up and took the leftover peach pie from the safe and cut two slices and served them up. He thanked me and dug in. But neither of us had taken more than a couple of bites when we heard the back door open and shut and in came Sue Dickinson.

Gave me a start, it did. It was rare she came in through the washroom, for she didn't favor mixing with servants. I figured it must be the rain brought her there. I jumped out of my chair. "Mrs. Dickinson, ma'am," I said. "Would you be looking for Miss Emily?"

"Is she in the conservatory?" Sue was giving Patrick an unfriendly look, her mouth pinched tight and her eyes hard as stones. He was the type of lad she had no use for. Tradesman, handyman, laborer—she didn't want to see nor hear them till they were serving her.

"Likely she is," I said. "I'll fetch her if you want."

"No need. I know the way." She gave Patrick another look and hurried out through the pantry, her skirts making the sound of dead leaves when winter's coming on.

Soon as she was out of sight, I turned on Patrick. "You'd best be off now. I'll tell the Squire you called." I was rushing, anxious to send him on his way. Emily didn't like meeting folks she didn't know. She trusted me to keep the house protected from outsiders. I didn't know what Sue might be telling her. But there was not much in this world I hated more than upsetting Emily. She had that effect on folks.

Patrick was doing his own frowning now, standing up slow. "You look like you just saw the Banshee," he said. "Fear's a bad habit and a stumbling block if you're wanting your freedom."

I didn't like being chided, especially by someone who didn't know me. "Sure, I'm not fearing anything," I said. "Just doing my job." I reached across the table for his teacup but he picked it up first and mine along with it and carried both into the washroom to set beside the sink. Real gentleman-like.

I felt a bolt of shame for directing him to the Amherst House and Northampton. One too costly and the other a long, long walk. "If you're still wanting a place to stay the night," I said, "you might go down the street to the railroad tracks. There's a couple nice houses beyond the depot. The one with the gables sometimes takes in boarders. You could try there. Ask for Ellen Kelley and tell her Margaret Maher sent you."

Patrick plucked up his coat and shrugged himself into it. "Thank you," he said, and smiled. It was as if the sun came out from behind the clouds—the room seemed that golden for a minute.

I opened the door and was glad to see the rain had lightened some. "Good luck to you, then," I said.

"And to yourself." He put on his hat. "Maybe we'll meet again sometime, Margaret." And as he stepped out, didn't he give me a wink over his shoulder?

For the life of me, I couldn't help smiling.

Chapter Ten

Soon as I shut the door on Patrick, I came to my senses and scolded myself. I was a fool to let him in. What if Emily'd come into the kitchen while I was sitting there chinwagging with a stranger? She'd not like being surprised in her own kitchen by a face she didn't know. And I didn't want to be the cause of her vexation. She had troubles enough, with her bad eyes and melancholy spells.

I was wiping down the table with my back to the pantry door, so I didn't know she was there. "Maggie?" she said. I didn't jump the way I used to, but the hairs rose on my neck. Emily was often catching me unawares. Not that she was sneaking about. It was just the way she moved through the house—quiet and smooth as the air itself.

"Miss," I said, turning.

"Sue says you invited a vagrant into our kitchen," she said. I couldn't tell if she was biting back a frown or a smile.

"He's gone," I told her. "And Patrick Quinn's not a vagrant. Just a lad with a message for your father." Soon as the words were out of my mouth, I realized I was talking as if he was a friend, when all we did was chat an hour. I felt the color coming up in my face. Didn't mean to mention Patrick's name, but I was cross and didn't like Emily slurring the lad's character without ever laying eyes on him. It nettled me the way Protestants talked about the Irish. Especially when most of us were doing our best to be American.

"Besides," I went on, "it's raining buckets and the poor lad was soaked to the skin, so I let him sit by the stove and dry out. No harm done." I went back to my scrubbing.

"I hope not," she said. "You know how I feel about intruders."

I nodded. I prided myself on taking precautions, mindful of Emily needing her privacy. No one was better at protecting her—she'd told me so herself.

"Well, tell him to take his message to Father's office," Emily said. "He'll likely be there Saturday morning."

"Tell him? How am I supposed to do that?" I stopped my scrubbing and bunched up the cloth. "Already sent him on his way, I did."

"More's the pity," she said, copying my accent. "Sure, if it wasn't raining, I'd be sending you after him." It always stung when she mocked me so. I knew she thought it comical, but it felt like a slap. Of course, a maid has to expect some buffeting by her mistress—it's the nature of things. And Emily never scolded or shouted—that was a blessing, surely.

"I'd look like a *gombeen* running after him all over Amherst now, wouldn't I?" It wasn't till then I saw her eyes glinting. "You're having fun with me," I said, feeling grumpy.

"*Gombeen*." Emily said it slow, like she was tasting it. "That's a word to raise a flag to. But what does it mean?"

I shook my head, feeling flustered. "Just somebody who's acting the eejit."

She raised her eyebrows and out peeked her secret Emily

smile. "I wager we're all *gombeens* from time to time," she said. "It's good for the digestion."

I couldn't think what she meant—it made no sense. But that's how it was with Emily. She sometimes said things in a way made me think I should be writing down the words and saving them like gold coins. Other times she was outright unkind. She was especially fond of mocking my accent—trying it on like a new shawl. I never knew what to say. I did my best to act and sound American, but it seemed my tongue had its own ideas. Once she said I reminded her of one of Vinnie's cats. "You look quite pleased with yourself," she'd told me. "Like Drummy-doodles when he's polished off a mouse-and-cream dinner or unspooled a ball of my yarn." Drummy-doodles was Vinnie's new favorite, and she spoiled him wickedly. It cut me, for who wants to be compared to a cat? I couldn't think of what to say, so I just stood there like a dolt. I knew she was teasing. But teasing can be a clever mask for cruelty.

Now Emily was trying to hide her smile, but I could see it anyway, looking like a tasty lump in her throat. She dipped her head and folded her hands together. "I didn't mean to torment you. I came to tell you Sue and I would like coffee in the parlor."

"Thursday's my afternoon off, miss," I said.

She nodded. "Of course it is. Never mind, Maggie. I'll make it myself." She smiled again—a true smile this time—and my hard feelings melted away.

"Sure, it's no trouble," I told her. It was Emily asking, after all. "Would you be wanting some peach pie too?"

"Thank you. You always wear the perfume of thoughtfulness."

"I'll bring it in directly, miss," I said, and listened to her feet whispering away.

It had stopped raining and the sun was peeking through wispy clouds by the time I popped off my apron and headed to Kelley Square for a chat with my sister. Mary wasn't in her kitchen but I found Tom sitting at the table over a cup of tea. He gave me a cheery nod. "What are you up to, lass? Are things so quiet at the Dickinsons you've come looking for trouble here?"

"Sure, that's not the half of it," I said. "The Homestead's thick with airs and graces today."

A chuckle came out of him. "Sounds like Sue's been visiting."

"She has indeed," I said. "Is Mary about? I'm mad as spit and in need of my sister's ear."

"She's looking in on Maureen O'Donnell up on Irish Hill," Tom said. "The poor woman's due any day now and big as a washtub. At her wit's end chasing those four young lads of hers."

My sister was the best midwife in Amherst. Fond of claiming she brought more babbies into the world than any doctor in town, and likely it was true. I could never depend on seeing her when I stopped by, for she might be called away any time of the day or night.

I poured myself a cup of tea and sat in the chair across from Tom. "Sure, I'm sorry to miss her," I said.

He nodded. His big hand curled and uncurled around his cup. "What did Sue do got your back up so?"

I shook my head. "'Twas nothing really. She came in through the kitchen looking for Emily when I was having a chat with a lad. It was clear as noon she didn't approve."

"A lad, was it?" His eyebrows went up.

"Nobody I knew. A tunnel worker looking for the Squire. I let him dry out before sending him on his way." I was wishing I hadn't said anything. Tom looked like he was going to make gossip of it. I drank some tea to settle myself. "He was needing a room for the night and I told him to talk to Ellen. So he might stop by here."

Tom shook his head. "Haven't seen a soul."

"Well," I said, finishing my tea, "if you see him tell him he can see the Squire Saturday morning in his law office. Name's Patrick Quinn."

"That I will." His smile was the knowing kind. Made me feel squirmy inside.

"Have you heard the students at the College are burning books from their hard courses again?" I said to change the subject.

Tom grunted and shook his head, and we chatted awhile about how pampered the lads are, till I remembered my promise to meet Molly Ryan and her cousin for a supper picnic. "I'd best be going along," I said. "Send one of your young ones up in the morning for what's left of yesterday's pie." I pushed away my memory of Patrick eating his slice. "The Squire's due home tomorrow, so Emily and myself will be baking."

"I'll tell Mary you stopped by," Tom said. "And I'll keep an eye out for your Patrick Quinn." And didn't he give me a wink, bold as a promise and sending the blood rushing into my face?

The sun was just rising but Emily was already in the kitchen when I came downstairs the next morning. "Good morning, miss," I said on my way to light the fire under the washroom kettle.

I never knew how it would be with Emily from one day to the next. Sometimes she spoke to me right off, cheery as a robin in spring. Sometimes she didn't say anything, just kept herself to herself. I learned to know which by the look of her and I could see today was a talking morning. Her apron was on and she was humming a tune and setting out her baking things—the big yellow bowl and glass measuring cup and silver stirring spoon. She had her own shelf in the pantry where she kept them. Didn't use ordinary wood and tin like myself. Vinnie told me it's what made Emily's bread so tasty it won prizes at the Cattle Show. I wasn't convinced, but who wants to be prying into another's cooking secrets? We all have our own ways to shine. I never told a soul the mysteries of my butter making. It was a skill I brought from Tipperary.

I started the fire and filled the kettle. When I came back into the kitchen, Emily was measuring her flour at the far end of the table. I banged open the cooker firebox and laid the kindling. The coals were still hot enough to catch shavings and newspaper scraps. "What is it you're making this morning, miss?" I asked.

"Rye and Indian bread—Father's favorite." She didn't look up from her mixing. "While it's rising, I may make a coconut cake, if the heat isn't unbearable." Sure, I wasn't surprised. She doted on the Squire almost as much as he doted on himself.

"He'll be pleased." I took my apron from its peg behind the pantry door and pinned it on. It was plain the Squire was partial to his eldest daughter. Proud as he was of Austin, and admiring of Vinnie's beauty and industry, it was Emily he favored. She was the only Dickinson who'd stand up to him—I'd seen it with my own eyes. Whenever he declared some new rule for the family, she'd commence tormenting him. "When were you elected king?" she'd say, and laugh and pat his arm. It annoyed him some, but not for long. Soon he'd be smiling and planting a kiss atop her head. Sometimes his tender ways with her set me remembering my own da, and more than once brought a tear to my eye.

But there were other times the two of them set me on edge. It felt like the air would spark between them—and their eyes fasten on each other in a fierce way. There was a wild force around them made me want to leave the room.

I filled a pan with kitchen scraps and went out to feed the chickens and collect eggs for breakfast. Yesterday's rain hadn't cooled the air any. Even the breeze was slippery on my skin. But the roses ribboning the garden path were blooming and casting their sweetness across the yard. I could even smell them in the henhouse.

The chickens were happy to see me, coming off their roosts and fluttering around my skirts. I shooed them outside and scattered the scraps so they'd keep busy while I gathered eggs. When I went back in the kitchen, Emily was scribbling on an envelope. I don't think she even knew I was there. She'd finished kneading—her bowl was on the windowsill with a dish towel over it. I got busy slicing ham and potatoes and chopping onions so breakfast would be ready when Vinnie and Mother Dickinson came down.

Pretty soon I heard Austin come in, clomping through the washroom and into the kitchen. He was smiling and rubbing his hands. "It smells appetizing," he said.

Emily looked up from her writing. "You're early." Her voice was raspy. It was never the same from one hour to the next. Like music, it was—sometimes soft as a lullaby, other times stern as a march.

"Good morning, Em." He plunked himself down in a chair next to her.

"Will you be taking breakfast here?" I asked, and he said he would. Lately he'd been at the Homestead so often I wondered was he spending any time with his own family? Emily got plates from the pantry and went to set the dining room table.

"Is Ned feeling better?" I asked Austin. The boy had taken sick with another fever the day before. "And Mattie—is she well?"

"Fit as a fiddle," Austin said. "And I'm sure Ned will pull through after a few days in bed." He didn't seem worried.

"A lad was here yesterday asking for your father," I said. "Came all the way from the Hoosac Tunnel."

"The tunnel?" Austin looked surprised. "What did he want?"

The hairs on my neck prickled. Didn't have to turn around to know Emily was standing in the doorway watching me.

"He wouldn't say," I said, stirring onions in the skillet, watching them sizzle in the melted butter.

"Probably to do with legislation." Austin picked up one of the scraps Emily had been writing on, turned it over, dropped it. "Father's going to be giving a speech next week. I hope the man didn't come to make trouble. Was he Irish?"

"He's American as myself," I said.

I heard Emily laugh, but when I turned to look, she was gone.

Chapter Eleven

The Squire came back to Amherst on the afternoon train. Settled himself in the library with Mother Dickinson and I brought them lemonade and slices of the coconut cake Emily made. He was grumbling about the other legislators when I came in, but he looked wrung out with the heat. He'd been frail all last winter, sick with one thing and another. By spring he'd been able to go back to work, but he still wasn't strong and all that misery left him tetchy.

"Welcome home, sir," I said, handing around the lemonade and cake. "How was your journey?"

"Barely tolerable." He glanced at me but didn't smile. I was used to that, to be sure. I wanted to tell him about Patrick Quinn, but with Mother Dickinson looking on, it was plainly not the time.

"That will be all, Maggie," she said. "Close the door behind you." I didn't have a choice but to leave.

I was uneasy all that day and night. Feeling as if dark clouds were rising and changing the light before a dreadful storm.

All weekend long I watched for a chance to ask the Squire if Patrick had talked with him. But the only time we were alone was Saturday night when he paid my wages and gave me a scold-

ing for putting too much salt in the gravy. I knew he'd not welcome me prying into what wasn't my business after all.

Just before I left for Mass the next morning, Sue Dickinson
walked into the kitchen with Mattie. Emily came down right off.
Must have been watching from her bedroom window and seen
them coming along the path between the houses. It seemed the
child wanted to spend the morning with her aunt instead of going to church. And wasn't Emily smiling, like she'd just been
given the loveliest gift? She whisked the girl off to her room
soon as Sue left. It made me think maybe Sue was after pleasing
Emily as much as Mattie.

It surprised me, though, for the Dickinsons always made a
grand show of getting dressed in their best clothes and trooping
off to the Congregational church together. All except Emily. I
did wonder why she never once went to church, not in all the
years I knew her. A few times I asked, but she never gave a satisfactory answer. Instead, she'd laugh and tell me some silly
thing—that she'd rather find God in her garden, or that any bird
in the yard could deliver a grand sermon. All I could think
of was the trembly holy feeling that came over me when the
Communion wafer melted on my tongue. I thanked God I was
Catholic.

On Sunday afternoons all the Kelleys ate dinner together, in one
house or the other. Whether the food was ample or meager, we
always had a grand time of it, trading tales and jests. That day
we were gathering at James and Ellen's. Mary caught me up on
news as we walked across the yard together. Seems Maureen
O'Donnell gave birth to twins, and both of them girls. A long,
hard labor, it was, but the babbies were healthy as piglets in spite

of sharing the one belly. Mary said Maureen was so pleased with herself for finally birthing daughters the tears were just running down her face. But her poor husband, Martin—he was beside himself, worrying how he was going to be putting food in the mouths of so many on a hod carrier's pay.

I had my arm linked through Mary's and my head bent to be hearing her over the children's noise, so I didn't look up till we stepped into Ellen's big kitchen. And there, sitting at the table with his chair pushed back and his arm slung over the rail of it, was Patrick Quinn himself. Talking with James, he was, and the two of them could have been long-lost brothers from the way they were going at it, such a fierce chinwag they were having. A little sound came out of me, like a squeak, for I'd reckoned he was long gone back to North Adams. I unhooked my arm from my sister's and smoothed my skirts. But before I had a chance to speak, Ellen came over and set a bowl of boiled potatoes in my hands.

"Would you be a love and take these into the dining room?" Ellen was a hardworking woman with a kind face, but she didn't abide lollygagging. Not much taller than myself but every inch of her all business. So off I went to the dining room, where two long tables were set together. They were already laid with Ellen's Sunday china and her daughter was putting out the flatware.

"I see you have a new boarder talking with your da," I said. "Do you know how long he'll be staying?"

But she didn't get a chance to answer, for Mary came in that minute, carrying the beef brisket. And didn't everybody follow till the room was stuffed with Kelleys and boarders? There was a great tapping of feet and scraping of chairs. When we were all sitting down, James said the grace, we blessed ourselves, and the eating began. Patrick was at the far end of the table next to

James, with my nephew Michael squeezed between himself and Ellen. I tried not to stare but I did glance his way more than once. He didn't look at me, though, and there was too much uproar to be getting his attention. In truth, there was enough laughter in that room to raise the dead. The little ones couldn't sit still and slid off their benches soon as they filled their bellies, while the older ones were making such a racket with their blather, I could scarcely hear what folks next to me were saying.

When the eating was done, I helped clear the table, thinking I could speak to Patrick where he sat. But before I got there, all the lads stood up and went outside, leaving the women and girls to the washing up. But on his way out the door Patrick glanced my way and gave me a nod. A little spark went from my head to my legs, knowing he recognized me. I was itching to go after him, but knew there'd be no end of teasing if I did. So I followed the women into the kitchen and busied myself scraping plates and heating water for washing. I was at the sink with suds up to my elbows when I finally got the chance to ask Ellen about him.

"How long will he be boarding?" I asked.

"He just paid for a few days," Ellen said. "Had some business in town. He's leaving tomorrow." She took the plate I just washed out of the rinse bucket and wiped it dry. "How did you come to be knowing him?"

"Sure, I'm not knowing him at all," I told her. "He stopped by the Homestead Thursday looking for the Squire. Did he mention me?" I dropped the last plate into the rinse water and pushed the potato bowl deep into the water.

"Now I can't remember, to tell you the truth." Ellen stacked the dinner plates and carried them to the shelf. She looked tired. "Seems like a friendly lad. James likes him."

"I saw that," I said.

One of the children started howling and Ellen went to settle the commotion. Mary took up the dish towel and commenced drying as she was telling me about a property Tom was looking to buy in Turners Falls. It was an investment, she said, and would soon be making all of them rich.

"It sounds promising." I was hoping she'd get around to telling me what she thought of Patrick. But she went on and on about Tom's ventures, and after a bit, I straight out asked.

"I only laid eyes on him two days ago." Mary wiped the bowl dry. "What should I be thinking?" She gave me a sideways look. "Don't be telling me you're sweet on him, Margaret."

"Don't be an eejit," I said. "How could I be sweet on him when I just saw him once?" But I was keeping my eyes on the washbasin.

"Happens all the time," Mary said. "I was taken with Tom the first day I set eyes on him, though we didn't speak for weeks. Patrick's a good-looking lad. I'll give you that." She finished her drying, snapped the towel in the air a few times, and hung it back on the rack over the stove.

"I amn't taken with anybody." I wrung out the dishcloth more forceful than usual. "I'm set on staying single." What I wanted to be saying was *single and free* but it would likely lead to a quarrel we'd had before. Ever since I got George Garrett out of my system, I'd resolved not to be getting myself tied down. I'd watched Mary bear one babby after another and had seen how they stole her sleep and wore away her liveliness. She had no money of her own, only what Tom provided. So whenever folks started in on how I should be finding a lad to wed, saying it was the duty of every Irish girl to marry and have children, I paid them no mind. Just because I liked the look of a lad didn't mean I wanted anything to come of it. *I'm American, not Irish*, I'd say, making them laugh and shake their heads. Besides, Patrick Quinn was leaving tomorrow and I'd likely never see him again.

I carried the basin across the kitchen and flung the water out the back door. I stood a minute, listening to the dishwater dripping off the bushes. I could hear the children calling and the men's rumbly voices from the porch out front. Kelley Square was never quiet, but it was a comforting place. No matter what happened other places, when I came here I felt safe and content.

With the washing up done, Mary and Ellen and myself headed for the porch. Patrick was sitting on the rail listening to Tom and James and drinking a pint. I sat on the steps with Mary and Ellen, but I was so twitchy Mary said something must be ailing me.

"I'm grand," I said. "Just need to move around a bit to settle that brisket." And up I got and took a walk—past the depot and across the tracks to the Crossing, where most of the Irish in Amherst lived. The houses were small, but well kept up. Nothing folks could be calling a shanty. Took my time going back but when I did Patrick was still sitting where I'd left him.

I went up the porch steps. "I see you're still in Amherst, Patrick Quinn," I called out. Made him turn and look. A smile came over his face.

"That I am, Miss Margaret," he said. "That I am." And I felt my color rising again. Sure, I was pleased he remembered my name.

We talked a minute, Patrick and myself. He thanked me for pointing him to Kelley Square and for sending the message that the Squire would be at his office on Saturday.

"Sure, I'm trusting your business here was a success," I said, hoping he'd say what it was about. But he just nodded and smiled some more and by then I was mindful of everybody watching the two of us.

"Ellen says you're leaving," I said. "Going back to the tunnel."

"I am, though I wish I could be staying longer. 'Tis grand spending time with Tipperary folk." He tipped his glass back and finished his pint. I was turning away when he said, "But don't you worry, lass. I won't be forgetting this place." He gave me a wink.

And didn't my heart commence banging away like a girl with nothing but fluff in her head?

It was almost dark when I got back to the Homestead that Sunday evening. The air was steamy and wet the way it gets when there's a summer storm brewing, the kind makes your sleeves stick to your arms. But the weather didn't trouble me. I was thinking of Patrick, wondering if he'd be coming back to Amherst soon. I turned in at the Homestead gate and shut it behind me. The Squire was particular about keeping the gate closed. When I first came, I thought it was himself being haughty and unsociable but later I learned he was doing it for Emily.

Walking up the drive, I glanced to my left and didn't I see the Squire himself coming along the path from the Evergreens? His head was hanging down and he looked like the oldest man alive, he was so slow and bent. I was about to call out, asking if he needed my arm to lean on, when a little wind came up, swirling the leaves around and tugging at his hat. He clapped his hand on it and the wind died the same minute.

God's truth, I knew a Faery Blast when I saw one. As far back as I could remember, I'd recognized those little gusts of wind the

Faeries make to warn the doomed. Rattled me, it did, though I didn't say anything, knowing the Dickinsons would think it a foolish superstition. Fretted about it all night, though, fearing the Squire would be sick by morning or even die in his sleep.

But on Monday he was his usual self—ate a good breakfast and went off to his office. I was busy with washing the bed linens and fixing the meals and didn't have time to be worrying about why the Squire would be having a Faery Blast or what Patrick talked with him about. It had rained overnight and cleared the air, so it was a grand day for drying. Emily baked a custard and Vinnie helped me hang out the sheets.

After dinner Mother Dickinson went off to call on Mrs. Jenkins and Vinnie went up to her room to take a nap. The Squire sat reading in the parlor. I did the washing up and took in the laundry. When I came back in, I heard Emily playing the piano, a quare thing for her to be doing in the afternoon. Going past the parlor on my way to sweep the front walk, I could see the Squire sitting in his chair with his eyes shut, listening. Must have done him some good, for he was uncommonly kind at supper and there was no lecturing or quarreling over the cold beef and cheese.

The Squire left right after breakfast in the morning, heading off to the depot to catch the milk train to Boston. In truth, I was glad to have him out of the house, for I worked better when I wasn't worrying about displeasing him. And I had a lot to do—Tuesday, it was, and laundry-starching day for me.

Mother Dickinson and Emily and Vinnie lingered over their supper that evening. The air coming in the windows was warm and sweet, smelling of roses. Mother Dickinson was livelier than usual, going on about supporting the cleanup from the Mill River flood. Vinnie said she'd take some old clothes to Northampton for relief. It was after six o'clock and I was biding my time in the kitchen, waiting for them to shift themselves so I could do the clearing, when in came Austin. He burst through the back door, his hair flying in all directions and eyes black as Satan. Holding a scrap of paper, he was, waving it like a flag at a parade.

"Where's Mother?" he shouted. I waved in the direction of the dining room and followed him in.

"Whatever's the matter?" Vinnie asked.

Mother Dickinson touched her throat.

"A telegram," Austin said, his voice breaking all to pieces in his throat. "Father's ill. Very ill." He handed the telegram to Vinnie. "We must go to Boston." He looked at his mother, at Emily. "Now. We must leave at once."

"Leave?" Mother Dickinson started to stand but sank back. She looked so pale I thought she was fainting.

"Father," I heard Emily whisper. "He's dying."

Austin touched his mother's shoulder. It was meant to calm her, surely, but it seemed a stiff and awkward gesture. "You and Emily will stay here. Vinnie and I shall go."

Vinnie stood up. I could see her hands shaking. "But hasn't the train already left?"

He frowned and then turned to me. "Maggie, go tell Tim to harness the horses. Immediately." His look told me to run and so I did, fast as I could, and heard no more of the family's talk.

Tim wasn't in the barn but I soon found him at the far end of the lawn by the vegetable garden, smoking a pipe. He sprang up the minute I told him the news, running as if to a fire and the scowl on him could have killed a demon. But when I got back to the house, he met me at the door and said word just came the Squire was dead.

The dining room was empty, the plates sitting on the table with food bits stuck to them. Sue came while I was clearing and the family clustered together in the back parlor. When I went in to offer tea, Mother Dickinson was rolling her head on Austin's shoulder, while Sue patted her hand. Poor Vinnie was wiping her eyes but it was doing no good, for the tears were gushing down her face.

Emily wasn't with them. Vinnie said soon as she heard the news Emily went straight upstairs and closed herself in her room.

She didn't come out for two weeks.

Chapter Twelve

Death is a terrible trouble for any family, but the Squire's dying was pure ruin for the Dickinsons. It threw them into a misery and confusion so wretched they couldn't think. Vinnie was the only one whose mind was at all sound. It was herself making funeral arrangements and writing letters and bearing the sympathy of visitors knocking at the door. And there were dozens, for it seemed all the Protestants in Massachusetts were grieving for the Squire. I didn't know how famous he was till I read his obituary in the papers.

Americans mourn different than the Irish. In Ireland the way folks talk about their dead is sweet with memories for laughing and sighing. In America they act like death is a thief instead of a friend. To my thinking, the pity of it wasn't the Squire's dying itself but the way he died—alone, without a soul to be holding his hand and pressing a cool cloth to his head or even saying a prayer.

It was Austin went to Boston and brought his father's body home on the train. At the depot lads from the hat factory and Kelley Square loaded the Squire's coffin onto a wagon and trundled it up Main Street to the Homestead. They heaved it up the front steps and into the hall, all polished and shining. Then Austin told them to open the lid. It was a solemn moment, to be sure, for looking on the face of death is no easy thing. But the Squire's body looked exactly like himself—stiff and solemn and grand.

Austin bent and kissed his father's forehead. Staggered me, it did, for I never saw one Dickinson kiss another in all my time there. When he straightened up, he had the strangest look on his face—tender and sad and angry mixed together.

In truth, seeing the Squire's body set me remembering how flinty and hard he was in his ways and looks and how he seemed to have no feelings. How I rarely saw him smile except at Emily. How he obliged me to work for him when I wanted to leave. How I stayed to keep him from hurting my family. How all that time my neck was under a boot.

Now, with the Squire's dying, the boot was gone.

The funeral was Friday afternoon. All the shops and offices in Amherst closed out of respect, and the air was so hot it made me feel flimsy and spent. Austin came before breakfast to attend his mother and was by her side the whole long day. I could see by the way his face twisted he was mighty distraught.

Emily hadn't stepped out of her room since the woeful news came, not to sit with the family nor give her mam a daughter's comfort, nor even to visit the privy. I thought it mean-spirited of her, but nobody in the family complained and Vinnie said it was for the best—Emily's nerves were fragile things. So it was myself going upstairs and down with the slop bucket, emptying her chamber pot. And it was myself bringing her meals and setting the tray on the floor in front of her door, for she'd not open it to my knocking. At first I felt sorry for her. Sure, I knew what it was to lose a father. But the truth is, I didn't have Vinnie's patience and after a while I commenced fretting. Any eejit knows it's not wise being by yourself after a death. It's a way of beckoning the Banshee to your own bedside.

"She's not eating enough to keep a bird alive," I told Vinnie. "She'll wither and die in that room of hers, surely." But when I saw worry jumping into Vinnie's eyes, I stopped my prattling, thinking it best to hold my tongue. At least till the funeral was over.

Tim made a proper bier and six lads from Kelley Square carried it into the Homestead. I covered it with a black mourning sheet and they set the coffin on it. The lads moved chairs from the library and parlor into the hall. They fetched benches from College Hall to set in rows on the front lawn. Neighbors came with flowers for the big vases in the hall and parlors.

Vinnie spent the morning of the funeral dashing in and out and ordering workmen about. As soon as they finished one task, she was giving them the next. Sue came at noon, bringing Ned and Mattie, dressed in black the three of them. Mattie seemed to know her grandfather was dead and wasn't going to be greeting her. But she kept looking for Emily. She even crept into the kitchen and stood in the corner watching me, looking the picture of a lost soul. I finally told her to go on upstairs and knock on her aunt's door. Maybe she could lighten Emily's grief, or even coax her out of her room. It was no secret Emily had a special place in her heart for Mattie.

Soon after the child went up, the mourners commenced filling the house with their black sorrow—Aunt Elizabeth, stiff and solemn in her mourning gown, Louisa and Frances Norcross, Fanny Boltwood, and President Stearns from the College.

Talked in low voices, they did, and sat lightly on the chairs. Vinnie greeted every guest and offered pastries and coffee. Mattie came downstairs, but Emily wasn't with her. Vinnie set the girl scattering flowers in the front parlor, and her little face was squeezed so tight she looked the most heartbroken person there.

When I opened the door to Judge Lord, Vinnie pushed past me to greet him. I remembered him from all the times I'd made up the guest bed for himself and his wife. He was a tall, proper-looking man with a great head of white hair, but something in his eyes was fierce and hungry.

Mr. Bowles came with his sickly wife hanging on his arm. He was editor of the Springfield paper and a great friend to Sue and Austin. A handsome man, surely, with a full beard and sparking eyes. The kind of lad could make a girl's knees crumple. When I answered the door, he surprised me by leaning down to talk in my ear.

"Where's Emily?" he whispered. "I must see her."

"Sure, she's not seeing anybody," I said. "Took to her room soon as word came of Mr. Dickinson's death and she won't come out."

He frowned. "All the more reason, then. Please let her know I'm here." He had a way about him, Mr. Bowles, made it hard to be saying no. But I tried.

"'Tis no use, sir," I said. "She won't even open the door to her own sister."

He looked at me, those jewel eyes shining. "One moment." He took a slip of paper and a pencil from his pocket, scribbled a note, and pressed it into my hand. "Be kind enough to bring this up to her. Slide it under her door if you must."

I went up feeling cross, but a bit sorry for the man too. It wasn't the first time I saw how Emily's solitary nature had a cruel side. I knocked and said I had a note from Mr. Bowles. I was bending to slide it under the door, when it opened and there she stood, with her hair unbound and her frock wrinkled and her face looking all broken. When I gave her the note I saw the tiniest spark of light in her eyes.

"Send him up, Maggie," she said. "And thank you."

Nettled me, it did. It wasn't right for her to turn away her own family but welcome Mr. Bowles. But down I went, found Mr. Bowles, and led him up the back stairs. Emily was waiting in her doorway. He bowed and followed her inside. The door closed again, all but a crack. It wasn't a bit proper but I kept remembering that light in her eyes when she read his note. Whether it was proper or not, I was glad somebody was with Emily at her father's funeral.

In truth, I never got used to the Protestant way of doing funerals. When Reverend Jenkins came from the Congregational church with his black robes and Bible, the lads opened the coffin and there it sat, smack in the middle of everybody. There was no music or incense or Communion and all the praying and reading didn't unlock the tears waiting to be shed. There wasn't even a cross on the bier, just a wreath of daisies.

There was so much gloomy quiet I slipped back to my kitchen to be breathing again. After a time I heard Mr. Bowles come down. He peeked into the kitchen but didn't speak to me, just went through to the hall. There was a scraping of chairs, and soon Mattie and Ned came and told me it was over. I shepherded them back to the parlor. Everybody had gone outside to walk to the cemetery. The family had hired no hearse but asked the important men of Amherst to carry the coffin through town. I stood at the parlor window with Mattie and Ned, wondering if Emily was watching from her own.

I hoped Mr. Bowles had consoled her but I knew she was likely still longing for some way out of her sorrow. It wasn't healthy she spent so much time alone. Sometimes folks who live by themselves take their own lives purely out of grief.

After the burial folks came back for the funeral collation and the house filled up again. My nieces were there to help, and Sue sent her second maid. We put out custards and cold meats and gingerbread and black cake in the dining room and served coffee and tea. I was in and out of all the downstairs rooms more times than I cared to count. Vinnie was busy as myself, acting the hostess and telling everybody who asked that Emily was bearing up as well as could be expected, though she looked like a ghost. Mother Dickinson sat in the parlor and received condolences like a forsaken queen.

By late afternoon most mourners had left. I was in the pantry resting my bones on a stool when I heard ladies' voices in the Northwest Passage. Took me a minute to figure out they were talking about me.

"So what are you suggesting?" It was Mother Dickinson, sounding worn-out with misery.

"Just that she bears watching." Made me bolt upright, for I knew that voice as well as my own—it was Fanny Boltwood herself. "She's skilled at what she does," Fanny went on. "And she can appear very competent—even reliable—for months and years. But she lacks loyalty. She has no allegiance but to herself. She's quite capable of leaving you on a whim, as she did Clarinda."

Her words tumbled me back to the memory of the day she cut me. Walked right past as if I wasn't there. How it filled me with humiliation and sorrow.

There was a silence before Mother Dickinson spoke.

"My dear Fanny, I do appreciate your concern. But I simply can't bear thinking about this at present." Her voice was splintering into sobs.

"Aunt Margaret?" It was young Nell, come into the pantry. I stood up, hoping I didn't look as stricken as I felt. But the way she took my hand and frowned into my face told me I wasn't hiding anything. "You look done in," she said. "Go up and lie down for a bit. We'll take care of things. Most of it's done."

Sure, I think Nell was surprised as myself when I went upstairs. I paused at the door to my room but something made me turn. It was my legs, not my thoughts, took me to the front hall to knock on Emily's door.

In truth, I didn't expect her to answer, but a quare panicky feeling came over me and I tried the knob. It turned smooth and easy under my hand and the door swung open. Sure, I thought I was in the midst of a Faery enchantment. It was a quick, bright thought, there and gone, tiny as a hummingbird. I went straight in. Without a notion in my head about what breaking a spell can cost.

Every window in Emily's room was flung wide open, the curtains wrinkling and floating in the breeze. Late-afternoon light spattered across the walls, making it look like the wallpaper roses were dancing. And wasn't Emily sitting in her chair, smack in the middle of the room, turning toward every puff, as if she was conducting a choir of the air? I stood gawking, every word I planned to say gone from my head.

"Maggie." Emily didn't take her eyes off the curtains.

"Miss Emily?" I had the spooky feeling what she was seeing wasn't the curtains at all but some invisible creature. I thought again of the Faeries and almost turned and left. I was that scared I might see something no human should set eyes on.

"What I don't understand," she said in a lonesome, gone voice, "is how the world goes on without him."

Soon as she said it, I stopped worrying about Faeries. For it wasn't my ears but my heart did the hearing and I knew there'd be no answering her with words. Hadn't I felt the same when my own father died? Hadn't I wondered how I could go on without him? I remembered holding his poor head in my arms when he took his last breath. I thought then it was a comfort to him. But now I knew it was mostly a comfort to myself.

I laid my hand on Emily's shoulder, tender as tears. She kept watching the curtains, so I watched them too. And after a bit I saw what she saw—the air lifting and filling the curtains like breaths, coming and going, in and out. It was kin to prayer, surely.

Time stopped then, or seemed to, while I was standing with my hand on her shoulder. Then her own hand came up and covered mine.

I don't know how long it was before I came to myself and slid my hand from under hers and crept out of her room. It could have been minutes or it could have been hours. But in that time that was not-time, we were bound together in a quare enchantment and I knew nothing would be the same again. For years I tried explaining it to myself. The closest I ever got was remembering the old tales of folks falling under Faery spells.

It was near a fortnight before Emily came out of her room. But her closed door never hindered me after that day. I went in and out free as the wind itself.

It's hard work tending the grieving, for they don't have their wits about them. And the dead always leave troubles behind for the living to mend. You might be thinking Squire Dickinson was the sort of man had his affairs in order, being a lawyer and all. Turned out, he never even wrote a will. So his property—the Homestead, the Evergreens, his fine horses, his land and rentals and his money, all of it—was thrown into confusion. Austin took over. Stepped into the Squire's place, became a landlord and the treasurer of the College while Mother Dickinson fell into a deep melancholy. Vinnie started singing to her cats and Emily took to walking back and forth in the Northwest Passage, sunk in a stupor of mourning.

The first time I came on her, it gave me a fright. It was the same as seeing a ghost—her in that white frock with her hair tumbled down.

"Where is he?" she said in a mournful voice. "I can't find him."

"And who would you be looking for?" I thought maybe she was walking in her sleep—some troubled souls do—so I took her arm gentle as I could.

She stared at me, her eyes looking big and black in that shadowy place. "Father," she whispered. "I don't know where he's gone."

Made the ice run down my back, it did. "Oh, miss!" My voice came out thin as a kitten's mewl. "Best you come in the kitchen and let me wet the tea for you."

But she shook her head and ran up the back stairs. Like a fearful rabbit scurrying to its den.

I went back in the kitchen, shaking my head. Something about Emily's grief I wasn't understanding. Something dark and sorrowing about the whole family. As if they weren't living in America but in Ireland in the grip of the Great Hunger. Starving for a scrap of mercy, every last one of them.

Chapter Thirteen

C hange is the one thing can be counted on in life, and it's no different if a person's rich or poor. Sorrow has its day but the tide turns and there's something new to be putting your mind to. It was as true for the Dickinsons as anybody else. Come the spring of 1875 some of the sadness eased away. Sue was expecting a new babby.

It was a great surprise to everybody, that news, for Sue was forty-four and it was known Austin and herself had a hard marriage. That was the way Vinnie spoke of it, calling it *hard*, though everybody knew she was meaning their roaring fights any time of the day or night. Sue had hired my niece as a second maid. Early on all the Dickinsons started calling her *Little Maggie*. Don't know why they couldn't have called her *Meg*, same as our family. But it cheered me whenever she turned up in the Homestead kitchen for a bit of rest and gossip.

Thanks to Meg, I found out right off whenever Sue and Austin had a row. Didn't mention it to Emily, figuring it would sadden her. In truth, though, I think she knew before I did. She was more somber than she used to be, so it was likely Sue told her everything in her visits.

One hot June morning after one of Meg's visits—when I was

mincing suet for a pork pie and shaking my head because Sue had turned out their laundress for leaving scorch marks on Mattie's night shift—Mother Dickinson came into the kitchen. Turns out, she was after scolding me for forgetting to close the gate when I came back from the butcher's. Though the Squire was gone, she still wanted everything done the same as when he was living. I told her I was sorry, it wouldn't happen again, but she was still scowling so hard I wondered if she had the headache. "Pay attention, Maggie," she said, shaking her head as she left. "I don't know what the Good Lord was thinking when he made the Irish."

I near dropped the knife, it stung me so. Good thing she left before I spoke my mind. Took me a few minutes to calm myself. I had to remember it was only Mother Dickinson treating me so. Emily and Vinnie sometimes teased but never scolded. Still, they were fond of mockery and I'd sometimes overheard the two of them going on about how lazy and crude the Irish were. I got to wondering if the only folks on earth who didn't look down on the Irish were Irish themselves.

And didn't Patrick jump right into my head when I had the thought? It's strange how a lad can haunt a sane woman just by stepping into her kitchen on a rainy afternoon and giving her a wink. He'd only spent a couple days in Amherst, so it made no sense I'd even remember him. But it seemed he was only waiting for the chance to step out of the shadows of my memory. Little things sparked my recollections—word of a coal miners' strike in Pennsylvania, or last week's newspaper story of another accident at the Hoosac Tunnel. A foreman this time, crushed to death by a chunk of rock. And didn't I recognize the name? James Gallagher, it was—the very lad whose message Patrick was carrying to the Squire. I never did find out what that message was, though it hardly mattered now. I remembered what he said about the brave Irish lads he knew in the Union Army, and how it was Irish workers in the Hoosac Tunnel did the risky jobs. How proud of himself he was for being Irish.

So there I was, thinking away, with my arms up to the elbows in the bowl of pork and paste, when there was a clatter and thump upstairs. I wiped my hands quick as I could and ran up. Mother Dickinson was lying on her bedroom floor, moaning and talking gibberish. Sure, I don't think she even knew who I was. It was clear as day she'd had a seizure.

Vinnie was out, so I ran to get Emily. Found her in the garden with her hands in the dirt, weeding nasturtiums. Soon as I told her she leapt up and flew across the lawn to the house. Later I thought it quare I was the one shaking that afternoon, not Emily.

We helped Mother Dickinson into bed and I went for Dr. Bigelow, who said she'd suffered an attack of apoplexy and would be a long time recovering. She'd be confined to her bed for months. After he bled her, Emily sat with her till she went to sleep. Vinnie and Austin came and looked in on her, then sat in the kitchen while I wet the tea. Emily came down after a while.

"Do you realize it's exactly a year since Father died?" she said, her face so pale it made me think of the moon on a winter night.

We all of us stared. Her words stood in the middle of the room like a coffin and not one of us had anything to say after that.

The last Sunday in June was warm and Ellen and Mary planned a big family picnic at Kelley Square after Mass. We all went around to the back of the house, where the lads had set planks on sawhorses for a long table. The older children brought out the food—platters of boiled ham, pigeon pies, stewed fruit, hard-boiled eggs, and bread. The conversation was lively—we talked about everything from the grand weather to whether Amherst would soon be putting gas lines in for streetlights. James had been to Boston and blathered on about attending High Mass at the new Catholic cathedral and seeing the Boston Red Stockings play baseball. I didn't listen close, but my ears perked up when he said he heard police were still looking for Fenians who invaded Canada in the 1870 raids. I'd listened to more than a few lively conversations about those raids back when they happened.

"What are Fenians?" asked my niece Katie. She was eight and stuffed with questions. A body couldn't move without herself wanting to know why.

Tom smiled across the table at his daughter. "They're a band of Irish lads who swore an oath to fight England after the War of the Rebellion," he said. "They're after freedom for Ireland, though they're living in America."

"Pure mischief if you ask me," Mary said. "It was five years ago. Sure, I'm glad that business is over and done with."

"Don't know that it is," James said. "'Tis said they're busy plotting again."

"Aye, I've heard that too," Tom said, nodding. "And I daresay we'd not be thinking they were just mischief if we lived in Canada."

Ellen shook her head over her plate. "Maybe not, but it was the Fenians got themselves killed now, wasn't it?"

"Made a laughingstock of the Irish, they did," I put in, remembering the Squire sitting at breakfast and reading newspaper articles about the raids out loud, his voice full of mockery, setting Emily and Vinnie laughing. Once Emily had asked me if

I knew any Fenians. I'd stood there with a bowl of stewed pears in my hands, having no words to answer and my face burning with shame. Knew she'd asked because I was Irish, though I'd never met a Fenian in my life.

"I hope the police arrest every last one," I said, helping myself to a slice of ham and passing the platter to Mary. "'Tis a sin, surely. Didn't the priest say they'd all be excommunicated?"

"That he did," Mary said. "'Twas the Pope himself condemned them."

"Sure, their hearts are in the right place, though," said James. "'Tis love for Ireland and the rights of tenant farmers driving 'em, after all."

I thought of Da and wondered what he'd be saying if he was alive. For years he'd been bitter about having the farm sold away from him, and who could be blaming him? But I'd never heard him talk about any Fenians or tenant farmers' rights.

"I'm thinking you won't be seeing them marching off to jail," Tom said. "They're a cagey lot. Keep their mouths buttoned tight, they do. Chances are, they won't get caught even if the Pinkertons try to roust them out."

"But Margaret's right," Mary said. "'Tis against Church teaching. They're risking their immortal souls, same as the Freemasons, for swearing an oath."

Ellen said it was a shame, but many folks didn't seem to care what the Church taught these days.

"Aye, that's the truth of it," said Mary, and went on to talk about a hired girl from Pelham who was carrying a child. "She's not yet fifteen," she said. "Won't say who the father is but most think it's a married man."

Ellen clicked her tongue. "Likely as not it's the man she's working for, more's the pity."

I shook my head at the shame of it, but I was glad they'd changed the conversation. In truth, I had no interest in hearing more talk of Fenians.

As her time grew near, Sue Dickinson stopped going out and about. In July she was sending messages to Emily instead of seeing her. Vinnie was wrought up with excitement. But it was plain Emily wasn't sharing her sister's mood. The closer Sue got to giving birth, the more agitated Emily grew. One day I came on her in the Northwest Passage, wringing her hands and pacing back and forth.

"What's troubling you, miss?" I asked, tucking my dust cloth into my apron pocket. "Did you get bad news in the mail?" Like most days, she'd got another stack of letters. I couldn't keep track of all the folks she wrote to.

She shook her head in a distracted way, like a horse shaking off flies. But it was plain she was distressed. The poor soul looked half lost in her own house.

"Come sit down and I'll pour you a glass of lemonade," I said. "It'll do you a world of good."

I was surprised she followed me into the kitchen. Wasn't her usual way. Couldn't remember a time we'd shared a glass of lemonade in the middle of the afternoon. Soon as she sat down, though, the truth came out—she was fretting over Sue.

"She's terrified of childbirth," Emily said. She turned her head to look out the window, where the path to the Evergreens was hemmed by a carnival of hollyhocks.

"Ah," I said. "'Tis no wonder. It's painful giving birth and Mrs. Dickinson knows what's ahead of her. But there's happiness at the end of it, surely."

She shook her head. "Her older sister, Mary, died in childbed. It horrified her. She never wanted to have children." I frowned, thinking of my sister and all the children she'd borne. Everybody knew bearing little ones was part of life for a married woman. A risk, to be sure, but the natural way of things. Mary never spoke of fearing it—she was strong and sturdy and a midwife as well. But I knew even she dreaded the births.

"I feel so cut off from her," Emily said in a low voice. She was still gazing out the window.

I'd never heard her say such a thing. And it wasn't the truth either—Sue had been sending her notes all week. "Well," I said, "that's easy to be fixing, now, isn't it? There's nothing stopping you from visiting her. She's just a few steps away."

She gave me a quare look and seemed to shrink back in her chair. "There are many kinds of distance," she said. And then, for no reason I could fathom, she started telling me how she met Sue. "Father and Mother brought her home from church one Sunday. It wasn't long after her sister died and she was grieving. We were both twenty—Sue and I. It seems so long ago now." She sipped her lemonade and a soft smile came over her face. "Father had been talking about her for weeks," she said. "He always had his eye out for remarkable young people. And he said she was extraordinary, with a rare gift for words. Of course, that excited my curiosity and I begged him to invite her to dine."

I was trying to imagine the Squire being interested in young folks. Always seemed to me he was mostly interested in himself.

"Father was right—she was the most extraordinary creature," Emily said. "From the first moment I saw her, I was bewitched."

Surprised me, the way she was talking. Made me think of how ladies in romantic novels spoke of their lovers.

"Even though she was deep in mourning, her beauty was astonishing." She finished her lemonade and flicked a look at me. "I've always been drawn to beauty, you know."

I did know that, surely. Anybody could tell from the way Emily studied flowers and butterflies and the undersides of leaves.

"She was lovely—oh so lovely." Her voice dropped. "A single star," she whispered. She was looking off in the distance, as if the kitchen walls were gone and there was nothing between herself and the sky.

I poured us both more lemonade. I didn't say anything, didn't want to interrupt her. But there were a thousand questions on the back of my tongue.

"We were inseparable from the first," Emily went on. "We belonged to each other. Like sisters. Like twins." She turned her head from the window and looked at me. It's as if she came back into her body from wherever she was. "Did you know we were born only nine days apart?"

"Sure, I did not," I said. My skin was prickling all over, like fleas biting me. I didn't know how much longer I could sit still.

"I couldn't bear it if I lost her," Emily said.

"She'll be grand." I stood up. I didn't understand what had happened just then, but it was a pure relief to be on my feet and moving. "Mrs. Dickinson's constitution is strong as anybody's I know."

Emily nodded. "God grant it to be so," she said. And didn't she sound like my mam? Those words could have come out of her own mouth. I cast her a closer look, wondering if she was mocking my way of talking again. But her face was earnest and her eyes were glistering with tears.

A week later, word came Sue was in labor. Emily was distraught. But when I tried to soothe her, she told me to go straight to the Evergreens and do what I could to help. She'd promised me to Sue, she said—as if I belonged to her instead of myself. Like a stick of furniture or a horse, to be sent off to another mistress without even being asked what I wanted. God's truth, it made me cross. I went, but couldn't be putting a cheerful face on it.

Sure, I'd seen my share of babbies born, so I didn't fret, though Sue was heaving and moaning. But what woman doesn't when she's pushing a new one into the world? Birthing always seems to take hours, even when it's quick. Dr. Bigelow was there and Meg and Eileen, the new maid. So there was little for me to do but watch and wait.

When the child was born Dr. Bigelow told Sue she had a son, turned the babby upside down, gave him a slap on his backside, and spilled him into my arms. I wiped him clean and wrapped him in a towel. Before I even gave him to his mam, he was rooting for the breast. The weight of his little body wriggling against my breasts made something unfold in the bottom of my chest.

"This mite's looking for his dinner," I said. God's truth, I couldn't take my eyes off him.

"I'll take him," Eileen said, and plucked him out of my arms.

And just like that, I felt robbed. It was so surprising, I stood there blinking. Struck by a fierce longing for a child of my own.

It was Mattie showed up at the Homestead a few days after the birth, carrying a note for Emily and the news they'd named the babby Thomas Gilbert. "But he's too small for a big name," she said, "so we're calling him Gib."

Eight years old, she was, with a habit of scowling that blunted her pretty looks. But she was all smiles that day, and after I served up some cake and a glass of milk, Emily whisked her off to her room. "So we can conspire to our hearts' content," Emily said with a wicked spark in her eye. She doted on Mattie like she was her daughter. Left me thinking it was a pity she never had young ones of her own.

Part III

Windows

Chapter Fourteen

1916

After Mattie D turns me out of the Evergreens, I'm raging the rest of the afternoon. It helps speed me through my chores, and by the time my boarders get home, the table's set and the smell of cooked sausage is filling the house. The lads come in together—all six of them—straight from the lumberyard on the far side of town. I stand at the door, see to it every last one of them scrapes his boots clean before stepping over the sill. Dan Casey's grousing as usual—this time about the weather—and I can't be blaming him, for it's spitting rain now and it looks like he's been in mud up to his knees. I make him take off his boots right there on the porch. Which sets him grumbling all the more.

As they troop upstairs to wash, the thought comes to me I could be buying the Homestead myself. Don't know why I didn't think of it before. The place will suit well for a boardinghouse, roomy as it is. In truth, it makes me smile, thinking of these Irish lads tramping through Emily's house, taking their tea in the double parlor and sitting on the veranda on warm Sunday afternoons. Would set Emily laughing, to be sure.

I'll go have a chat with Tom after the washing up. He'll know how it's done. He's been buying property of one kind or another since he came to America.

At supper the lads are stirred up about the war in Europe. Jimmy Brennan says his brother is fighting with the Irish Sixth Battalion. "The Huns are using poison gas now," he tells us. "It chokes the breath from the lads and burns like Hell itself. 'Tis the Devil's own creation."

I give him a frown, for the lads know I don't tolerate crude talk at my table.

He scoops another spoonful of colcannon and sausage into his mouth. In truth, I don't know how he can eat at all, thinking of his poor brother. "Sorry, ma'am," he says. "But you'd be agreeing with me if you read his letter. Harms every living thing that breathes it, the gas does." I expect he's right—Germans are brutal as the English, surely. I've no taste for war, and all the tales I've ever heard of battles are dreadful. Yet it seems some lads are born to relish the fighting. It's the same the world over.

"Why are Irish lads fighting an English war? I'm asking," Dan says. "Let the English do their own brawling."

"When they come home victorious, they'll be given Home Rule and you'll be singing a different song," Jimmy says.

Several of the lads are nodding. Then Martin O'Day speaks up. He's usually the quiet one, Martin—keeps a tight bridle on his tongue—so when he has something to say, we pay attention.

"Won't be any Home Rule without a fight," he says. "We need a rising." His voice is low and raspy, but we hear every word. The lads look at Martin and one another, but not one of them says anything.

I put down my fork. "There's been talk of a rising for years and years. Folks were blathering on about it when I was a girl. There's been risings here and risings there. But the end is always the same—Irish lads in prison or dead, more's the pity."

"Freedom's a long time coming, surely," Dan says. "But 'tis a new century now."

"That it is," I say. "And I'm hoping you're right. No one wants to see a free Ireland more than myself."

"Amen to that," says Jimmy, and there's nodding all around.

I take up my fork again. "Now finish what's on your plates, lads. There's apple torte for dessert."

I make short work of the washing up and hurry across Kelley Square to Tom's place. He's alone, smoking his pipe and warming himself by the parlor fire. I feel the same jolt I always do seeing himself instead of Mary in the old rocking chair. She's six years in her grave now, and Tom's days are long and lonesome without her. His rheumatism vexes him and his bad legs bind him to the house, after he spent his whole life coming and going. It's plain he's glad for the company, especially since Nell has gone off to the moving picture show for the evening. She's the one takes care of him and helps out at the boardinghouse when I'm needing an extra pair of hands.

We chat awhile and I tell him about being turned out by Mattie D and that I'm wanting to know how to go about buying the Homestead. I remind him I've saved money from selling the New Mexico land my brother Tommy gave me. He looks doubtful, says it'll likely be costing a lot more than I'm expecting. Says I should apply for a mortgage at the bank and tells me how it's done in his careful way, till my head is spinning with the particulars and the clock on his mantel is striking nine.

When I go out the door I'm more cheered than when I came in. I never gave any thought to buying a place on Main Street before today, let alone the Homestead. But Tom makes it seem possible. Sure, it's not the first time chatting with him has lifted my spirits.

Still, I'm feeling edgy walking to the Savings Bank in the morning. I've been inside it more times than I can count, but never with the thought of begging for money that wasn't my own. If there's one thing galls me, it's being on the unfortunate end of charity. Asking rich folks for money—even when I'll be paying it back—is mortifying. But I'm wearing my new hat and it makes me feel lucky.

There's a black automobile in front of the bank—sides so shiny I can see my reflection. Gives me a pang, seeing a machine where a horse and buggy should be. Nell is always reminding me times change and I need to get used to things. I try, but can't help noticing the world was not so frantic in earlier years. Ever since the War of the Rebellion, things have got louder and more wearying.

A sober feeling comes over me whenever I go in a bank. A bit like a church, it is, though not so holy. The walls are always fresh painted, no matter the season, but half the property is behind bars. Wouldn't like to work in such a place myself—sitting in a cage all the day long. I tell the bank teller I've come about a loan and he directs me to a chair where I wait till I'm summoned. Takes twenty minutes before a woman comes out of a back room and asks me to follow her. Twenty minutes of myself sitting on a hard chair, all stirred up and fretting over what I'll be saying.

The woman looks like Kate Grady's daughter—with the same

big hands and snaggy left eyebrow and black hair frizzing out of her bun. She leads me through a door and down a hall to a tiny office where a round-faced man is sitting behind a desk. He has dark eyes behind his spectacles, but it's his mustache strikes me. Thick, brown, and lush as a mink's pelt. Can't stop staring. It's the spitting image of Alexander Bianchi's.

The man tells me to sit down, and when he asks how he can help, I come right out with it. "I'm after buying the old Dickinson place on Main Street," I say. But before I get a chance to tell him how much I've saved, he's shaking his head and telling me I've come to the wrong place.

"You'll want to apply to the Realty Company on Main Street," he says. "They're handling the Dickinson mansion sale through a New York lawyer."

"New York?" I say. Seems unlikely. What would a lawyer from New York have to do with the Homestead?

"Indeed." He gives me a tight smile and stands up quick. And I see the look on him I've been seeing my whole life in America—the belief I'm a stupid Irish woman, not worth another minute of his time. The shame is old as I am and drops over me like a shroud. I'd thought I'd be putting that behind when I left domestic service. My knees give a loud creak when I get up and I walk out feeling stiff and old, hoping my hat shades the red of my face.

Hoping I'll have more luck at the Realty Company.

Chapter Fifteen

1877

Three years after the Squire's death, I'd almost forgot Patrick Quinn. Things happen in a town to keep you occupied if you're a servant. The Dickinsons kept a quieter house than most, but they still had their visitors, and the town its scandals. The Lothrop girl ran away from home and took refuge in Reverend Jenkins' home across Main Street from the Evergreens. Her cruel father was all anybody in Amherst wanted to talked about. Then Austin came down with the ague and lay sick in bed for weeks. The College president died and was laid in his grave not far from the Squire. Mary Scannell, wife to the Dickinsons' new stableman, died from typhoid, leaving poor Dennis to bring up six little ones on his own. In the fall, Sue took Ned and Mattie and Gib to visit relations in Geneva, New York, and Austin moved into the Homestead for a month. Emily and Vinnie and his mother made a great fuss over him, but it was myself emptying his chamber pot and scrubbing his sheets.

Emily was still grieving her father, talking about what a lonesome place the world was without him, asking quare questions out loud. She'd say, "How is he faring without a body?" and

"Doesn't the snow make his resting place too cold?" She called the grave his *house of marl* and I had to ask what she meant, for it sounded like some heavenly palace. Turned out *marl* was her fancy way of saying *dirt*.

Judge Lord and his wife visited the Homestead at least twice a year. They'd roll up the drive in their grand carriage and everybody from both houses would come out to greet them. They were like kindly relatives, sitting with Mother Dickinson and chatting over dinner about the latest news from Boston and Salem. The Judge favored conversations about politics and literature. Austin and himself would get into lively quarrels, while the others would listen and smile. Evenings he and Emily would read poetry in the parlor. Seemed Emily and himself shared an affection for Shakespeare's writings and sometimes sat in the library reading plays out loud. I began feeling sorry for Mrs. Lord, wondering what she thought of such goings-on. It made my heart sting, though she never complained. If I'd been Emily's mam, I'd have chided her for being too familiar with the Judge, but it wasn't my place, and if Emily guessed my thoughts, she never said so.

That spring Tom was all stirred up about his daughter Meg because a lad from Palmer was sweet on her. "Word is, he's been stopping by the Evergreens every day," Tom said. He was perching on a stool in my washroom, balancing a cup of tea on his knees, while I finished the ironing. It was a fine May afternoon and I was wishing I could be outside in the air, for it was sugary with apple blossoms. "She'll get herself sacked if she keeps letting him in the door," he said.

I let him go on a bit. A father's got a right to keep an eye out for his daughter. In truth, though, I'd met the lad and had no quarrel with him.

"Meg's a good girl," I reminded him. "And clever too. She'll not be shaming you. Besides, she's a woman grown now and knows her own mind." I smoothed a pillowcase over the board and picked up my flatiron. "What's happening in Kelley Square?" I said to change the subject.

Tom sipped his tea. "Been quiet this week," he said. "Only news is that lad Patrick Quinn's turned up again. Came on the train two nights ago."

"Patrick Quinn," I said as if trying to remember who he was.

"Aye, the Tipperary lad who worked on the Hoosac Tunnel. He came to town just before the Squire died." Tom emptied his cup and went to the kitchen for more. When he came back he said, "It was just a couple days. No reason you'd remember."

"I'm guessing I do," I said. "What's he here for this time?"

"Looking for work," Tom said. "The tunnel's done now. Ellen's rented him the attic room while he's searching."

"So he's staying on awhile, then?" I tried to sound like I didn't care one way or the other.

"I'm guessing it depends on where he finds a job," Tom said. "He's a restless lad. The wandering sort who won't stay put long."

"Maybe I'll be seeing him Sunday," I said.

"Maybe you will," Tom said. "I'd best be going. Mary's after me to fix the door to the shed."

"Give her my love," I told him as he went out the door.

Tom had a knack for sizing up folks. He was likely right about Patrick's roaming. I had a restless side of my own, so I'd not be faulting a lad for what came natural. But I couldn't keep myself from hoping he'd be at Kelley Square come Sunday afternoon.

"Eejit!" I yelped, for I'd scorched the hem of the pillowcase

when I wasn't paying attention. It was a bad omen and I was out of sorts the rest of the day—twitching between vexation and excitement.

Nobody noticed except Emily. She made a jest of it—said I'd been spending too much time fussing over the new Cochin hen Austin had added to the flock. I'd have to stop feeding her buttermilk, Emily said, or she'd soon be fatter than the pig. Sure, the hen was a beauty, though she didn't lay well. But her feathers were soft as velvet and there was no chicken with a sweeter temper. A person could do worse than learn manners from a Cochin.

I didn't see Patrick that Sunday, nor the one after. But the next Tuesday I happened on him in town. I was coming out of Cutler's Store and there he was walking toward me, bold as life. I went up to him with my basket on my arm.

"If it isn't Patrick Quinn himself," I said. My face was likely pink as Emily's roses.

He gave me the kind of smile made me know he couldn't put a name to myself. "I'm maid to the Dickinsons," I said. "Margaret Maher." And I held out my hand for him to shake.

He took it. "Sure now, how could I be forgetting such a pretty face?" And didn't he bend down and kiss my hand? Made my skin tingle all the way up my arm.

We stood talking about this and that. I told him about the Squire's dying and his funeral—the biggest Amherst had seen in years. I asked how he was settling in at Kelley Square.

"Sure, I have a grand view of the railroad tracks." He winked and laughed, and I laughed with him. Out of the corner of my eye, I saw Fiona McGhee walking by and glancing our way. In truth, I liked being seen with a handsome lad.

Patrick said he'd found a job with a carpentry crew building a mansion in Northampton. Sounded to me like it would keep him near Amherst for a while. I was just telling him how Henry Paige had had to move his fish market out of Gunn's Hotel because of the stink, when the hat factory lunch whistle blew.

"Sure, I'd best be off," I said. "Will I be seeing you next Sunday after Mass, then?"

"I'm thinking you might," said Patrick, and winked again. And wasn't my step light as angels all the way home?

I soon learned Patrick rarely went to Mass, more's the pity. And often as not he'd be gone off somewhere Sunday afternoons, so I'd not see him at Kelley Square either. The truth of it is I never knew from one week to the next when we'd meet.

The times we did, though, they were lovely, to be sure. Sometimes I'd sit next to him at Sunday dinner and we'd flirt. When he laughed at something I said, the pleasure ran all the way down to my toes. It cheered me, seeing him—I thought it a bit of good luck to be starting the week. But we were never alone long enough to have an interesting chat like we did the rainy day we met. I still remembered things he'd said, and what I'd said back, and how his teasing had made the air crackle in the kitchen.

Sure, I wasn't the only girl keeping an eye on himself. Betsey Doyle and Katie Murray who worked for Mr. Hills, and Peggy Lynch from up on Irish Hill made no secret of doting on him. He was a charmer and that's the truth of it. Friendly to everybody and handsome besides. Ellen said it was a wonder he didn't have a pretty young wife and a house full of children. He was always flirting with one girl or another, but nobody steady. It was plain as a pikestaff he wasn't looking to marry.

Like all Catholic girls, I knew it was a blessing for a woman to marry and have babbies. I'd watched Mam and my aunts laugh as they dandled little ones on their knees. I'd seen Mary rock her wee ones and found comfort in rocking them myself. I'd liked coddling Clarinda Boltwood's children, and doling out sweets to Mattie and Ned and little Gib. The pleasures were plain enough. But troubles came with marrying. Some men were mean when they'd had the drink. And some were mean without it. I'd known women to flee with their children so they'd not get mangled or stabbed. Secrets and whisperings and shame brought down more families than I could count. And it was mostly the men who did the beating and the women who were the beaten.

Some days I felt downcast about being single, but mostly I was content. It's a sorry waste of time to be moaning after what you don't have.

The first big snow of winter that year came a week after Thanksgiving with flakes floating down like Faeries falling from the hawthorn trees. When I went to the barn to milk the cow and feed the chickens, Vinnie's cats came with me and didn't we make pretty prints? But all our tracks were filled by the time I was done. It snowed all day and all night but the next morning the sky was clear and blue as Factory Hollow Pond on a summer day. The sun was blinding on all that white, the snow so deep it came halfway to my knees. Lads brought out the big town rollers and pushed them up and down the lanes to flatten the snow so horses and sleighs could pass. By afternoon the street was a lively place with folks wrapped in wool and furs and gathering to chat.

I boiled beef and potatoes for dinner, served with a bowl of summer peaches Emily had canned. Emily fed Mother Dickinson, Vinnie went off in the sleigh to visit a friend in Sunderland, and I did the washing up. After, I took a few minutes to look out the front parlor window and watch folks in the lane. Sure, it looked like everybody was having a grand time.

Emily came into the room and stood beside me. "It's like alabaster wool, isn't it?" she said. "Soft as fleece."

"The snow?" I said, but I saw what she was meaning—how the snow hid all the bumps and edges of things, like a down quilt. "Sure, it does have a comforting look to it."

"Beautiful yet without mercy. Like the Angel of Death." It was almost a whisper.

Her words sent a shiver down my back. Seemed a foolish thing to be saying, a way of bringing down troubles, surely. *"Whist!* You'll be provoking the Faeries." I said it playful-like, though I was serious enough.

Emily smiled and put her hand on my shoulder. "There's nothing to fear today," she said. "It's a festival out there. You must take the afternoon off, Maggie. Go be with your friends and enjoy this fine day. We've no need of your services before supper tonight. And Vinnie will be late for that, in all likelihood."

God's truth, I didn't wait for her to be changing her mind.

Indeed, it was like a festival—everybody was in a mood for celebrating. Folks laughing and talking, children racing up and down, dogs barking, the tang of woodsmoke in the air. I was standing in the street chatting with Molly Ryan when folks started coming up from Kelley Square—Nell and Kate bundled in red scarves and hats, laughing and tossing snow in the air and chasing each other.

"Looking for lads to flirt with, surely," I said to Molly.

She laughed and went on with her tale of the Lowells' rooster escaping its coop and freezing solid to the rooftop overnight. I spied James and Ellen over her shoulder. And who was with them but Patrick Quinn? He was pulling a sled with my nephews Jamie and Willie tucked up warm as toast under a fat wool blanket.

Patrick came up to Molly and myself. "We're off to Irish Hill now for coasting," he said, "and Willie says his auntie Margaret must come along." He nodded to Molly. "And yourself as well."

Molly shook her head. "Ah, I wish I could. But I've a pile of ironing big as myself to be doing." And off she went.

"We're going to have great fun," Jamie cried. Willie was wiggling, making the sled rock back and forth. "You must come, Aunt Margaret!"

"There, now," said Patrick to me. "'Tis plain you have no choice in the matter." And with himself smiling into my eyes, how could I say no? Sure, there wasn't a dithering thought in my head, though I'd not been coasting before in my life. So off we went to the hill, where it seemed the whole town was gathering. A long hill, it was, running down to the street between two rows of rickety houses. Patrick pulled the sled, and I walked along beside, jaunty as you please.

Sure, it was a glorious afternoon. Up and down the hill we went, taking turns on the sled, first Patrick and then myself riding with the young lads. Standing on top I could see the whole of Amherst. Halfway through the afternoon Mary and Tom showed up with another sled. Only my brothers being with us would have made me happier. We grown ones shared Tom's sled, doubling up and laughing and shrieking down the slope—Patrick and Tom, myself and Mary, Ellen and James. But wasn't I surprised when, late in the afternoon, Patrick pulled me down to sit in front of him without so much as a word of asking?

It was a wild and thrilling ride, with Patrick so close I could feel his warmth right through my cloak. His two arms wrapped around my waist with his long legs beside mine. The sun was in my eyes and the wind whipping my face when we hit a rut and the sled went flying off the track. Patrick yelled, "Hang on tight!" and I grabbed his knees, for there was nothing else to hold. Back and forth we went, veering this way and that as Patrick tried to steer. But it was no use—we were plowing our own new path down that hill. We swerved round a shed and came near crashing into a wall. Then we hit a ridge and our sled tipped on its side and buried itself in a drift, tossing us off, with myself still wrapped in Patrick's arms.

My cloak was twisted around my waist, and one of Patrick's legs caught in my skirts, but neither of us moved at first, both just lying there, laughing in the snow. I was still trying to catch my breath when Patrick freed his leg and got up.

He stood there with his hands on his hips, grinning down at me. "Sure, you have the pinkest cheeks in Amherst, Margaret Maher. As pretty as a picture, you are." And he smacked his lips like he'd just downed a pint.

My heart thumped hard. "Late is what I am," I said, sitting up quick and pulling down my skirts to cover my legs. Patrick grabbed my hands and pulled me up. Then, to my surprise, he kissed my cheek.

I burst out laughing. "Is it flirting with me you are now, Patrick Quinn?"

"That I am," he said. "And it won't be the last time. So you best be ready." Then off he went, laughing, to dig the sled out of the snow.

"Do you think I have nothing better to do than listen to your boasting?" I called after him, for I couldn't be saying what I was feeling. In truth, I was well and truly flustered by his attentions. I'd been sweet on him for months but was scared to let my heart run free and think he might be sweet on me too.

Yet here he was calling me *girleen* and giving me kisses. It set my brain spinning, to be sure.

God's truth, I was cheerful that night. I made a late supper for Emily and Vinnie and fed Mother Dickinson myself before helping her into her nightgown and tucking her up in bed. I stoked the fire in the dining room so Emily could knit while Vinnie lay back on the sofa with Tabby on her lap and read out loud from a novel. It was a pleasing picture, to be sure, and it made me feel content as that purring cat.

I brought them hot chocolate and slices of gingerbread and some for myself too. I sat at the table, thinking of Patrick and paying no attention at all to Vinnie's reading. The warm fire and chocolate soon made my eyes too heavy to stay open and I nodded off. It was Emily tapped me on the shoulder and said I ought to get myself off to bed. Sure, I was dragging as I finished the washing up and banked the fires.

But before I went upstairs I stood a minute at the back door, looking out at the yard, all blue and lilac-colored under the half-moon. Seemed to me the hard corners of the world were all smoothed away and only beauty and peace endured.

Chapter Sixteen

Patrick wasn't at Mass the next Sunday and Tom said he'd gone off to Northampton again. I was disappointed, to be sure. At Kelley Square I played checkers with Jamie and Katie. Nell had a pair of skates and was begging me to buy a pair myself, for the ice on Factory Hollow Pond would soon be solid. When I told her I didn't know how to skate, she promised to teach me. Set me thinking what fun it would be to go skating with Patrick and wondering when I'd be seeing him again.

Mary was weary, for she'd been out the night before helping a new babby into the world. I made her sit while I wet the tea and chopped cabbage and onions for supper. And because I couldn't stop thinking of it, I started talking about the lovely time we'd all had on Irish Hill.

"Sure, you've been blathering on about it ever since Mass ended," Mary said. "And it wasn't the grand weather excited you. 'Twas Patrick Quinn himself, and that's the truth of it." I turned and saw her chuckling and twinkling at me.

"He's a bit of a flirt, to be sure," I said. "But there's no harm in that, now, is there?"

"Just sets me wondering if you're wanting a family of your own after all," Mary said, and I felt a pang, but pushed it away.

"I'm thinking maybe you've changed your mind about staying single," she went on. "You're thirty-six and 'tis no secret a woman's seasons are numbered."

"If it's marriage I'm wanting, do you think I'd be setting my sights on the likes of himself?" I went back to my chopping. Mary's words nettled me, for all my bold talk. I didn't like being pitied for not marrying.

Willie ran in, whining that Jamie was teasing him, and Mary went off to sort things out. By the time she came back, the meal was half made.

Mary folded herself into the rocking chair with a sigh. "The headache's still with me and Jamie's not a bit of help," she said. "The boy's too high-spirited and that's the truth."

I nodded, thinking she was going to be going on about what Jamie'd been up to. But she went right back to talking about Patrick. "You could do worse for a husband. He's a handsome lad and good-natured, from what I can tell."

"Pshaw!" I said, for I didn't want to be talking about him anymore. Still, it took some of the soreness from her earlier words. Like putting honey on a bee sting.

That night I went back to the Homestead, promising myself I'd spend less time thinking about Patrick. Hoping I could keep that promise.

Deciding not to think about a lad is a sure way to be carrying him around in your head all the day long. Patrick kept popping into my mind when I wasn't expecting it. And Mary had been no help, with her deciding I was wanting my own family.

She was right about my age. Everybody knew a woman who waited too long to be having children could end up having none at all. But long ago I'd seen the value of a single life and was in no rush to marry. Seemed to me a woman should be somebody herself before she became somebody else's. By the time I was twenty, I'd seen for myself how many wives were doing the same work I was as a maid and getting nothing for it but bad knees, a lame back, and a houseful of hungry children. No wages nor any days off. My sister, for all she was blessed with a lovely husband and children, was worn out by the time she was forty. So I wasn't yearning after her happiness, surely. I didn't need the bother of a lover, let alone one who'd pester me to marry.

But a maid's life is a lonesome one, even with her sister living close by. I was mindful of what I was missing—the thrill of a lad's sweet kisses, the pleasure of his smiling eyes, and the comfort of lying in strong arms at night. No matter how many times I reminded myself I didn't want to give up my freedom, I wasn't always believing it. There wasn't much freedom in domestic service, truth to tell. I was bound by the whims of other folks.

Sure, these thoughts worried me early and late and in the middle of the night. But even as I puzzled over them, I knew their foolishness. For the truth was no lad was asking to marry me, was he? Least of all Patrick Quinn.

December came in hard with biting winds, the kind that froze the laundry stiff on the line and stabbed my fingers when I took it down. Emily liked to say we were feeling the back of the Old North Wind's hand slapping our cheeks. Sometimes I wondered if she had Irish blood, she liked playing with words so.

News came in the middle of the month that Judge Lord's wife, Elizabeth, had died. The poor woman had been so broken down with rheumatism and winter fever, it wasn't a surprise. But it struck the Dickinsons hard. They'd long prized his friendship and Emily especially felt the blow. She was certain the Judge was bowed low with grieving. She wrote him consoling letters so long they made the envelopes fat.

Christmas was soon on us. Austin and Ned cut a small tree to set in the corner of the Homestead parlor and Vinnie and Emily trimmed it with ribbons and strings of beads and colored glass balls. Set an angel of creamy wax atop the tree, looking like Saint Gabriel himself. It was lovely when I drew back the drapes and let the sunlight in.

I was helping Emily twist red ribbon through evergreen boughs on the fireplace mantel when she asked who my sweetheart was. Came out of the blue, her question, though it shouldn't have surprised me, with the close way she watched folks. Took me a minute to answer.

"Sure, I don't have a sweetheart, Miss Emily," I said.

"Oh, but I have reason to think you do." She tilted her head. "For you're looking as happy as if you'd just received the sacrament."

I blinked at her blasphemy, and I must have blushed too, for she laughed and said, "Come, it's nothing to be ashamed of." She tucked the end of the ribbon behind a bough and stepped away to see the effect. In her white frock she looked a bit like the tree angel herself. Something graceful and light in the way she held her body made her almost beautiful.

"Have you ever been in love, miss?" The question came out without my wishing it, born of wondering and that unsettling angel look.

"In love?" Emily tapped two fingers along her bottom lip. Her smile started slow and opened like a flower. "I would have a quicker answer if you'd asked have I ever *not* been in love. For that condition I have no memory of at all." She looked back at the mantel. "Truth to tell, I don't know how to avoid being in love with *someone*."

I tried to unpuzzle her words. "Is there somebody you're loving now, then?" I asked.

She turned to face me again. The flash had drained out of her eyes and they went round and sad—I'd never seen that look on her before. "Oh, my dear Maggie," she said. "There are so *many* someones, I wouldn't know whom to pick."

What a quare strange thing to be saying. I couldn't think what to reply, so I just nodded and quick as I could went back to the kitchen to comfort myself peeling potatoes. But it set me thinking hard about what she meant. For the life of me I couldn't work it out. Or maybe I didn't want to—maybe I was fearing what I might find if I thought too hard. It was easier sometimes just to tell myself Emily was a riddle and not go poking around in the shadowy corners of the truth.

With the turning of the year the cold settled in and the snow came down and piled up against the door. It was a hard winter—one affliction following on the heels of another. Vinnie fell sick with a slow fever, keeping her in bed for weeks. Mother Dickinson grew weaker and weaker. She'd been confined to bed since her attack. At first she couldn't speak, nor feel anything at all on the right side of her body. I made broths and teas and milk toast and oyster soup, and Emily and myself spooned them into her mouth like she was a babby. We moved her into the room next to Emily's. There was a door between, so Emily could hear and tend her in the night. When she could finally talk again, Mother

Dickinson's mind was a hundred miles from nowhere. She'd ask and ask if the Squire had come. "Why isn't he home yet?" she'd say, tossing on her pillows. "I don't understand what's keeping him." And she'd beg Emily to watch for him. "Someone needs to wait up," she'd say. All the color would wash out of Emily's face and she'd look like she'd been stricken herself. Near broke my heart, seeing it.

"Hush now," I'd say, taking Mother Dickinson's hand and giving a nod to Emily. "No need for Miss Emily to be losing her sleep. I'll wait up and see him in myself." It seemed to soothe the poor woman.

At the Evergreens, Ned had falling fits. Then came word Samuel Bowles had died. Emily looked as if she'd been struck by a plank. She staggered around the house and spent hours in her conservatory though it was bitter cold. In truth, I was puzzled why she took it so hard. He was a friend, surely, and the only mourner who sat with her through the Squire's funeral. But she hadn't laid eyes on him since then. Molly Ryan speculated they'd been secret lovers years back. I told her it was a foolish idea, but more than once I wondered.

It was near the end of February before I saw Patrick again, and that on a sunny Wednesday afternoon when I was going about my errands in town. The snow was melting into puddles of slush, wetting my hems and chilling the toes in my boots. But the sky was blue and the sun was pouring down and my misery disappeared when I saw himself stepping out of the Amherst House.

I had my market basket on my arm and it was heavy with a pork loin and a three-pound sack of rice and other sundries. But it could have been made of mist for all the notice I took of it as I stepped up to Patrick. "I've not seen you at Mass," I said. "Where have you been hiding yourself after all?"

"Ah, Margaret," he said in his cheerful way. "Don't you know I've been out and about doing the Lord's work?" And didn't he laugh like he had the wittiest tongue in Amherst?

"Now it's blaspheming you are?" I said as if his words shocked me. "Be off with yourself, then." And I started to turn away but it was all make-believe, for I was laughing myself. Seemed I couldn't keep a stern look on my face when he was near.

He leaned closer. "'Tis good to see you, truly it is. Though I have to confess"—I caught a whiff of the whiskey on his breath—"it's not the Mass I'm missing but your sweet face shining like the dawn itself."

"Get away with you!" I said, laughing. His boldness, for all it flattered, made me a bit sad, as I knew it was likely coming from the drink as much as from himself. Irish lads were as fond of their liquor as they were of flirting, to be sure. But in truth, I was pleased to see him. "Would you be heading back to Kelley Square now?" I asked. "For I'm walking to the Dickinsons' and wouldn't mind the company."

"Sure, I'm happy to provide it, *a chara*," he said, and took the basket from my arm like a proper beau.

At the back door of the Homestead, he put down the basket and leaned toward me. "You're a handsome woman, Margaret," he said in a soft voice. His eyes were shining. "And I'm thinking it's time I was giving you a real kiss." I saw the crinkles at the corners of his eyes and my heart flipped upside down. I took up the basket and fumbled with the door latch.

"Will you be going to the dance in Northampton on Saturday night?" he said.

Meg had told me about the dance, for James McKenna was

taking her. I looked back at Patrick. "Are you asking me to go with you, then?"

"I am indeed." His smile was warm as sunshine.

"Sure, I'd like that, Patrick Quinn," I said, and fled into the house, feeling like a young bird on the rim of a nest, working up the courage to fly.

Chapter Seventeen

Saturday morning I was making breakfast when Emily came in from outside, smelling of cold air and melting earth. Surprised me, for I'd seen the crack of lamplight under her door the night before and knew she'd stayed up till the small hours.

"It's a fine brisk day," she said. "And if I'm not mistaken, there's a ribbon of spring in the wind." She pulled off her gloves and rubbed her hands together. "March is coming."

"A ribbon?" I was cutting slices of ham for the skillet.

"Haven't you ever noticed how certain scents flutter around us, Maggie? Like ribbons in a breeze."

"Perhaps 'tis your imagination, miss." I dropped a slice into the pan, where it sizzled in a happy way.

"Not at all. Come. You must smell it yourself." She took the knife from my hand as if breakfast didn't matter and pulled me out onto the piazza. There I stood in the wet cold, shivering while she waited for me to catch the smell she was talking about.

But it was no use. I didn't have the clever nose she did, nor the patience that morning to try. I shook my head. "Sorry, miss. I amn't smelling any ribbons this morning."

She laughed. Tipped her head back and chortled at the sky. It wasn't the first time she'd laughed at something I said. The soft humiliation in it I'd learned to ignore as time passed. But that morning it nettled me—maybe because my mind was mostly on Patrick. Even as I hurried back into the warm kitchen, I was thinking of what I'd like to be saying if I wasn't a maid. If I was free to speak my mind.

When Patrick came knocking just after seven o'clock, I was ready—wearing my blue calico and burgundy shawl, my heart thumping away in my chest. Soon as I opened the door he looked me up and down, and then he bowed.

"Sure, you're the prettiest girl in all of Hampshire County." He stepped over the sill, took my cloak, put it around my shoulders, and bundled me out of the house. His cosseting made me feel a proper sweetheart. God's truth, it was lovely.

He and his friends had rented a horse and cart for carrying everybody to Northampton. The cart was so full the poor horse had a hard pull. All of us were jumbled close, but it kept us warm. Soon I was laughing and talking without a thought for how icy my face was.

The dance was in the basement of the town hall. We went in a side door and down some steps into a great room bright with gas lamps. Three fiddlers were playing a reel at the far end of the room. Some wooden chairs stood against the walls and there was a long table of refreshments—bowls of lemonade and pink punch and plates of cakes and biscuits. I was smelling the sugar just stepping through the door, my arm locked through Patrick's and my feet already itching to dance.

Didn't I have a grand time? Patrick and myself danced and talked all night. Between jigs and quadrilles he brought me cups of punch and slices of cake. And every time we danced a waltz, he held me closer. By the last one his chest was pressing tight against mine. God's truth, it was rousing to be in his arms.

Late in the evening the dancing turned to singing—those sad, sweet ballads that always pull at Irish hearts. "Green Bushes" and "Eileen Aroon" and "Mo Ghile Mear." Near the end of the night, a lad stood up and sang a ballad I'd never heard before—the tale of a lad longing to go back to the valley of Slievenamon. Sure, it took me straight back to Tipperary, for I knew that mountain so well it was carved on my heart. I remembered walking on its slopes with Michael, picking flowers for our mam. Michael was only two years younger than myself and we did everything together. Close as twins, the pair of us. Thinking of those days made me so homesick, my tears spilled over. Patrick put his arm around my shoulder, and when I looked up, I saw tears running down his own cheeks too. So there the two of us stood, crying like babbies. And I do believe I was never happier in my whole life.

It was quiet most of the way back to Amherst, for we were all weary. At the Homestead, Patrick handed me down and walked me to the door. Before I could open it, he took both my hands and drew me against himself. "I'm thinking it's time I was giving you a real kiss," he whispered. I knew I should be stepping away, but I didn't move an inch when his mouth came down on mine. Made me so weak in my bones I could barely climb the stairs to my room.

Sure, I don't know what made me stop before I went in. Maybe it was the sound of Emily's footsteps—though it was rare as teats on a hen to hear them. She was usually all silence and glide. More ghost than woman, I sometimes thought. But something made me look up and there she was, not four feet from me in her nightgown and shawl, her hair streaming down.

"Miss Emily?" I said. "Is something wrong?"

She shook her head and stepped closer. "Did you have a good time at the ball?"

"Wasn't a ball, miss," I said. "Just a plain old Irish dance." I kept my hand on the doorknob, for I was reeling with weariness.

"Coquetry pays no deference to class," she said. "One can flirt as easily at a barn dance as at a ball."

"Sure, I try not to flirt, miss," I said, though it was a lie. Most of my time with Patrick was given to flirting.

"Oh no, you must! It's one of the great pleasures of life!" Even in the dark I could see her eyes sparking mischief. "And who better to flirt with than a handsome Irish rogue?"

I took my hand off the knob. "Patrick's not a rogue," I said. "I'll be going to bed now if you have no need of me. I've Mass in the morning."

"Every man's a rogue if you give him the chance," she said, smiling, but before I could answer she was gone.

"I like him," I said to Mary. "And that's the end of it. So don't you be telling me what a blackguard he is." I was too cross to look at my sister, though I was standing in her kitchen, washing her dishes in her sink. "I'll not be listening to Amherst gossip."

It was two weeks after the dance and I'd walked out with Patrick three times since. We went to a fiddlers' contest, sat through a lecture about the railroad strike in West Virginia, and took a long stroll out to the Agricultural College, just the two of us. Each time he took me back to the Homestead, we kissed on the doorstep. Sure, his kisses were growing longer and sweeter and making me hunger for them when he wasn't around.

"'Tis not gossip I'm telling you." My sister's tone was easy. "I saw him with my own eyes from the parlor window. Kissed Anna Breen on the cheek in broad daylight. If the girl had any self-respect, she'd have slapped his face."

I swirled the dishcloth over the last plate and dropped it in the rinse bucket. "A charmer he is and that's the truth of it," I said. "But he means nothing by it. 'Tis just his way in the world."

I didn't tell Mary, but I *did* mind Patrick kissing Anna. She was Ellen's cousin and fresh from Galway, not a day older than twenty with black hair and blue eyes and skin smooth as cream. She was looking for work as a maid. I was hoping she'd find a place soon—and not anywhere near Amherst.

Mary changed the subject. "Did you hear John O'Hara's been beating his wife?" She took the broom from the corner and began sweeping the floor.

"Meg told me," I said, wringing out the dishcloth. "'Tis said the poor woman's been knocked about more times than a body can count." I carried the basin out the back door and tossed the dirty water onto the gravel beside the tracks. The snow was mostly gone and the frost coming out of the ground so my shoes got muddy just going across the yard. I had a clear view of the boardinghouse, so I took my time wiping them off. But there was no sign of Patrick coming or going.

When I went back in, Mary had done sweeping and was wiping down the long shelf. She was fierce in her housekeeping, my sister. Didn't tolerate a smidgen of dirt nor clutter. But a strand of hair was coming out of its bun and looking at it gave me a start. For the first time I saw it was going gray, though for years it had been the same brown as my own. It had been a long time since I thought about how much older she was than myself. But now I saw the gap—that had seemed so big to me when I was young but hadn't mattered in years—was going to mean something again. I pushed away the thought of my sister growing frail and sick. But not before it caught in my throat a minute. I dropped the basin back into the sink.

"You go put up your feet in the parlor now," I said, taking the wiping cloth out of her hand. "I'll finish in here. Won't take me a wink."

Saint Valentine must have been watching that minute and decided to bless my good deed. Not two minutes later, I heard the back door open. And when I turned around wasn't it Patrick himself standing there and smiling to beat the Devil?

"Margaret, *ma chree.*" He put his hands on his hips. "You're a feast for my eyes and that's the truth of it. Come over here and give me a kiss."

The heat came up in my face. I flicked the wet cloth in the air and smacked it down on the shelf. "You'll not be telling me what to do," I said, though my legs were weak with wanting to go to him. "I'll do what I like."

He laughed. "Ah, sweet Margaret, you know how much I like the Irish spirit in a girl, don't you, now?" And he dropped his hands off his hips and came to me. God's truth, I couldn't stop myself from sliding into his arms any more than a mother could stop from picking up her crying babby. He wrapped himself tight around me and gave me a long, deep kiss. So long I near ran out of air. When he finally let me go I was breathing like I just ran up Irish Hill.

I'd never been kissed that way before. It seemed the sort of kiss a man would only give when he was in love.

"Patrick," I said, "if it's an easy woman you're after, you won't be finding herself in me." It seemed a foolish thing to say after enjoying his kiss so, but my brain was fuddled and cottony.

"Sure, I've known that for months now." I fancied his cheeks looked flushed. "'Tis one of your attractions, love." And didn't he chuck me under my chin like I was a babby?

My feelings scurried about like a litter of new-weaned kittens. I wanted to slap him. And I wanted him to kiss me again. Instead, I sat him down at the table and wet the tea and soon we were chatting away. We talked about this and that and he told me the sad tale of his mother dying in Ireland just days before he emigrated. Then he asked me the name of the town I came from.

"I know by your accent it was County Tipperary and I'm guessing it was in the south somewhere," he said. "Clonmel, maybe?"

"Sure, I'm not from Clonmel," I said. "And I don't want to be talking about it." I was thinking of the misery I saw when I was a girl. "'Twas a long time past and makes no difference to me now, does it?"

Patrick's eyebrows went up. "No difference?" he said. "'Tis the place that made you, Margaret. 'Tis the marrow in your bones, just as Ballingarry is the marrow in mine."

"Ballingarry?" I said. "Sure, I've heard of it since I was no bigger than a sparrow. My da took us there once for the Whitmonday fair."

"Did he, now?" Patrick said. "Sure, if I'd seen you, I'd have danced you off your feet."

I laughed. "I'm thinking not. I was just a wee girl then."

"It's a famous place, Ballingarry," he said. "There was a battle there during the Great Hunger. Right in the middle of Widow McCormack's cabbage patch. 'Twas a great day for rebelling." His eyes were shining. "I watched the fighting from the attic window when I was a boy. Young as I was, I could already smell a free Ireland."

"And yet she's not free, is she?" I frowned. "The English boot is on her neck and never coming off. Dreaming it will change is nonsense."

"Margaret." He reached across the table and took my hand. And didn't a shiver go up my arm? "It's not nonsense at all. 'Tis the truest thing I know. There are thousands of bold Irishmen and -women after making that dream come true right now." He looked straight into my eyes. "Come, tell me, love." His thumb was stroking my palm. He was being too familiar by half. He shouldn't be touching me that way and I shouldn't be letting him. But I didn't draw my hand away. "Isn't where you came from the place of your true heart's longing?"

I couldn't deny it—hadn't I wept with him at the dance, listening to the old ballads? A wistful feeling came over me. In truth, I still yearned for the view of Slievenamon from Da's farm—those lovely green and yellow fields folding themselves away to the purple slopes of the mountain. "We lived near Kiltinan Castle—outside Fethard," I said. "Da was a tenant farmer. A big farm, it was—forty-nine acres—so we weren't starving. There was enough to send myself and my brothers to school."

Patrick made a soft whistle with his lips. "Forty-nine acres," he said. "Not everyone was so lucky."

"Sure, I know that." I pulled my hand from his and poured myself another cup of tea.

"So why did you come to America, then," he asked, "with such a grand farm to be running?" He was looking like he knew the answer.

"The land was encumbered," I said. "Squire Cooke sold it, so we had to leave."

Patrick nodded. I could see he wasn't a bit surprised. "It's always the same. Another man's livelihood stolen away. Another injustice, with all the rest. Aren't you angry about it, Margaret? Wouldn't you like to see all of Ireland free?"

I looked away. I didn't want to admit it. I'd spent years telling myself what happened in Ireland didn't matter anymore—I was American now. But I was angry, to be sure. God's truth, there's nothing sweeter in this world than freedom.

Chapter Eighteen

When Emily first started talking about Judge Lord, I thought she was just passing the time. Then I began noticing he was coming to the Homestead more and more. Every two or three weeks he'd show up on the doorstep and I'd have to be making up the guest room again. Sure, he didn't look too grief-struck to me. And I'd have been a fool not to see he was spending most of his time with Emily. The pair of them were always taking walks in the garden or reading to each other in the library or laughing in the parlor over some clever thing one of them had said.

In truth, I didn't care for the Judge. For all his titles and importance, he wasn't the sort of man you'd expect to be seeing in a court. He was more of a rascal than a magistrate—overfond of jesting and bawdy more often than elegant, with a tongue on him like a whip.

When Emily told me she felt safe with the Judge—safe in a way she hadn't since her father died—I thought it quare, for though he was older than herself, he wasn't fatherly in his ways. Took me a while to see Emily was beguiled by love. But it was plain enough once I figured it out. She was always saying how wise he was, how much he made her laugh. And there was a blizzard of letters flying back and forth between the pair of them. So many Vinnie started teasing. Emily usually gave as good as she got when it came to poking fun, but when Vinnie mentioned the Judge, Emily'd blush instead of bantering. Still, it was a surprise when she asked me to post her notes in secret and pass his letters to her when nobody was about.

It's rousing to be in on a secret, and that's how I felt when I first began hiding the Judge's letters in my pocket and running them upstairs to Emily's room. But as time went by, it began to trouble me. I didn't like the look of it. Secrets are tinder for lust. There's good reason for keeping God's commandments. Passion's flames can jump the grate if not damped.

Then Emily started calling the Judge by his middle name, Phil, and giggling like a schoolgirl whenever he was mentioned. I told Patrick about it when we walked out on a sunny day in March. "Sure, it's like being in a novel," I said. "Posting love letters and keeping secrets." I was wearing my new shawl, a red wool paisley I bought for keeping warm and feeling lovely. We crossed a field and went along a path into the woods. The trees were budding but hadn't leafed out yet, so the sun was bright and warm on my back.

"Secrets get the blood pumping, surely," Patrick said. The path narrowed and curled around a boulder. I went ahead but he was so close behind I could have reached back and touched him if I'd had the notion. "And what would you be knowing about a novel, a working lass like yourself?"

I knew he didn't mean any insult but I felt a sting. "Miss Emily lends me books," I told him, letting the barb push into my voice. "She likes to talk about them when I'm done reading."

"What? The Myth and yourself are friends now?" His voice

was choppy from holding in a laugh. "Does she give you flowers and send you cunning verses in her notes too?" I'd told him about the care Emily took writing letters to her friends. His teasing made me cross.

"Don't be daft," I snapped. "I know my place." And I walked faster, just to show I couldn't be trifled with. Still, his words rolled around in my brain. I wondered if there was some truth in them I didn't care to admit. It's often the way of things.

The path widened and Patrick came up beside me again. The sun was melting the snow into dark winking puddles. I heard a dove calling close by. A lonesome sound if ever there was one.

"If I knew you liked secrets so, I'd be giving you a few for safekeeping." Patrick scooped my hand into his. His voice was low and sweet but there was merriment in it. Was he still teasing? Or was he meaning something else? Was this a new riddle to be solving?

His fingers brushed the circle of bare skin on the underside of my wrist. Something fluttered in my throat—a warning of danger, maybe—but I didn't draw my hand away. "The only secrets I'll be keeping are my own, Patrick Quinn," I said, sounding bolder than I felt.

"Ah, but you don't need to be keeping secrets from me, *girleen*," he said. Quick as a snake, his fingers slid under my sleeve. Made me shiver all over and a hard ache grew in the pit of my belly. I thought of all the secrets in *Jane Eyre* and how often I'd imagined Mr. Rochester looked like Patrick.

"*Girleen* are you calling me now?" I said. "You ought to have your eyes checked, lad. I'm no more a *girleen* than you are. Or haven't you noticed?"

He laughed. "Indeed I have, Margaret. Indeed I have." He

stopped walking. I knew I was putting myself in the way of sinning. For weren't his fingers still inside my sleeve, stroking my naked skin? The ache in my belly grew fierce, spreading to my knees and turning them to jelly. I took a sharp breath and leaned toward him and then he smiled, let go my hand, and pulled me into his arms. Sure, there wasn't a thought in my head as he kissed me and kissed me. And for every kiss he gave, didn't I give him back two?

Patrick could turn the dreariest day into a sunny one just by walking into a room. He did that very thing one Thursday morning in June when I was just done washing the fresh-churned butter. My hands were still slippery when he stepped over the sill and stood looking as pleased with himself as one of Vinnie's mousers.

"Take off your apron and fetch your shawl," he said. "There's somewhere I want to be taking you."

"Don't be daft," I said, scooping up the butter and packing it into the crock.

"Come, lass." He stepped behind me and slid his arms round my waist. And didn't it give me a tingle from my neck all the way to my backside? "'Tis your afternoon off and surely you can be spared an extra hour. You're not a prisoner, love. I promise I'll have you back before dark." I could hear the chuckle in his voice.

"Back from where?" I said.

He kissed my neck. "From the adventure we'll be having. Just the two of us."

"Hush your blather," I said, but I didn't mean it. Sure, I couldn't have resisted if he was related to the Devil himself. Which I sometimes thought he was.

~

The sky that day was the color of dirty dishwater with a chilly drizzle coming down. But it could have been raining sunshine the way I felt with Patrick. He whisked me off to Northampton, where he led me past a row of shops, down an alleyway, through a door, and up two flights of stairs. We stepped into a great room with a platform at one end and folks sitting on benches before it.

"What is this?" I said.

Patrick tucked his finger to his lips and whispered, "'Tis the adventure I promised, lass." He led me to an empty bench and pulled me down beside him.

I looked around at the other people—a mixed lot, more women than men, and not high-and-mighty folks. I was glad of that, for I was wearing a plain green calico and straw bonnet. A stocky lad two rows in front of us turned and nodded to Patrick, who nodded back. Then a woman in a blue frock stepped up on the platform. She was tall and wide at the hips with a pretty, open face. I admired her hat—it was red and set forward on her head under a spray of bright feathers.

She lifted her hands to hush the crowd. The minute she began talking, gooseflesh came up on my arms. It was like listening to music, the way she said things. She told us she was Maria Dough-tery from Worcester, and a great admirer of Fanny and Anna Parnell. If we didn't already know about the Parnell sisters, we'd be hearing about them, she said. They'd soon be famous as their brother Charles for their Irish courage and valor. Few women alive could measure up.

Sure, I'd heard the name Parnell batted round from time to time, but figured it had naught to do with myself. Miss Dough-tery's speech changed my mind about that. She told us of a new famine in Ireland. Didn't have anything to do with the potato blight, she said—all the fault lay with the landowners themselves. She reminded us the Irish had suffered centuries of misery and poverty. Their rights and liberties had been trampled by the English aristocracy, who took their land and stripped Ireland of her riches. Those who tended the soil were evicted to make room for sheep and cattle, and exiled across the ocean.

Of course her words made me think of Da—how could they not? Seemed like she was talking about his own life. I had a raw memory of the day he came through our cottage door with the terrible news the farm was to be encumbered—every acre fenced for pasture. There was no future in Ireland for Michael Maher's family, he said. Like a bolt to my heart, it was—shame and fear mixing together. Didn't know what the future would bring any of us.

Listening to Miss Doughtery brought all those feelings back. But she told us this time there'd be a different ending. "Irishmen and -women won't be driven away from their land anymore," she said. "It's worth fighting and dying for. And it will likely come to that, for concessions are only wrung from England by force." She stepped close to the platform edge and lifted her arms. "Charles Parnell and those who support him are raising Ireland toward freedom!"

Everybody cheered. Folks were leaning forward and I was leaning with them so I wouldn't miss a single word. She went on and on for near an hour and every minute stirred my heart. My blood was rising and, from the look on his face, so was Patrick's.

Near the end her voice got raspy. "No American with a drop of Irish blood can fail to see their duty! The sacred fire at the altar of liberty has been kindled and we must not leave our Irish brothers alone in their fight!" We all jumped to our feet, cheering and clapping. My heart was pounding in my throat. Folks swarmed the platform. When Patrick turned his smile on me it was big as the world.

"Maybe we should be heading back now?" I was surprised there was still light coming through the windows. I felt as if I'd been away for hours and hours.

Patrick took my hand as if he owned it. "We'll not be leaving till you meet Maria," he said, and pulled me into the crowd.

"Miss Doughtery?" I said. "Do you know her, then?"

I don't think he heard me, the palaver was so loud. I followed him, my blood glowing as I recalled how Miss Doughtery called us Americans of an Irish stripe. Hearing those words wiped away the shame of where I came from.

The man who'd nodded to Patrick walked up and clapped him on the back. "It's good you came, lad," he said. Then, in a low voice, "Did you hear the news?"

Patrick gave his head a shake.

"They arrested him," the man said. "Came knocking on his door at night and carted him off to jail. He's to be tried come September and it's rumored the authorities are hounding his friends—looking for some poor devil who'll testify against him."

"'Tis vile," Patrick said under his breath, looking sober as I'd ever seen him. "Sure, there's no end to the persecutions."

I looked from one to the other but couldn't think who they were talking about. I'd heard of no arrests, seen nothing in the papers. And it seemed odd Patrick hadn't introduced me. My mind was churning, surely.

"Well, if it isn't Patrick Quinn!" It was Maria Doughtery herself smiling and coming up to us. "I was wondering if you'd be here." And she gave Patrick a kiss on his cheek, bold as you please.

Patrick laughed his big warm laugh. I might have felt jealous if not for his hand resting so easy on my back. "Maria, this is my friend Margaret Maher."

"'Tis a pleasure to be meeting you," I said, giving her my hand to shake. "'Twas a grand speech. Stirred my blood, it did."

You'd think I'd given her the blessing of the Pope himself from the smile she turned on me. "I'm gratified to hear it," she said. "Welcome to the cause. I'm hoping you're as true a warrior as Patrick."

"Sure, I'm no warrior," I said, wondering if she was jesting.

Patrick laughed. "*Whist* now, Maria. I'm still recruiting her."

Others were clamoring around us. A woman came up and drew Maria away, and we left, going out the door we came in and down the steps to the street. Patrick was in high spirits as he drew me along the sidewalk. "I'm thinking we should celebrate," he said, walking fast. "Let's have a cup of tea." He stopped before a red door and opened it with a flourish. A strap of hanging bells made a tinkling sound when we went in.

Sure, the tearoom was an enchantment. There were seven tables dressed in white linen and on each one stood a vase of flowers. Three women sat at one, every one of them wearing an elegant hat and shawl. A waiter came up and led us to an empty table. Patrick ordered a pot of tea and a seedcake, and soon as they came, I started asking questions. "How did you meet Miss Doughtery?" I said. "And what did she mean about myself being a warrior? Sure, I'm not a warrior nor ever could be."

"But you were roused by Maria's speech, surely." I watched him drop sugar into his tea. Brought a memory of our first chat at the Homestead.

"I was that," I said. The look of the cake was making my mouth water.

"And you've a warrior's soul—there's no denying it." He smiled across the table and cut into the cake.

My mind conjured the old stories Da told of warriors and heroes and how he once said I had a heart strong as Cú Chulainn's. But I couldn't imagine a way to fight for Ireland's freedom when I was in America. I was still getting used to the idea of being of the Irish stripe.

The seedcake was sweet and buttery. Every piece melted on my tongue. I asked Patrick about the lad who spoke to him after the speech.

Patrick was busying himself cutting more cake. "An old friend from the Hoosac Tunnel," he said. Something in his face made me wary of asking more. He shifted a wedge of cake onto his fork. "Sure, let's not spoil the day with talk of old times," he said. "Let's enjoy the time we've got." And his smile warmed me top to toe.

Chapter Nineteen

Patrick and myself kept walking out together, and the times I was with him, I felt pretty and young. He'd worked a charm on me, to be sure. I saw how other women from St. Bridget's Parish looked at the pair of us when we strolled on the town common. He took me to the Cattle Show and more dances in Northampton. Once he rented a buggy and drove us out to Pelham and back. And didn't I feel grand sitting by his side?

He talked a good deal about Ireland and how much the country suffered. He told me he dreamed of going back—for it's best to be amongst your own kind, he said. He told me how hard things were the first years when he came to America. New York City was a wicked place then, plagued with cruel and murderous lads who'd rob you quick as look at you. He'd had a hard time finding work at first—taking one odd job after another, everything from ratcatcher to street sweeper. When war came he was glad to sign up for the Union Army, just to get himself out of the city.

He never spoke much about the war itself. What I found out was in dribs and drabs. It was a dull life mostly, he said. Soldiers were most of the time just sitting around or marching to the next fight. Sometimes a memory would tighten his lips and set a bleak cast to his eyes. I learned not to press him, for when I did he'd go all quiet and gloomy. Once we saw a one-legged lad coming along Amity Street on crutches and Patrick told me he'd seen a friend's arm blown off in battle. "A shell took it clean off at the shoulder," he said. "The poor lad died where he fell."

"Lord have mercy," I said.

But before I could ask questions, he sank into what Emily called a *brown study*—with his eyes turned down and his mouth a thin line—and I knew he must be thinking dark thoughts. Not for the first time I was certain he was keeping some dreadful secret. But any eejit could see it wasn't a good time to be asking.

Patrick had his secrets, surely, and was fond of keeping them close. There were times I wondered if it was his most powerful charm.

Judge Lord came again and Emily went about in a happy daze. The two of them closed themselves into the parlor for hours and I could hear them laughing behind the door. When I called them for dinner, they came out blushing.

As they came into the dining room, the Judge bent and tugged at a ruffle on Emily's skirt.

"Why do you wear such frippery?" he said.

She laughed. "It seized your attention, didn't it, Phil? That's answer enough."

"My dear, if it's my attention you desire, you must take it off altogether. And be assured it'll be more than my attention you'll be seizing." And didn't he slide his arm around her waist and pull her against him?

Sure, it made me blush and it should have made Emily blush too, especially with his hands on her that way. Instead she said,

"Why, Judge, sir, don't you know that what you see not, you better see?" And she laughed all the harder.

But the next time the dressmaker came to the Homestead to be making her frocks, Emily told her to leave off the ruffles and ribbons. Twice a year, it was, Mrs. Noyes and her cloth occupied the dining room for a week. Emily and Vinnie always had a grand time of it, choosing their patterns and fabrics. Vinnie favored the color lilac and sorted through swatches of silk and cambric and velvet for hours, setting them next to one another and holding them up to her face, asking if they flattered her complexion.

In the fall of 1878 Vinnie decided I must have a new calico. Don't know what was wrong with my old ones, but I wasn't about to object. "What do you think, Maggie?" she said, waving a swatch of dark blue sprinkled with yellow and gray flowers.

"She must have more than one, now that she has a suitor." Emily smiled in that sly way she had.

"A suitor?" Vinnie dropped the swatch back into the pile. "Oh, Maggie, you must tell us everything!"

"Sure, there's nothing to be telling," I said. "Patrick's a friend, is all." And I pretended there was a pot on the stove needed tending. But I heard them laughing together when I hurried off and I feared they were mocking me again.

Later Emily came to the kitchen looking sad. "I'm sorry if I spilled a secret," she said. "I didn't mean any harm. You're our own dear Maggie, so to make it up to you, you shall have four new dresses." She took my hand and led me back to the dining room, where Mrs. Noyes showed me patterns she said might suit. I was glad to have new calicoes, but I would have traded them all for one silk frock, just for the slip of the cloth under my fingers.

On Christmas Day I wore the prettiest calico I had—dark red

with lilac and pink flowers twining across it—and my best wool shawl, the color of cream. Vinnie clapped her hands when she saw me and Emily pronounced it a glory and tried to look solemn. But it was the smile on Mary's face when I walked into her kitchen filled my heart that morning.

We had our dinner at Kelley Square, sitting around the big table, young and old alike. Mary wouldn't let me serve, made Nell and Meg do it, said for once I'd sit and be waited on. We laughed and told stories and feasted together—and what more could I be wishing for?

Patrick gave me a gift that day. A rosary wrapped in a square of white linen. The beads and cross were the color of honey.

"It's been blessed in Ireland," Patrick said. "'Tis made of cow's horn." I could hear in his voice he was proud of himself.

I didn't have the heart to tell him the only rosary I'd ever pray on was the one my mam gave me. So I looped it around my palm and kissed the crucifix before I put it in my pocket. Then I gave him a kiss on the cheek in front of everybody.

When he walked me back to the Homestead that night, there was a ribbon of ice on the edge of the road and a ribbon of stars above our heads. I shivered when I opened the Homestead gate, and Patrick said, "You're cold!" and wrapped his arms around me so I felt swaddled tight as a babe. My bones went soft as pudding. I didn't resist or push him away when his mouth came down on mine. God's truth, I welcomed his kisses, sinful as I knew they were. For a blaze was running through me, fast as fire climbs a curtain blown too close to a lamp. If it had been the fire of Hell itself consuming me, I wouldn't have noticed. I was that far gone.

He didn't let me go but drew me through the gate and up the drive. Took both my shoulders and kissed me again, hard. My whole body was quivering with wanting him.

"Don't leave!" I whispered, my words sounding like a scandal even to my own ears. But I didn't take them back.

"Ah, sweet Margaret," Patrick whispered. "I'm not wanting to leave you, but what would you have me do?"

I had no answer for his question but couldn't bear the thought of parting. So my body said what my tongue could not. I took his hand and turned away from the house and led him to the barn.

The mare lifted her head and nickered for attention when we stepped inside. Then Patrick pulled the big door shut and the warm straw-and-animal smells folded around us. I heard the cow moving in her stall and the sleepy chucking of a few hens on their roosts. We kissed again—long and sweet—and made our way to the back of the barn where hay was banked high against the wall. Patrick slipped his hands around my waist smooth as butter. Then he was laying me down and himself beside me. And whatever was about to happen, I welcomed it, that I did.

This is love is all I was thinking as Patrick kissed me and his hand moved on my breast and slid up under my skirts. He touched my bare thigh and I shivered and let out a little moan, for my flesh was near melting with the heat of his fingers.

It was that very minute an unwelcome thought popped into my head—seeing Emily and Judge Lord the last time he came, the way he fondled her neck and slipped his fingers under her collar when they didn't know I was looking. He'd pried open her top button and she'd laughed and leaned against him for a bit before gently pushing him away. It was as if the two of them were in the barn with us, just a few feet away. And both of them laughing at myself. I was washed all over in shame. I rolled away from Patrick and stood up.

"What is it, love?" He tried to pull me down again, but I slipped my hand from his and headed for the door.

"Sure, I don't know what I'm doing," I said. "Go home now, Patrick. Leave."

He was right behind me. "Don't be getting angry now. 'Tis loving you, I am." His voice was sweet and sad in my ear and his breath was warming my neck and then he was turning my face and kissing me again. I almost gave in, but mustered the will to push him off and open the door. He kept following. Even as I was stepping out into the cold he was touching me, trying to draw me back into the barn, calling me *darlin'* and *ma chree*, and all the sweet words he could think of. And the truth of it is my body wanted to stay the whole long night with him and give myself over to his caresses. Even though it would blacken my immortal soul.

He followed me across the yard to the back door and stole another kiss before I could pull it open. I hissed for him to go and gave him a shove so hard it set him lurching off the step. I told him if he was any kind of man he'd be respecting me instead of stealing kisses. And I said I didn't want to be seeing him again.

God's truth, it was the biggest lie I ever told.

It was Dennis the stableman found my shawl next morning, lying where I left it in the straw. I should have been glad it wasn't Austin or Ned spying it, but I was so agitated when I saw the lad coming from the barn with that lovely cream wool hanging off his shoulder like an old sheet, I lit into him for being careless.

"*Eejit!*" I yelled, yanking it out of his hands. "'Tis my best shawl and look what you've done! Soiling it like some old rag."

"'Twas soiled where you left it," he said, which was true, but the bold look in his eye told me his meaning had layers I didn't want to think on. *Innuendo* was what Emily called such talk. I was turning away when he said, "'Tis not the only thing you've lost."

Sure, I whirled around in a fury, thinking he was meaning my virtue. But there was the rosary Patrick gave me dangling from his fingers. "Should be thanking me, I'm thinking," he said. "I'm guessing you'll need to be saying some extra prayers after what you did last night." And he smiled.

It was all I could do not to spit. Wouldn't it be just the thing, having it noised all over Amherst the Dickinsons' maid was too free with her favors? I couldn't bear the thought of Mary hearing such gossip. I was too old for such goings-on, she'd say, and she'd be right. Too old and too careless of my reputation. Which I knew as well as the next woman was the only treasure worth keeping.

So instead I took the rosary and mumbled, "Thank you," and invited Dennis into the kitchen for a slice of cake.

I washed the shawl and hung the rosary Patrick gave me on a nail over my bed. I wasn't myself the rest of the week. I fretted over the oven being too cold and the cakes not rising. I complained about the gloomy weather and the damp in the walls. And all the while I was thinking of Patrick. I wanted to have nothing to do with him and I wanted to be with him—both at the same time. I fancied what I'd say when I saw him and wondered what he'd be saying back. Should I let him kiss me? Should I walk out with him again? I longed to talk to somebody. But what happened in the barn was too troubling to share with anybody. I knew I'd have to confess it to the priest sooner or later, and even that thought was beyond bearing.

So I prayed. I said ten decades of the rosary instead of five. I prayed to the Blessed Virgin for fortitude and forgiveness. I prayed to Saint Patrick for mercy and wisdom. And I did everything I could to avoid Patrick Quinn.

God's truth, it wasn't easy. Staying away from him was the hardest thing I'd ever done. For the truth is, that night in the barn left me wanting more. I missed the dazed way his kisses left me feeling. I remembered the sweet fire that rose in the pit of my belly when his hand slid up my leg. I yearned to feel it again. But I was afraid of what I might do if I did.

It was three weeks before I went to confession. And a hard confession it was, for my poor knees were hurting that day and my head aching as well. Getting the words out near tore my throat. It was a great relief to have it done, though. Father Barry reminded me sinning was contagious and told me to pray for strength. I mustn't give in to Patrick's wiles. A woman should only lie down with a lad when she's his wife. And he gave me a hard penance so I'd not be forgetting.

After that some of my shame fell away. But the thought of being in Patrick's arms again still had a glow to it, like living in a happy dream.

Chapter Twenty

Life went on in its normal way and I tried to be glad I'd seen the back of Patrick. Amherst had its share of excitement to keep my mind off what I didn't wish to be thinking. There were always stories about misfortunes, sickness, accidents, and arguments. There were woeful fights at the billiard hall with Irish lads arrested for brawling. And terrible fires. It seemed some part of town was always going up in flames. As if the feverish spirits of America sent the sparks flying. The whole Phoenix Block burned one year, turning barns and houses to ashes. And so many chimney fires I could have marked the weeks of the calendar by them. Many were blaming Irish lads from the Crossing and Irish Hill. Seems it's always the poor getting blamed for a town's hard luck.

Winter settled toward spring and the snow melted away and the mud came up in the road. Then Patrick turned up at Mass on Easter Sunday. I tried not to be glancing in his direction but I saw him give me a long look and it gave me such a pang I almost left. Soon as Mass was done, I hurried away. Mary came after me, asking what had happened between us, but I said I didn't care to be talking about it and she let the matter go. Patrick didn't show up at Kelley Square that afternoon and for that I was grateful. Mostly.

It was two weeks later Tom came by on his way to town and said Patrick wanted to see me. "The lad is suffering," he said. "He's done his penance long enough. It's time you stopped punishing him."

I took Tom's words to heart. Sure, I didn't like to think of Patrick suffering. And truth to tell, I was suffering myself. For all my determination to avoid sinning again, my heart was yearning after him.

Next day Mary came to chat. While I wet the tea she told me Anna Breen had left her post and was back living with James and Ellen. "And Patrick Quinn's been giving the eye to Katie Murray."

"Are they stepping out?" A hot feeling came over me.

"Sure, I don't know," Mary said. "'Tis just gossip. Likely it's Katie herself spreading it."

"Or himself, knowing it'll make me jealous," I said.

"Aye," Mary said. "I wondered about that. What happened between the two of you? Did you give him the back of your hand?"

"Maybe I should have." I was thinking hard thoughts that day and letting the tea steep too long. It was bitter as my tongue when I finally got around to confessing the truth to Mary. She was more understanding than I expected and told me I'd done the right thing. Respect was a requirement for love, after all.

"To tell you the truth, I've been troubled by things I've heard Patrick saying," Mary told me. "Snippets of chat here and there. Some twaddle about a rising in Ireland. Does no good nor never did, is what I say."

"Sure, Patrick may be wrong about some things, but he's

right about that," I told her. "I heard it myself at a lecture. And it's not just lads saying so." Next thing I knew, I was telling her about hearing Maria Doughtery speak. How her words had stirred me and started me thinking new thoughts about being Irish. "And she's a respectable woman," I assured her. "With a taste for fashion, if you can judge from her hat."

Mary laughed. "'Tis the best way of judging, surely."

I went shopping in Northampton with Molly Ryan the next week. Molly was after buying a new hat for her honeymoon. She was soon to be married to a lad from Worcester—William O'Shea. In truth, I was happy for her but sad for myself, for she'd been a dear friend, and after she moved, I knew I'd rarely be seeing her.

We stopped in front of an emporium where the window was filled with handsome spring bonnets. We admired them a minute and Molly said she was for buying the hat with the red feathers, and in she went. As soon as I stepped through the door who did I see but Maria Doughtery herself, standing by the counter, holding a green bonnet in her hands?

Her face lit up when she saw me. "You're Patrick Quinn's friend," she said. It pleased me she remembered, though I wasn't certain it was still the truth. I introduced Molly and the three of us chatted a bit. I told her how much I'd liked her speech. "Don't you live in Worcester?" I asked.

"I do," she said. "But I have family in Northampton, and whenever I'm here, I visit the local hat shops."

I was puzzled. "Surely there are milliners in Worcester."

She laughed. "I'm a milliner myself," she said, her eyes sparking. "With my own shop on Main Street. So I like to see what others are selling. Are you looking to buy a new hat?"

"Sure, I'm always looking," I said, laughing myself. "I've got my eye on that blue bonnet. 'Tis stunning, isn't it?"

"It is," said Maria. "And it would suit you well. The color will set off your eyes."

The hat was the latest fashion, a pert brim with ruffles tucked under, a pink silk rose, and a satin ribbon for tying. Had to pull my eyes away or I'd have bought it on the spot.

"I must be going." Maria put the green hat back on its stand. "I hope you'll come and visit my shop sometime," she said.

I nodded good-bye and watched her leave, admiring her bearing and the way she moved. *Like a warrior*, I thought. Later Molly confessed she was as taken with Maria as myself, the woman was that friendly. Said I must come to visit once she'd moved to Worcester and we'd visit Maria's shop together. It was a grand idea, to be sure, but I left without buying the hat.

A week later Patrick showed up at the Homestead. Walked right into the kitchen without knocking. I was feeding wood into the stove firebox when he said my name. I stood up straight as a plank. "What are you doing here?" I said.

He was standing with his hands tucked behind his back, just smiling at me. His dark eyes were so lovely I couldn't stop myself from smiling back. Took every drop of my will not to cross the floor to himself.

"What is it you're wanting?" I asked. I wanted to say he wasn't welcome here, but couldn't make my tongue form the words.

He took his arms from behind him.

"What's that?" I said, though it was plain as the nose on my face he was holding a hatbox.

"It's for you," he said.

"Sure, I have work to be doing," I said. "And don't you have a job of your own to be going to?"

He didn't answer, just stepped closer. "Open it," he said.

"Go on with you now," I said, but it was only a minute before I was taking the lid off that box, though I knew it was a fool's business. Lying there in a blanket of tissue paper was the blue bonnet I'd admired in the Northampton shop.

I looked at him, looked back at the hat. Shook my head.

"Try it on," he said, his voice so sweet it made me catch my breath. "See if it fits."

"Go on, be off with you. I've no time for your *figary*." I had to make myself say it, for those weren't the words that wanted to be coming out of my mouth.

"'Tis no *figary*." He put the box on the table and took the hat out, all in one motion. "If you won't be putting it on yourself, I'll do it for you." And didn't he set the hat on my head and tie the ribbon under my chin as if he'd done it a hundred times?

I knew I likely looked a fool, standing there in the kitchen in my old calico and dirty apron with that dainty lady's hat perched on my head like a pretty bird. I knew I should be snatching it off. But my hands were shaking and tears were coming up in my eyes. "How did you know?" I said.

"That would be telling, now," he said, grinning. "A lad needs to be keeping some secrets. Even from the prettiest girl in Hampshire County." He reached to touch my cheek and I didn't stop him. "Ah, Margaret," he whispered, "'tis breaking my heart not to be seeing you anymore."

Sure, that was all it took. The pleading in his voice broke my own heart and my tears spilled over. I let him put his arms around me and kiss me right there in the kitchen. When he let go and stepped back, I felt so bereft I started to pull him back. Then I saw he was looking past me at the door to the pantry.

"Good morning, Miss Dickinson," he said in a thin voice.

I turned and there stood Emily watching us. She was smiling in that way she had, as if she was understanding everything—both what could be seen and what could not.

I pulled the hat off quick as a burn. But from the minute I saw her smile, I knew I'd be hearing about that bonnet for days. And so I did, for Emily was a great tease and liked poking fun. I suppose I should have taken her mockery for a sign of affection, and looking back I think that's how she meant it. But that day just knowing what she saw riled me.

"'Tis not what you're thinking," I said, putting the hat on the table and giving Patrick a nod toward the back door. When he left, I poked another chunk of wood into the firebox and clanged the heavy door shut. I knew my face was bright red and it wasn't from the fire.

Whenever Judge Lord came to Amherst he spent every day and every evening with Emily. It was the sort of goings-on the Squire would never have allowed and it was plain Mother Dickinson, tucked away in her room, had no knowledge of. Vinnie, though, was merry as a robin. Nothing seemed to scandalize her as long as Emily was happy.

One afternoon while Emily and the Judge were in the parlor, Vinnie said we must polish all the silver. I helped her lay out every piece on newspapers on the kitchen table and we spent hours rubbing away tarnish. She chattered on about the latest fashions and gossip. Told me of a lady who used to live in North Amherst and was arrested in Boston for poisoning her husband.

"He's not the first husband she poisoned either." Vinnie put down her cloth and leaned close. "She was married before and that husband died of dreadful spasms in the middle of the night. She couldn't bury him fast enough." She said the famous Mr. Emerson from Concord might be coming to Amherst. "There was a day Emily would have given everything she owned to meet him," Vinnie said. "Now it's always *Phil this* and *Phil that.*"

Her eyes danced and sparked and next thing I knew she was telling of a man who courted her years before. Joseph, his name was, and they had had an understanding about marriage. He was handsome with curly hair and eyes so blue they dazzled her. "Tragically, he died." She looked sad a minute, then brightened. "But I'll never forget his kisses."

I smiled, thinking of Patrick's kisses. He'd been coming around again—every day or two he'd turn up at the back door, we'd share a cup of tea, and he'd steal a few.

A log shifted in the cooker stove and the fire made a whoosh. I got up to check on it and shoo a cat off the shelf. Then I went upstairs to check on Mother Dickinson. When I came back in the kitchen, Vinnie was whimpering and covering her right eye. Saw right off what likely happened—a speck of polish lodged in her eye. I hurried her into the washroom and rinsed her eye, but she was still in pain.

"I'll fetch Miss Emily," I said, for nobody is better at calming a woman than her sister. Off I ran without a thought except Vinnie's relief. Didn't stop to knock at the closed parlor door, but burst straight in. And didn't I clap both hands over my mouth at what I saw? There on the sofa with her bodice open and her skirts up to her thighs was Emily herself, lying atop the Judge.

I murmured, "Pardon me," and ran back the way I came. But I didn't go quick enough to flee the chime of Emily's laughter. Sure, I wanted to run all the way to Kelley Square. I wasn't just ashamed for Emily. I was ashamed for myself. Hadn't I been in nearly the same state in Patrick's arms just a few months ago?

It wasn't till the next morning I was able to look Emily in the eye. From what I could tell she felt not one whit of shame. In truth, I was feeling envy of her carefree ways, for it still fretted me how close I'd come to sinning with Patrick. Was it because I was Catholic? From the looks of it, Protestants, for all their talk of righteousness, did what they wanted and never felt a bit of guilt.

The next day the Judge went home to Salem. Looking pleased with himself too. And wasn't Emily happy as any lark on a summer morning all the rest of that day? You'd think she'd been blessed by the Faeries themselves.

About noon Tom stopped in the kitchen on his way home. He said I looked quare sickened and wanted to know what was troubling me. Sat me down for a chinwag, he did. So what could I do but tell him what I saw?

He listened close and tugged on his ear. "Ah, Margaret," he said, "there's no judgment on you for the sins of your betters. 'Tis just the way the world works and you won't be changing them no matter what you do." He shook his head, smiling. "Miss Emily's had a wild streak ever since I've known her. She'll do what she wants, make no mistake about it. She always had the Squire wrapped around her little finger. And now she's got the Judge there, from the sound of it."

"Sure, I don't know what she sees in him," I said. "He's not a bit handsome and he takes shameful liberties. It's wicked for her to be loving himself."

He laughed, a deep burst of it, and put his hand on my shoulder. "Love has its own ways, darlin'. And there's no unpuzzling it—you'll just be wasting your time."

Part IV

Doorways

Chapter Twenty-One

1916

The stairway up to the Realty Company office is lit so dim, I stumble and crack my shin against a tread. So I'm limping when the clerk shows me into the office where a little man with sparse gray hair is sitting at a desk behind two stacks of paper. He looks up smiling and then wipes the smile off his face. Don't know who he's expecting but it's plain it's not myself. Sure, any eejit can see I'm not off to a good start.

Soon as I say who I am and why I've come, he holds up a hand and clears his throat. "Let me stop you before you go on," he says. "There are certain stipulations on the sale of that house. Madame Bianchi isn't selling to someone off the street."

"Sure, I'm not off the street!" I'm half out of the chair, I'm so provoked. "I have my own boardinghouse, sir."

He gives me a doubting glance. "Permit me to be candid, Miss Maher." He straightens his shoulders, makes himself a wee bit taller. "Madame Bianchi is looking for a buyer suited to the neighborhood, if you catch my meaning."

God's truth, I'm raging. I know his meaning, to be sure. "My money's good as anybody else's," I say. I know my accent gets more Irish the more vexed I am, but I can't help myself. "And maybe she won't be so persnickety if word gets around there's ghosts in the old place."

"Ghosts?" Gives me a surprised look, the man does.

I lean over the desk. "Folks don't like buying a haunted place," I say. "And I won't be shy of telling them."

His eyes go narrow. "Why would *you* want to buy it if it's haunted?"

It's a surprise, his question. I sit back, touch my hat to steady my nerves. And then I hear myself saying what I didn't know till this minute.

"It's *because* it's haunted I'm wanting it," I say.

He blinks. "You're an interesting woman, Miss Maher. Unfortunately, your pursuit of this matter is futile. Madame Bianchi is already in negotiations with a buyer." And he stands up, making it plain it's time for me to go.

The news rocks me, surely. Don't know why he didn't tell me straight off instead of spewing all his nasty blather about myself not being suitable. Takes me a minute to gather my wits. I get up slow. "Who's buying the place, then?" I ask. I remember Rosaleen mentioning Dr. Bowen.

But he won't give me a name. Just stands holding the door open, waiting for me to leave.

Outside, the clouds have the look of silver needing a good polish, telling me it's going to rain any minute. I hurry back to Kelley Square. Keep my head down and walk past the Homestead fast as I can. My shin still stings from stumbling on the stairs. I expect I'll have a big black-and-blue patch on my leg in the morning. Haven't felt this low in months.

The smoke curling out of Tom's chimney is good as a finger beckoning. I hurry up the porch steps just as the rain starts bucketing down and find Tom in the kitchen wetting the tea. His face brightens when I come in.

"How was your visit to the bank?" he asks.

I shake my head and tell him what happened, mention there's already a buyer. He's a good listener, Tom is. He sits me down at the table and pours me a cup of tea and then sits across from me with his own. The sound of the rain ticking on the windows makes me feel cozy in the warm kitchen. Eases my disappointment, it does, and brings up happy memories.

"I'm sorry the luck wasn't with you today," Tom says. "Truly I am. 'Tis hard thinking of somebody else owning Miss Emily's house."

I nod and drink my tea. It's a sweet thing, hearing him say the thoughts I'm thinking.

"Can't say I'm surprised there's a buyer already," he says. "'Tis a handsome house and sturdy built. With grand grounds."

"And the garden," I say, to keep the tears from wedging up my throat. "I remember all those times Miss Emily sent me out to dredge a rose or a lily she could be sending in a letter. She had so many friends it's a wonder her garden wasn't stripped bare."

Tom laughs. "She had friends, all right. Everybody who knew Miss Emily loved her. Like a sprite, she was."

I nod. "Aye, there was a force about her, to be sure," I say. "A kind of shining. Made me think of the way hoarfrost glimmers on the trees when the sun comes up. When I first started working at the Homestead I thought she was like a ghost—living in that big house, but hardly there at all."

Tom chuckles. "She had her ways of disappearing, to be sure," he says.

"But I was dead wrong about her hardly being there." Even as I'm talking I'm feeling the old tingle. "That house was filled to bursting with herself. It was as if she was in the walls and folded into the light coming through the window glass." I pour myself more tea and offer some to Tom but he shakes his head. "Times I thought she'd bewitched me. Wherever she was—in the house or garden, or even the barn—she made that place part of herself. I don't know how she did it—she wasn't just living in her body but in the bricks of the house. The dirt of the garden."

We sit quiet a minute. Tom and myself do a lot of talking about what's past. Sure, who else can I be sharing those times with? Everybody we knew has passed on. But we talk the way folks tell the old Irish tales—as if we have all the time in the world.

"Remembering's a sweet thing, surely," he says after a bit. "Looking back, seems most of the days were good ones. Though I don't recall feeling so at the time."

I laugh. "That's the truth of it," I say. "But it's always grand chatting with you."

"Don't you be fretting about the Homestead now," he says. "When the sky falls, we'll all catch larks." And doesn't he make me laugh again and think of Da, who was forever saying those very words when my spirits were low?

We rattle on and lose track of time. So it's a surprise to the both of us when the back door opens and in walks Nell, carrying a sack of groceries. Though the rain is dripping off her, there's a smile on her face. Pretty as a lass of thirty, she is, though she's well past fifty now.

"Guess who's bought himself an automobile." She sets the sack on the counter and starts pulling things out. She tells us about a professor at the College who sold his two horses to buy a Knox Touring Car. She says it can travel forty miles in an hour.

"Surely not," I say, trying to picture an automobile going faster than a horse at a gallop. Infernal machines, they are. Making a rattling racket and spouting foul smoke wherever they go.

"He swears to it," Nell says. "He says he took his wife for a ride and it knocked the starch right out of her." She finishes emptying the sack and pulls a towel from the drying rack over the cooker and wipes her face and hair. "You'd like it, Aunt Margaret."

"I would not, to be sure," I say. But Tom laughs and next thing I know I'm picturing myself sitting in an automobile, roaring along the road at an unholy speed. An adventure worth having, maybe.

"What's the news in town?" Tom asks.

Nell starts bustling about, clearing away the empty tea things, putting away the groceries. "All anybody's talking about is the grippe contagion," she says. "Nobody knows how it's spreading but some say the stables in the center of town are the cause of it."

Tom *humphs* and takes out his pipe. "Next thing you know, folks'll be saying horses are a health menace."

Nell shrugs. "What have the pair of you been up to?"

"Having a wee chat," Tom says. He leans back in his chair and looks at me. "Seems there's a buyer for the Homestead."

"An outrage, it is, selling the place," I say. "Mattie D's got no respect for Miss Emily's memory. Not a care for what the rest of us might be thinking."

"Don't rile yourself, Margaret," Tom says. "I've said before—she's likely got a good enough reason."

"Oh, she does," Nell says, pouring herself a cup of tea and sitting in the chair next to me. "She's been swindled."

"Swindled?" I say. It's a shock, this news. "By who?"

"Her husband, the captain," Nell says in a breezy way, as if everybody in town knows. "Apparently he's robbed her blind. Remember hearing several years ago about that woman from New York who sued him?"

I nod, though the memory is misty. Tom looks as puzzled as myself.

"Well, it turns out Captain Bianchi had been spinning a web of lies for years," Nell goes on. "He used his Dickinson connections to get folks to loan him thousands of dollars. In payment, all he sent were bad checks. He finally ran off to Europe. Came as a terrible blow to Mattie D. But the scandals kept coming and he kept begging for more money and she sent what she could until it ran out. By the time her mother died most of her fortune was gone."

I feel a pinch of pity. "Why didn't I know this?"

She gives me a surprised look. "I assumed you did. It's not a secret. It's been in the papers."

Tom slaps his hand down on the table. "I was right, then—she had no choice but to put the Homestead up for sale. She's had a hard life, she has."

Nell nods. "She had that nervous collapse after Miss Vinnie died and that's why she went abroad—her doctor prescribed it. It was right around that time she met Alexander and he swept her right off her feet. He must have reminded her of the dukes and earls she wrote about in her novels. By the time she learned who he really was, they were married."

It's uncommon when words fail me, but I can't think of anything to say. An ocean of tender feeling is swirling in my brain.

Seems that Mattie D wasn't stonyhearted when she turned me away. She'd been hoodwinked and robbed by her rogue of a husband and was only after protecting her pride. I know a thing or two about how that feels.

"She's always been a good steward of Miss Emily's work," Nell says. "Remember that collection of her poems she published a couple of years ago?"

"I never knew why she called it *The Single Hound*," Tom says. "But it's a noble book and honors her mother along with Miss Emily."

I nod. I have the book myself, on the nightstand by my bed, where I can open it when I'm yearning to read Emily's verses. I remember finding a mention of myself in the preface. *An archaic Irish servant* were the words Mattie D wrote. I had to look up *archaic* in the dictionary. *Old-fashioned*, it means. *Out-of-date*. It was hurtful at the time. But I suppose there's a truth to it. And I'll not be ashamed of keeping the scruples I was raised with.

One thing is certain—Mattie D's hard-heartedness doesn't excuse my own.

"I think I've made an awful mistake," I say after a minute. "And it's up to myself to be fixing it."

Chapter Twenty-Two

1879

Sometimes it seemed I was always going in and out of doors that didn't belong to me. The only time I didn't feel so was at St. Bridget's. I belonged to that place, surely. In truth, I'd given some of my wages to its building ten years back. Stepping through the door made something light and sweet open in my chest—a holy feeling. I always thought Mass was more devotion than obligation. Patrick saw it the other way around.

But my heart gave a little leap whenever he did show up for Mass. One Sunday in late June I was kneeling in my pew when he surprised me by squeezing in beside me, bold as you please. I crossed myself twice for strength and protection, as he shifted closer and closer again. By the Sanctus, his arm was against mine and his leg was wrinkling my skirts. I was mindful of the musky smell of himself. Sure, my body had a will of its own that paid no heed at all to my soul.

He took my arm soon as Mass was over and hurried me outside. We were the first ones out the door. Didn't seem respectful to be rushing off right after Holy Communion, but I didn't complain. I was liking the way my arm tucked into his. The morning was lovely with the sun shining out of a pure blue sky and the bushes full of flowers. Wasn't just pleasing to the eye, but to my nose too. The air smelled grand.

"We've got to hurry," Patrick said, pulling me along.

Sure, I don't like being told what to do on my day off. "What's got into you?" I asked.

"I don't want to be late." He slid his arm free of mine and put it around my shoulder. "I've made plans for us this day, love."

"What plans?" I was wary but gooseflesh was going up and down my back.

"If I told you, it wouldn't be a surprise, now, would it?" He was sucking on his teeth to keep from laughing.

"I'm not always liking your surprises," I said. "There's a wild streak in you, Patrick Quinn." But the truth was, I liked it. His wild side was one of the reasons I couldn't resist him when he was with me—and why I craved being with him when he wasn't. "Tell me where you're taking me or I'll not be going." And I stopped, right there in the street.

"Ah, love, you're spoiling the fun," he said. "We're about to be having a right *spraoi.*"

Spraoi. It was a word I hadn't heard for years. It brought a pang, reminding me of the times Da took our whole family on a lark. Happened at least once a year—climbing Slievenamon or dancing at the Fethard Fair. Walking to Killusty and picnicking by the River Anner.

But in spite of the tingle in my back and the tear in my eye, I didn't budge, so Patrick had to confess. Turned out, he'd bought two train tickets to Worcester and we were off to attend an Irish fair. And how could I say no to that?

~

The fair was at a big brick church not far from the train station—St. John's, Patrick said it was. "'Tis where I went to Mass when I was working here." He gave me a wink. "Can't promise you it was often."

"You worked in Worcester?" It was one more thing I didn't know about him.

"For a few months after the war," he said. "The factories were only hiring Yankees, so I laid track like every other Irish lad." He shook his head. "It's hellish work but it's filled many an Irish belly, so I was grateful to have it. Then I heard about the good wages at the tunnel, so I left."

Not for the first time, I was struck by how Patrick was always leaving one place and going to another. A restless lad, surely. Made me wonder how long before he'd be leaving me too, and a sad feeling came over me. But it didn't last long, for the fair was a wonder, with the smell of roasting meat in my nose and the music of fiddlers and drummers in my ears. The sun was shining and the women's frocks were bright and I couldn't have been thinking sad thoughts if I tried.

Patrick bought hard-boiled eggs and scones and pork pasties from a woman who looked like my aunt Johanna. We ate our lunch sitting on a patch of grass, watching a juggler and a potato sack race. Later we joined a crowd singing the sweet, sad songs of Thomas Moore. Made me homesick for Ireland, it did. And I wasn't the only one with tears wetting my face before it was done.

After the singing, a priest stood on a platform and talked about a new famine in Ireland and how we should collect money to send our Catholic brothers and sisters across the water. He had a golden tongue and music in his voice. The palaver at the edge of the crowd quieted, till everybody was listening. "Now, I know some of you are ashamed to be seeking charity for our beleaguered homeland," he cried. "But we lovers of Ireland have set our minds and hearts on freeing her. The land system has been corrupt for generations and it's squeezing the tenant farmers ever tighter. We're determined to reform Ireland. She must rule her own affairs!" Patrick and myself stood up and cheered along with everybody else. My own heart was beating hard, and I couldn't help thinking how Da would have admired such noble words.

There were more speakers, and when a charity basket was passed around, I put in half my wages from the week before. I was in such a state of excitement I felt no surprise when we came on Maria Doughtery tending a booth. Patrick bought cups of lemonade and the three of us chatted till the sun was low in the sky.

Sure, I was as reluctant to go as Patrick when we headed back to the station in the soft blue twilight.

I spent most of the next day in the washroom, mangling a tubful of sheets and frocks, expecting Patrick to walk in any minute. Imagined him sweeping me into his arms and kissing me till I couldn't breathe. But instead of Patrick, it was Emily who walked in. I'd been scrubbing a stain from her hem for the best part of twenty minutes, but no matter how hard I rubbed, it wouldn't come clean. In she came, looking fresh as daisies in her white wrapper, just as I was dipping her frock in a pan of bluing for the third time. I wiped the sweat off my face and tried to tame my tongue but I was cross at Emily and disappointed with Patrick and had neither wit nor will to keep my mouth shut.

"Will you tell me one thing, then?" I said. "Why, for the love of God, are all your frocks white? You're not a nun, after all."

Emily's eyes went round and she took a step back. I could see from the way her face shut she didn't want to answer—maybe didn't even have an answer to give—and I was sorry I spoke. But I knew better than most that words spoken can't be unheard.

"I'm sorry, miss," I said, scrubbing harder. I couldn't bring myself to look at her. I tried to gentle my voice. "It's just that white is the color of death where I come from. I know it's not like that here in America, but it troubles me."

"*Death?*" she said in a choked voice. The startled look was on her still, but joined now by something that chilled my blood. After a minute she said, "I guess you'd have to call it a fancy. It makes me feel myself." She murmured something else I couldn't make out and left the washroom.

I hung the laundry and started peeling potatoes and carrots for dinner. By noon I knew for certain Patrick wasn't coming.

In the afternoon Meg came by to gossip about Austin and Sue. She said they'd had another screaming bout the night before. All about Sue's wasteful spending. "Those parties of hers are wicked," Meg said. "She invites all the fancy ladies in town and they smoke cigarettes and tell sinful stories the whole night long. They keep me up till the wee hours waiting on them. Then I have to do the washing up after they're done."

"Sure, I'm sorry to hear it," I said. I was aching to talk about my day at the fair with Patrick, but my niece's head was full of doings at the Evergreens and she didn't stay for a second cup of tea.

Later, putting away dishes in the pantry, I saw the spice tin had been moved to the windowsill. It was where I stored paper scraps of Emily's writing I found in her pockets on laundry day. I'd never looked at them close, but I was feeling out of sorts.

There was only a pinch of guilt troubling me when I plucked off the lid and took out one of the scraps. Emily's handwriting was small and broken; most of the letters stood alone, not joined with lines and loops like mine. It took some time reading and even when I figured out most of the words, I couldn't unravel the sense of it. There was *a cube of the rainbow* and *the arc of a lover's conjecture* and the quare word *eludes*. It was as if she took chance ideas and stuck them together willy-nilly to make a word bouquet. It was pleasing to my ear but bewildered my mind.

Then I thought of the pretty glass drops and boxes hanging on threads in Emily's room. They sometimes caught the afternoon light and cast it on the wall over her bed. The first time I saw the little rainbows scattered among the wallpaper roses, I squeaked with the surprise of it. She showed me how the glass dangles caught the sun and made a fan of colors.

"A tiny box of rainbows!" I'd said. "How clever!" The way Emily smiled straight into my eyes made me feel like I was shining myself.

I dropped the scrap back in the tin and shut the lid tight. Through the pantry window I saw the wind blowing in low clouds from the north. Like curtains those clouds were, with the sun winking in and out between them. It looked like rain. I grabbed the laundry basket and hurried outside. I unpinned the sheets quick as I could and brought them in to fold for Tuesday's ironing.

I was making gravy when Emily came down the back stairs. I'd not been able to stop puzzling over her poem. I was stuck on the line about the lover's conjecture—it took me back to thinking about Patrick and the confused feelings knocking around my heart. When she stepped into the kitchen I blurted out what was in my head—a confusion of arcs and conjectures and rainbows.

"What are you talking about?" she said. Then, "Have you been reading my verses?"

"Only one, miss," I said, quick as a bird flitting off a branch. "Caught my eye, it did. The one about the rainbow cube."

I thought she was going to be cross. But all she did was nod. "I'd forgotten. Did I leave it in my pocket?"

"You did. I laid it in the spice tin with the others. Saw it just now when I was putting away the china." I was rattling on for no reason but to fill the room with sound. To make my voice lift the curtain between us. When she tilted her head, I stopped.

"And you thought I'd written it for you?" she asked.

I put down my spoon. "Not for me, no. But remember we talked about the glass dangles in your room? Shaped like boxes and cubes, you know? So I wondered if what I said made you write it. But I don't understand about the lover—" I stopped again, for I couldn't find my way to the end of the thought.

"Dangles?" she said, and then she laughed. "Oh, you mean the prisms! Yes, I remember. It's actually meant to be a mathematical verse of sorts. I was having a little fun."

I felt a bit collapsed. I liked thinking I gave her the idea.

She was looking at me like I was a book she was reading. Then she said, "Perhaps I do have you to thank for the poem's genesis. I get my ideas from so many places—it's like sifting air."

I blinked. "What does it mean, then? The poem? The part about the lover?"

"Ah, the lover's conjecture. Of course—you're thinking of your beau." She got the spice tin from the pantry and brought it into the kitchen. "I suppose I was thinking of him too, in a way. It could as well be Patrick as anyone. There's always mystery when it comes to love, don't you think?" She opened the tin and turned it over so the scraps fluttered down on the table. They lay in a jumble of shapes and soft colors. I was glad I'd shut the windows so a chance wind couldn't blow them all over the kitchen. "Poems are about anyone," Emily said. "Or everyone. At least the good ones are."

So the poem was about everybody. And finding my own story in it gave me a bit of pride. I watched her pick up a scrap and read it to herself. "The muse assaults me at odd times, Maggie. So I must be ready. That's why I always carry my pencil." She swept the scraps into her hand and put them in her pocket. Looked like I'd likely be saving them from the laundry again next week. She popped the lid back on the tin and smiled at me. "It's good of you to rescue them. I think I shall anoint you Steward of the Verses." She put her hand on my head, like a priest giving a blessing, and tried to look solemn, though her mouth was tugging up at the corners. "Now it's your duty, Maggie, to preserve and defend them. They are my entire estate."

I knew she was jesting, but something in her words touched me. There was a coin of truth in them, bright as a silver dollar. That's always how it was with Emily.

When I got to Kelley Square Thursday afternoon, Mary was on the porch, sorting through a bag of old clothes. "Jamie's outgrown every single hand-me-down I've got," she said, inspecting a ragged pair of boys' trousers. "And I've patched these till there's nothing left but lint."

"Time to be making new," I said, knowing she took satisfaction in her needle.

"Aye, if he'd hold still long enough for the measuring." She dropped the trousers into her ragbag. "You're bursting to tell me something," she said. "I can see it in your face. Spit it out, lass."

And so I did, filling her ears with what I'd seen and heard at the fair. The more I talked, the more excited I got about the cause of Irish freedom. It wasn't till I ran out of breath did I notice Mary was frowning.

"Sounds to me like Patrick's been leading you down the primrose path," she said.

Now I was the one frowning. "Sure, I don't take your meaning. 'Tis fighting to free our brothers and sisters from English oppression I'm talking about."

"*Wisha!* You sound like a Fenian," she said. "You can't believe such blather, surely."

"And why not? I'm asking," I said. "Maybe it's yourself should be believing it too."

She shook her head and the look on her face made me feel small, like a girl again. That was the trouble having a sister so much older. I loved her but she tried my patience.

I would have said more if the train whistle hadn't tattered the peace of the afternoon. I near jumped, which wasn't like me, for hadn't I been hearing that awful noise for years now? Truth is, it felt like my insides had broken to pieces, the way a dish shatters when it's dropped. And right there, on Mary's porch, my mind flew back to the time Emily took a chipped plate the Squire had been complaining about and smashed it on the flagstones outside the kitchen door. Remembering that left me thinking how quare it was my thoughts so often linked themselves to Emily. We were as different as day and night. But sometimes it felt like I was living inside her life as well as my own.

Chapter Twenty-Three

Judge Lord came in August, bringing his nieces. They took rooms at the Amherst House, and while the Judge was with Emily, the girls hired carriages and went riding over the hills or off to Northampton to shop. I was surprised the Judge gave them the freedom to do whatever they took into their heads, for his court judgments were always stern and sometimes harsh. But I was glad the nieces weren't underfoot all day, for wherever they went they left a clutter behind them I had to be cleaning.

The last day of the Judge's visit I spent cleaning the cooker. I fettled the flues and ventilators, swept out the ashes, blacked and buffed the box and warming oven, and rubbed the brass hinges till they shone. Took me most of the afternoon and left my apron and frock in such a state there was nothing to be done but put on fresh ones. I had my foot on the stairs about to go up when Patrick came in with a spray of flowers in his hand. He held them out to me. "Sure, I've been wasting away with missing you, *agra*," he said. "'Tis killing me, it is. Give me a kiss." He leaned over the bouquet in a funny way so it looked like his head was stuck in the middle of it.

I laughed but my heart was thrumming. "You must be daft,"

I said. "Even a *gombeen* knows to leave a girl alone when she's been blacking a stove."

He must have heard what my tongue wasn't saying, for he dropped the flowers right on the floor and wrapped me up in his arms. And didn't he kiss me soundly, stove black and all?

"Now look at you," I said, pushing him away. "You're a sight, you are. Looking like a chimney sweep after spring cleaning!"

"Aye, and if it weren't for your cheeks being red as berries, we'd be a matched set." He leaned in to kiss me again.

It was that minute Emily came into the kitchen with the Judge behind her. The flowers were still on the floor. I picked them up and hurried them to the sink.

"I've just blacked the cooker, miss," I called over my shoulder. "Haven't finished cleaning up yet, so mind where you step."

Emily moved back and bumped into the Judge, who gave a little grunt. And didn't she burst out laughing? Clapped her hand over her mouth, but there was no stopping it. That laugh slipped right through her fingers. Next I knew, the Judge was laughing too. There they stood, the pair of them, having a grand hilarity like a couple of schoolgirls.

"Fair enough, Maggie," Emily said. "Sure, 'tis your kitchen and that's the truth of it." Used my accent, she did, instead of her own, which set the Judge laughing again and herself joining in.

Her mockery struck me like a stone hitting my chest. Rocked me back from the force of it. I saw Patrick's eyes go narrow and felt a dark shame flood me. More than once I'd boasted to him of my situation. Told him the Dickinsons were good people for all their quare ways. I'd not mentioned Emily's love of ridicule.

Patrick came and touched my shoulder and bent his head near my ear. "They may not be English, but they're after acting it through and through," he whispered.

I gave him a shove toward the door and out he went. God's truth, I wanted to follow.

I commenced pumping water with such a fury it soaked my sleeves. As soon as Emily and the Judge left, I ran upstairs to put on a new frock and apron and calm myself. But there was no forgetting the humiliation.

Patrick wasn't at Mass Sunday but I found him waiting at the corner when I left. He fell in step with me and took my arm as I headed to Kelley Square. His look was gentler and more tender than before, and I wondered if it was because he'd seen Emily mocking me. When Emily ridiculed my accent she wasn't insulting only myself but all Irish folk.

He asked me the question I'd been wondering myself—what did Emily see in the Judge?

"He seems a bit of a *shoneen*," he said. "Too full of himself to see his own wickedness."

"I'm thinking it's a family trait," I said, and I told him about the Judge's fancy nieces, how they'd taken a dislike to Emily. "They act like she's no better than a servant. Rude to her face, they are. And the Judge—he doesn't seem to notice."

"Maybe she's deserving it," he said. "Tasting her own medicine, she is."

"Maybe so," I said. "But I'm thinking nobody deserves being mocked."

"So, tell me about himself," Patrick said. "How'd he get to be such a puffed-up piece of shite?"

"Sure, that's no way to be talking about your betters." I didn't say so, but the truth was, I thought he was right.

"He's no more my better than a drunken lout lying in the

gutter. He's the lot who sent Dr. McDonough to jail because he was Catholic and wouldn't kiss the Protestant Bible."

This I hadn't heard, though it didn't surprise me. From what I'd seen of the Judge he was like every other aristocrat—using money and the law for protecting himself and his own kind.

"Never mind him," I said. "He's back in Salem with his nieces now. And I'm glad for it, surely."

"Good for you, lass." Patrick put his arm around my shoulder and gave it a squeeze. "I have a surprise for you waiting in my room."

I gave him a long look. "Sure, I'm not going in your room, Patrick Quinn."

He laughed. "Didn't expect you were, so I'll be bringing it to you after dinner."

"What is it, then?" I asked.

He laughed. "That would be telling, now, wouldn't it?"

We passed the Homestead on the far side of the street but I didn't even glance at it. Turned the corner and walked past the depot and went up the steps of Mary's house arm in arm, like sweethearts. I clean forgot to chide Patrick for not coming to Mass.

After dinner, I sat on the porch steps while Patrick went up to his room. He came out holding a package behind his back. And didn't he have a big grin on his face?

"Are you going to give it to me or not?" I said.

"After you kiss me, I am." I didn't think it was possible, but his grin got bigger.

"Making me pay for it, are you?" I said, but my skin was sparking all over and I was standing up.

"That I am," Patrick said, and he kissed me with his hands still behind him.

"There," I said, giving him a little push. "Now what have you got?"

He presented a package wrapped in brown paper and tied with string. Looked for all the world like a book. I gave him a look, for of all the gifts I dreamed Patrick might be giving me, a book was never one of them.

"Open it," he said.

And so I did. It was a book, to be sure. A thick one with a dark green cover and etched on the cover a shiny golden harp that made me think of the giant Dagda's. The book was just printed, from the look of it. I turned it to read the title on the spine. *Knocknagow.*

"It's lovely," I said. "I never heard of it, but I'm liking it already."

"'Tis brand-new," Patrick said. "Straight from Dublin. Look inside."

The title page read *Knocknagow; or The Homes of Tipperary by Charles J. Kickham.* Under it Patrick had written *To my sweet Margaret.* Tears came up in my eyes. Patrick offered me his handkerchief, but I pressed my face into his chest instead and welcomed his arms around me.

He told me everybody in Ireland was reading *Knocknagow*, and he could hardly wait to hear what I thought. Charles Kickham was a true Irish patriot, he said, working for freedom and justice. The book was a story about the struggles of regular Irish folk. "Like yourself," he said.

I started to tell him I was American, not Irish, but it seemed an old, wearisome song I was singing. And the truth is, I wasn't sure I believed it anymore.

~

Patrick walked me back to the Homestead that night, and when we reached the doorstep, I slid into his arms easy as falling. He held me in such a cherishing way, made my knees go soft. "Sure, you're the cleverest lass I know, young or old," he whispered. "And you have the brains not to take any nonsense from the Dickinsons. Nor anybody else who makes the mistake of thinking they're better than you." He stepped back and took my face between his two hands.

"Are you including yourself?" I asked, feeling saucy.

He laughed. "Ah, Margaret, you'll be the end of me, you will."

"Don't fret yourself," I said. "Haven't I been listening to Maria Doughtery and reading the words of the Parnells? In truth, Mary's thinking you're filling my head with Fenian notions."

"Is she, now?" Patrick's fingers were moving on my neck in a mighty distracting way.

"She is, and I'm thinking she's right." I raised my face to his as he bent to kiss me.

But our lips didn't meet before the back door opened and there stood Vinnie with a lamp in her hand. I jumped away from Patrick.

"Thank the Lord you're home, Maggie!" Her pretty face was all pinched so she looked like one of her cats. "Emily's in a bad way."

"Emily?" My heart banged in my chest. Sure, I think it was understanding Vinnie's words better than my brain.

Patrick stepped into the light. "Can I be helping?"

Vinnie raised the lamp and squinted at him. But it was me she spoke to, her voice shaking. "When I came home from church I found her down in the cellar. Sprawling in the old rocking chair. I feared she was dead."

I felt a bit shaky myself.

"Dr. Bigelow says she had some sort of fit." She moved back and waved me into the house. I cast a look at Patrick but he was already leaving. "She sleeps and wakes and sleeps again," Vinnie said.

I didn't even take off my shawl before running up the back stairs. It didn't surprise me Emily had been in the basement. She went down there sometimes when she felt stirred up or overcome. It was cool as a cave and she'd once told me it eased her eyes and her mind. Struck me how she favored both the cupola and the cellar at times. I didn't dither at her door, just walked straight in and there she was in bed with the sheet drawn up to her chin.

"Maggie," she whispered. "I'm glad you've come."

"Miss Emily." I smoothed the sheet over her. "Been giving everyone a scare, you have." I patted her hand lying on top of the blanket. "I'll be getting you a cup of tea, then."

But she caught my hand as I stepped away. "Stay," she said. "I need to hear one of your Irish tales. Please."

I did what she asked. Of course I did. I sat by her bed and held her hand and told her the old stories till she fell asleep. Wasn't till I left her room did it strike me I hadn't given a minute's thought to Patrick since Vinnie opened the door. My thoughts of him had floated away like they were part of a dream.

Emily stayed in bed for a week, and when she was up and about again, she moved like an old woman careful of her bones. I never saw Emily so frail before and it troubled me. I wasn't the only one. Vinnie kept a close eye on her whenever she was in the room and fretted when she wasn't. She had me cook strengthening broths and egg custards, same as I made for Mother Dickinson. If the fussing bothered Emily, she didn't complain.

The season turned and the snow came down. I read the whole of *Knocknagow*. It told a tale of Irish pride and showed the goodness of Irish hearts even in the midst of suffering and sorrow. Near every line brought a Tipperary memory. I read it in my room at night before saying my prayers. I read it in the kitchen after the washing up. I read it while waiting for the water to heat. When I finished I was mournful it had ended, and wanted to read it again. For the first time since I set foot in America, I was proud of coming from Ireland and glad I still had my accent.

Patrick and myself often talked about the book. He told me the author had been part of the rising at Ballingarry and later edited a newspaper till they put him in jail. It was a sorry tale, he said, for he was locked up fourteen years and it ruined the poor man's health. But in spite of his ordeal, he still had the patriot fire in his heart.

"Was he a Fenian, then?" I asked, curious.

"Aye, he was that," said Patrick. "And proud of it too."

I didn't know what to think about Fenians anymore. Most folks I knew thought them sinful or worse. But I'd been stirred by the speeches in Worcester and Northampton and defended their ideas to Mary and Tom. *Knocknagow* had opened my heart and I was feeling sympathy for the cause. It's a quare and wondrous thing, how a book can change the way a person sees the world.

The weeks untwined as weeks do. Children were born and old folks died. There were scandals and pleasures. The son of the College president shot himself. A traveling menagerie came to town and there was a grand parade. Reminded me of Emily and myself watching the circus stealing away in the middle of the night. Austin came down with the ague and lay in bed for weeks. Meg was the one dosing him with quinine and broths.

In April, the hat factory burned, the flames so close to Kelley Square they cracked three windows. The Hills brothers built a new factory. It went up fast—a grand building, spread over a whole block and topped with chimneys so tall I could see them on the far side of town. Mary complained the brick walls vexed her, made her feel closed in and trapped. She began talking of Tipperary and its fields and bogs so much she made herself lonesome with the longing. Surprised me, for she'd always said she never wanted to go back. I told her about *Knocknagow* and how it warmed me and made me want to walk up Slievenamon with Michael one more time. She sighed and said she wished she knew how to read. So I promised to read it to her, a few pages every Sunday after Mass.

Emily recovered and was happy as I'd seen her. That spring and summer the Judge came so often Tom jested he was likely going to be moving from Salem to Amherst.

On Independence Day Patrick and myself walked out to the fairgrounds and strolled on the racetrack. "Like a couple of grand racehorses we are," Patrick said.

I laughed, liking the way he tucked my arm into his. "More like a couple of plow horses, I'm thinking. Plodding along."

"Now, lass, I'm not the plodding kind myself. And I'm thinking you're not either." He let go my arm and danced around to the front of me. I didn't stop, so he had to walk backward, but he was laughing and giving me a wink. A regular charmer, he was. "You're needing a new adventure, love. And I'm just the lad to be giving you one."

I stopped walking. "An adventure," I said. For some reason, his words put the thought of California in my head again, after so many years. I set my hands on my hips. "And what adventure would you be suggesting now?"

He slipped his hands around my waist. "Come with me to Brooklyn."

That surprised me, to be sure. "Brooklyn? In New York? Why would I be wanting to go there?"

"It's a city, full of shops and parks and houses and good Irish folk. And I'm guessing you know about the bridge they're building. 'Tis a wonder of the world." His grin was near as wide as his face and the warm splay of his fingers through my shirtwaist was giving me dithers.

"I've heard of it," I say. I didn't want to sound too eager. But in truth, the idea of spending a day there was exciting.

"There are good prospects in Brooklyn," he said. "For a working lad such as myself."

The breath went out of me like air from a pricked balloon—all at once and in a rush. A score of thoughts ran through my mind, like rabbits in a meadow scattering before hunters.

"What prospects?" I said. A shade slipped across his face and settled around his eyes. Sure, I'd seen that look before—when he'd been away for days and didn't want to tell me where he'd gone.

"Tell me true," I said, pushing away from him. I could see he was planning on telling a lie.

He looked straight into my eyes and changed his mind.

"There's a factory looking to hire lads like myself. The wages are too good to pass up."

"A factory? Why would you want to be working in a factory?" I tried to imagine Patrick toiling all day at a dusty factory bench. It didn't sound like a thing he'd be doing for long.

"Manufacturing," he said. "Look, a lad's recruiting me. Says I have the skills they're looking for."

"Carpenter skills?" I asked.

He didn't answer, but his hand was on my waist again, moving around to the small of my back. It was distracting, surely. "Say you'll come with me, *acushla*." He was always using sweet words with me, but I wondered if I really was his darling.

"Is it proposing you are, then?" I said, my voice scratching along my tongue so it didn't sound like my own.

"Now, what else would I be doing?" He leaned in to kiss me.

I couldn't tell if he was teasing or true. "I'm thinking you might be looking for myself to be your maid," I said. "To do your cooking and cleaning so you won't be having to."

He laughed. "Sure, Margaret, you're so contrary you make the Devil look obliging. I love you and that's the truth of it. Just say yes and give me a kiss." He took my hands and smiled into my eyes. Sure, that minute I saw he meant it. My insides started swirling like water going down a drain. I was excited and cross and sad all at the same time. Needed to clear my head and figure things out before making any promises.

"What can I do to be convincing yourself?" His voice was sweet as glazing on a cake. He pulled me in for a kiss and I didn't stop him. In truth, I kissed him back.

"You've muddled my brain, Patrick Quinn," I said. "I'm needing time to think before giving you an answer."

"I'll wait you out, lass," he said. "Time and patience will bring the snail to Jerusalem."

It was an old proverb, but the way he said it made me feel like a rabbit destined for the snare. So I said, "I'll not be getting on any train with you till I'm sporting a wedding ring."

"That sounds like a yes to me, surely." There was a laugh in his voice.

"Something must be wrong with your ears, then," I said, feeling snappish. "Because it's not. So best not be counting your coins before you're earning 'em." And I hurried back to Kelley Square, with himself following me like an eager pup.

Chapter Twenty-Four

Trouble was, when Patrick turned on his charm, I couldn't resist him for long. By twilight we were sitting on the boardinghouse steps, sighing and kissing, when I should have been thinking and praying about whether to be giving him the yes he was after. When Ellen came out on the porch, we jumped up, and I'm certain we were looking guilty as we were.

"James is hoping to share a pint with you before bedtime," she said to Patrick.

"Tell him I'll join him after walking my sweetheart home." He squeezed my hand.

"Sure, there's no need," I told Patrick. "I'll be taking myself home tonight. Go on with you now." He looked sorrowful, but I knew a pint would cure him quick enough. And it saved me from committing a sin that night. For I'm certain if he'd walked me back, he would have pressed me to lie in the straw with him again, and I'd not have the will to resist.

I gave him a quick kiss on the cheek, left him to his drink, and started back to the Homestead. But there was Mary sitting in her rocker on her porch, so I stopped and had a word. "Sure, Margaret," she said, "your cheeks are bright as if you'd been standing over a hot stove."

"Are they now?" I went up the steps and plunked myself down in the chair beside her. With the sun gone down, the air was lovely and cool.

"They are indeed," she said. "I've known you from the day you slid into this world. You've never hid your feelings. 'Tis Patrick, isn't it?"

I didn't say yes and I didn't say no, but my eyes slipped past hers, which was as good as admitting she was right.

"Sure, 'tis no surprise. The two of you shine like the stars themselves." She gave me a glimmering smile. "It won't surprise me if he's asking you to marry him one of these days."

"He already has." I wasn't planning to tell her, but it slipped out and I confess it was gratifying to see the staggered look on her face. "But I've not given him an answer," I added, quick as a minute.

Her surprise gave way to a laugh and then she was crowing. "Didn't I tell you?" She stood and gave me a hug. "'Tis what I've been praying for. It's what we all wanted."

"What you wanted?" I said. "I remember clear as day you telling me Patrick was a rogue. Not the marrying kind, you said."

"Sure, I'll not deny there's a bit of the rascal in him," Mary said. "But I'm guessing he'll settle down once he has a wife and little ones. It'll content me, knowing you're married and living close by."

I couldn't look at her for wondering if I should tell her Patrick's plans. She'd not be so pleased if she knew he was taking me off to Brooklyn. "I'm still deciding." I didn't want her prying deeper. She had a way of uncovering my wickedest thoughts. "I've got to be getting back to the Dickinsons. Tomorrow's a washing day if the weather holds." I stood up.

"Don't keep him waiting too long now," Mary said. "Luck has a way of slipping through the fingers."

"Sure, that's the truth." I gave her a kiss and went down the steps.

Walking back to the Homestead, I was thinking of the times I'd planned on leaving the Dickinsons' service. Wondering why the way was opening for me now.

After he proposed, Patrick stopped by the Homestead every day. "Are you ready to give me your yes?" he'd say, coming up behind me and sliding his arms around my waist. I'd feel his breath at the back of my neck and the smell of himself, soapy and clean and fresh with outside air. And my spine would go soft as a pudding.

I told him I was still deciding. He'd have to give me time.

"How much time, *agra*?" he'd whisper. "You can't keep a lad waiting forever."

"You've been talking to my sister." I'd laugh, shaking him off.

What I didn't say—what I didn't know how to tell him—was how uneasy I felt about moving to Brooklyn. And I couldn't figure out why. Didn't I love an adventure? Hadn't I been the one longing to go to new places and see new sights? Living in Brooklyn would be all those things, surely.

But the times I'd thought about marrying Patrick, I'd always imagined living in a house in Amherst. On Irish Hill maybe, or at the Crossing. Maybe even at Kelley Square. A small house, with a little garden and a yard for children. I tried to picture keeping house in a city flat looking out on a noisy, crowded street. The air would be thick with dust and smoke. There'd be no gardening there for me. And—worst of all—no sister just down the street.

It must have been Tom told Emily about Patrick proposing. She brought it up in her own peculiar way one morning while she was kneading bread, her hands dusty with flour and the smell of yeast on her apron.

"I had a chat with a wren early this morning," she said, not looking at me but working away at the dough with her head down and wisps of hair floating around her face.

"A wren, was it?" I was pounding allspice and rosemary into a saddle of mutton and only half minding what Emily said. It wasn't the first time she'd talked about chatting with birds.

"He came to my window and shared a disquieting tale." She stopped kneading and rounded the dough into a ball.

"Did he, now?" I lifted the meat and settled it into a pan.

She covered the dough with a dishcloth and wiped her hands on her apron. "He told me someone's been trying to convince you to marry."

I near dropped the pan. It was all I could do to open the oven and slide it in. I couldn't think of anything to say, but there was Emily turning her twitchy smile on me and expecting my confession.

"I understand love, Maggie," she said. "And I know the attractions of marriage, but—"

I cut her off. "If you're meaning Patrick, I haven't told him yes or no." I shut the oven door with a bang.

"Good for you, Maggie. Be brave." Her smile opened and the flicker in her eyes made me feel tender and sad at the same time. "I wouldn't have you caught in his snares."

"Snares, is it?" I went in the washroom to clean the grease off my hands. Pumped the water hard to settle myself.

"I suspect it is," she said. "Men are fond of snaring their prey. And what better place to set a snare than in a woman's heart?"

I stopped pumping. I didn't like to think about Patrick that way. It made him seem scheming and cruel. But he'd set himself in my heart, to be sure. I dried my hands and went back in the kitchen.

"Is that in the Bible?" I asked. She knew her Bible, Emily did, and was fond of quoting it.

She laughed. "Not the one you're thinking of. A Bible of Life, perhaps."

"'Tis from one of your verses, then," I said.

"You know me too well." She shook her head slowly back and forth but she was still smiling. "But in this instance, no. Not precisely. Though the sentiment lurks."

I remembered times we'd talked about love—its pleasures and confusions. And because they were there in my mind, the words came out without my meaning to say them. "Judge Lord," I said. "Hasn't he set a snare in your own heart while I've been sighing after Patrick?"

She gave me a look she'd never turned on me before—admiring and respectful. Then she tilted her head. "How wise you are, Maggie. Perhaps he has."

August came and I still hadn't given Patrick an answer. But all of a sudden Mary stopped pressing me to marry. She began acting as if there was nothing at all between Patrick and myself. Talked as if he was just another Irish lad boarding with Ellen and James. It was puzzling, for she'd been overfond of reminding me he was my last chance for having babbies. "And I'm knowing better than anybody how much you like children," she'd say with a nod.

One Thursday afternoon I was in the midst of telling her how Patrick had once worked in Worcester, when Tom cut in.

"The lad's had quite a life, he has," he said. "And knows how to tell it too. A couple weeks ago he had a bit too much of the drink and blathered on for an hour about being with the Fenians on one of their raids back in eighteen seventy. They all marched up to Vermont and crossed the border into Canada. Armed to the teeth, he said. But it turned out to be a bloody business for the Fenians. Some were shot dead and their leader was arrested before their very eyes."

"They're a cowardly lot, Fenians," Mary said, sending a look in my direction. "Wicked and wild and ungodly. Hooligans, surely. Looking to rile up the countryside and wreck the order of things."

"Likes a bit of mischief, Patrick does." I poured myself another cup of tea. "You ought not be believing every word he's saying. Likely he read something in the papers and was acting the maggot." My words were bold, but Tom's words rattled me. It was one thing to be wanting the freedom of Ireland. It was another to be killing folks. I didn't like hearing Patrick might be mixed up with that. Worse, it troubled me he was confiding to others what he never told me.

Tom gave me a look. "He had a lot of information for somebody who wasn't there, Margaret. I'm telling you, the lad has a past."

"Not one to be proud of from the sound of it," said Mary.

"Everybody has a past," I said. "Doesn't mean it's one to be ashamed of." But in truth, I didn't know what to think. If what Tom said was true, I was hurt and angry Patrick didn't tell me himself. I'd always been inspired by tales of wild courage and action. And thinking about Patrick being so bold stirred me now.

I decided to ask him about the raid. The next time I saw him, I promised myself. But when he turned up in my kitchen Saturday afternoon, the thought went flying straight out of my head. For he came to say he was leaving Amherst.

"I'll be back in a few weeks—maybe a month." He pulled me close, paying no mind to the great splatters of grease across my apron. There was a faint smell of sweat about him. "I'm after giving you a chance to sort things out—decide if you'll be marrying me. Truth is, I've grown as weary of nagging you day in and day out as you are of hearing me. So I'll not be pressing you anymore. But much as I love you, I can't wait forever. So when I come back I want your answer, yes or no."

I looked up at him. He was gazing at me with such tenderness I almost said yes on the spot. Instead I asked, "Where are you off to, then?"

"I'll be visiting a friend," he said.

I pushed out of his arms. "Does it happen your friend lives in Brooklyn?"

He glanced away a minute and then looked back at me. Didn't have to say yes for me to know the answer. "I'll give you the address. You can send a letter if you like," he said.

I didn't fancy the idea of himself leaving, or setting a limit on my time for answering, but I'd dithered so long I had only myself to be blaming. And here he was standing in front of me with his arms at his sides, looking regretful.

Sure, I couldn't be cross at him more than a minute. "All right," I said. "I'll have your answer in a month, then." And I reached for his hands. I was thankful when he took mine and drew me back in.

His good-bye kiss was so slow and sweet my whole body ached when he left.

A letter came from my brothers the next week. Four pages, it was, reporting how they were moving from mine to mine, working their way into New Mexico Territory. They'd stayed together and their luck had been good. It was risky, though—there were terrible accidents in the mines and plagues in the camps. Michael had suffered a bout of typhus that laid him low for weeks, but he was recovered and the pair of them in good health.

Folded into the letter was money for Mary and the children. Mary told me to write back telling them she wasn't in need—her Tom provided well for his family—so she'd be putting it in the charity box at church. I added a whole paragraph about Patrick. How handsome he was and all the places he'd lived and things he'd done. How he'd asked me to marry but I hadn't decided. I ended that letter like I ended them all—begging them to quit the mining life and come back East to settle down in Amherst. *We're all missing you*, I wrote. *Come home soon.*

Then came a cool, bright morning with a soft wind riling the rye in the meadow and a bite of fall in the air. Before breakfast my chickens escaped the coop and I had to chase them clear to the end of the garden. Sure, it was plain it was an unlucky day and I'd have to be taking extra care with knives and fires. At eleven o'clock Emily was making custard in the kitchen and I was washing pans at the sink when we heard a loud knocking on the front door.

"I'm not receiving anyone today," Emily said. "Unless it's Phil." The bell of her voice followed as I went to answer.

The young lad on the doorstep wasn't anybody I knew. I was about to order him around to the back when he pulled a yellow envelope out of his pocket. It was stained and wrinkled but I knew what it was—a telegram. And they rarely brought good news. I figured it was likely for Vinnie, since she had a friend in Boston with consumption. But then the lad spoke my own name like a question, and when I nodded, he gave it to me. My hand was shaking when I took it. As if I already knew what was inside.

I didn't want to read it. I slid it into my pocket and went back to the kitchen, where Emily was pouring her custard into molds. I was walking slow, which wasn't my usual way. She looked up with a little frown on her face. "Who was it, Maggie?"

I shook my head. "'Tis a telegram, miss. For me." I took the envelope out of my pocket and stared at it.

She didn't say anything, didn't ask why I wasn't opening it, didn't turn away or leave the room. She just waited. As if she knew I'd be needing a shoulder to cry on.

Finally I sat down and opened the flap and pulled out the paper. *Western Union* was written at the top in fancy letters. And below were the words I was dreading even before I knew there was anything to dread:

MICHAEL DIED AT 10 YESTERDAY MORNING IN MINE
EXPLOSION. TUNNEL COLLAPSED. REMAINS NOT RECOVERED.
WILL TRAVEL EAST SOON AS POSSIBLE. TELL MARY AND TOM.
YOUR GRIEVING BROTHER TOMMY.

My mind unraveled that afternoon there in the apple green kitchen. For the life of me I can't recollect what happened next. It was as if a great crack opened in the ground and I fell in. A few things I remember, though they're more like sparks of light in the dark than memories—the telegram fluttering to the floor. Emily's hand on my arm, then on my shoulder. The rattle of a carriage going by the house. But I don't know if those things happened anywhere but in my mind.

I can't tell you how long I sat there or how I managed to stand. I don't know who fetched Tom from Kelley Square or what he said when he put his arm around my shoulder. I don't remember praying my rosary with him there at the table, though Emily said I did.

I do remember thinking I would surely die.

And then wanting to.

Mary took the news hard as I did. She was part mother to Michael after all, just as she was to myself and Tommy. At Kelley Square we held a wake though there were no remains to be waking. All the Irish in Amherst came and we keened and drank and sang for hours. I couldn't stop thinking of Michael's poor body crushed in that broken earth. I took the daguerreotype of himself and Tommy out of its frame and tucked it inside my bodice, close to my heart. At night I dreamed terrible dreams and woke up gasping. I missed Patrick and was cross at him for not being near when I yearned for the comfort of being wrapped in his arms. Days I stumbled through my chores half blind. I burned roasts and boiled the kettle dry. I dropped plates and scorched linens on ironing day. I overchurned the butter and forgot to feed the cats. I felt as if my heart was ruptured and my insides were washed in blood.

After a week I wrote Patrick a short letter telling him the news. Sure, I would have written more if I'd not felt so empty and lonesome. It was as if I'd been crushed in the mine beside poor Michael.

Vinnie didn't scold and Emily was kind and tender. She brought me flowers from the garden and told me not to worry about housekeeping—she and Vinnie would be doing it for now. She distracted my mind by reading stories out loud and leaving little notes pinned to my door. Her cousin Frances sent me cheering letters. Even Mother Dickinson seemed to understand what had happened and said she was sorry for my loss.

Then Tommy came home.

Twelve years had come and gone since I'd laid eyes on my youngest brother, but it didn't take a minute for all that time to disappear when he walked into the Homestead kitchen with Tom. It was pouring rain outside and both men were soaked to the skin but I squealed like a babby and threw my arms around Tommy and burst into tears. I stayed so long weeping into his neck, he had to pry me off and sit me on a chair, and even then I wouldn't let go. Hung on his sleeve like it was a promise.

The lads took off their jackets and passed a towel back and forth, while I found a dry one to wipe away my tears. And didn't Tommy look lovely? Handsome as ever he was—the same face that was in the daguerreotype though now he was sporting a beard. His skin was seasoned like old wood, glazed tawny by the Western sun. Once my tongue came unstuck from my throat, I couldn't stop asking questions.

Seeing Tommy alive and in the flesh swept away my sorrow. Felt like a miracle, it did, sitting with him in the same room. Tom, it was, put the kettle on and wet the tea, and we sat talking. I lost all track of time and would have left dinner to get itself if Emily hadn't come into the kitchen.

"Miss Emily, you must come and sit with us," I said, as if it was my own house. I bustled around and pulled out a chair, introduced her to Tommy, and poured herself a cup of tea. I thought Tommy might be feeling shy sitting down with the mistress of the house. But he chatted away like she was one of his own family. Maybe living out West all that time had him believing his betters were his equals.

Emily didn't take offense. She asked him near as many questions as I did, laughing at his jests and making some of her own. It was the happiest I'd seen her since the Judge's last visit. Sure, I couldn't hear enough of Tommy's tales and felt a pang when Tom stood up and said they had to be heading back to Kelley Square. Mary would be getting fretful and cross, for she hadn't spent more than a couple hours with Tommy before Tom whisked him off to see me.

A lump came into my throat from knowing I'd probably have to wait till Sunday before seeing my brother again. But then Emily said I must take the rest of the week off. "We can get along without you for a few days," she said. "Vinnie and I are perfectly capable of taking care of Mother and preparing our own meals." She stood up and carried her cup to the sink.

When I didn't move—for my poor head was still spinning—she got my cloak. And didn't she put it around my shoulders and pull me to my feet and draw me to the door?

"Go along now," she said, and she squeezed my hand like a sister.

I turned to thank her.

"Ah, Maggie," she said, "Heaven comes so rarely near us, we must visit when it does."

Chapter Twenty-Five

Who should turn up the day after Tommy returned but Patrick? I was sweeping dead leaves off Mary's front porch when I saw him coming across the yard. It was a shock, to be sure. My first thought was he was after his answer. I backed away as he climbed the steps and I'm certain my face twisted in a quare way. "'Tis only two weeks since you left," I said. "I've no answer yet."

But he shook his head, took the broom out of my hand, and pulled me to him, holding me like he wouldn't let go. He kissed the top of my head and said, "I got your letter," into my hair. "'Tis the only reason I came." Sure, it was good to snug my face into his chest and listen to his strong heart beating. My tears came up fast and I couldn't stop them flowing.

We went for a long walk out to the Agricultural College, himself holding my hand and listening all the way. I told him all my memories of Michael till my heart was too sore to hold anything but sorrow.

Patrick was by my side the next three days. A true comfort, he was, with his tender ways and soft touches. He didn't press me for kisses, though he was happy to give them when I asked. Nor did he talk about marriage. Said he'd ask me after a month, like he promised.

He liked Tommy, said my brother reminded him of some of the good lads he'd met in the Irish Brigade. Fearless, they were. Best fighters in the Union Army.

When he left to go back to Brooklyn, I saw him off at the depot and stood waving him out of the station. It felt like a cold wind had blown up all of a sudden, though it was a warm, golden day. I stayed for a long time looking down the tracks at where the train had disappeared. Thinking I'd be giving Patrick the answer he wanted when he returned.

Eight days Tommy stayed in Amherst, and every one of them Mary and myself begged him not to go. But he had business in the West needed tending and said he couldn't linger. I saw he was restless. Reminded me of Patrick that way. Maybe something about moving from place to place and working outside under the open sky made settling hard for lads. Patrick had complained of feeling cramped and itchy when he stayed in one place too long. Once he told me living in Amherst was like being locked in a box with a bunch of mosquitoes. I thought it funny at the time and laughed, but seeing Tommy looking the same helped me understand.

Tommy talked about Michael for hours, told us tale after tale of how well-liked he was in the mining camps and towns and how much he loved the Western life. Always talking about striking it rich, Michael was. Which was why he kept moving on, looking for the next lode when one petered out.

Tommy said he was at the bakery the day of the explosion. When the church bell started ringing, everybody in town dropped what they were doing and headed for the mine. He ran all the way, wanting to be part of the rescue crew. But when he got there, it was plain it was too late to save the miners—the entry had fallen in along with the tunnel. He grabbed a shovel anyway and started digging alongside the other lads. It was the only way to keep the grief and horror away, he said. He dug all day and night and into the next day, till he couldn't stand up anymore and his friends had to carry him away.

I listened with my head hanging and my tears running down. There was nothing for it but to pray, and so we did. One day Father Barry came all the way from Northampton to bless Tommy and say a requiem Mass for Michael.

We were sitting on the steps at Kelley Square a quiet Sunday afternoon, chatting about one thing and another, when Tommy told me about a girl he met he was wanting to marry. He hadn't asked her yet, but he was planning to. Beautiful, he said, with bright blue eyes and a big smile and every inch of her Irish. I asked what he made of Patrick, told him he'd proposed and I'd not decided whether to say yes. Thinking I likely would. "He was sweet to come when I wrote about Michael," I said. "But I'm not certain I want to be living in Brooklyn, though he has his heart set on it."

Tommy turned to face me. "Do you *want* to marry him? I remember when you were working for the Boltwoods, you were always telling me you weren't going to wed anybody. Planned to stay single and free, was what you said."

"That was more than ten years ago," I said. "I hadn't met himself yet."

Tommy grinned. "Love makes fools of us all, now, doesn't it?

Remember how demented you were for George Garrett?" he asked. "I thought you'd run off with him, surely."

I laughed. "God's truth, I thought about it. I wasn't much past twenty, with the mind of a silly girl. But it would have broken Da's heart if I'd yoked myself to a Protestant. And sparked a scandal besides."

Tommy was nodding. "Sure, Brooklyn isn't California, but it'll be an adventure, I'm guessing."

"It will, won't it?" I said. My brother was always able to see the bright side of things—and it brought out the spark in me. It was another reason I was wishing he'd stay East.

"Best thing about Brooklyn is you can stop being at the beck and call of the Dickinsons and their like," he said. "I was surprised when you stayed with them instead of following me to California."

I was quiet a minute. "'Twas your letter persuaded me," I said.

"My letter?" He was frowning.

"The letter you sent to the Squire saying it was too dangerous for me to be going to California and I should stay in Amherst. When he showed me, all my fight drained away," I said. "Seems like something you'd remember."

He tapped the beard on his chin, just a little tap, then closed his eyes. A dark flush came up in his face. That fair Maher skin had betrayed all of us, more times than we could count.

"I do," he said, his voice gone soft. "In truth, I could see the sense of his thinking. Mining towns were rough places when I first went out there. Some would as soon cut your throat as look at you. And then there was the cholera."

I thought about what he said. "What do you mean, you could see the sense of *his* thinking? It was your letter—your handwriting was on it. The Squire showed it to me and I recognized it right off. Wasn't I the one helped you learn your letters?"

"Aye, you did," he said. "And it was my writing. But not my idea." He wasn't looking at me anymore.

"I don't understand," I said.

He took a breath in, let it out slow. Almost like smoking a pipe. "The Squire sent me a telegram asking me to write to you. Telling me what to say. Vowed it was for your own protection."

I looked away at the train depot, where a man was standing beside his horse and buggy. I thought about what Tommy was saying. The Squire was behind it all. From the first, he'd been scheming to deceive me, using his money to get what he was after. He'd not only threatened my family in Amherst—he'd got Tommy to do his bidding.

"Why?" I said. "I don't understand why you did it. Did he pay you? Threaten you?"

"'Twas a long time ago, Margaret." Tommy shook his head, making a curl fall over his brow. "He didn't pay me, but he was mighty convincing. It was best for you to be staying, surely. With Mary close by and needing your help."

"I like making up my own mind," I said. "And I had my heart set on running a boardinghouse."

"Aye, I remember," Tommy said. "God's truth, I've been wondering why you didn't open one right here in Amherst, you wanted it so."

I gawked at him. "Sure, I never thought of it," I said. "And for the life of me, I don't know why."

Tommy laughed. And didn't I laugh with him and give him a hug as well? I thought of how Emily was fond of saying it's easy to invent a life. But that day I was seeing how life was inventing *me*.

~

I didn't think I could bear parting with Tommy. Spending those fall days with him had calmed something in me, taken a bit of the sting out of Michael's death, and brought me back to myself. But too soon the day of his leaving came and we all got up with the sun and gathered on the depot platform, waiting for the train. Mary and myself were clinging to him like babbies to their mam. Sure, that's no surprise, for there's no bond stronger than family. When I heard the whistle and the train chuffed up, blowing and screeching, my tears came up. The car doors opened and the steps came down and I hugged Tommy tight and bid him good-bye. Felt like he was being swallowed by a steaming monster and I'd never be seeing him again.

Soon as the train left I went back to the Homestead, for I knew sitting with Mary would only sharpen my grief. A memory came to me—of a summer day I found Emily staring out the front window an hour after the Judge left. She turned and gave me a sad smile. "It's the transitory nature of life that makes it so sweet, don't you think, Maggie?" she said. "The knowing each moment that it will never come again."

I didn't make sense of her meaning then. But now the truth of her words was so plain, I blessed myself, right there on the street.

Grief is a long season and my sorrow over Michael's dying lingered. Vinnie and Emily were understanding, mindful I was mourning. Emily was especially tender. One day when I was low, she found me sitting on the bench outside the kitchen door. She sat beside me and we watched a few leaves drift down from the apple trees. After a time she asked if I wanted to talk. And my thoughts just came tumbling out. I told her I was feeling awful for never going to California like I planned.

"I was set to," I said. "Had my ticket and everything. Michael was so excited I was coming." Tears came springing up in my eyes. "It's been years and years since I laid eyes on him. And now I'll never be seeing him again."

"Oh, Maggie," she whispered. I looked at her and there was pity all over her face.

All at once I was angry. It wasn't her pity I was wanting. I wanted things to have been different. "It's blaming your father, I am," I blurted. The skin of my face was hot under the tears. "It was himself stopped me. Told me he'd hurt my family if I left. Said he had to have me—no other maid would do. I'll not forgive him, though he's dead and gone." I pressed my face into my handkerchief.

"He did it for me," Emily said in a quare voice.

"For you?" I looked at her.

She bowed her head. "*I* was the one who insisted you stay. I knew from the first week what a treasure you were. A pearl without price."

I flashed on the memory of Mam telling me my name Margaret meant *pearl*. Remembered Emily said she wouldn't call me by it. For a minute I couldn't breathe. "It's wrong to get what you want by hurting somebody," I said. "'Tis a sin."

Emily nodded. "It is. I thought he convinced you of the benefits of staying. I didn't know he threatened you. I'm truly sorry."

I looked at her. Saw the tears in her eyes. Heard how heartfelt her words were. And the anger flowed out of me. God's truth, I was still under her spell.

Patrick came back to Amherst the next week. Walked into the Homestead kitchen on a Saturday afternoon. I had my hand in the oven, checking the temperature. When he said my name, I jumped and shut it with a crash.

"*Agra*," he said, stroking my cheek, "you're looking prettier than ever." The skin under his fingers tingled. I sighed and leaned toward him, expecting him to kiss me. Instead he said, "I'm guessing you know why I'm here. I've come to collect the answer you promised." He smiled a slow smile. "And much as I want to, I'll not be kissing you till I get it."

It nettled me, himself being smug that way. I felt my anger spark and went to the table, where I'd left a clutch of potatoes. I tried to settle myself—I owed him an answer, and till that minute, I thought I had one.

"I was hoping you'd have got Brooklyn out of your system by now." I started peeling potatoes.

He made a little laughing sound, but I could tell I'd unsettled him. "*Achushla*," he said, and his voice was like honey, all golden and sweet. "You promised."

I couldn't deny it. And I wasn't a woman who went back on promises. I jabbed an eye out of the potato I was holding. Then I looked at him and saw the worry on his face and my heart melted. All I could think of was himself coming all the way from New York to comfort me when Michael died. That he'd waited so patiently for me to accept him. That was true love, surely.

I nodded and put down my knife and went to him. I put both my hands on his chest.

"Yes," I said, smiling. "My answer is yes."

God's truth, Patrick was happy. His smile was wide as the sky and he wouldn't stop kissing me till Vinnie came in the kitchen looking for Drummy-doodles.

～

I made a pitcher of lemonade and we went out to the piazza and sat on the bench, where we looked at the Pelham hills, all purple and red with the turning leaves. It was one of Emily's favorite views.

Patrick told me about things he'd seen in New York, the great bridge they were building in Brooklyn and the Grand Central Depot in the city. Best of all, he said, was the grand parade and picnic to celebrate a holiday for laborers. His keenness made me feel keen too. But when he mentioned attending a lecture about Irish Home Rule, I suddenly thought of Fenians and remembered what I'd planned to ask before he told me he was going off to New York. So I asked him outright—had he been with the Fenians who raided Canada?

"Tom said you were," I said. "So I want you to tell me true. I'll not be listening to any blarney."

He was quiet a minute, looking at the last of the lemonade in his glass instead of myself. "I did go, more's the pity. But it was more than ten years ago and I've been trying to put it out of my mind ever since. Not something I want to be talking about." He closed his eyes as if to show how much it hurt him to remember, but I didn't say anything.

He gave out a long sigh. "After the war I lived with some other lads from the Irish Brigade. Most of us couldn't find work, so we spent our days swapping tales and talking about Ireland. But when it came to good news about the old country, there was none to be had. No matter our talk about independence and fairness, it was clear England wasn't going to lift Ireland's yoke. When some lads joined the Fenian Brotherhood, I did too." He finished his lemonade and poured himself another glass. "Word came of a plan to bend England's will by taking territory in Canada."

"So you joined in," I said.

He gave me a look. "Sure, I did not. That was back in 'sixty-six and I was weary of war. It wasn't till four years later I had any part in the fighting. By then I was just wanting to get out of the city—'twas a fearful place full of gangs and hoodlums in those days. And the only job I could get was as a cartman clearing night soil out of tenement outhouses. So I went north with Captain John O'Neill and his army. And it was grand at the start. We were near a thousand strong and raging like stirred-up wasps." He was looking at the hills. "We crossed the border into Canada and were advancing to a bridge when our flag bearer was shot. Died where he lay, the poor lad." He was quiet a minute, looking down into his glass. "Before we had time to blink, the Canadians were on top of it, raining down fire. We all ran for cover. I lay down behind a stone wall and said my prayers."

In truth, I was stirred by his tale. Admiration was leaking through my vexation.

"We made our way back across the border, though it wasn't easy with dodging bullets all the way and having to leave the wounded and dying behind." He shook his head. "'Twas a shameful thing, Margaret. O'Neill upbraided us for cowards and told us to rally and redeem ourselves. Sounded to me like he wanted to send us all to our deaths. Before we could heed him, a US marshal arrested him. After that we all ran away. One lad turned his jacket inside out to show he wanted no part of the Fenians anymore."

"So you quit them?" I said.

He shrugged. "It was more like disappearing. I took the Hoosac Tunnel job. Went belowground, like a rabbit to its den." He gave a small laugh.

"Disappearing," I said. "Was it the shame of it?"

He drained the rest of his glass and put it on the bench between us. "Let's talk about something else now, lass. I've done enough remembering for one day."

I scowled. Vexed me, the way Patrick was forever hiding secrets. I didn't like himself not trusting me. A flash memory of the day we met came to me, when he wouldn't tell me his message for the Squire. I still didn't know what he was hiding all that time ago. Made me wonder what else he'd been hiding since.

"Sure, I've no more time for chatting today." I stood up and took the glasses inside.

"Margaret—*agra*," he said, following me. "This is a day we should be celebrating—not fighting."

He was right, surely, and so I let him kiss me. But then I told him I had work to do and he'd best be on his way.

"You've made me the happiest lad in America," he said, and tried to kiss me again.

"Go on now," I said, ducking and pushing him away. "We'll talk after Mass."

First thing I saw when I stepped inside St. Bridget's the next morning was Patrick. On his knees with his hands folded and his head bowed. I curtsied to the altar and slid into the pew beside him. When he lifted his head and looked at me, his face was so hopeful it touched my heart. Wanted more than anything to see his carefree, rascally smile again.

So I leaned close to him, right there in the sanctuary at the beginning of Mass before the Gloria. Leaned close to his ear and whispered I loved him and was as happy as himself we'd soon be married. The smile that came up on his face was so wide I nearly fell into it.

Chapter Twenty-Six

I f Emily guessed what had happened between myself and Patrick, she never said. I tried to find a good time to tell her we were engaged, but the next week she sickened again and took to her bed. Vinnie sent for Dr. Bigelow and Emily didn't argue, though she didn't like seeing anyone—not even Sue—when she was having one of her spells. Worried me, they did, those spells, for they were coming more often and lasting longer.

The doctor said she must take to her bed for a fortnight and dosed her with laudanum and belladonna. So I had to be nursing Emily as well as Mother Dickinson. Made my days long, and dreary too. A cold snap came for a week and I kept fires going in all the stoves and heated blankets for comforting. Emily, whose tongue was sometimes sharp as a knife, was sweet and grateful and sad. Seemed like the only cheer she welcomed were letters from Judge Lord. When I brought her one she'd ask me to leave and close the door behind me. She said she wasn't being unkind—she just needed to keep herself to herself for a while. I understood, to be sure. When it comes to love, all women need to cherish it in their hearts.

Emily missed her writing, and some days she talked on and on about her letters and verses. On days she felt strong enough, she had me prop her up with pillows and bolsters and set her lap desk over her knees so she could scribble away. I fretted she'd weary herself and begged her to rest. I made a point of trying to tuck her in every night before going off to bed myself. Times I wanted to be prying those papers out of her hands, for it seemed to me the writing stirred her up and troubled her spirit.

One night I came right out and told her. "Rest is what you're needing, miss," I said, taking her lap desk from her and smoothing the blankets back in place. "'Tis plain all this writing is distressing yourself. Wears you out, it does."

She gave me a look I'll never forget, as if I were a ghost come to haunt her into madness. "You're right, Maggie," she said in that slow, whispery voice she sometimes used. "It drains my soul. And the worst of it is there's no point. My ink might as well be invisible for all that comes of it."

"Ah no, miss," I said. "It's not what I'm saying. I just don't like seeing you so weary."

She put both hands to her forehead, covering her eyes. "I don't know what drives me but I must do it." Her voice was like a lonesome child's, dropping into the silence of the room. "I'm powerless before it. My poems are an obsession."

"Poems are born of yearning, surely," I said, thinking of all the poems and tales I'd heard growing up. "I'm familiar with the sting and hunger folded into them. 'Tis ofttimes said Tipperary grows as many poets as potatoes."

Her hands fell away and she was staring at me. "Yes," she whispered. "'Sting and hunger.' That's it precisely." She shifted on the bed, propping herself higher on the pillows. "But mine have all come to nothing. Ashes to ashes and dust to dust."

I didn't like hearing her talk that way. "I've read them, miss. They're not dust and ashes, to be sure."

"You've read them?" She frowned. "That's impossible."

I smoothed her top blanket again, for she'd rumpled it shifting. "Haven't I been rescuing them from the laundry for years? I've read dozens, surely."

Sick as she was, she laughed. "Oh, those are just scraps," she said. "Musings and notions. There are hundreds of real poems, Maggie. More than you can imagine. More than anyone knows."

This seemed unlikely. "Hundreds, is it?" I gave the blanket one more pass with my hand. I waited for her to tell me she was jesting, but instead she nodded.

"Possibly more." She slid deeper into the bed. "Though I don't know why I keep them all. I'm running out of places to hide them and I should probably throw out every last one."

"'Tis your fever talking," I said. "Why would you be hiding them? Folks want to read them, surely. They're so clever and sharp."

"Ah," she said, sighing. "I fear not. There's no market for singularity. And my poems are nothing if not singular."

I didn't know what to say. I wasn't even sure what she meant. But I knew Emily was different, and if that was the same as *singular*, then she was singular, surely. Yet now what she needed was sleep and I feared all the talking was only getting her stirred up. "Don't be throwing them out," I said, turning out the lamp. "Not before I've read them."

"You shall have them all," she said into the dark, her voice bitter. "Every last one. I'll bequeath them to you and let you read them to your heart's content, as long as you promise to consign them to the fire when you're finished."

I didn't answer, for she needed her sleep more than she needed my talking. But I was thinking I'd not be promising anything of the kind.

In truth, I didn't give Emily's poems another thought till the next afternoon when she put me to work gathering them together. They were everywhere—tucked into old hatboxes and spilling out of satchels and stacked in piles on her closet shelf. She sat propped in her bed watching while I dragged them out and piled them in the middle of the floor. By the time I was done all the words in my head had left me. There I stood, ringed around by her poems. In truth, I was flabbergasted.

"You see my dilemma," Emily said.

"But when?" I said. "How did you write so many?" I turned in a circle to face her.

She was looking at me close. Made me remember the time she showed me how to look at a leaf under a magnifying glass. "I've been writing at night," she said. "For years. Father encouraged me when I was young."

I tried to imagine the Squire encouraging anyone. He hadn't been the encouraging sort. Yet I knew—everybody knew—he was awfully fond of Emily. If anybody could get him to do something against his nature, it was herself.

She made an open gesture, sweeping her hands around the room. "They are my children. But sadly they've all come to a bad end." The darkness was in her voice again.

"Sure, I'll help you put them in order," I said. "Not all helter-skelter like this."

She nodded. "Together we'll prepare them for a proper burial. Shall I order a casket?"

I didn't like her jesting. Poetry was the marrow of speaking and there were books and books of poems in the Dickinson library. A whole shelf of them. "If they were made into books with pages of print and fancy covers, folks would be paying to buy them," I said. "From the look of it, you've all the poems you need for making dozens."

She laughed, but it was a bitter laugh. "You don't understand. No publisher will print my poems. They're not considered suitable."

"Sure, that can't be true." I took a page from the nearest hatbox. Her handwriting was spiky and hard to work out. I read it three times before putting it back. "It doesn't look unsuitable to me," I said. I didn't tell her it was a puzzle no matter how many times I read it.

Emily smiled. "You're very kind to say so, Maggie. But you don't understand the world of publishing."

My cheeks got hot and I turned away to clear my anger. I opened a hatbox and found a stack of booklets. There must have been dozens. Bits of string fluttered from the sewn edges. I lifted them out and placed them on the end of her bed.

"These are clever, miss," I said. "Did you make them?" I held up one of the booklets.

"I did," she said. "They're like the manuscript books we made in school." Her eyes were weary-looking but sharp. "I don't mean to make sport of your kindness, Maggie. For a time I endeavored to share my poems with the world. But the cost is too high." And she closed her eyes as if to make an end to it.

This made no sense to me. I didn't know what costs she was talking about but I wanted to help her. "I could be putting them in order for you," I said. "Finding a safe place for them."

She sighed. "I ran out of places long ago. My closet is bursting, as you know."

"Why not in the library?" I said. "I can make room on the

shelves. And there are empty drawers in the desk." I was the one who'd cleared Mr. Dickinson's things from the cupboards and drawers and I knew all the empty nooks and crannies.

"No, no. I can't have them out where they could be found." She placed one hand on her forehead. I suspected a headache. "You're the only one in the world who knows they exist, Maggie. You must make a solemn vow to keep it so."

This seemed unlikely. "Why would you be keeping them secret?" I asked.

She sighed and looked out the window. "A good deal of my life has been hidden. Perhaps it's simply become a habit."

"Habits can be broken," I said. "With confession and penance."

She gave me one of her quare looks, and for a minute, I thought she was going to laugh. Instead, she said, "Not easily. I've long suspected habits are the price of our humanity. God's little joke, if you will. Or perhaps the key to grace." She made an odd sound in her throat—halfway between a sob and a laugh. "The truth is, I can't bear the thought of them lying around. They'd be frightfully exposed. I'd fear for their virtue. They're better off as ashes."

I tried to stretch my mind around the idea of poems having virtue. If anybody else said such things, I'd think them cracked. But it was the way Emily talked—as if the whole world and everything in it was alive with feelings and thoughts. It was a peculiar notion, but when I didn't study it too hard, it made a kind of sense.

Then I had an idea. "I can put them in my trunk," I said. "It's near empty—just sitting under the window with nothing to do." It struck me I was talking the way she did—as if my trunk had a will of its own. "No one will be finding them there. Who would be looking in a maid's trunk?"

The quirk of her mouth made me laugh, and for just a minute, I thought she was going to say something spiteful. Then she nodded. "Yes," she said. "I do think they'll be quite comfortable there."

It lifted my heart, seeing Emily satisfied and happy. It was too rare a thing.

I laid Emily's poems in my trunk later that afternoon—forty booklets she'd stitched up with string, and fifteen more she'd yet to stitch. It seemed a pity to leave them undone, but I hadn't the time nor skill to be sewing them myself.

Three days in a row Emily made me promise to keep them secret. Sure, it went against my inclination, for it seemed to me a poem wasn't quite real till it's shared. And it was plain she once wished them published. It was why she wrote so many letters to the editor Mr. Higginson, surely, and why he visited all those years back. Emily herself told me she wrote to him first. Her letter had been so coy and flirtatious he came to Amherst to find out who she was. But he never promised to publish her verses.

A deep sorrow was in her whenever she spoke of them. Like she was speaking from the bottom of a well, her voice echoing through the water and darkness.

After I said yes to his proposal, Patrick came by the Homestead every day. I'd wet the tea and we'd chat in the kitchen. On my days off we'd go on long walks in Amherst or take the train to Northampton. One Sunday we went all the way to Holyoke. It brought back memories and I told him how, when I first came to America, myself and the other Catholics in Amherst would walk to Holyoke for Mass because it had the only church around. When I mentioned it's where Mary and Tom were wed, he started pressing me to set a day for our own wedding.

"It would have to be at St. Bridget's," I said. We were walking beside the Holyoke Canal, admiring the reflections of the mill buildings in the water. "And St. Bridget's is a mission church since Father Brennan left. So we have to go to Northampton and talk with Father Barry. And then there's banns to be read. That takes a while."

Patrick stopped and picked up a wee stone on the path. He turned it over in his hand. "Or we could get married in Brooklyn." He was looking at the stone. Not wanting to look me in the eye.

"Not if it's myself you're marrying," I said, and went on walking. He knew better than to suggest such a thing, surely. He was Catholic himself and knew we'd have to be married in our own parish church. Besides, I wasn't about to get married among strangers when my own friends and relations were living in Amherst.

After that day he began nagging me to speak to Father Barry. I said he should talk to him himself. He said I was the one who went to Mass regularly so I knew him better. The more he pressed, the more I balked.

"Don't know what the hurry is," I said. "We waited this long. A few more weeks won't harm us, surely."

Then came a sunny Thursday afternoon when we were sitting on the porch in Kelley Square, with Patrick plaguing me about the marriage date again. The Brooklyn folks were getting impatient, he said. "They'll not wait much longer. I have to be telling them this week whether or not I'll be taking the job. And I can't bear the thought of leaving you, truly." He put his arm around me and kissed my ear.

"Then tell them you won't," I said. "There's plenty of jobs right here in Amherst and Northampton."

He let his arm drop. "Are you changing your mind about marrying me, then?"

"I'm saying I don't know why you're so set on going to Brooklyn," I said. "What's so grand about a factory job that you'll give up the life we could be having here? Is it the money?"

He shrugged. He wasn't looking at me. A question came to me then, and soon as it did, I wondered why I hadn't thought it before.

I twisted so I could see his face. "What is it they're after making in this Brooklyn factory anyway?"

I saw him blink, then look away toward the depot. Even though we weren't touching, I could feel his shoulders tightening.

"You'd best tell me," I said. "I know you're hiding something."

He tried to take my hand then, but I slapped him away.

"You're trying to charm me with a smile and a kiss and a cuddle," I said. "But it will do you no good. You've got to be telling me the truth, Patrick. Now or never."

He was quiet a long minute, hunching over himself. Then he sat up straight. "All right," he said. "I'll tell you. But I can't tell you here. Not where somebody might be hearing us." He looked twitchy and the shiver I felt was more fear than excitement.

"We'll go for a walk, then," I said. "Right now."

The air had the feel of a storm coming on as we walked up Triangle Street. We went in through the gate of West Cemetery and walked along the path among the stones. I knew the path was shaped like the number eight—curving out and back and around on itself. I remembered Emily once telling me it was the same shape as the symbol for infinity and that was a good thing to have in a graveyard.

We passed the Squire's grave—upright as the Squire himself, it was—and went on to the older part of the cemetery, where the slate stones were slanting in crooked rows. I stopped walking. "There's nobody here," I said. "And it's past time you were telling me."

He let out a long breath. "Before I do, you have to promise not to tell another soul." He looked straight into my eyes. "It must be kept secret, or my life is in danger."

"Your life?" I thought he was jesting. But there wasn't the usual glint in his eye and he looked as grave as I'd ever seen him.

"Promise me, Margaret." He sounded miserable.

I wasn't sure I believed him, but I promised. God's truth, I didn't like doing it. Keeping secrets has a way of leading to ruin.

And so he told me. A lad he knew when he lived in New York had recruited him to help with a secret plan. "It's a kind of school," he said. "They've asked me to teach."

"Teach?" I said. "I thought it was a factory job. Teach what?"

He looked down and reached for my hand but I tucked it behind my back.

"Tell me," I said. "You promised the truth."

He let out a long breath. "When I was working on the tunnel, I was one of the lads who set the dynamite. I'll be teaching others how to make it."

"Dynamite?" I'd read about dynamite, knew it was deadly and wicked. "What lads?"

"I can't tell you," he said.

I took a step back. "And that's the reason you're after going to Brooklyn? To make dynamite?" I felt the anger boiling in me, pumping through my body. "You lied to me. Said it was a factory."

He didn't answer, didn't move.

All at once, I understood. It struck me quick as embers jumping from a grate. "They're Fenians, aren't they, these lads? They'll not be making dynamite to dig tunnels. It'll be for blowing up buildings and hurting people. Killing them." My words were coming out fast, all in one breath. "Are you forgetting my own brother died in a blast? If it wasn't for dynamite, he'd still be alive."

I couldn't read the look on Patrick's face. I took another step away. "What I don't understand is why you wanted me to go with you. What would make you think I'd want to be any part of such a plan?"

He gave his head a shake, like he was just waking up. "Because you've got a fighting spirit. Because you love Ireland." He took a breath. "Because you love me and you're going to marry me."

I felt sick. I stared at him, wondering if anything he said was true.

"I'm not," I said, oddly mindful I was standing between two broken gravestones. "I won't marry a man who makes dynamite for killing folks. I've lost one lad I love to the infernal machine and I won't be losing another. Our engagement's done."

He stood like a statue, looking at me.

"Leave," I said. "I don't want to be seeing your face again. Ever." He took a step toward me, but it was uncertain. "Don't touch me," I said. "Just go."

And so he did.

Chapter Twenty-Seven

I didn't go back to Kelley Square that day. Walked straight to the Homestead and shut myself in my room. My heart was beating too fast and my skin felt flushed. Wasn't from the walking—came from the riotous feelings thrashing inside. They tumbled in waves—anger, regret, relief, sorrow.

I kept thinking of Patrick's face just before he walked away. Searing, it was—near stopped the breath in my throat. I'd watched him out of sight before I moved. Now one minute I wanted to take back what I said and marry him next week. The next I was so angry I couldn't bear the thought of seeing him again. I wondered if I should tell a policeman or a judge what he was doing in Brooklyn. I knew it must be against the law. Then I wanted him to hold me in his arms and tell me it had all been a grand prank to make me laugh. Seemed like every feeling in the world was my very own.

Didn't take long before my tears started coming. I sat on my bed, bent over my knees and weeping. I was sorrier than I'd ever been in my life. Yet I knew I'd done the right thing sending Patrick away. I could never marry a man who made bombs. No matter how I cared for him. No matter how noble the cause.

I prayed a long time—prayed for myself and prayed for Patrick. And for all the folks who might be wounded and killed by his dynamite. I was getting off my knees when I spied my trunk and thought of Emily's poems lying there. I opened it and stared down at them—nestled against the side with its fading red and yellow paper. I took out one of the booklets and commenced reading.

I read slowly. Sure, I couldn't have read fast if I'd wanted to, for Emily's writing was so hard to work out. I read on and on, and when I finished one booklet, I took up another. I didn't try to get the meaning of the verses, just let the music of them wash over me like a tide. God's truth, I sat up half the night in the pool of light from my lamp, her words scattering through my mind. Like sparks they were—tiny scraps of light. I didn't half understand them. Yet for some reason they filled my heart.

"He wouldn't say a word to anybody," Tom told me. He was shaking his head over Patrick as I walked with himself and Mary back to Kelley Square after Mass the next Sunday. It was a bright fall day with the leaves flaring red and yellow against the sky. "Had the look of a lad condemned to the gallows, he did. Bowed low like an old man carrying a weight on his back. Didn't seem like himself at all."

"I don't want to hear it," I said. "He's gone and that's the end of it." I knew Tom and Mary were blaming me for Patrick's misery. I'd told them we had a fight and broke the engagement and he went off to Brooklyn. But I hadn't told a soul what he'd be doing there, and had no plans to. Now everybody was asking why he left so sudden and I was struggling to find a good enough answer.

Mary, who had her own doubts about the lad, tried to console me. "You're well rid of himself," she said. "I knew he was a rascal and a rogue the minute I laid eyes on him."

In truth, her opinion of him had changed more than once, but I nodded and said I should have listened to her in the first place. "Don't know why I couldn't see it," I said.

"Sure, there'll be other lads," she told me. "There are as many good fish in the sea as ever came out of it. And you're young yet."

But the both of us knew that wasn't true.

There was nothing for my sadness but plunging myself into life at the Homestead. I'd been doing my job all along, but half my mind had been on Patrick—wondering when I'd see him, where we'd go together next. Now I was free of all that.

But in truth, it's not so simple a thing, casting a lad out of your mind when he's been living there for years. He haunted me, Patrick did. I kept seeing his sorrowful eyes the day he told me the truth. And my dreams were troubled by his kisses. I'd wake up in the middle of the night with my lips warm from tasting his. Took a powerful determination to turn my mind away.

I was wearing out. It was slow but I could feel my liveliness thinning as the strength drained out of me. All the lifting and bending and climbing and kneeling were crowding my muscles and melting my bones and I woke up aching every morning. My belly hurt and I lost my appetite. I could look at a sweet cake all morning and not want to take one bite.

When the fever came I knew the typhoid was back. It's a terrible scourge and takes all the strength from your bones. I could scarcely walk across the kitchen without needing to sit down and rest. So it was off to Kelley Square for me, where Mary could nurse me proper. Stayed the whole month of October, I did.

Mam used to say it's a dangerous month, October. The curtain between the worlds is thin and the Faeries can slip through to plague even a saint. It's best to keep your body busy and your mind clear and stay on guard for accidents and hauntings. But I was flat on my back and feverish besides, with nothing to distract me from the terrors. They came at night, all the demons and dark spirits I'd heard of in tales as a lass—Pookas and Changelings and Kelpies from the sea. When the crisis passed, I was limp as a bird just hatched from its egg. It was a long, slow mending but I healed. And as my body healed, so did my mind. The thoughts of Patrick eased and stopped scorching my heart.

By November I was strong enough to go back to the Homestead. And didn't Emily herself meet me at the door and pull me into her arms like I was her long-lost sister instead of a maid? Made me blush with the surprise of it. It pleased me, to be sure.

The seasons went round—a wet fall turned into a winter bleak and bitter as they come, with snow up to my knees and ice under the eaves, then a slow spring following. But by April the snow was melted and we were on our way to summer.

When it came it was glorious. Meg gave her notice at the Evergreens and married her sweetheart, James. Emily was well enough to spend long, happy hours in the garden with her birds and flowers and the music of poems in her head. Mother Dickinson was cheered by the warmth and seemed stronger. And St. Bridget's Parish was growing with so many baptisms and confirmations it was hard to keep count.

Sue Dickinson took a new couple into her circle—Professor David Todd and his pretty wife, Mabel. They were young and handsome and fresh from Washington, DC. Soon they were all the rage among the better sort in Amherst. Vinnie was particularly charmed by Mabel. All I was hearing from her was *Mabel this* and *Mabel that,* how musical and artistic she was and how she was soon to be calling at the Homestead. It seemed Mabel was longing to get to know the Myth of Amherst, and praying for an invitation. Vinnie begged Emily to come with her to the Evergreens so they could meet, but Emily would not.

Then word went round Sue had told Mabel a scandalous tale about Emily. Said she once walked into the Homestead parlor and found her lying in Judge Lord's arms. Vinnie was raging at Sue for spreading such nonsense, but it gave me a chill, for I couldn't forget walking in on them myself.

When Emily heard what was being said, the summer glow went out of her like water running from a bucket with a hole in it. She stopped sending notes to Sue and refused to see her. It was a terrible thing, for Emily trusted no one more. She'd always tried her poems on Sue, something she never did with another soul. I prayed the trouble between them wouldn't last. But they'd have nothing to do with each other for months.

Vinnie said Sue made up the story because she was jealous.

"Sure, who could she be jealous of?" I asked. We were cleaning the parlor, which surely needed it. The open windows let in dust from the street, and it sifted down on everything in a gray-brown mist.

"Why, Judge Lord, of course!" Vinnie straightened from the chair leg she was dusting. "Emily's in love with him and Sue don't like being replaced."

"Replaced?" The word squeaked out before I could stop it. Such a foolish idea.

"Oh, those two." Vinnie attacked the piano with her duster so fierce I saw feathers flying. "It was always *Emily and Sue, Sue and Emily* from the minute they met."

Sounded to me like Vinnie was the jealous one. Surprised me, it did—she'd always been devoted to Emily. But it seemed there was a bit of spite buried in her. I felt for her, to be sure. I knew how it was to be the younger sister—to always feel a little lower, to long for the respectful glance, the promise of fairness.

In September Mabel Todd finally came to the Homestead. Austin, it was, brought her, and she was handsome as Vinnie said, with her fancy dress and big eyes and the dainty air some mistake for innocence. But I saw right off she was up to no good. I know a minx when I see one and Mabel knew how to cast her eyes about, to be sure. Betty, the new maid at the Evergreens, had already told me Mabel was fond of flirting with young Ned. Said he was half gone on her, the poor lad.

Vinnie was lovely that night, decked out in blue. She was desperate for Emily to meet Mabel and sent me three times to get her, but Emily stayed shut in her room. So Austin and Mabel and Vinnie sat in the parlor while I served coffee and gingerbread. Then Austin asked Mabel to sing for his mother's pleasure and sent me upstairs to sit with her while she listened.

God's truth, the music was lovely. Mabel was a grand singer and knew how to work her voice and the keys same as she knew how to work a man's desire. When she was done and I started back downstairs, Emily's door opened a crack and she whispered me over. Pressed a note in my hand and said I should give it to the singer. I said it would make Vinnie happy if she gave it herself, but Emily closed her eyes and shook her head and never did come down to meet Mabel.

Not that evening nor ever.

Not long after, Mother Dickinson caught a bad cough and started failing. Some days she seemed not to know where she was or the names of her own daughters. Every day she asked when the Squire was coming home. Tore my heart, it did. "Soon," I always told her, and it was not a bold lie, for it seemed she'd soon enough be with him again. Like Emily said, the hardest part of caring for somebody wasn't the work of it but the need to be pleating the truth.

In the morning Mother Dickinson had to be lifted from her bed and put in her chair, and she was such a tiny stick of a woman by then it was no trouble for two of us. Usually it was Vinnie and myself moved her while Emily aired the bed and smoothed the sheets and plumped the pillows. Once a week she'd tuck a sachet of fresh lavender under the mattress.

In November came the day we all were dreading. I was lighting the kitchen fire when Vinnie called me upstairs. Her mother had waked early after a fretful night and was moaning about her aches and pains. Sure, I was surprised, because it wasn't like Mother Dickinson to complain. She'd been good lately—even had an appetite, swallowing every bite of the custard I made her the day before and asking for more. But even after Vinnie and myself carried her to her chair, she was mewling. Emily came in from her room, looking weary as her mother.

"Go back to bed, Miss Emily," I said, placing the pillow behind Mother Dickinson's head the way she liked. "I'll tend herself this morning."

Mother Dickinson gave me a tiny smile, looked at Emily and then at Vinnie, who was opening the curtains.

"Don't leave me, Vinnie," she said in a loud voice. Then her eyes closed and a long rattling breath came out of her.

I knelt down and crossed myself right there, for I knew she was gone. In truth, it was a blessing. A slow dying is the saddest kind, and the poor dear had been suffering for years. Vinnie cried, "Oh no!" and Emily made a choking sound. But neither one of them moved. It was as if they were struck to stone. Indeed, it was a cold, lonesome morning and that's the truth of it, but it was sorrow froze them, not lack of a fire.

Sure, I never blamed anybody for taking a death hard. It's not for me to judge, especially if they're not Catholic and don't have the solace of the True Faith. But the death of a woman's mam— that's the worst calamity there is. And I didn't have room in my heart that day for anything but love.

A death in the house makes for more work at a time when folks aren't thinking clear. So it falls to the maid. I was the one laid the body out after giving Austin the sad news. Emily and Vinnie tried helping, but their minds were drifting too far, poor things. It wasn't only their tears were shed that day, but my own too. In the years of tending her I'd come to think of Mother Dickinson as part of my own family. It's curious how families grow wider the longer you live. A person can hold many dear and not all the same blood.

After dressing Mother Dickinson in her best gray gown and brushing out her white curls for the last time, I fetched the undertaker. Her body was laid in its coffin, carried downstairs, and set in the hall where the Squire's had been. The house filled up for the funeral, for many loved her and many more wanted to honor the family. Emily didn't come down, but nobody expected her to.

Mabel Todd sat herself in the family row beside Austin and Sue. Surprised me. It wasn't proper at all—seemed to me she should mind her place at a funeral. At the collation after, she went from room to room, mingling with the Amherst notables, like she was the hostess. Made me cross, it did. So I was in no mood to put up with her nonsense when I was carrying an empty tray from the library and spied her halfway up the front stairs.

"What are you doing?" I said. Put down my tray on the hall table and marched right up those steps. "The collation's downstairs, ma'am," I said. I took her by the elbow. "I'll show you the way, if you're lost." Lord, I was angry.

She gave me a look would cut the Devil himself. "Don't touch me!" She shook me off like my hand was corrupted. "I'm just having a look around. I'm not harming a soul."

I scooted past her so I could block her from going higher. "No one's to disturb Miss Emily," I said. "That's the rule here. Always has been. And always will be, while I'm maid."

She gawked at me, her eyes like stones in her face. "What an insolent servant!" She was near spitting when she said it too. But she turned around and went mincing back down the stairs.

I wondered if Emily heard us from behind her shut door. It didn't matter. I was doing my duty.

It was midnight before I finished that day and dragged myself upstairs, knowing there was still work to be done in the morning. Funerals always make a mess of a house and folks who are grieving are best aided by order and cleanliness. I'd just finished saying my prayers when there was a tapping on my door.

It was Emily standing there in her nightdress with her hair down and her face looking weary as my own.

"What can I do for you, miss?" I asked.

Her smile was soft as a shadow. "I came to thank you for what you did today," she said. Sure, I didn't know what she was meaning and it must have showed on my face, because then she said, "In thwarting Mrs. Todd's designs. Your fierce protection is priceless, Maggie."

"You're welcome, miss," I said. "But you should be going back to bed now."

Instead, she stepped into my room. She was looking all around, as if my simple things were interesting to her.

"How lovely!" she said. She was staring at the rosary hanging on the wall—the one I'd taken to calling Patrick's because it was himself gave it to me. The beads had caught the lantern light and were winking like tiny amber stars.

She touched it with a finger so the crucifix trembled. "I've never seen you use this one, Maggie."

"No, miss." I was surprised she noticed, but too tired to be explaining. In truth, I wondered why I still kept it on the wall. "You really should be sleeping now. 'Twas a hard day."

She nodded. "I shall sleep soon enough," she said. She was still looking at Patrick's rosary.

Sure, I was ashamed I said it, knowing how she coupled sleep with death. And she'd just lost her mam. Felt awful, I did. "Oh, miss," I said, "I'm dreadful sorry. I was only thinking you're needing your rest."

She nodded and a sigh came out of her. "It's all right, Maggie. I know what you meant." Then she smiled. "I know your heart."

I was staggered—tears sprang into my eyes. I was desperate to soothe her, to take away the pain. I quick took Patrick's rosary off its hook and put it in her hand. Didn't know what else to do.

She stared at it. "Oh no," she whispered. "You mustn't—"

"I want you to have it," I said. "I'll not take it back. Besides, the beads are the color of your eyes. Now go along to bed."

She took my hand then with her empty one and folded it into hers. She'd never done that before. "You're my guardian angel," she said. Then she left, in that whispery way she had. And I was alone.

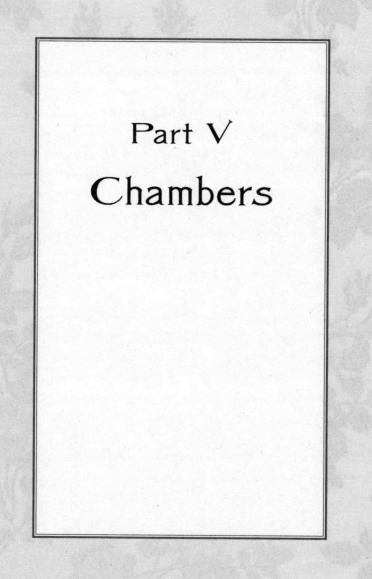

Part V

Chambers

Chapter Twenty-Eight

1916

Strange, but it's easier for me to get a thing done when I'm raging and righteous. It makes me bold and saves me from fretting about what other folks will think. But knowing I need to mend my squabble with Mattie D is giving me qualms. I spend most of a week working up my courage and planning what to be saying so she'll let me in the door.

It's Friday by the time I've had enough of my own dithering and set my mind to the task. In the morning I make a loaf of gingerbread, wrap it in my best kitchen towel, and tuck it into my market basket. Just after the noon whistle blows, I put on my coat and hat, take a deep breath, and head out the door with the basket on my arm. The day is sunny and warm. The crocuses Nell planted in front of Tom's porch are blooming and daffodil shoots are poking through the dirt. I spy two robins hopping about on Mrs. Hills' lawn when I pass. By the time I open the Evergreens' gate, I'm feeling hopeful.

But when the big front door opens to my knock, it's not Mattie D standing there—it's her maid. I've not seen the woman before—she's wide waisted and stern faced with a look telling me I've just spoiled her whole day.

"What do you want?" she says, glaring. In truth, she reminds me of myself in the days when I was guarding the Homestead from intruders.

I tell her I've come to see Madame Bianchi. She doesn't ask who I am or if I've got a message for her mistress. Just shakes her head and says she's gone out.

"I don't know where she's at," she says. "So don't bother asking." And she swings the door shut, quick as that.

Feel foolish, I do, standing on the doorstep with my gingerbread and nobody to be giving it to. I go back down the walk and feel the pull of the Homestead soon as I come to the path between the houses. Like an enchantment, it is. It takes all my self-control not to hurry over like I did so many times.

Instead I go out the gate and head up to the town center. Figure since I've got my basket with me, I might as well do a few errands—stop in at the post office and get some fruit at the grocer's. Maybe take a look in the new Hastings Store everybody's talking about. But when I come out of the grocer's, who do I spy but Rosaleen Byrne? She's across the street chatting away with two women in front of the Amherst House and she's surely the last person I want to be seeing this morning. I quick turn right and head up North Pleasant Street.

It's a grand day—more like the end of April than March—and my walking turns into strolling, the sun and soft air on my face. When I pass St. Bridget's, I figure it's time to be heading home, so I cut through West Cemetery since it's the shortest way.

The grass is starting to green around the gravestones. There's a riot of daffodils along the fence. I remember Emily once telling me she lived next to this cemetery when she was a girl and it's easy to picture her walking amongst the stones. "I liked it there," she said. "It was a soft place. Visited by birds and dreams."

Her grave is in the middle of the cemetery, a small stone marked *EED* set beside the Squire's grand one. I stop in front of it. I haven't been here in years, though I used to visit quite a bit after Emily died. Many a Sunday I stopped here after Mass to pay my respects and say a prayer for her soul.

There's a footstep in the duff behind me—I barely hear it, it's so soft. When I turn I'm face-to-face with Mattie D.

"Miss Mattie!" I feel like my hat's flown off my head, I'm that surprised. She has a peculiar look on her I can't read. I try to remember the words I planned while I was walking to the Evergreens, but every one of them is gone. So instead I try being friendly. "A fine spring day," I say.

She gives me a tight nod. "Maggie," she says, and steps up beside me to look down at Emily's stone. Sure, it's plain she doesn't think I belong here. I can feel her vexation—like heat rising off a stove. She's expecting me to leave but she won't say so—won't ask. Guess she fancies herself too much of a lady.

I don't move. Keep trying to think of how to say what I planned on my way to her house, though it seems disrespectful in front of Emily's grave. I slide a glance at her. She's still looking down at the stone, but there's no sign she's praying. Her eyes wide-open and no sorrow on her face.

"I stopped by the Evergreens to bring you some gingerbread," I say after a minute. "Your maid said you were out but I didn't expect to find you here."

She sighs. "I'm not going to change my mind. I'm selling the Homestead." She won't look at me.

I decide to come right out with it. "I know about your husband," I tell her. "I know he left you and swindled you out of your fortune." I don't have the heart to say she's well rid of him.

She raises her chin, like she's studying the sky. I've seen her do so before when she's tried to keep tears inside. Even as a girl, she'd look up when I scolded her for stealing a sweet or bothering Emily when she was writing. She takes a breath in, like she's going to say something, but nothing comes out. A wee flurry of wind pulls at my hat and there's a shiver at the top of my spine—as if somebody is standing behind me, laying two hands on my shoulders. *Emily?*

Mattie D's shoulders sag suddenly and her face softens. There are tired circles under her eyes and it's plain she's suffering. Then she looks at me, and God's truth, I'm certain she's seeing Emily's ghost, her face is so pale.

She closes her eyes. "I don't know where he is. I've heard nothing at all for months, despite begging for word. Even his friends can't find him. It seems he's disappeared from the face of the earth."

"Sure, that can't be," I say. But in truth, I know it can—since I was a babby I've been hearing about folks disappearing without a trace. Some snatched away by Faeries, some just walking across a meadow into the mist and never seen again.

Tenderness has always been stronger in me than hard feelings. I reach out and touch her arm, very gentle. "I'll not torment you. I'm here to listen if you're wanting to talk."

She doesn't say anything. Looks the picture of misery—this tall, stately woman standing before me.

"Let's go sit over there for a bit," I say, nodding to a wooden bench a few feet away. I loop my free arm through hers and turn her. It's an old habit—acting bold when a woman's too stubborn to admit she's needing help. I used it more than a few times on Emily.

I'm expecting her to draw herself up and tell me to leave her alone. So it's a surprise when she lets me guide her to the bench and sit her down. I sit beside her. "Why don't we have ourselves a bite of gingerbread?" I say. "'Tis Emily's recipe and it will do us both good."

She looks puzzled but doesn't stop me when I set the basket on my lap and fold back the towel. The loaf is still warm, so the dark-ginger-and-molasses smell is strong when I break off a chunk. I cast a glance her way. As a girl she loved gingerbread. All the neighbor children did, but Mattie was the first to come knocking on the back door whenever Emily made it. As if she could smell it baking no matter where she was.

I hand her the piece and break off another for myself. And there we sit, filling our mouths with sweetness and neither of us saying a word.

"I've been thinking," Mattie D says after a while, her voice riffling the quiet. "Aunt Emily should have a more attractive stone. One that represents her as a poet." She's looking over at the stone. "I've been reading some of the family papers. Her last letter was a note to Fanny and Louisa Norcross. *Called back* is what she wrote. That's all. It's so like Aunt Emily." She turns her head and looks at me. "What do you think? Wouldn't it be appropriate for her stone? Just her name and dates and the words *called back*?"

God's truth, I can't believe she's asking my opinion. Isn't like her one bit—nor like any of the Dickinsons except Emily herself. I look at the Dickinson plot set on its little hillock.

"Aye," I say, nodding. "It sounds exactly like Emily. *Called back* would be fitting, to be sure."

"I'm glad you think so," she says. For a minute I wonder if she's mocking me. If this chat is just an entertainment to her. But then she gives me a kindly look. "I'm also planning to write a book about her—a sort of biography using the family letters Mother collected. There's been quite a lot of interest since *The Single Hound* was published."

This is good news—makes me happy for Mattie D—and for Emily too. I think about the three volumes of Emily's poems Mabel Todd printed—and how that woman traveled around, giving lectures on Emily. How so much of what she said was pure blather.

"'Tis a grand idea—writing a book," I say. "There's a lot of rumor and nonsense bandied about. Would be nice if somebody who knew herself set the record straight."

Mattie D nods. "You knew her," she says as if the thought just came to her. "Quite well, I suspect."

"I did indeed." In truth, I'm surprised she knows.

"I have some questions that you might be able to answer," she goes on. "Perhaps you'll have tea with me some afternoon and we can chat."

Now I'm staggered. Never once did anybody from the Amherst gentry invite me to tea. And the last person I'd expect it of is Mattie D. "Sure, it sounds lovely," I say. "I'll be happy to help. All you have to do is ask." Comes right out of my mouth, like I'm talking to a friend.

"I'll do that," she says as if she's feeling the same. "And thank you for the gingerbread. It does take me back."

I can't help smiling. "I thought it might. I remember the times

Miss Emily took you down cellar to her baking cupboard and fed you her sweets. Thrilled you same as Christmas morning, I'm thinking."

Mattie D nods and she's smiling too. "Aunt Vinnie warned her over and over that gingerbread was too rich for children, but she might have been talking to the sky, for all the notice Aunt Emily took of it." Her face has gone soft. "Do you know Ned used to call her gingerbread *a rich*?"

I nod. "I do, to be sure."

Seems the both of us are warm with memories, and we go on for a while. There's a comfort in how our talking reminds me of chats I had with Emily. The thought startles me—because of course it's not the same. But I'm even more surprised when she asks if I'll do her a favor.

"Aunt Emily spoke more than once about your sound judgment," she says. "'Maggie has a stern good sense,' she used to say. I met a man last week who wishes to buy the Homestead and he's made a compelling offer. He seems pleasant enough but I would hate to sell it to someone who'd dishonor the place. I'd appreciate knowing what you think."

"Me?" God's truth, I'm stunned. She might not be thinking my judgment's so good if she knew what I was thinking of her just a week ago. "Is it somebody I'd be knowing?"

"I doubt it. But perhaps you could contrive a way to find out about him." She has a hopeful look in her eye. "He's the new rector at Grace Episcopal Church—Reverend Hervey Parke. I'd be most grateful for your opinion."

Sure, I don't know what to say. I'm flattered she'd be trusting me, though I don't know how my view of the man will make a difference. I study her face. Surely she knows I'm not disposed to liking anybody who's after buying the Homestead. But God's truth, I'm curious. And I'm always willing to help a friend. Seems to me Mattie D's become one.

"I'm glad to be helping you," I tell her. And next thing I know she's reached over and is squeezing my hand.

Chapter Twenty-Nine

1883

I didn't see Patrick's rosary after the night I gave it to Emily. I didn't expect her to use it. But she'd admired it, so I thought she'd be hanging it on her wall or keeping it on her mantel, where she could look on it from time to time. God's truth, I was glad it was gone from my wall, though. Ever since Patrick left, seeing it hanging there had made me sad, reminding me how my future changed in an afternoon. Giving it away helped put those feelings behind me.

But things started happening that made me worry it had been a mistake—giving the rosary to a Protestant. Patrick came creeping back into my dreams at night. I'd wake up longing for himself. Wondering where he was, hoping he'd found a clean boardinghouse or rented an apartment with a nice view. One that didn't look out over railroad tracks or factories.

I got a letter from him—a short one on clean paper. His handwriting was crooked, but I had no trouble reading the words. He wrote he was sorry for keeping secrets from me, that it wasn't too late if I wanted to change my mind and join him in Brooklyn. He still loved me. I wrote an answer, short as his own and meant to hurt, but I stopped myself from posting it. He wrote again, but after the third letter came and I still didn't answer, he stopped writing.

When I saw a column in the *Boston Post* about making dynamite, it felt like Patrick had laid his hand on my shoulder. I read it all the way through, though I couldn't understand the half of it. It was too confusing with all its particulars. I clipped it out of the paper and hid it in my chest of drawers with his letters, but it gave me a sad shiver whenever I glimpsed it.

Later, I began seeing news about dynamite bombings in England—attacks on police barracks and government buildings and explosives hidden on ships. It was Fenians doing it, so the papers said. And the Fenians weren't denying it. Felt sick to my stomach, knowing Patrick was the one likely teaching those lads how to make the bombs.

I never told a soul about the Dynamite School. Thought it better to be keeping that sorry news to myself. But it made its way into the Springfield paper and Tom put two and two together and figured out why Patrick had moved. Of course he told Mary and it was herself who outright asked me one Sunday afternoon while we were washing dishes.

"That Dynamite School's where Patrick Quinn went off to, wasn't it?" she said, looking troubled. "I knew he was a rascal, but I didn't think he was a murderer."

"He didn't murder anybody," I said, though I wasn't as sure as I sounded.

"Teaching other lads to murder's the same as doing it yourself," Mary said.

"It's not, surely," I said. But it wasn't the first time I'd had the same thought. I felt the tears coming on, and Mary saw them even before they started falling. Next thing I knew, she had her arms around me and was patting my back like I was one of her own babbies. God's truth, I surely felt like a babby that day.

"You're still loving him, aren't you, dear?" Mary said.

I shook my head but she paid me no mind. Made me sit down while she wet a new pot of tea, as if tea would cure my ailing heart.

Whenever there was word of Judge Lord in the papers, Emily grew lively. She'd read the reports to me out loud, going over every word as if it were a riddle to be solved. When the Judge visited, the two of them didn't try to hide their kissing and cooing, and I did my best not to think about what was going on when they were alone. Emily glowed and giggled all day. Wasn't herself at all.

And didn't she smile and laugh when she got his letters? She spent hours writing back, page after page. Her envelopes were so fat I feared the seals would pop. I don't know what they wrote to each other, but I'm guessing there was some wickedness in them. He was a witty man with a tongue saucy as her own.

Then came a cold morning when I went in to light her fire and found her propped on her pillows wide awake.

"I have a secret for you," she said, her eyes glinting. She was smiling like a cat with its eye on a saucer of cream. "But you must promise not to breathe a word. Not even to Vinnie."

Truth is, I like nothing better than a secret whispered maid to maid over the back fence. But when your mistress tells you something shouldn't be spoken of, there's always a danger it might slip out when you're tired or cross or have an extra pint at Christmas. I knew plenty of secrets from the folks I worked for—bits and pieces of talk—and I'd never shared a one. But those were things I overheard or guessed. I'd never had a mistress offer one. Like a temptation, it was—not to be trusted. Made me wary.

I got on the floor and started laying her fire. "Now, who would I be telling your secrets to, miss? But if you can tell me, you can be telling your own sister, surely." I was thinking she was too old for such foolishness, but I didn't say so.

"Don't spoil my fun, Maggie," she said.

I looked at her over my shoulder. Her mouth was making a little pout. "What is it, then?" I asked.

"Judge Lord has asked me to marry him." Her eyes were sparking.

I couldn't think of one word to be saying. The Judge was at least seventy. "You're jesting, surely," I said.

She shook her head. "I'm not."

"Did you give him an answer?" I lit the fire and stood up, wincing from the twinge in my right knee.

"Not yet." There was a wistful look on her face.

All I could think of that minute was Patrick and all that time I'd kept him waiting for an answer when he proposed. How he wanted to take me to Brooklyn.

"Will he be moving to Amherst, then?" I asked.

She blinked. "I assume we'll live in Salem."

I tried to imagine Emily moving to Salem. I feared it would be the end of her. In truth, I couldn't picture her living anywhere but this house.

"I'm thinking you'd not like it much," I said. "Living in Salem. Away from your sister." Didn't try to stop myself saying what I was thinking, but soon as the words were out, it struck me I was

talking about myself. All those foolish long-ago ideas about having a grand adventure when the good life was right here in front
of me.

"Father never wanted me to marry, you know." She said it
dreamy, like she was talking to herself. "But I think he'd understand. Judge Lord reminds me so of him."

"Surely not, miss." I couldn't think of any man more improper
than the Judge. I'd heard enough to know he had a tongue on
him would make a decent man blush. Seemed he thought nothing
was more satisfying than being saucy. How in the name of
Heaven could he remind her of the Squire? For all he'd vexed me,
Mr. Dickinson had always been proper and dignified.

"I fear he does." She raised her eyebrows and gave me a quare
smile. "Love reckons by itself alone," she said as if that settled
things.

Betty, it was, first told me Mabel Todd was making trouble in
the Dickinson family. Seemed Ned, who was twenty-one now
and feeling his oats, had gone sweet on her, and she was welcom-
ing his attentions. She danced with him at Sue's fancy parties,
had long chinwags, and went for walks, just the two of them. The
poor lad was head over heels. And small wonder, since Mabel
was using every womanly wile to charm him. But then he found
out his father was taking her for long rides in the country and
reading her poetry and the two of them were putting their heads
together over books of art and landscaping. Wasn't long before
Ned told his mother and word flew through town that Sue and
Mabel had a falling-out.

At Kelley Square we talked about it for weeks. Had a good

laugh over how surprised Sue's set was when she cut Mabel out of her circle. It was a blow to the ladies, for they admired Mabel, with her liveliness and cultured ways. But nobody was blaming Sue, for it was plain the sort of woman Mabel was. Liked beguiling a man, she did, crooking her little finger and seeing him come running. She didn't seem to mind how old or young he was.

Anybody could see things were heating up between Austin and Mabel. Mary said it was shocking the sinful things rich folks did behind the doors of their grand houses. I'd seen enough to agree.

After a while Mabel went to Sue and they patched things up. Don't know what Mabel said—likely said it was all a misunderstanding and her friendship with Austin was innocent—but for a time, Mabel was welcomed back to the Evergreens. She started paying special attention to Mattie, gave her piano lessons and took her for sleigh rides. Meanwhile she was doing all she could to stay friends with Vinnie, praising her cats and sending her notes and taking tea with her in the afternoons. It did Vinnie good—it plainly roused her spirits. I guess she was sometimes lonesome living with Emily. And no wonder—Emily kept herself to herself so much, always writing and reading and fussing over her plants.

But Mabel didn't mend her ways. Austin and herself kept meeting, ofttimes at the Homestead. Seemed harmless at first—Mabel would be chatting in the parlor with Vinnie, and Austin would stop by. He'd act surprised to see her and they'd chat for a bit. But then the two of them started taking walks in the garden or sitting side by side on the parlor sofa. She'd be throwing her smiles his way and he'd be watching her like she was a cake he couldn't wait to eat. Before long they drew Vinnie into their scheming and the three of them worked out a plan to

trade notes without Sue knowing. Sure, it sparked Vinnie's liveliness. Anybody would think she enjoyed the trickery and
scheming.

I wanted no part of it and told Vinnie so. Said I wouldn't deliver their notes. I pointed out Mabel was young enough to be
Austin's daughter and the pair of them carried on without a care
for virtue or honor. But Vinnie just smiled and said true love was
the only thing made life worth living and she'd not be the one
standing in its way.

After a while Sue figured out what was going on. Most wives
aren't eejits, after all. Betty told me Sue and Austin had a great
row, roaring and shrieking and throwing things. Said Sue was
raging so, she scratched gashes with her fingernails down the
hallway wallpaper. Must have scared the children, especially
young Gib, who wasn't yet eight years old.

I could see Emily was vexed with her brother. Every time
Mabel and Austin met at the Homestead, she was downcast. She
began sending notes to Sue again and soon they were going back
and forth like old times. I was glad, for I never saw two people
take more solace in each other's words.

One spring morning Emily came into the kitchen, looking for all
the world like she'd met a ghost on the stairs. When I asked
what was troubling her, she shook her head and went into the
dining room. I followed and found her fiddling with the vase of
daffodils on the sideboard.

"I had a dream," she said in a quare, strange voice. "Or a pre-
monition. I'm not sure." She looked down at her fingers, then slid
into a chair—the way she did it made me think of silk running
through a lady's fingers. "I was writing a letter when a dreadful

feeling came over me. As if Judge Lord had died." She took a fluttery breath, then waved her hand. "But it was probably nothing. A phantasm of fear, a wisp of dread." She gave me a thin smile. "It went away."

"Likely it was last night's sausage," I said, knowing how fond the Dickinsons were of blaming their afflictions on digestion. Myself, I always suspect the Faeries might have a thing or two to do with troubles. Emily nodded in a muddled way and then stood up and went to the pantry to get flour and molasses for making gingerbread.

Not twenty minutes later Vinnie came bustling in. "Emily, did you see this morning's paper?" She was flapping it like a fan in front of her.

Emily put down her measuring cup and wiped her hands on her apron. "How could I when you're holding it? Tell me." Her voice was raggedy.

"Judge Lord—he's very sick." Vinnie stopped fanning and laid the paper on the table.

Emily went ghost white and swayed on her feet just as Tom came in the back door, looking for a cup of tea. Sure, I thought she was going to faint. She looked at Vinnie, then at me, as if she'd lost every sense she had.

"Miss Emily?" said Tom.

She swung around. And didn't she run to him and press her face into his chest, like he was the comfort she was needing?

"'Tis Judge Lord," I told him. "He's come down ill. It was in the paper."

Tom patted her back with his one arm. "He'll be better, Miss Emily. Don't be crying now. I wouldn't see you cry." Sure, there are few lads tender as Tom Kelley, more's the pity.

The next day Emily asked if I'd pray for the Judge and I promised I would. But it fretted me. Should I say a rosary? I knew the Judge was Protestant and Protestants didn't have much use for the Blessed Mother, though Emily kept a lovely picture of her that Sue gave her. I'd prayed for Protestants before—Emily and Mother Dickinson and Vinnie—but always in secret, with nobody knowing. This was the first time I'd been asked.

Maybe I'd just say the Our Father. Protestants said it, though they stuck some words on the end. I turned the puzzle round and round in my head, like a riddle I couldn't solve, until I finally decided to ask Emily herself.

She was out in the garden. It had rained the night before and there was no sun to dry things out, so my shoes soaked through just crossing the grass. I found Emily on her knees, clearing sticks and leaves from the rose beds.

I squatted beside her. "I've a question, miss," I said. "About praying for Judge Lord. I don't know what a proper prayer is for a Protestant. Is it allowed to pray the rosary?"

She laughed. As if I'd just said the most comical thing. My face flamed hot and I rose up. But when I turned to go back to the kitchen, she grabbed my skirt. "I'm sorry, Maggie. I meant no harm." But the laugh was still fairly bursting from her mouth and she was making a foolish face to keep it in. "Your question simply took me by surprise. And now I'm imagining what Phil would say if he knew rosaries were being said for him." And she started laughing again, making a lie of her words.

God have mercy, I was more than cross. "Miss Emily," I said, yanking my skirt from her hand, "'twas yourself who asked me to pray for him. If you were jesting you should have made it plain."

She sat there on her heels, blinking up at me. I should have shut my mouth then and gone back to my work. But the fury was in me and I couldn't contain it any more than Emily could her laughing. So I kept talking.

"I know it's common to correct servants and even shame us. We know to expect it and are used to putting up with it. But I won't be suffering mockery of my faith. Or the place I was born," I added. And didn't I cross myself in front of her and turn on my heel and march straight back to the kitchen?

Chapter Thirty

I apologize." Emily stood in the kitchen doorway, her cloak half off, her garden gloves smeared with dirt, and her hair coming out of its net. She was tattered as a wet dog. Sure, it wasn't like her not to look tidy. She even slept neat. "Sometimes I don't think of—" She stopped. "Truly, I don't mean to be unkind."

I didn't say anything at first, but I was thinking her mockery was beyond unkind. It was mean, a kind of heartless cruelty. The way folks treat an animal. In truth, though, she'd done it before. Why did it tip me into outrage this time when I'd borne it so many times in the past?

"I can accept you're my better in society," I said, speaking slow, being careful with my words. "But before God we're both the same. I have feelings and thoughts. Being Irish doesn't make me an animal to be petted or kicked as you see fit."

All the color left her face. She pulled off her gloves and dropped them onto the table. "I'm truly sorry, Maggie. I feel ashamed to have treated you so. But I sincerely intended no insult to your faith. Your question simply surprised me. I don't think of prayers the way you do."

Can't deny it, her apology touched me. I put down the bowl I was holding. "How do you think of them so?" It was my way of making peace, I suppose—trying to find a path through the hurt.

She shook off the rest of her cloak and draped it over a chair. "They're not words to recite. Or things we say to God. I don't think they're words at all."

I frowned, wondering if what she was saying might be heresy. Sounded like it. But I stood there anyway, out of the long habit paying my wages.

"Sometimes I go up to the cupola," she said. "It's quiet there— the sounds of the house and street are distant and soft. When I climb those steps I feel I'm leaving all my cares behind. And I just sit there. No words, no thoughts. Only light." She sank into the chair. "That—to me—is true prayer."

I felt a flutter in my spine. "Sure, you're making no sense," I said. "I know what true prayers are—I say them every morning and every night. Just like attending Mass on Sunday. 'Tis an obligation. A duty."

She gave a little shrug. "I don't believe prayer is a duty. It's more of—" She stopped and opened her hands and I could see she was trying to think of words she wasn't finding. It wasn't like Emily, and I saw it worried her. Words were her treasure. She cast me a pleading look and what was left of my vexation melted just that fast.

"Maybe you're meaning an act of adoration," I said.

"Perhaps," she said, nodding. "That's closer. Yes."

"But there are words to be saying," I said. "Like music, they are, to God. The Church gives them to us. To help us keep the tune."

Emily was staring at me in her quare way. I didn't know what she was thinking. I picked up the bowl again.

"I prayed a great deal during the war," she said after a minute. "Formal spoken prayer. The way I'd been taught. But I don't see that it did any good. It was such a distressing time. The dying just went on and on. There was no end to the blood."

I remember Patrick telling how he watched his friend bleed to death. I shook the thought away. Everybody'd heard terrible stories. Death was always in the news in those days—college lads who went off to war and came back in coffins. Farm lads who threw down their plows and volunteered, just to be shot to bits in terrible battles. Brave Irish lads whose bones were tossed into pits right on the battlefield. And saddest of all—the lads who came back with broken, mangled bodies, lost and restless in their minds.

"I prayed and prayed in the midst of all that misery," Emily said. "But it was as useful as a bird's stamping on air. Maybe it was the wrong kind of prayer. Or maybe I was praying to the wrong kind of god."

Her words shouldn't have affected me the way they did. Wasn't it more heresy? But here came tears into my eyes and one was even running down my cheek.

"So I stopped. Or tried to." She sat at the table. Her voice was low, barely more than a whisper. "Eventually I came to understand— to experience—God as a great and holy silence. And the only response to that is wonder. Adoration, as you say." She raised her face and gazed at me. Or through me—I wasn't sure which. "Which is what my poems are, Maggie. If prayers need words, *they* are my prayers."

I looked back at her. She was waiting for me to say something but all I could do was nod and glance out the window.

"I think it's coming on rain again," I said, and went to get more wood.

~

Emily changed that day. She never mocked me again. Nor any other Irish person, for that matter. And it seemed to me she listened closer when I was talking. Respected me more than before. She even asked me to call her Emily.

"*Miss* is a title," she said. "It doesn't feel as if you're talking to *me*. Couldn't you see your way to simply using my name?"

I thought about it a minute. I'd been calling her *miss* for years but all along I'd been thinking of her as *Emily*. I said, "I can try. Especially if you can see your way to calling me *Margaret* instead of *Maggie*."

She blinked. Then she laughed, a burst of gleeful knowing from deep in her throat. "That may be too steep a mountain to climb," she said when she calmed down. "Perhaps some things are best left as they are."

I saw the truth of it. And she never did call me Margaret. But the quare thing is, from then on I sometimes called her Emily without thinking.

I thought a good deal on what she'd said about prayer and poems. There was something holy in her writings, hard as they were to understand. A sacred shine on them, surely. Instead of seeing her as one of the Faery Folk, I began wondering if she was something like a saint. To be sure, it was unlikely a Protestant could be a saint. But one thing I knew about saints—they weren't always the folks you'd be expecting God to choose.

At night I took to opening one of her booklets and reading her poems slow, one and then another. Like fireflies, they were— sparking in the dark. They made me think. They made me shiver and look at things and listen. They dazzled my heart. I saw what

Emily meant about them being her prayers. God's truth, they were becoming mine.

It was plain Emily was fretting over Judge Lord. And no wonder—he wasn't a young man and healing is a chancy thing. But she was dragging herself through her days, her nerves stretched so tight they wore her out. I did what I could to ease her thoughts away from himself, but there was no taming her mind. It was wild as the wind itself.

Praise God, it turned out Tom was right—the Judge didn't die. The crisis passed and he rallied. By late summer he was able to be out and about.

Outside the leaves grew bright and rattled in the trees. Inside Emily was more herself. We went back to our morning chinwags in the kitchen, talking about this and that, whatever struck our fancy. One day I asked if she'd ever answered the Judge's proposal. She was in a playful mood, bending over the table kneading bread, and when she spoke there was a thrumming in her voice.

"Not yet." She laughed. "I think it does men good to make them wait, don't you? It teaches them patience and protects them from pride." She gave me a quick look. Her eyes were sparking. "At least one hopes so."

"*Wisha*, you make it sound like a game," I said.

"And so it is," she said. Then, "Didn't you keep your own beau waiting for an answer?"

I was staggered. Couldn't think how she knew. It was three years since Patrick left and she'd never said a word in all that time. "I did indeed," I said. "But it wasn't to be teaching him patience. 'Twas my own undecided heart kept me from saying yes." I took up my knife and started chopping parsley for the mutton stew. "Maybe it's the same for yourself."

She stopped her kneading and wiped her hands on her apron. I wondered if I'd been too bold. Tried to mend it quick. "Or maybe it's not. For myself, 'tis all in the past now. I'm done with love."

"I don't understand how it's possible to be done with love," she said after a minute. "In my experience, it's never past. I've tried locking it away in a drawer, but the key never leaves my pocket."

I wondered who she was talking about—what love had she tried locking away? I tried to think. Maybe Samuel Bowles, the newspaper man who sat with her during the Squire's funeral? It surely wasn't Mr. Higginson—for all her pleasure at his letters, I'd seen no sign they were lovers. Nor even heard any rumors. For some reason, Sue Dickinson popped into my head. Maybe she was more than Emily's friend. Don't know where that thought came from, but it wasn't a pretty one.

"Sure, it wasn't that way with Patrick and myself." I wiped my knife clean and scooped the parsley flakes into the pot. Wished I had a pint of ale to give it more flavor. "Not certain it was true love at all, to tell the truth," I added. "But it's just as well. I've always been shy of getting married. It can shackle a woman, surely." She didn't say anything and I was glad of it. I wanted her to stop talking about love. Didn't like where it was taking my mind. "It's not for everybody, I'm thinking. There's a deal of freedom in staying single." I carried the pot across the room and set it on the cooker.

Had my back to Emily when she spoke. "For my part, I'm glad you didn't get caught in his snare, Maggie. I can't imagine happiness without you close by."

Surprised me, it did, and melted my heart. I felt the heat run up my neck and into my face. "You're very kind," I said.

"I'm many things, Maggie—legions, perhaps. But I've never masked sincerity with kindness." She said it in a low voice. "I need you so that I can be myself. When you were sick with typhoid, I was miserable—terrified that I might lose you." Her voice split.

I turned to look at her. "'Tis all right, Emily. I'm not going away."

A long sigh came out of her and she leaned toward me. So I opened my arms and let her fall into them. I felt the sorrow and happiness coming from her. Such a quare perfume, it was—sweet and bitter, mixed.

Austin was spending more and more time at the Homestead. When he wasn't trysting with Mabel Todd, he'd sit and talk with Vinnie and Emily about Sue. She was too sociable, he'd say, always putting on grand receptions, theatricals, and fancy picnics. It wearied him and cast him down. What he liked was quiet and a book to read or a fruit tree to graft. He was a solitary like Emily, something Sue didn't respect.

I was rolling my eyes hearing such nonsense. If there was ever a man who was loud, it was Austin Dickinson. Had a booming voice and a heavy tread and always tramped across the floor like he was in army boots.

But Emily would sigh and say she understood his sensibilities and Vinnie would pat his hand and tell him Sue would soon see the error of her ways. Sure, it seemed to me he was leaving out his own part in the situation. Didn't look to me like he was a bit solitary—not when Mabel Todd came around, surely.

Came a morning Vinnie showed up in the kitchen and sat herself down at the table, slumping her shoulders like a schoolgirl in a mood.

"What's troubling you?" I said, for it was plain she wanted me to be asking. I served up her breakfast and poured myself another cup of tea. Figured I was likely in for a long listen.

She looked at me. "Did *you* know Emily's received a proposal of marriage?"

I couldn't think what to say, for hadn't I promised Emily not to tell? Yet I'd never been certain Emily was serious. Luck was with me, though, for Vinnie didn't wait for my answer.

"Judge Lord asked her months ago, Maggie. Months!" Vinnie's fork clinked on the plate. "All in secret. She never told a soul." She was quiet for a minute. "Maggie, he's an *old man*!" Her voice was all lonesome and sorrowful, like she was going to start keening. "He was our *father's* friend."

"She's happy enough when she's with him," I said.

She shook her head and waved her hands about. "It's always been all flowers and birdsong with Emily. Everything pretty and sweet."

Sure, I knew that wasn't true. Emily had her share of troubles like everybody else. And there was nobody with a sharper tongue. Even her poems were full of needles and blades. And the Judge was the same.

"She's not thinking clearly," Vinnie went on. "Can you honestly imagine her living in Salem? She hasn't even walked past the gate in years." And she burst into tears.

"Oh no, Miss Vinnie—you musn't cry!" I did what I could to comfort her, and after she calmed a bit, she told me Emily had come to her room and showed her a coral ring and bracelet the Judge gave her. Undid the clasp and pointed to an engraving on the inside of the bracelet.

"*Little Phil*, it said! Can you imagine?" Vinnie wiped her face with the back of her hand. "I suppose that's another one of her jests, since Judge Lord is as tall as they come. But it made my skin creep, Maggie."

I was nodding and patting her shoulder and making tender sounds. Didn't tell her I'd heard the Judge call Emily Jumbo and knew the nicknames were a joke between them, for she was small as he was large. I told Vinnie I'd surely know if Emily promised the Judge she'd marry him. And, in truth, I didn't think Emily would be going anywhere. "A woman who waits long to be answering isn't likely to be saying yes," I said. I gave her my clean handkerchief to wipe her tears and blow her nose.

"I don't know, Maggie," she said. "She's changed since Mother died. It's as if something came loose inside her."

I hushed her again and poured her a cup of tea. Sometimes there's nothing more useful can be done.

Chapter Thirty-One

In September Judge Lord was well enough to come to Amherst again. Emily was in raptures to see him and the pair of them filled the house with their laughing for a week. After he left, I kept a close eye on her, and she went back to writing letters and poems and tending her plants, though she seemed more downcast than usual after the visit. One day, when we were in the garden cutting back dried lily stalks, I asked what was troubling her.

"I was just musing about how glorious these lilies were only a few weeks ago," she said. "Like triumphal banners. And now every one of them is dead."

"Aye," I said, "but I'm thinking it's not the reason you're in low spirits. 'Tis something else on your heart."

She gave me a smile that wasn't really a smile.

"Is it Judge Lord, then?" I said. "Is it himself you're fretting over?"

"He's very dear to me," she murmured, but the way she said it told me it wasn't the reason.

Took a while, but she finally came out with it—she was missing Sue, who'd stopped coming by the Homestead, fearing she'd meet Mabel Todd. Sure, I should have known it all along. Emily couldn't be happy if Sue was sad.

At the end of the month, Gib came down with a fever and dysentery. Dr. Bigelow said it was typhoid. Sure, my heart went out to the tyke, for I knew too well what that was like. The whole family was tormented with worry and no one could sleep a wink from one night to the next. Austin went around scowling and Sue's face was red from crying. Dr. Bigelow came every day but the poor lad kept sinking, and at dusk on the fourth of October, Betty came bursting into the Homestead to tell us the crisis was on him.

Emily was beside herself. Up and down the kitchen and along the Northwest Passage she paced. She was wringing her hands and the sounds she made were close to keening.

I tried to settle her but she would not be settled.

"I can't bear it," she moaned, staring out the kitchen window, though it was too dark to see the Evergreens.

"Would you be wanting to go over, then?" I asked, knowing her likely answer would be no.

But she turned and looked at me, her face lit like a candle. "Yes," she whispered. "Yes, I want to go."

"I'll take you across." I got her shawl before she could change her mind, plucked up the lantern, and led her out into the dark.

Night was Emily's natural element—gentle on her eyes and heart. But she looked a ghost in her white dress, gliding along the path with the yellow lantern light falling on her hem. The house was cold as a tomb when we stepped inside. I followed her up the stairs to Gib's room. My nose stung from the smells— ammonia and fever and vomit.

Vinnie was sitting just outside the door. When she saw Emily she gasped and stood up. "What are you doing here?"

Emily paid her no mind but went straight in where the poor lad was thrashing and moaning. Sue sat beside him, weeping with her head in her hands. Austin, who was standing at the foot of the bed, brought a chair from the corner and set it next to Sue. Emily swayed and sank down.

The poor child was not in his right senses. He cried out and fell into a terrible silence, then cried out again. It was plain his fever was raging. I couldn't bear doing nothing. I spotted the basin of water and a cloth on the washstand and wrung the cloth out and laid it across his forehead, but he dashed it to the floor. Dr. Bigelow loomed in the doorway, his long face grim as ever I saw it. I plucked up the wet cloth and stepped out to give the doctor room, for there was little to be had with the lot of them hovering around the bed.

I watched as he drew back the sheet and pressed his listening tube to Gib's chest. He took the poor boy's pulse and poked his belly. His mouth made a straight line above his beard and his eyebrows fluttered up and down like white moths. It was plain the boy was sinking and even a doctor can't give hope when there's none to be had. It was in God's hands now and all of us knew it.

I crossed myself and whispered an Our Father. Emily was talking to Gib in that sweet way she always had with the lad. She promised him an extra slice of gingerbread when he got well, and told him she'd seen an owl in the pine tree outside her chamber window that very morning. She stroked the blanket over his legs. He stopped thrashing and lay still. Seemed like magic, it did. She went on talking, telling him how dearly he was loved and saying he must lie still and get well or she'd not be bearing it at all. Sure, I don't know why he attended so to her voice.

Then she started shaking. She'd not taken her eyes off Gib since she went in the room, except to cast a worried look at Sue. Dr. Bigelow closed his bag and backed away. I had the feeling he felt himself bested by Emily's spell. The only sound in the room was Sue's sobbing. Emily pulled a handkerchief from her sleeve and pressed it to her mouth.

"Emily?" I said, but she seemed not to hear.

Gib cried out and rose up on his elbows, then sank back on the bed. Austin groaned and reached for him but the lad thrust his father's arm aside. "Open the door—they're waiting for me!" he said in a high, clear voice.

His poor mother looked up, her face white as Emily's dress. And didn't everyone in that room stare at the doorway to see who he was meaning? But there was only myself. It was ghosts he was seeing, surely. I remembered my own typhoid fever visions and they were so bitter I would have run if Emily hadn't reached for me.

"I'm going to be ill, Maggie," she said, her voice shaking like her hands. "Help me."

I hurried her down the stairs and out the door, where she retched into the rhododendrons before we went back the way we'd come, with herself leaning on me every step. I put her straight to bed and there she stayed. Late the next afternoon Vinnie came in with the awful news Gib had died in his mother's arms just before five o'clock. All of us were buckled with sorrow. It harrows the whole world when a child dies.

I fixed my strength on caring for Emily, who was sick as ever she'd been.

The Dickinson family was in shambles after Gib's dying. Emily stayed in her bed, barely able to lift her head off the pillow. What strength she had she used writing notes to Sue. Note after note she wrote, and my poor feet complaining with all the running back and forth to the Evergreens I was doing. There was no more talk of Emily's romance with the Judge.

It was Christmas before Emily was up and about, but nobody had the stomach for festivities. I was glad for my own family in Kelley Square, where the mood was brighter. The laughing and singing and sweet cakes were welcome after so many bleak days.

I think Austin was shattered as Sue by Gib's dying, but instead of mourning with her, he turned to Mabel. And she was keen to comfort him. Any fool could see where things were heading. Saint Valentine's Day, it was, Mabel came rapping on the front door. When I opened it she walked in and plunked herself down on the parlor sofa. Kept glancing out the window, so I knew right off she was looking for Austin. Vinnie came in from the library and told me to brew some coffee and settled herself next to Mabel. Sure, it was plain she was in on Mabel's scheme but I wasn't in the mood to be smiling on their frolics.

When I came back with the coffee, Mabel was chattering away about decorating the house she and her husband were renting. Austin came just after four and up she jumped and went right to him, even put her hand on his chest in plain sight of Vinnie and myself. And didn't he cover it with his own?

"Will you be having coffee?" I asked him.

"No, Maggie," he said without looking in my direction. "I've something important to show Mabel." He gave her a bold look anybody with a brain in her head could catch the meaning of. And he swept her out of the room.

The pair of them closed themselves in the dining room for two hours. They surely knew I was in the kitchen, just the other side of the wall. I would have plugged my ears if I could, for the wanton sounds coming through that wall near turned my stomach. When they finally came out, glowing with their immorality, I couldn't look at them. Good thing they didn't say anything to me, for I couldn't have bit my tongue hard enough to be civil.

After that, they met two or three times every week. It got so they didn't even try to straighten the dining room before they left. When I'd go in later to set the table for supper, I'd find sofa pillows tumbled on the carpet, and the afghans Mother Dickinson had made strewn about the room. Like regular appointments, their meetings were. We all knew to expect them. If Emily was in the kitchen, a knock on the front door sent her scurrying upstairs while Vinnie hurried to greet Mabel with a cheery laugh. Within the hour Austin and Mabel would be closing themselves into the dining room and I'd be spending the next three hours pretending not to hear what was plain to any creature with ears.

Sue took on Emily's habits and wouldn't leave her house. Betty said she kept to her room with the drapes drawn and wore only the deepest black night and day. Sure, I felt sorry for the poor woman and even worse for Ned and Mattie. They were grown by then—Ned a college lad of twenty-two, and Mattie lovely and stylish at seventeen. Both of them missed Gib awfully and were cross and bitter with their father, blaming him for hurting their mam. To be sure, I blamed him myself. I'd never liked him much and now I couldn't respect him either. I cast down my eyes when I saw him so I didn't have to look at his face. And Mabel Todd—I couldn't look in her direction at all. Sin is still sin even when it's dressed in silks and furs.

Then came a doleful day in the middle of March with the rain coming down so hard it looked like gray blankets dropping from the clouds. A knock on the front door turned my heart to stone but I went to answer. It was as if I knew I'd be finding bad news on the other side. And I was right about that—there stood a lad with the wet dripping off every inch of himself though he was holding a big umbrella. When he handed me the telegram and I saw it was for Emily, that stone rolled over in my chest. I gave him a quarter from my pocket and told him if he'd come around the back he could dry off a bit and there'd be a slice of cake for him. But he said no, and who could blame him? Nobody wants to be in a house when Death comes calling.

I took the telegram straight up to Emily, who had already got up from her writing desk when I opened the door. The look of dread she gave me was the same as my own. She opened the telegram and I think she read it, though she was staring as if she couldn't understand the words. Then she crushed it against her breast and sank down in her chair.

"Emily?" I said.

She shook her head and closed her eyes. But she was holding it out to me. So I read it.

Judge Lord was dead.

I believe a sound came out of my mouth, like the mewl of a kitten. But Emily, she made no sound at all.

Chapter Thirty-Two

We shuttered the house for a month, draped mourning crepe over the front gate, and closed the doors to all but family. One good thing came of that—it kept Mabel Todd out. Austin and herself had to do their sinning elsewhere.

Emily was almost invisible, hardly leaving her room for days. Times she did, she'd float through the house, in and out of shadows. It reminded me of the weeks after the Squire's death, when she'd startle me by coming around a corner like a ghost.

But she kept writing. It was all she did besides caring for her plants. She wrote for hours and hours at the little desk in her room. She had Dennis put a table in the conservatory so she could write there. Page after page she wrote. Every day I carried her letters to the post office and every day I collected a stack to carry back to her. But her poem scraps were so full of sorrow I stopped reading them.

April came and the crocuses bloomed and a new clutch of chicks hatched out. Dennis spaded and raked the flower beds for planting. On warm days Emily put on her garden gloves and went out to weed, though it was plain her heart wasn't in it. She'd kneel down and poke in the dirt a smidgen and then she'd be up and walking back and forth, drifting the way a butterfly does, from one plant to the next. One afternoon I was churning butter on the piazza and saw her walking the same way she did when she was with Judge Lord. Even listing a bit to her left as if she was leaning on his arm. Gave me a chill, it did. I even stopped my churning. Took me a minute to turn back to my work.

That spring my nephew Willie turned thirteen and started plaguing his parents with wanting to go West and join his uncle Tommy working the mines. Tom wouldn't hear of it and Mary said it would break her heart. But I saw the love for adventure gleaming in the lad's eyes, same as my own at that age. Took a special shine to him, and gave him a bigger slice of cake when he stopped by the Homestead kitchen. I served up a lesson or two of my own while he was eating—made it plain to the lad that family was the only treasure worth having.

In May Mabel Todd and her husband rented a house on Lessey Street behind the Homestead. A grand one, it was, with columns and trees and a wide lawn. Not five minutes it took Mabel to walk from her door to the Homestead. She came every day and Austin was always there waiting. The trysting was so regular I knew the hour to start looking for Mabel. Soon I was arranging my chores to take me upstairs and outdoors between two and four thirty in the afternoons so I couldn't hear their cavorting.

Mabel began noising it around town she was great friends with Emily Dickinson. Said Emily admired her and told her secrets. I don't know where she got such a notion. She didn't know Emily at all, let alone her secrets. Maybe Mabel was just so full of herself she figured everybody believed her. I know she fancied herself a great artist. She used to paint flowers on her collars and the fronts of her dresses. She even showed them off to me, and I murmured nice things and pretended I was dazzled by her talent.

But in truth, my nieces, every one of them, could draw flowers more real than Mabel's.

In the middle of June, Emily had a fainting fit in the kitchen. I was making a coconut loaf cake with her, the two of us working away and chatting. Since the Judge died she wanted my help when she baked. She'd weakened and was sometimes dizzy and having trouble remembering the recipes. That day she was standing at the table cracking eggs into a bowl when her legs gave out and she sank right down to the floor.

I spoke her name, but the way she lay so still told me she couldn't hear. She closed her eyes and a blue cast came into her skin.

I ran for help.

Dennis came and carried Emily to her room while I went for the doctor. When I got back to the Homestead, Vinnie had come back from her marketing but there was no change in Emily. She lay on her bed, and only her breathing told us she was still among the living. Dr. Bigelow took her pulse and looked in her eyes. He said she had no fever but somebody should sit with her till she woke and then summon him. So I said I would.

Emily was insensible for hours. When she finally opened her eyes, it was twilight and the birds had all gone quiet except for a lonesome phoebe singing outside her window. *Maybe that's what woke her* is what I was thinking there in the gloom by her bed. As soon as she sat up, she was sick all over her sheets.

When Dr. Bigelow came, he pronounced she was suffering from revenge of the nerves. Likely from all the deaths in the family, he said. Sure, he didn't know the half of it. The truth of it is we were all scared, every one of us thinking Emily was at death's door. And it was plain she thought so herself, so weak she could hardly turn her head on the pillow.

Sue came first thing the next morning and sat with Emily till afternoon. I don't think they talked much, for Emily could barely whisper, but I saw their hands were clasped together the whole time.

All summer Emily was confined to her bed. Sue came and went. Sometimes she just sat watching Emily sleep. Sometimes they whispered together. Vinnie took to reading to Emily in the mornings and Austin visited every day after work. It was August before she was strong enough to sit up and write a letter. We all of us felt we'd been spared a fresh sorrow.

By fall Emily was up and about, though still feeble. Instead of working in the kitchen, she sat on the veranda watching squirrels and birds and looking across the grounds to the Evergreens. On days she felt stronger, she walked in the garden or worked in her conservatory.

In October Mabel Todd put on a grand afternoon tea and invited all the best people in Amherst. Vinnie went, wearing a new frock in rose silk and white taffeta with pleats and tucks and flounces. She looked very grand indeed. She came home with her cheeks flushed, eager to be telling what she saw. She dragged Emily out of the conservatory and I wet the tea for us all.

Even before the kettle boiled, she had Emily laughing. It wasn't till that minute I realized how long it had been since I'd heard that happy sound.

"She served chicken salad, Em. Chicken salad! On chipped plates with cups of apple compote." Buffy, Vinnie's big tomcat, came wending into the room and jumped on her lap, bumping her arm and sloshing tea onto the tablecloth. I reached for him but Vinnie draped an arm around him and shook her head. Emily gave me a wink and dabbed the spot dry with her napkin.

"Tell us more, Vin," she said. "Tell everything."

So Vinnie unspooled the afternoon's happenings, setting them out like gifts for our pleasure. "Mabel's mother was there—Mrs. Loomis. An elegant woman, very proper. If she knew what Mabel was up to—" A giggle caught Vinnie and she had to take a sip of tea to stop it. She went on petting the cat, who was purring away loud as you please. Vinnie had to raise her voice to be heard, which made Buffy just purr louder. Soon I was biting my tongue to keep from giggling myself.

"When Mrs. Loomis learned I was Austin's sister, she wanted to know how friendly he was with the Todds and why Sue wasn't at the party. Said she was surprised her daughter could afford the house rent on a college professor's salary. I'm convinced she knows what's been going on between Mabel and Austin. I told her they were only friends, but I don't think she believed me."

"What would Father say if he knew his sweet Vinnie was telling lies?" Emily was frowning but it was plain she was pretending her concern.

"It's our house now, Em." Vinnie tossed her head back in a smart way as if she were still a young lass. "And I'll not do anything to stifle Austin's chance for happiness. He's had little enough."

"And what of Sue's chance for happiness?" Emily's voice was sharp. "Austin's supposed unhappiness in his marriage is Mabel Todd's invention and you know it." She stood up, holding the table to steady herself. Ever since her fit, she'd been shaky.

I jumped up and took her elbow. "Shouldn't you be lying down now?"

I thought she'd be resisting me, but instead she whispered yes and leaned on me while I helped her upstairs to her room.

In truth, Emily never came back to her old self after the fit that summer. More and more she kept to her bed. She caught all sorts of coughs and fevers and dyspepsias. She slept late and rarely came down for breakfast. Most of her waking time she was writing letters. Sometimes when I went in early to light her fire, I found her sleeping with the lamp still lit, her lap desk on her knees and a half-written letter fallen to the floor. Twice she spilled ink on the bedspread. The stains set so, scrub as hard as I would, I couldn't get them out.

She started refusing to see Dr. Bigelow. She said it wasn't medical treatments she needed but birds and sky and light. A few times she let him watch from the hall while she shuffled past her open door. She said it should be enough if he was any good. I knew she was teasing and told her not to be a silly *gombeen*, let the man do his job. But she just laughed and declared she'd always secretly been a *gombeen*, though I was the only one who recognized it for what it was.

But no matter how I scolded and fussed, she wouldn't agree to a proper examination. It vexed the doctor and soon enough I learned he'd spread the story all over Amherst, making Emily seem foolish and cracked.

Set me raging sometimes, the way some folks will twist the truth and strew it about, without a care for how hurtful it is.

∽

Emily started asking me to sit with her afternoons. She liked me to read out letters from her friends. My voice soothed her, she said—my way of speaking made her feel safe and cherished. Sometimes the letters were enchanting as a book. One winter day she had me read a note from a friend staying in California. The lady's words made the place a wonder of bright flowers and warm breezes over a silver sea.

"Sure, it sounds like the Garden of Eden before the Fall, now, doesn't it?" I said, sliding the letter back into its envelope.

Emily smiled. "I've thought a great deal about Eden. But I don't think you'll find it in California."

"Sure, I don't either," I said. "Not anymore. Though it would have been nice to see the place. There was a time I thought it came close to Heaven."

"Oh, Maggie." The smile was on her still. "Heaven's not just close—it's the very air we breathe. I believe most of the time we live within its gates unknowing. Sometimes—if we're very lucky—the veil is lifted, and we *see*."

I didn't understand what she was meaning that day. Thought maybe her weakness had muddled her brain. Like her poems, her talking was a riddle took me years to untangle.

Emily starting confiding things she told no one else. I don't know if it was because I was always there. Or because her sickness made her do it. But I wanted to believe it was because we were close as sisters and she trusted me with her secrets.

Whether she was trusting me or not, many things she said were surely secrets—surprising and troubling and some of them sweet. Those long hours linked us. And sitting with her in that room filled with afternoon light, I spilled secrets of my own. As the days opened into weeks and the weeks into months, I began to understand my destiny hadn't been my own for years, but was forever bound to hers.

I told her about Patrick, about his work in the Dynamite School and the bombings in England and Scotland. I told her about the arrests and trials of the bombers. I told her it made me ashamed to know what Irish lads were doing. Yet the truth of it was I had no dearer wish than for Ireland to be free.

The way she listened told me she was giving me all her attention—her eyes never strayed from my face for a minute, and she even winced hearing the sad parts. I could feel the worry coming from her, same as my own. There's something about being listened to that way gives a person relief.

"But he was brave," she said. "And that's a quality I admire. For all his faults, it appears your Patrick was a warrior."

A warm flush came over me. I remembered Maria Doughtery calling Patrick a warrior after her lecture in Northampton. Hadn't thought of that in a long while. At the time it worried and confused me, but now I was feeling pride in the recollecting. "A warrior, yes," I said. "But I'm thinking he was a rogue too."

She laughed. "It's the easiest thing in the world to fall in love with a rogue, isn't it?" Emily was looking past me, at something that wasn't there. She'd been doing it so often lately it had stopped giving me a chill. "They're practically irresistible. It's the wildness in them, I think. It makes you want to live"—she paused and looked at me again—"incandescently," she said slowly. "Yes, that's what it is. You have some of it yourself, Maggie. There's a wildness in you that keeps my heart buoyant when you're near."

I stared at her. "Sure, I'm no wilder than one of Miss Vinnie's house cats."

Emily smiled. "Ah, but you have put your finger on it. Every one of them has teeth and claws and an untamed heart, no matter how they purr and preen."

I didn't know what to say to that. Wondered if I should take offense, but in truth her words warmed me. I saw the rightness of them, surely. For after all those years of training myself to be a proper American woman, I'd become more Irish than I was before. Emily was the only one to have known it, maybe. But it was a sweet thing to finally be seeing it myself.

I wrote a letter to Patrick that night. Three pages long, it was. I thanked him for giving me *Knocknagow* and for introducing me to Maria Doughtery and for taking me to the Irish Fair in Worcester. I thanked him for being my friend and for wanting to marry me. I told him what had happened in Amherst since he left—the Phoenix Block fire, my long bout with typhoid, the coming of Mabel Todd to town. I told him about Mother Dickinson dying and the calamity of little Gib's death. I asked how he was and said I was sorry for not writing sooner. On the last page, I wrote that I missed him. Things weren't as lively since he left town. It was as if some color had gone out of the sky. I pondered a long time how to sign it. And my eyes were blurry with tears when I finally wrote: *Your own Margaret.*

One afternoon in April when I was sitting with her, Emily showed me the last letter she had from Judge Lord. It had been folded and unfolded so many times there were tiny cuts in the creases. "It's a message from the grave," she said. "We never had a proper farewell, you know. When we parted the last time, neither of us imagined it was the end." She pressed the letter to her breast a minute. "I suppose that's the way Death most often comes, isn't it? Yet his very last words were *a Caller comes*. When I first read it I thought a visitor had interrupted him, but now I believe the caller was Death. He knew when he wrote it he was dying."

I nodded, for it was no surprise to me a man might hear the knocking when Death was at his door. Hadn't I heard the Banshee screaming myself—and more than once? "Some say 'tis a blessing not to be taken without notice."

She blinked. "It would be a great blessing to join him," she whispered. "And I believe I shall before long."

"Don't say so!" I grasped her hand as if it might hold her. There was no thought in it—just the needing to protect her.

She smiled and laughed a little. "Honestly, it will be a relief when the end comes, Maggie. I have lost so many. Nearly everyone I've loved and who loved me." I squeezed her hand but I didn't know if she noticed. Tears were coming up in her eyes, ready to spill. "All gone into eternity ahead of me."

"There's Vinnie," I said. "And Sue." And then, because I couldn't contain it longer and because it was so, "And myself. Don't be leaving us yet."

But I don't think she heard me. She was staring out the window, where the sunset was streaking the sky pink. Same color as her Damask roses just before the petals fall. "It's all come to nothing," she murmured. "All my hopes gone like smoke. All my dreams turned to ashes."

Ashes and smoke? Her words chilled me. "It's not so, Emily. 'Tis your sickness talking."

She shook her head. "I mean my poems, Maggie. Do you still have them?"

I nodded. "Aye, they're safe in my trunk," I said. "I know they're precious to you as children and you couldn't bear it if they came to any harm. But my trunk's a lucky one, it is. Came all the

way from Ireland with nary a scratch." I patted her shoulder.
"Sure, they're safe as houses. Nothing will be harming them."

She shook her head. "I want you to promise me something,
Maggie. You must swear to it."

"I'll do anything you say," I told her, not thinking for a minute
what she was about to be asking.

"Promise me you'll burn them when I'm gone," she whispered.

I think I flinched. I know I sucked in my breath and drew
back my hand. "Oh no!" I said. "Don't be asking such a thing."

She shook her head. "You must. They belong in eternity
with me."

"Eternity?" I wondered where she thought eternity was and
how her poems would get there if I burned them.

"Swear it." She was looking into my eyes, holding them with
her own. And now it was herself squeezing *my* hand. Her face had
a begging look I'd not seen before—so forlorn I couldn't refuse.

Still it took me a minute before I nodded. "I promise," I murmured.

"Bless you." She raised my hand and kissed my fingers. I felt
her lips fluttering over them soft as a butterfly. Then she turned
my hand over and kissed my palm. Right in the middle of it.
Brought tears to my eyes, it did. And all the rest of that day my
hand burned like it was singed.

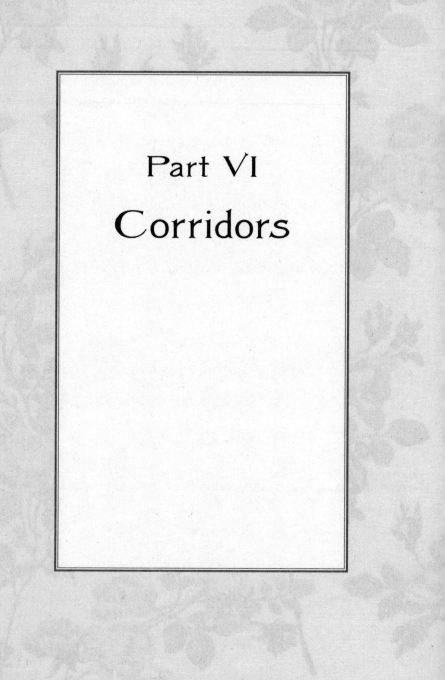

Part VI

Corridors

Chapter Thirty-Three

1916

After promising Mattie D I'll find out what I can about Reverend Parke, I start asking around town. Nobody has ever heard of him. But then I don't know a single soul who goes to the Episcopal church, so it's not surprising.

In truth, I don't have a plan for meeting the man. I don't even know what he looks like, so I wouldn't know if I passed him on the street. On my everyday errands in town, I start making a point of walking up Spring Street so I can pass the church, thinking maybe I can spot him. Surely a rector would be dressed different than an ordinary man. But I don't like going that way because I have to pass the Dell, the big house Austin designed and bought for Mabel Todd. Three stories tall, it is, with more than a dozen rooms—a jumble of arches and gables and quare windows. As ugly a place as I ever saw. It's a blessing the Todds aren't living there anymore so I don't have to worry about running into Mabel. But for all my trouble, I've not laid eyes on the rector. And I'm starting to grow vexed at myself for dithering.

On the last Saturday in March, I'm outside pegging work pants on the line when a quare thing happens. It's a grand, bright day with the birds flitting about. I drop a clothespin and bend to pick it up, and out of the blue, Patrick Quinn pops into my head. Haven't thought of him in months and months. But now, as I'm shaking out a pair of heavy cotton drill trousers, I'm seeing himself laughing, his head thrown back and his mouth open and a great hoot coming out of him.

"And what would you be laughing at now, you big gack?" I say. Right out loud too so anybody looking over the fence will be thinking I'm daft. And maybe I am—for there's no one here, let alone a lad who for all I know is dead and in his grave. If I'm talking to anybody, it's likely a ghost.

God's truth, I spent too many years with Emily, where nothing was fixed, and the edges of things were so thin and supple and it was hard to see them at all. I shake my head to get Patrick out of it, and train my mind on what's in front of me. But even as I'm hanging the last collar, I hear his voice in my ear—*When did Margaret Maher grow so timid?*

And just like that, I know I've got to find the rector and talk to him direct. I know nothing about his habits or even where he's living, but he'll surely be at his church on a Sunday. I can see him before Mass.

Sunday morning is blowy with high clouds scuttering across the sky. Grace Church is the size of St. Bridget's, but fancier. A gust of wind comes up as I'm climbing the steps and I have to hold my hat or risk losing it. Can't deny I'm feeling guilty going into a Protestant church, worrying the taint of heresy might fall on me like dust and everybody will know what I've been up to.

Inside it's shadowy as a winter twilight and near as cold. Strikes me right off what a fool I am for coming. But then I hear footsteps and see a man walking toward me through the gloom. He's wearing a long black cassock, like a priest.

"Hello," he says. "Can I help you?" He steps closer, into the light cast from the big round window over the door. For a minute it looks as if he's surrounded by it, like a great halo. Reminds me of a picture of Saint Finbarr Molly Ryan once showed me. He's a nice-looking man—younger than I expected—with a liveliness about his eyes. But it's his smile surprises me—it's so kindly I stand there gawking.

He leans closer. "Are you all right?"

Sure, I must look a sight with my hat askew and my hair flying out of its bun. It takes a minute to unstick my tongue. "Are you Reverend Parke, then?" I ask.

"I am." He nods, still smiling, but there's a question on his face now. "And you are . . . ?"

"Margaret Maher," I say. "I won't be keeping you, sir. I'm just wanting a minute of your time."

"Why don't we sit down?" He nods me over to a stone bench set against the plaster wall and waits till I settle before sitting next to me. Treating me like a lady, he is, though he's surely heard my accent and knows I don't belong in his church.

"'Tis about the house," I say.

"House?" He's looking flummoxed.

"The one you're wanting to buy. The yellow brick place on Main Street." I almost say *Emily's house* out loud. God's truth, I'm not feeling like myself at all—the words are tangling in my throat and turning into knots. Can't get them out right to save my soul.

"How did you know about that?" he asks, and I'm thinking his kindliness is gone now. No surprise in that, surely. I look a midden mess and here I am asking what's none of my business.

"'Tis what folks are saying." I'm too flustered to look straight at him. "And I know Madame Bianchi, who's put it up for sale. Word is you're buying it."

Sure, he surprises me with a chuckle. "I didn't realize it was public knowledge. But, yes, I'm hoping to purchase that house for my family. It's a fine place. And as handsome within as without, I must say. Have you ever had the pleasure of stepping inside?"

"Aye," I say, "I know it well, for I lived there thirty years." God's truth, it gives me a niggle of pleasure seeing the surprise on his face. I daresay he doesn't expect an old Irishwoman to be laying claim to such good luck. "I was the Dickinsons' maid for thirty years," I go on. "Had my own room over the kitchen. But"—and I pull myself up taller—"I run a boardinghouse now. For those needing a roof over their heads." I don't tell him I'm only taking in Irish. He doesn't need to know everything.

"Thirty years," he says in a musing way. "Then you know how magnificent it is."

"I do, to be sure." I try to think of a question Mattie D might want me to be asking, but he commences talking before I have the chance.

"How fortunate!" he says. Makes me wonder what he thinks a maid's life is like, if he's calling me fortunate for being one, but I've no time to ponder, for he's rattling on. "I must admit, I was charmed by the property from the moment I saw it. 'There's an impressive house,' I said to my wife, and she agreed. She's from New York, and knows a fine home when she sees one." He's got that soft look comes over folks' faces when what they're thinking makes them happy. "I've always longed for a house like that—a modest estate, of classic proportions, in its proper setting. As if it belonged there and nowhere else. It's how I always imagined my home would be—a house to be treasured for generations. A place our five children will cherish when they're grown. A family homestead, if you will."

I suck in a breath. "Yes," I say, my own voice near soft as a whisper. "It is that." The feelings are tumbling around in me, like clothes churning in a washtub. I'm certain it's a sign—himself using the word *homestead*. As if Emily herself is telling me she approves this man. It's a bit quare, thinking of Emily's house filled with young ones. They have a way of occupying every nook and cranny of a place. I picture them running through the rooms and banging open cupboards and closets. Yet Emily liked nothing better than chatting with children and was forever giving them treats. Can't remember seeing her so happy as when she was playing games with Ned and Gib or conspiring with Mattie to play some trick on Vinnie.

I give him a nod. "Thank you, sir." I smooth my hair and straighten my hat and stand up.

He gets up too. "I apologize. I'm afraid I've waxed overly enthusiastic. I believe there was something you came to talk about?"

"Aye, there was." I feel kindly toward this man, who's so enchanted with Emily's house. "I know how you feel about the place. In truth, I feel the same. But—" And I stop a minute, not sure what I want to be saying.

"Go on," he says in a gentle way.

"It's only—" I take a breath. "I think you should know—there's ghosts there."

"Ghosts?" He blinks once, his mouth crinkles up into a smile, and next thing I know he's laughing. "Ghosts!" he says again, and he's rubbing his hands together. "How delightful!"

Sure, I'm staggered. Don't know if he's jesting—or just reckless. "Well," I say, "good luck to you, then." I give him a nod and go out the way I came in. Sure, I don't know what to think about a man without the good sense to be wary of the spirit world. It's plain he's got no Irish in him.

Nell comes after Mass to help me get Sunday dinner on the table. While I'm peeling carrots and she's mixing up a pudding, I tell her about meeting the rector, how I like him even though he fancies ghosts.

"I guess the Homestead is the right house for him, then," she says, laughing.

I give her a side-look. Not sure my niece understands the nature of ghosts. "What have you been doing this week?" I ask.

She tells me she stopped by St. Mary's Cemetery when she was in Northampton Friday. "The grass is looking nice on Uncle Tommy's grave," she says. "I said a rosary for him while I was there."

"That was kind of you." I feel a prickle at the back of my eyes. "'Twas hard seeing him go into the ground with myself the only Maher left remembering the farm."

After a minute Nell says, "I'm glad he came back East before he died. Gave the rest of us a chance to know him. Remember Kate asking who he was? Thinking he was a stranger?"

I laugh, remembering my youngest niece's puzzlement. "I guess he was. That day's a sweet memory, to be sure." Indeed, all my memories are sweet when it comes to Tommy. I just wish there were more of them. "It was a hard life he had, though. Don't think I'd have stayed long if I'd gone with him back in eighteen sixty-nine like I planned."

"But you liked it when you visited in eighteen ninety-four," Nell says. "You said it was grand."

I nod, remembering the excitement I felt the year I finally went to California. With Vinnie's blessing and a new trunk, I took a year off from working at the Homestead to travel. "It was an adventure, surely." I finish with the carrots and start peeling potatoes. "Especially when Tommy took me to the Midwinter Fair in San Francisco. The 'Forty-nine Mining Camp was great fun, though he warned me the real camps were full of sickness and dirt and cruel bosses, the work so hard it broke many a lad. 'Tis why he went into ranching, he said."

I go quiet, thinking. Most dreams come and go like the wind, but some stick hard to the timbers of a life. I was lucky to go to California after dreaming of it so many years. But by the time I did, I wasn't looking to live there—I just wanted to see the place.

Turned out, Tommy was hoping I'd stay on, help him out on his ranch in the New Mexico Territory. But one look at the place and I knew it could never be home. After just a few months, I was already looking to be back in Amherst.

I remember something Emily once said. I'd been talking about wanting to go West and how I'd never stopped hoping I would. She was sewing that day and put down her needle to look at me.

"Hope is a clever glutton," she said. "It feeds on our dreams but leaves us empty in the end."

Seemed a quare thing to say at the time but now I'm guessing she was thinking of her own dream of having her poems printed. And her sorrow knowing she'd never live to see it come true.

Chapter Thirty-Four

1886

It was a hard winter, and Emily so sick Vinnie didn't venture from the Homestead. Austin came often to sit with Emily in the evenings, and he stopped his trysting in the dining room with Mabel Todd.

Emily spent most of her waking hours in bed, reading or writing letters. A little book of Mrs. Browning's poems always lay close at hand. Lovely, it was, slim and blue with gold letters on the cover. Many a time I came in and found her reading it. She touched the pages the way Vinnie petted Buffy, her fingers loving what was under them.

Once she said, "You must hear this, Maggie," and read a verse out to me.

> Earth's crammed with heaven,
> And every common bush afire with God;
> But only he who sees, takes off his shoes,
> The rest sit round it and pluck blackberries,
> And daub their natural faces unaware.

She sighed and closed the book. "Doesn't it steal the very breath from your lungs?"

I said it was a fine poem indeed. Then I saw her face was slick with tears. "Are you in pain, miss?" I asked.

But she shook her head. Her fingers danced over the gilt letters. "This," she said, her voice gone wobbly, "this is an *immortality.*"

I didn't understand her meaning and worried maybe her fever was back or she was about to have another fit. I took the book gently and put it on the table and smoothed her pillow.

I didn't think more about it then, for I was busy settling the tray on her knees and picking up the papers and letters she'd strewn across the floor. But later, after my chores were done and I was brushing out my hair before going to bed, I remembered the way the late-winter sun came in Emily's room that afternoon while she was filling herself up with Mrs. Browning's words. I thought how quare it was that a faraway English lady wrote words that could have been skipping straight from Emily's heart.

Though Emily was frail, she was still Emily—gripped by newspaper stories of court doings, as if the Judge were still alive and she'd soon be discussing them with him. She blistered Vinnie with questions about a murder trial whose defendant had the name Dickinson. And she couldn't stop talking about a traveling juggler tried for poisoning a lady he'd romanced.

"It would make a fine novel, wouldn't it?" she said one day while I was collecting her tray after dinner. "That story about the juggler and the lady."

"Sure, you didn't touch your potatoes," I said.

She laughed. "Maggie, I thought we were having a conversation about *art*, and all you think about is potatoes."

"Potatoes aren't to be scorned," I said. "A good potato's brought many a man back to health. There are worse things to be thinking of, surely." I didn't say what those worse things were. Figured Emily could fill those in on her own. She'd always had a melancholy turn of mind.

"Set the tray down and tell me a potato story, then." It was good to see her smiling after so many sorrowful days. I put the tray back on the table.

"The only potato story I know is too sad for the telling," I said. "'Tis the misery of the Great Hunger. You wouldn't want to be hearing it."

"But I would," she said. "I want to know *everything*. I'm woefully ignorant about the world."

That wasn't true, to be sure, for Emily read every book she put her hand to and was the cleverest woman I knew. But there was so much pleading in her eyes, how could I refuse? So I sat myself down and told her about the famine—what I remembered and what Mam had told me. How I saw with my own eyes ragged children dying by the road. How good lads and their families were bundled out of their houses. How there were grain and oats and food enough to feed the starving, but it was all shipped off to England. And didn't she listen to every word? Sure, I watched the tears come up in her eyes and one spill down her cheek.

I reached to pat her hand. "That's enough sadness for one day, I'm thinking. And with yourself still languishing. 'Tis not the sort of tale likely to be lifting your spirits." I stood up.

"I've had it wrong," she said, sunk deep in her pillows. "All those years I thought the Irish ignorant and empty-headed. But I was mistaken."

A spider of mischief crept into my head. "And here I've been thinking you believed I was only good for cleaning and scrubbing." I was waiting for her to laugh, for she surely knew I didn't mean it. But she just looked at me with those sad eyes.

"'Tis true," I said. "We Irish seem a sorry lot sometimes. But it's not an easy thing, living where we don't belong. Times I've thought I should be going back to County Tipperary and living out my days among my own kind."

She frowned. "What do you mean, your own kind?" she said. "*We're* your own kind, Maggie. Everyone here in Amherst. You're American now, not Irish."

I think my face must have flushed pink as the roses on her wall. "I would have given half my wages to hear you say that seventeen years ago, miss," I said. "But God's truth, I'm Irish to the bone. And proud of it too. There's not a country on earth more persecuted nor a people more noble and spirited." I stopped, realizing I was reciting Maria Doughtery's words. "Like all Irish folks, I came here to make a better life for myself and my family. Family's what truly matters in the end."

She nodded. "It is." Her eyes were shining. "And life has taught me that a woman's true family is vaster than those she's related to."

I thought about that. I wondered if she was including me in her true family and it set me wondering who might be in my own true family.

She locked her eyes on mine. "Will you forgive me?"

"Me?" I said. "And what would I be forgiving you for?"

"For misjudging the Irish all these years," she whispered. "I was so misguided."

Her tears came in earnest then, washing down her face. There was naught to be done but put my arms around her. I rubbed her back and wiped her cheeks with my own handkerchief and kissed her tears away.

A letter from Patrick came a week later, addressed to me at the Homestead. Surprised me, it did, for I hadn't heard anything from him since I wrote after Emily's fit. I took it straight to my room and closed the door. There were three pages, and though the words were easy to make out, I read them slow. Tasting every one, the way Emily did.

My Dear Margaret, he wrote.

> *It has been six years since I last looked on your sweet face, and I have not forgot you. I am well and prospering, living in Brooklyn and working at construction. I left my job at the Dynamite School after a year working for Professor Mezzeroff. You may have heard the name of Jeremiah O'Donovan Rossa. He was the brave lad who recruited me and he remains my friend. But I have learned Professor Mezzeroff is a fraud and a trickster who cannot be trusted. He knows about dynamite but not about honor. The truth is, he's not from Russia at all. Even his accent is a sham.*
>
> *Brooklyn is a grand place, full of shops and parks. There is work here for anyone who wants it. You could find a job in a minute if you came. I think you'd like New York, for it's as thrilling as the grandest adventure.*

A flush came over me and I felt myself falling into the old sweet yearning. I remembered the way Patrick's arms felt around

me, and how good his mouth tasted when we kissed. The pit of
my stomach filled with heat. Then I turned to the last page.

> *I have some news you will want to hear. I am to be*
> *married in June to a lovely Irish lass. She came two years*
> *ago from County Cork. Her name is Nora Sullivan and*
> *she's a true patriot. After the wedding we will move to*
> *Dublin and do what we can to free Ireland.*

He signed it, *With affection, Patrick.*

The news staggered me. I'd wondered if Patrick might marry,
but now I was having trouble taking it in. I read the letter
three times, then sat on my bed a long spell. There was no hint
of himself resenting me. He didn't accuse me of wronging him.
He was the same Patrick as ever, charming and lively. Still
fighting for the cause. It was who he'd always been—who he'd
always be.

I told Mary about the letter, confessed I sometimes still had
regrets for not marrying him, for who doesn't want a lad's comforting arms around her from time to time? Mary *tsk*ed and
shook her head and said the saints had been looking out for me,
surely. What sort of life would I be having in Brooklyn and Ireland, so far from my family and friends?

I knew Mary was right, but it was Emily who gave me true
comfort. When I told her what Patrick wrote, all I saw was com-
passion on her face. "The heart spans distances and time," she
said. "But gives no quarter to the mind."

"Is that one of your poems?" I asked.

She shook her head and smiled. "It just came to me while I
was listening to you," she said. And she opened her arms and
gathered me in.

My time for wild adventures was over. I wanted excitement of a
different kind now—adventures of the spirit. And the hours with
Emily on late-winter afternoons were mighty adventures, to
be sure. Every conversation started the same, with news and
weather and the health of her plants, but they soon found their
way to deeper things—faith and love and hope.

As the days went by, Emily talked more and more about
death. I didn't want to hear it at first, fearing it would be opening
the door to new troubles. But it was always on her mind, so I
listened. It didn't surprise me, surely. Her poems were filled with
mourning. So many people she loved had gone, it was no wonder
she was bowed low. Death tries to crush us all, doesn't it? I've
done my own share of grieving, to be sure.

When someone you love dies, you first feel sorrowful, then
lonesome, and after a while, jealous. It feels as if Death has stolen
your heart and will never give it back. For most of us the jeal-
ousy fades with time and the hole in your heart is filled by others
and the sorrow turns into a kind of peace. But with Emily nothing ever faded. The pang of loss went on and on, fresh as its first
strike.

Spring came with its birds and flowers, and I was hoping Emily
might revive, for it was her grand season when she usually grew
lively and bright in the long-stretching days. The birds at her
window did cheer her and she talked of walking in her garden,
and twice declared herself *ecstatic*. But she never ventured from
her room. Walking from her bed to her writing desk and back
took all the strength she had. She complained of losing her *veloc-*

ity. I thought it a quare word till I got to thinking how she used to flit about the house. It was the perfect word for how she used to be. But now she was slow as a snail and leaned on my arm when I was with her.

She talked and talked about her garden. Came a morning she begged Vinnie and myself to take her outside, though every step taxed her. "I must salute the crocuses," she said. "Their pretty parade is as martial as a drum."

Vinnie fretted and I scowled, but we did what she asked. For she was Emily after all, and the iron in her soul was fierce as her body was weak. We half carried her downstairs and wrapped her in a cloak, though the sun was bright and the air soft as a kitten. She leaned on each of us by turns and tasked me with picking a spray of daffodils for her windowsill. But it wasn't more than an hour before she asked us to help her back to bed.

Like sunshine in her room those daffodils were, and I added new ones every day. When the daffodils were done it was the turn of the fritillaria, with their checkered pink bells hanging down like the heads of guilty boys. After that it was blue hyacinths, Emily's favorite. But as the bouquet changed from yellow to pink to blue, it seemed to me Emily's health was slipping away with it.

Chapter Thirty-Five

It was plain Emily was sinking. She was sleeping both early and late and complaining of pains in her chest and back and eyes. Her writing slowed and her letters grew short—barely a sentence or two. But she still wrote them and had myself delivering them all over Amherst, tucked in my basket along with flowers from her garden or conservatory.

Sue came, still in the black mourning she'd worn since Gib died. Her visits always cheered Emily. Sometimes she stayed for hours and the sound of their murmuring voices was a comfort when I passed in the hall. One rainy afternoon I heard her singing a lullaby Mary sang to her little ones when they were new. The tune was so familiar and Sue's voice so sweet I couldn't stop myself peeking in. Sue was sitting on the bed cradling Emily in her arms and stroking her hair, like the tenderest mam.

In spite of Sue's devotion and all my prayers, Emily didn't rally. She slid from a bright hope in early spring to sober forbearing by mid-April and finally—as her garden burst into full, bright glory—to calm acceptance. I'd sat with the dying before, so I knew the grace and comfort of that kind of peace. But I couldn't stop thinking of a verse from one of Emily's poems—about hope being a bird that never stops singing.

The climax came early on a Thursday morning. I was just back in the kitchen from feeding the chickens when Vinnie called from upstairs, leaning so far over the banister I wondered she didn't fall.

"Run and fetch Austin!" Her face was twisted and pinched together, her voice full of tears.

Instead, I ran upstairs, knowing Vinnie's dramatics got the best of her sometimes. But before I even reached the room, I could hear Emily's breathing—like an engine, it was. She was lying in bed with her left arm thrown over the side, as if she were reaching for the hyacinths on her windowsill. Her eyes were half open but I knew she wasn't seeing anything.

"She's had another fit," Vinnie was saying, foostering around the bed like a fretful hen. "I can't wake her."

"I'll go for the doctor," I said, already halfway out the door.

"Fetch Austin first, Maggie," Vinnie said, her voice gone wobbly. "Please."

So I hurried down the stairs and ran to the Evergreens. And wasn't the grass on both sides of the path filled with blue violets, as if the world hadn't rocked off its hinge?

Austin was reading the paper but he jumped up soon as I went in. "Is it Emily?" he asked, and went straight out the door when I nodded. Didn't even put on his hat.

Emily's dying was a terrible thing. Two long days it took. Even when I wasn't in the room, I could hear her rasping and shaking. Dr. Bigelow gave her chloroform and olive oil to ease the fits, and then she lay limp as a rag, though those awful sounds were coming from her poor throat. I was shaking myself, just listening.

The doctor kept saying she felt nothing, but I knew it couldn't be true. It was plain Emily was suffering. At night I prayed three decades of the rosary before going to sleep. Early in the morning I crept into her room, stood by her bed, and whispered the Our Father—three times for the Holy Trinity. Seemed to me her breathing gentled a bit, but maybe it was just my wishing it to be so.

Austin sat with her day and night, while Vinnie and myself went in and out of her room, too restless to stay in one place. Sue came every morning and Vinnie's friend Marriet came in the afternoons to comfort her.

An hour before sunset—with gold light flooding her room—Emily stopped breathing.

I had just come into the room with an armful of fresh linens. The quiet was so quick and sudden I felt struck deaf. Then Vinnie moaned and the hat factory whistle sounded, so I knew it wasn't my ears. Marriet helped Vinnie from her chair and led her out. Austin stood looking out the window with his back to Emily, saying nothing at all.

I heard Dr. Bigelow coming up the stairs with his heels cracking the floorboards like gunshots, and a powerful fury rose in me. I wanted to stand at the door and keep everybody away from Emily. Hadn't it been my job for seventeen years? But in he came and laid two fingers on her neck and shook his head. And didn't a sob come out of my throat?

Soft as a whisper, I put the linens on top of Emily's chest of drawers. Tears were running down my face and I didn't even wipe them away. Seemed disrespectful somehow. Austin turned from the window, took a long look at Emily, then left the room. The doctor drew the bedsheet up over her face and went after him.

I was alone with Emily. I pulled back the sheet and knelt beside her. I couldn't bear to see her dear face covered while I prayed for all the saints and angels to be coming quick to carry herself straight past Purgatory to Heaven. Then I opened the window nearest her, hoping it wasn't too late for her soul to get out, and I crept downstairs to fetch cloths for the laying out.

As I washed her, my tears dropped onto her face and I had to wipe it. Yet it was comforting, surely. I'd washed her so many times those last months, her body was familiar as my own. I dressed her in a clean nightgown, fitting her arms gently into the sleeves and drawing the hem all the way to her ankles. Then I brushed her hair, folded her arms across her bosom, and pulled the top sheet to her waist.

Just as I was folding back the hem in the pretty way she liked, a slice of light fell across her hands. Like a long gold knife. God's truth, I jumped back, it startled me so. I turned. Through the west window I saw ribbons of gold and purple clouds with the sun peeking out beneath. Had the uncanny thought Emily had arranged it so to comfort me.

I couldn't bring myself to leave her room, so I sat with her till my tears stopped. Took a while. Finally, I closed the window and drew the curtains so her spirit wouldn't be coming back and making mischief. For I knew she would try. Emily had a talent for mischief and I wasn't so foolish as to think Death would be stopping her.

Downstairs, I burned the cloths in the kitchen stove. Tom came up from Kelley Square and I told him Emily had died. He said he already knew and put his arm around me and kept it there for comfort while the light drained away. Later, I wiped my eyes with my apron and touched the empty sleeve where his arm used to be. It offered a quare comfort, made me think how his

accident was the reason I stayed in Amherst and started me on
the path of working for the Dickinsons.

We went through every room in the house, covering the mir-
rors. Everybody but Vinnie had left. She was still in the parlor,
sitting with two kittens on her lap, stroking them for all she was
worth. She pretended Tom and myself weren't there. But we were
used to that. It's the way of some not to see what's right before
their eyes.

Emily was different, though. Emily paid attention to everything.

In the morning Sue came to help Vinnie with the funeral arrangements. The two of them hadn't been friendly since Austin
and Mabel started their trysting, but both loved Emily dearly
and she'd made plain how she wanted to be buried. She must be
wrapped in a white robe and buried in a white coffin. Like her
father, she'd be borne on foot to the cemetery. But instead of
parading up Main Street, she was to be carried through the barn
and over the fields by lads who'd worked for the Dickinsons.
Irish lads all, and Tom the head mourner.

Austin shook his head at the plans, saying they weren't at all
proper for a Dickinson funeral. But it was what Emily wanted,
so there was nothing he could do.

Sue ordered a robe of white flannel but I was the one putting
it on Emily. It made me think of the Irish wakes I'd told her
about. She'd asked a hundred questions and I'd told her about the
praying and weeping and keening and laughing. I'd told her
about the toasts and storytelling and how the dead were wrapped
in white shrouds. I think it would have pleased Emily to see the

coffin—painted white, with canvas handles, and the inside lined with Russian flannel, white and soft as a cloud.

The morning of the funeral the sun came up like a pearl through clouds and fog. The undertaker's lads brought Emily down in her coffin and put her in the library. Austin came and went all morning. But after eleven he slipped away, telling me on his way out the door he was after some private time with Mrs. Todd. As if I approved.

By noon the clouds burned off and it turned into one of those grand spring days Emily loved. When Sue came she went straight into the library and closed the door. I didn't trouble her—though I longed to give the library one more dusting before the mourners came. After a time, she came into the kitchen and said she was going home—she'd not be at the funeral. I must have looked shocked, because right away she said, "*She* will be here, won't she?"

"I'm guessing she will," I said, knowing she meant Mabel Todd.

"Well, then." Sue was sometimes cold and pretended she didn't see the servants. But that day the lonesome smile she turned on me would have broken any woman's heart.

Later, when I went to the library to draw the curtains and make sure everything was proper-looking, I saw Sue had placed a knot of violets and a lady slipper at Emily's throat.

Mr. Higginson came and he stood over the coffin, looking down at Emily for a long time. Her face was ghosty in the dim light but her red hair was bright as a sunrise in all that white cloth. "There's not a trace of gray in her hair," he said. "She could be thirty." He passed his hand over his eyes.

Vinnie came in, carrying two sprays of heliotrope, and laid them atop Emily's hands. "To take to Judge Lord," she whispered.

The vanilla smell of the heliotrope filled the library. Made me think of Emily baking. Made me think of love.

The funeral didn't take long. Emily's coffin stayed in the library. She would have liked that, I think—lying amongst all those books. Mourners sat in the hall and some in the parlor. My family came from Kelley Square, wearing their Sunday best. Vinnie sat with Austin on one side and Marriet on the other. Mabel Todd was behind Austin, dressed in the blackest gown I ever saw and her veil so thick I wondered she could see anything at all. She sniffed into her handkerchief and poked it up under the veil again and again, as if she was trying not to cry. But it seemed to me her grieving was all for show.

Mr. Higginson read a poem Emily liked and the new minister of the Congregational church read from the Bible. Reverend Jenkins came all the way from Pittsfield to say a blessing at the end.

Everybody stood up while the coffin was carried by friends of Austin down the hall and through the back door, and set on a bier covered with violets and pine boughs. Then Tom and the other lads lifted the coffin and carried it past the garden and through the open barn, just like Emily wanted. We all followed in a sad parade, masters and servants alike—for Emily's death made us equals in sorrow.

As we came out of the barn, a strange thing happened—a

crowd of orange and yellow butterflies rose up and fluttered around the coffin. And didn't they attend Emily the whole way? Like they were mourning too. We walked cross-lots through fields of buttercups and violets to the cemetery. The sky was bright blue and all the birds were singing.

When I saw the open grave was lined with pine branches, my sorrow lifted a bit. I knew it was Sue's doing—for she was the one who'd be making sure there was a soft, sweet-smelling place for Emily to rest.

I looked at Vinnie, standing at the side of the hole, the toes of her boots poking out over the edge. The look on her face frightened me and gave me the thought she was yearning to follow her sister into the grave. I moved behind her, close enough to catch her if need be.

The minister said a prayer. I stood with my hands folded and my eyes wet, watching Emily go down into the earth all in white, tucked like a tiny bird into her nest. It was a kind of poem itself.

Chapter Thirty-Six

Took all my strength to raise myself from my bed the morning after the funeral. Out of habit, I went to light the fire in Emily's room. Gave me such a start seeing her bed empty, it shocked me wide awake and a terrible lost feeling came over me.

I stood looking around the room—at her table and chair, the lamp and candlesticks, her basket and chest of drawers. For some reason it was her wallpaper struck me. In truth, I'd seen it so many times I'd stopped noticing. But that morning in the half-light, it looked like the roses were alive. The vines all greeny-blue and yellow with those great pink roses hanging off them, the kind you bury your nose in if they're real.

I straightened the stack of books on her mantel, though they didn't want straightening. Just habit, I guess. I opened the top book and a scrap of paper fluttered down—the flap of an old envelope. When I picked it up I saw it had Emily's writing: *Take all away from me, but leave me Ecstasy.*

I tucked it down into my pocket to put it with the others in my trunk, wondering when she wrote it. Could have been anytime, but I'm guessing it was a morning in spring.

Vinnie was in the kitchen pouring cream into the cats' saucers. It was odd seeing her there—the morning kitchen was Emily's space. She didn't speak, but scooped up Buffy and rocked him like a babby. He squirmed and switched his tail. I tried to summon the pity I'd felt for her at the cemetery. But all I saw was a silly old woman pampering her cats.

I asked how she'd slept. She said she hadn't, and was glad it was finally daylight. Said she still felt the night chill on the back of her neck. She didn't need to say she was missing Emily. The house felt hollowed out and cold even with the sun lying in a sheet on the floor and already starting to creep up the wall.

I got busy, lighting the fires, pumping water, and filling the wash kettle. When I went back in the kitchen, Vinnie had moved across the room to the west window, rubbing her face on Buffy's head and purring like a cat herself.

I set a pan of oatmeal on the stove. I couldn't help wishing she'd choose another window. That was Emily's window—the one she looked out of when she was making her bread. She once told me she liked looking west because the sun was heading that way, so it was a way of seeing into the future. I wasn't persuaded it was her real reason—figured it was more because it was the direction of the Evergreens, where Sue lived. But her words always made me think. Sometimes she'd recite one of her poems. "I'm tasting the words on my tongue," she'd say, as if they were tuneful as little songs. In truth, her words were more like hammers, opening holes in the walls of my heart.

Already I was missing the sound of her.

"I suppose we should sort out Emily's room," Vinnie said.

I didn't say anything, it surprised me so. I stirred the porridge hard. After a minute I said, "'Tis too soon to be thinking about that. There's cleaning to be done first. The house is a terrible mess." I opened the firebox and threw in another stick of wood. "I'd best be setting the table." And quick as Hell can scorch a feather, I hurried into the pantry to get the plates.

The truth of it was I dreaded sorting Emily's things. If I had my way, we'd be locking the door to her room—same as Sue did after Gib died—and never setting foot in there again.

The next two weeks were heaving with work. I aired out the downstairs rooms, sorted the linens, polished brasses, blacked the cooker, made the meals, did the washing up, and was out and about all over Amherst shopping and carrying notes for Vinnie. I visited the Evergreens every day to see if Sue was needing anything. Vinnie's friends were in and out and I was busy feeding them. It was a whirlwind, surely, but at least it kept my mind off grieving.

It was strange caring for the Homestead without Emily in it. She was like a perfume that still filled the air. Sometimes I'd glance out the window and spy a flutter of white amongst the stalks of purple foxglove in the garden. It didn't give me a ghosty chill like you'd expect, just made me smile, thinking of herself flitting about.

Then came the day I was dreading. At breakfast Vinnie said we couldn't delay any longer. We had to start sorting Emily's room. She wouldn't listen to my complaining it was too soon. *Stalling*, she called it. She ordered me to lay a fire in Emily's stove so we could burn her letters when we found them.

"We?" I said. "Emily didn't tell me to burn any letters." I wasn't going to be part of that. It was bad enough I promised to burn the poems.

Vinnie gave me a sideways look. "Do you think I *want* to do it? Do you think I would if I hadn't made a sacred promise?"

Sometimes the dying ask too much is what I thought. But I didn't say so, not to Vinnie. "I'd best get busy, then," I said, and started clearing away the breakfast things.

It was a bright morning, with birds singing outside the windows. The hens were clucking away near the back door and there was the sound of a buggy passing on the street. I wondered how many letters we'd find, and if Vinnie would be reading them before putting them in the fire.

I took as long as I could with the washing up and kitchen chores, so it was nearly ten when I went upstairs. We started our sorting in the closet, hauling out Emily's frocks and laying them on the bed. They were made of wool and cotton and linen, every one of them white as chalk. Some were trimmed and pleated with a bit of lace, but most were simple styled. There was not a flounce to be found. Plain as my own work dresses and wrappers, they were.

"What shall we do with them all?" Vinnie said, shaking her head in a mournful way.

"Likely the Poor Farm will take them," I said.

Vinnie's face pinched together. "Not Emily's dresses!" she whispered.

I rubbed her back to steady her. "Of course not," I said. "Sure, I was acting the maggot."

"You must take them," Vinnie said. But neither of us moved to do anything. We just stood looking down at all those white frocks stretched across the bed where Emily died.

Vinnie found the first bundle of letters in the top drawer of the chest and the second in a hatbox in the closet. Some were tucked in envelopes and tied with ribbons, but it was plain they'd all been read again and again.

Vinnie plucked up a handful and held them out to me. "Put them in the fire, Maggie."

I didn't take them. "Aren't you going to read them first? See what's inside?" I moved so I was standing between herself and the stove.

"Read them?" She looked like I'd blasphemed.

I felt sad and desperate. It struck me that if Vinnie spared the letters I wouldn't have to burn the poems. "Shouldn't we be sending them back to the folks who wrote them? That's the way it's done, I'm thinking."

She shook her head. "I shall keep my promise to my sister. I couldn't save her, but I can at least abide by her wishes."

It was plain there was no stopping her. She was set on doing Emily's bidding, no matter how it pained her. I should have known—she'd spent her life doing what Emily wanted. But I tried one last time. "You don't have to burn any today," I said. "There must be more somewhere. Why don't we collect them all first?"

She stared at me, like she was wanting to agree. But then she frowned and stepped around me. I heard her open the stove, a fluttery sound when she threw the letters in, then the fizz of flames whooshing up.

I didn't turn to look. I went quick to the bed and piled up the frocks. "I'll take care of these," I said. "Then I'd best be making dinner so you can keep up your strength." And without looking back, I hauled them out of Emily's room and down the hall to my own.

Soon as I dropped them on my bed, I knew I'd been foolish to carry them off, for I'd no idea what to do with them. I looked around the room, at the wall pegs over the chair, at the little chest of drawers stuffed full of my things. At my trunk under the window.

It was empty except for Emily's poems. The ones I'd promised to burn. There was plenty of room for the frocks. I took care folding them and opened the trunk. For just a minute I stood looking down at the booklets. I'd dipped into them so many times I knew some of the lines by heart. If I meant to keep my promise, I'd gather them up right now and throw them in the kitchen fire and be done with it.

Instead, I laid the frocks over them. Gentle as a mam laying a babby in a cot. When I closed the lid, there was a catch in my throat, as if Emily was going into the ground all over again.

Three weeks it took me to sort through Emily's things. I had to do it alone—Vinnie said she didn't have the heart after burning the letters. She told me if there was any small thing took my fancy, I should keep it. But Emily didn't have much to suit me—a brooch and a bracelet, some pretty shawls. One afternoon as I was cleaning out her chest of drawers, I chanced to wonder why I'd not come across the rosary I gave her. If she'd thrown it out I would have seen it in the trash. Sure, I was glad I hadn't, for it would have torn my heart. But I was flummoxed by what became of it. Seemed there was no end to her riddles, even after she was gone.

When her room was sorted, I worked my way through Emily's frocks, dyeing them one at a time in an old laundry barrel when the weather was clear. Near brought tears to my eyes each time

I dropped one in the dye. A quare thing, for I'd complained so
many times because they were white and now I couldn't bring
myself to be coloring more than half of them. When I was done,
I took the lot to Mary for making into dresses for my nieces. The
last one I ironed and put back in Emily's closet. It was a way of
keeping part of herself tucked away in the room she loved.

Now all that was left in my trunk were her poems. They were
safe there. Nobody knew about them but myself. That would
satisfy Emily, surely.

But I kept remembering the look on her face when I swore I'd
burn them. How relieved she was. How she kissed my fingers
and whispered, "Bless you," like a priest giving absolution.

First thing every morning I'd see my trunk and shame would
come washing over me for not keeping my promise. I'd scold
myself for failing my duty. I was certain Emily would be thinking I'd betrayed her.

I tried convincing myself it made no difference to me if the
poems were burned to ashes. But I'd spent years watching Emily
write them, seen her reaching for those words, rolling them
around in her mouth, finally finding the right ones. I'd seen her
scribbling in a fever, right beside me in the kitchen. Her eyes
would spark with excitement. Sometimes she'd ask a question.
"What do you think, Maggie—*fasten* or *sanction*—which sounds
better?" Since she seemed to be expecting an answer, I'd pick a
word. Sometimes she'd smile and say, "Of course!" and sometimes she'd frown and shake her head and scribble some more.

She worked and worked those poems, like a dressmaker working her cloth—sewing a seam and studying it and measuring
and ripping it out and sewing again. Her body near quivering
with the passion of the chore. Those poems were treasures, dear
to her as life. Each one a pearl.

~

Came a hot June morning when I saw something glinting at the bottom of the kitchen waste bin. I picked it out. Fit right into my palm, it did—it was in one of those little picture frames that opens like a book, trimmed inside with red velvet.

It was a likeness of Emily as a girl. Looking serious and waifish with a flower in her hand and not a hint of her rascally smile or the spark in her eyes. I'd seen it before, but nobody in the family liked it, not even Emily. I once heard her complain it made her look like a goose.

Vinnie must have thrown it out.

I tucked it in my apron pocket and there it lay all day, bumping my leg when I moved. That night in my room, I opened it and looked at it for a long time. It was scratched and faded and didn't look much like Emily, but I was glad I'd found it. It was something.

I propped it open on my trunk. Gave me a familiar feeling, Emily watching me. Like she was standing in the shadows, the way she did.

I resolved to burn her poems in the morning.

Soon as I got up, I took all the booklets out of the trunk and laid them on my bed. They'd burn quick, kindling to the fire, make a lively start to the day. By the time Vinnie came down, every last one would be ash.

I pulled on my dress and put up my hair. There were streaks of gray in it now—made me glad to be binding it to my head. I fussed with my collar and peered into the looking glass. I was dithering, and I knew it. Took a deep breath and gathered up the poems. A raw, sick feeling came over me as I started down the back stairs. Just at the turn I saw something white flicker at the bottom. I told myself it was likely one of the cats. But didn't I go cold all over?

I stood still a minute, listening for footsteps, but there was nothing. A terrible dread came over me. I turned around and ran back up the stairs, straight to Emily's room. Don't know what I thought I'd be finding—herself sitting at her writing desk?

But nobody was there, neither ghost nor Faery. I stood in the middle of the room, cradling the booklets. Wasn't much trace of Emily left. Only her one white dress in the closet. The mantel and sills I'd swept clean, put her books on the library shelves and her plants in the conservatory. Even the top of her chest of drawers was empty—all her little bottles and pots thrown away. I knew there were still a few things in the top drawer—combs and ribbons, a silver hand mirror, a corset Emily never used.

And it was then I knew what to do. I slid open the empty bottom drawer and shoved the poems inside, all helter-skelter, as if Emily had tossed them there herself.

They filled that drawer right to the brim. I had a time getting it closed. But I felt better when I left the room. I knew Vinnie had a habit of going in there, spending an hour dusting and tidying, though there was nothing to tidy anymore. I knew it was her way of healing. Sooner or later she'd find the poems. And I knew she'd treasure them. There'd be no more burning Emily's things.

Two weeks later I was cleaning the parlor when Vinnie came running down the front stairs, flapping one of the booklets like a flag. "It's Emily—poems of hers," she gasped. "They were in her bottom drawer. I don't know why I never opened it. There must be hundreds." She crumpled onto the sofa. But it was only a minute before she popped up. "I must go tell Austin. He'll be so surprised." And before I could say anything, she was out the back door.

A sick feeling came over me. All I could think of was Emily saying she didn't want her poems found. It was why she gave them to me, trusting I'd obey.

Instead, I betrayed her.

All that day the guilt nagged me. I saw Emily's ghost in the shadowy corners of the house and flitting past the rosebushes when I fed the hens. Late that afternoon Sue and Mattie came through the back door and found me scrubbing pots and crying a rainstorm. I pulled my hands out of the dishwater and dried my tears and asked what I could be doing for them.

"Maggie, what on earth is the matter?" Sue had a kindly side she rarely showed to servants, but that day she showed it to me.

"'Tis Miss Emily's verses," I told her. "I couldn't burn them. No matter I promised her."

"Maggie!" Sue's voice turned snappish. Didn't take much to make her cross. "What *are* you talking about?"

"Her poems that were hid in my trunk. Miss Emily didn't want anybody to be finding them," I said. "She made me swear I'd burn them after she died."

Didn't Sue's eyes spark so? "Burn her poems! What a dreadful idea!"

"I promised her." I was mumbling.

"I'm sure Aunt Emily didn't mean it," Mattie said. "Her poems were her legacy." She was twenty now, lovely and elegant too. But as she stood there by the pie safe, twisting her fingers together at her waist, all I could think of was herself as a girl and how much Emily loved her.

I started crying again.

"They were indeed," Sue said firmly. She pulled her handkerchief from her sleeve and gave it to me. "Now, dry your tears, Maggie, and tell me everything."

And so I did. It all came pouring out while Sue listened. When I was done, she put her hand on my arm. "Maggie, you've done the right thing. You mustn't feel guilty. It was Emily's mortal shyness that made her extract such a distressing vow. I'm grateful you couldn't bring yourself to fulfill it. Those poems were Emily's children and it's our duty to care for them."

Her dark eyes were warm and glinting with tears. Her love for Emily was all over her face. I thought of all the notes I'd passed between the two of them and how often I'd come on them with their heads bent together in the Northwest Passage. I knew they loved each other but I told myself it was because they were sisters-in-law. Now I saw it was something more—something fierce and stubborn and lively as fire.

"Thank you, ma'am," I said. I saw Mattie's eyes were red. Seemed my tears had started her own. "Would either of you be wanting some gingerbread?" I asked. "I made it fresh yesterday. 'Tis Emily's recipe."

That night I dreamed I was weeding the roses in Emily's garden. There were masses of blossoms—pink and red and white and gold, all bouncing over my head. Below them was a great tangle of weeds—tall leafy ones with yellow undersides and roots like spiders' legs. They were killing the roses and I was frantic to pull every last one. But the faster I pulled, the faster they grew around my fingers.

Then Emily was there. She was holding something out to me so bright I couldn't make out what it was.

"Emily?" I took my hands out of the dirt and wiped them on the grass.

"This is my letter to the world," Emily said, and I knew from her voice she was smiling. She let go what she was holding and it fluttered down like a bird and settled on my lap. It was a little book, slim and pale and smelling of hyacinths. The cover was white as her dress except for the words *Poems by Emily Dickinson* spelled out in gold letters. Took my breath away, it was so lovely. I picked it up and opened it. The pages were warm under my fingers. When I looked up Emily was gone.

The dream woke me with such a start, I sat up straight in my bed. My heart pounded and my ears rang. It was dark but I got up and went to the window. It was a clear night with the Milky Way glistening and a thin slice of moon caught in the trees. It made me think of the time I'd sat all night with Emily and we'd watched the circus leaving town. A secret between us. So many years ago. And then I remembered how, just a few months back, Emily had said a book was a kind of immortality.

I stood a long time at the window, still smelling the roses and feeling the weeds furring along the tips of my fingers. In the dark it seemed like I was even now holding the warm, satiny book, its gold letters winking under my palms. Seeing Emily's smile.

Part VII

Porches

Chapter Thirty-Seven

1916

Word comes in the middle of April the Homestead is sold. No matter I'm reconciled to Reverend Parke living there, I feel a pang that it no longer belongs to a Dickinson. But I keep the feeling to myself, and when folks ask, I tell them the rector will be taking good care of the dear old place. Mostly I'm grateful Mattie D has the means now to live her own life and look after Emily's poems and letters.

Two weeks go by and there's no sign of Reverend Parke moving in. The Homestead still stands empty in the spring rain and sun with the only sign of life the slow-greening grass. I wonder if Emily's crocuses came up this year, if they're blooming by the back door, all bright and new. "Don't they remind you of soldiers," she used to ask me, "standing so brave and martial in the cold?" Sure, I couldn't see it then. But now I can't lay eyes on a crocus without thinking of soldiers.

Seems I'm not the only one thinking of soldiers. There's more and more talk of the great war in Europe—my boarders bring it up every time they sit down to a meal. Some are saying America will soon be joining in.

"If they start drafting lads here, it's back to County Cork for me," Dan Casey says. "I'll sign up with the Sinn Féin if it comes to it."

"What do you know about Sinn Féin?" There's a dark side to Martin O'Day—I warrant he knows more than he ought about wicked goings-on.

Dan gives him a quick frown. "I know they're for an independent Ireland," he says. "'Tis enough for me."

Martin shakes his head and puts down his fork. For a minute I'm afraid he might be planning to land a blow on Dan's nose. But he just crosses his arms and leans back in the chair. "Sinn Féin is falling apart, lads. You'd best be joining the Irish Republican Brotherhood if you're after dying for Ireland."

"You don't have to go back to Ireland for that," says Joseph Connor. "You can be joining *Clan na Gael* right here. They're all of them Fenians."

Hearing the word brings up feelings I thought were long gone. For a minute seems like Patrick himself has walked in the door. "All right, lads," I say. "That'll be enough fighting talk today. If you've nothing cheery to say, best tend to your eating."

They are all of them good lads and eager to be pleasing me. And from the looks on their faces, I'm guessing they're as glad as myself to stop talking of Fenians.

The next day is grand with wind and sun and leaves budding out on the trees. Nell has promised to help make tonight's supper, so I take my time doing the afternoon errands. I'm on my way home from Murphy's Drugstore with my basket on my arm when who should bump into me but Mabel Todd herself? She's coming out of the jewelry store, not looking where she's going, and jolts me hard with her elbow. I rock back a bit. Though I haven't seen her in years and her hair's gone white, there's no mistaking her—her eyes are big as ever and she has that look on her face like she's the Queen of Amherst in spite of the stutter in her step from the stroke she had a few years ago.

Something twists inside me—a sparking vexation rising from my belly. I flash on the months Vinnie sent me to the Dell to do Mabel's cooking and cleaning so she could be editing Emily's poems. How I witnessed every day the sinning between herself and Austin. How I found Emily's booklets taken apart with the papers and strings strewn all over Mabel's desk. How I saw Mabel had scribbled changes to the verses she didn't like. Puts me in a mood, it does, so instead of going on my way, I step in front of her, bold as a bucket, and say, "Bless me, if it isn't Mabel Todd."

"Maggie," she says, all cool and proper. But the scorn on her face is plain as day. Just makes me crosser.

"Sure, I've not seen you since the trial," I say. "Fine weather to be out and about."

Her eyes go hard and I feel a fizzle of satisfaction. It's plain she remembers the trial that cold March in 1898 when she and Vinnie sued each other over the strip of Dickinson land. I'll never forget the fancy hat she wore in court with its silly white bird wings. Looked a proper fool, to be sure. Vinnie's lawyer made her admit she didn't buy the Dell—Austin gave it to her. He got the truth out of her about Emily too—that Mabel had never laid eyes on her except as a shadow flitting down the Northwest Passage.

I don't look away from her like she wants me to. I know the things she's said about me since the trial—called me a liar and a fool. Said I was a cowardly traitor, a nobody. Just a worthless Irish Paddy.

Didn't find out till later it was my deposition made her lose the case. Testimony I gave a whole year before the trial. All I ever did was answer the questions put to me. Told the truth of what I saw with my own two eyes. Didn't have a choice, for I swore an oath. If Mabel didn't want things to come out, she shouldn't have been doing them. Secrets don't stay hid forever. Instead, she spread her vicious lies all over town.

In front of me, Mabel wrinkles her nose like she can't bear my smell and moves sideways to go past. I take a step at the same time, but it's the wrong direction so I end up blocking her again. Wasn't my intention but now I've done it, I'm not sorry.

"Excuse me," she says in her haughty voice. "You're in my way." She folds her lips so tight her mouth disappears when she hitches herself past me. I watch her sway her way up the street and feel a shudder of pity at the sight. Surprises me, for she's the last person in Amherst I'm wanting to be sorry for. But here I am, feeling tenderhearted.

I walk on down the street, past the Evergreens. Soon as the Homestead looms beyond the hedge, I feel its enchantment come over me again, strong as ever. And then I see the carriage gate standing wide open. Stops me right there on the sidewalk. All the years I've lived in Amherst, it's been closed. Soon as I get close I can see workmen milling around outside the house.

Makes me cross, it does. I was certain Reverend Parke loved the place as it was—didn't he tell me so? But it looks like he's after making changes to the property. I'm feeling as vexed as if he broke a bargain we'd struck.

I head up the drive. Gives me a shiver, surely. It's been years since I stepped on the property but they all vanish in a minute.

As I round the corner I'm half expecting to see Emily herself coming out the back door, carrying her basket of garden tools, so when there's a flash of white at the corner of my eye, I'm not surprised. But it's not Emily—just the old pear tree in full bloom, a cloud of white. Lifts my heart to see it—the pear was always the first tree to bloom at the Homestead and I'm comforted knowing it still is.

It's then one of the workmen spies me. He's carrying a ladder past the old grape trellis and he puts it down and shakes his head at me—it's plain he's wanting me to go. I can see the trellis is collapsing and the barn roof sagging. A sadness comes on me, but I've no time to nurse it, for the lad is glowering at me now. "You're trespassing, ma'am," he calls. "This is private property."

I walk over to him. "Indeed it is. And I'm knowing every inch of it too. Looks to me like it's falling into ruin. I'm guessing you're here to be fixing it."

His eyes go wide and his scowl melts away. "You're Miss Maher." He says it like he's certain, but I can't think how.

"I am," I say. "And who might you be?" Now I'm closer he looks a bit familiar, but I can't place him for the life of me.

"It's Jerry O'Shea," he says, putting his hand on his chest. "Molly's youngest son. Don't you recognize me?"

Soon as he says her name I do, for he has his mother's eyes. Gives me a burn in my own, for my dear friend Molly Ryan passed away eight years ago. I must have seen him at her wake.

"Jerry?" I say. "I'm remembering you as a rascally *spalpeen*. But you've grown into a handsome lad, to be sure."

"You look the same as you always did." His grin couldn't get any wider if it was Heaven's gate itself he was standing before.

"*Wisha*, you'll be turning my head with your blarney," I say. "Now tell me what you and your mates are doing here."

"We're renovating the place before the new owner moves in," he says. "It'll be a challenge too, for he wants it done by July."

"What's he after doing?" Even as I'm asking I'm thinking maybe I don't want to know.

"Ah, it's a long list," says Jerry. "Sandblast off the yellow paint to show the red brick. Raze the barn and build a garage. Take off that boxy room in the front—the one with all the windows. It don't fit with the rest of the house, he says."

"The conservatory?" I feel a hot stone in my chest. I think of all the hours Emily spent there, how happy she was tending her plants. How I'd smell the sweetness of flowers coming off her the rest of the day. I try to picture how the house will look without it, when the bricks are red instead of yellow. How the yard will feel without the barn. "'Tis a pity, surely," I say. I feel like the rector's betrayed me, though in truth he made no promises. I hope it won't be too distressing for Mattie D. She's invited me to tea next week and I'm certain we'll be talking about it. Maybe I'll bring her another loaf of gingerbread.

"I wonder if I could take a peek inside," I say. I wait while he's studying the idea. Likely makes him uneasy, for it's surely against the rules. "Just for a minute," I add, the need boiling up in me. Urgent. Hard.

Most lads admire a bold woman, no matter her age. So I'm not surprised he says he'll let me have a quick peek inside the Homestead. He even promises to guard the back door so nobody will be stopping me. He's a good lad, Jerry is. A credit to his mam.

Stepping over the doorsill sets me remembering my first time doing it, that snowy morning near fifty years ago. It's as if the smell of split wood is in my nose again and I can see pots stacked in the sink waiting for their washing. I stand still a minute, letting the place fold around me. There's a sweet, melty feeling in me—like warm honey filling my chest.

After a minute I walk through to the kitchen. My footsteps sound quare, echoing off the bare walls. Most everything's been cleared out. The missing cupboards have left dark patches on the floor and the big worktable is gone. There's nothing at all on the pantry shelves—not even a broken plate. The windowsills are empty of everything but dust. I run my finger along the one Emily liked to look out and it comes up dark gray.

I promised Jerry I'd hurry but every step is heavy and slow. The Northwest Passage is shadowy as it ever was. I stumble twice for no reason—like I'm tripping over things that aren't there. I keep stopping, listening for echoes and stirrings—listening for ghosts. But there's no sound except myself.

The front hall is fringed with light and I see water stains over the front door and a long smudge running down the wallpaper. I wonder how many times I opened that door to strangers I then turned away. For Emily's sake.

The parlor's bare—the carpets and drapes gone. All the paintings taken off the walls. The only thing left is a blue and white vase on the front windowsill. It isn't one I've seen—it must belong to one of the tenants—and it's covered in dust. When I pick it up I see why it was left. There's a crack running from lip to base. A knot rises in my throat and I put the vase back on the sill, thinking of the broken things folks leave behind when they move on.

In the library the Squire's desk is gone and the shelves are empty of books. Likely the books and furniture are stacked somewhere in the Evergreens. But it feels like the room's been defiled. I go through into the conservatory, where those shelves are empty too. All that's left of Emily's plants is a faint smell of mold and dust.

Upstairs, I look into my old room and there's my bed in the corner, topped with its thin mattress. Didn't expect that, surely. Whoever cleared out the place must have thought it as useless as the cracked vase. I sit on it for a bit. It's lumpy as it ever was, but it comforts me some. I look out the window, see the apple trees are starting to bud. There's a scatter of purple underneath and I smile—Emily's violets and wild hyacinths, surely. A couple of workmen are walking along the hedge behind the fence. At the end of the orchard, they turn and one of the lads sweeps his arm toward the garden. The other one's nodding and pointing to the house. Feels like he's pointing right at myself. Gives me a shiver, it does. Makes me feel like a ghost.

I save Emily's room for last. In truth, I'm shaking when I open her door. Don't know what I'm expecting to find, but it's bare as the rest. Only thing makes me think of herself is the wallpaper—all those roses rioting up the wall.

I stand in the middle of her room for a long time, watching the light slide into the trees west of the house. Tears prickle but I still stand listening, waiting for something that doesn't come.

Don't know how long it is before I hear footsteps in the hall below and come back to myself. Likely it's Jerry, come looking for me. I turn and leave Emily's room, closing the door soft and slow behind me. The hollow sound telling me she's gone.

I have every intention of going down. Last thing I want is to get Jerry in trouble. But right in front of me are the stairs to the attic, and when I look up, I think I'm seeing something move at the top of them. A shadow—and then a sound, soft as a whisper. The skin on my back is swarming with gooseflesh, but next thing I know, my feet are carrying me up all on their own.

There's not much light here—just what sifts in from the gable windows on the east and west. There are a few crates under the eaves and a big steamer trunk. The place smells of dust. In all my years with the Dickinsons I was only up here a dozen times. Once when Mother Dickinson asked me to fetch an old basket for a picnic. Another time when I was chasing one of Vinnie's cats. Soon as I remember that, I know it wasn't a ghost drew me up here, but a cat. Don't know where it's got to now, or how it found its way into the house, but every cat I ever knew had secrets.

I take a look around, walk the length of the attic and back again, but there's no sign of the cat. I'm about to leave when something makes me turn and look behind me. God help me, I don't know why, but without even thinking I start up the stairway that goes to the cupola. Something's drawing me—as if a cord is stretching from my heart to the tiny room at the top.

I step up and into the cupola, holding the newel post to steady myself. The place is just as I remembered—silent and light struck. The old chair is still sitting square in the middle. And for the first time since I walked in the back door, I feel Emily is near.

I take a deep breath and let it out slow. After a minute I walk around to look out every window. It's just a step and a turn to move from one pair to the next. I look at the Homestead lawn sloping away from the house—the orchard and what's left of Emily's garden. I see the hat factory chimneys and the Pelham hills—at the next window the barn and the grand houses beyond that the College bought on Lessey Street. There's a flash of gray and white when a bird flickers by. It's not till I turn to face the west windows that I see it. Hanging from a nail driven into the sash and glowing in the light. The rosary I gave Emily.

Near knocks me to the floor, the sight of it. There's a sharp buzzing in my ears. I sink down on the chair, for I'm shaking too much to stand. Don't know how long it is before I hear Jerry calling my name.

I get up slow. Feels like I'm standing in a crown of light. I draw the rosary off its nail and tuck it in the pocket of my skirt.

It's just after four when I get back to my house.

Inside it's quiet, with the still, roomy feel a woman's home has when she's the only one in it. *Spacious*, Emily called it. I close the door behind me and listen for the click of the latch like Emily did when she shut herself in her room. For years I didn't understand why she took pleasure in shunning the world—thought it was a kind of sin. Took owning my own home for me to know she wasn't shutting out anything at all, for she carried every bit of life in with her.

She had a spacious heart, Emily did.

In the kitchen, I wet the tea for myself and sit at the table by the window where the afternoon sun's coming in. Birds are singing their supper songs in the trees. It was Emily's favorite time of day, an hour before sunset, when the air turns gold.

"Do you see how the world shines?" she'd ask me. "How everything in it is alive?"

In truth, I didn't see it then. But now it's plain as the tea in my cup. I wish I'd thought to tell her she was shining too. It's what she did with her poems—reflecting the brightness she saw back to the rest of us. And truth be told, I did my own shining by saving her poems and setting them where Vinnie would find them.

I remember something Emily said not long before she died. It was an afternoon like this, with the sun coming in. I was dusting her room and she was telling me about Carlo, the dog her father gave her when she was young. How she took him on long walks in the countryside. How he made her feel safe. "There was never a more steadfast companion," she said. "When he died the world broke to pieces."

Across the room, I felt her sorrow. "We had dogs on the farm," I said. "My favorite was Rory. He went everywhere with me, even to school. He'd lie down outside the gate till lessons were done. Never saw such patience. I loved that dog, surely." I wiped the heavy sandglass on her mantel and slid it over so I could run my rag underneath. "Sometimes I remember Rory and myself running across the upper field—the memory so sharp I can smell the green of Tipperary itself. Feels like I'm still there and we could run forever."

"Yes," she said softly. She was quiet a minute. Then she said, "Eternity is behind us and there's immortality to come. But for now we have the bliss of memory."

I stopped my dusting and looked at her. She was sitting up, hugging her knees in that gold afternoon light. Her smile was dazzling. There was nothing to be said to that. I was overcome by love.

I take the rosary out of my pocket and hold it in my hand. The horn beads wink and shine at me—like amber pearls.

I finish the last of my tea, though it's gone cold while I've been musing. Soon Nell will be here. She'll be telling me about her day and asking about mine. I'll talk a bit about my errands in town and how the boarders are all worked up over Fenians and a rising in Ireland. Maybe I'll tell her about seeing my friend Molly's son. I'm thinking I won't say anything about going inside the Homestead. Some things are best cradled in the heart.

I pour myself another cup of tea. Maybe I'll take it out to the porch and sit there till Nell comes. The sun will be slanting across my rocking chair, making a pool of warm light.

I open the door and step outside.

Author's Note

Every novel has a history. *Emily's House* began more than seven years ago with a curiosity about Emily Dickinson. Like so many, I was drawn to her poetry and fascinated by her eccentric and reclusive habits. I knew focusing a novel on such an intriguing and unusual character would be challenging. But one of the pleasures of writing I enjoy most is discovering story lines and working out the puzzles of a character's experience. So I eagerly dug into researching her life and the lives of her friends and family. I read everything about the poet and her world I could get my hands on. It began to look like Emily was the still center in a swirling family drama, especially after Mabel Loomis Todd's arrival in Amherst.

But then I read Aífe Murray's *Maid as Muse* and encountered Margaret Maher. I knew right away I'd found my protagonist. Margaret's pivotal role in sharing Dickinson's poetry with the world inspired me to give her a voice and a story. From that point on, I was committed. I found her tone early and she quickly emerged as the energetic, ambitious woman Emily described as "wild and warm and mighty."

The real-life Margaret Maher was born in 1841 in County Tipperary, Ireland. As a child, she lived through the Irish potato famine, and as an adult, she was companion and confidante to the woman whom many consider America's greatest poet. Her story is an immigrant's story of overcoming obstacles through determination, perseverance, and strength of character. One can only be awed by the scope of her impact, and the impact of others like her, on the American story.

While there's a wealth of information on Emily's life, as well as numerous theories about her motivations and intentions, Margaret's experience during the Dickinson years is not well documented. I've taken the liberty of giving her a vibrant life apart from her service to the Dickinson family, including an interest in Irish Home Rule, a passion common to many Irish Americans in the last decades of the nineteenth century.

As in my previous novels, most of the major characters are based on real people. An exception here is Patrick Quinn. The cryptic comment in one of Emily's letters that "courageous Maggie is not yet caught in the snares of Patrick" prompted me to create a man in Margaret's life. His story and his relationship with Margaret are entirely my invention. However, I have based his life on the Irish immigrant experience of that time, including the long struggle for Home Rule, the Fenian raids on Canada, and the establishment of the Brooklyn Dynamite School.

Until recently, the primary source for most biographies of Dickinson has been the papers of Mabel Loomis Todd. This has resulted in what I believe is a distorted portrayal of Emily's sister-in-law, Sue Dickinson, and the near complete erasure of Margaret's presence and role. Mabel never met Emily face-to-face and, because of her long affair with Austin Dickinson, had reason to disparage Sue's reputation and importance in Emily's life. She also resented Margaret's role in exposing the affair through a legal deposition, and verbally belittled her later in life.

To balance this bias, I relied on the reminiscences of Emily's niece, Martha Dickinson Bianchi. It was Martha who wrote the eyewitness account of Margaret's agitation over Emily's order to burn the poems following her death.

In her 1897 deposition, Margaret testified under oath that the booklets (labeled *fascicles* by Mabel) were hidden in her trunk. The fact that Vinnie is the one so often credited with "finding" the poems inspired the idea that Margaret moved them to a place where Vinnie could find them. Before this "discovery" no one in the family, with the possible exception of Sue, knew the extent of Emily's writing.

After Emily's death, Vinnie became fixated on getting the poems published. She first turned them over to Sue for editing, but grew impatient with her sister-in-law's slow progress. She then gave them to Mabel, who transcribed and edited them with Thomas Wentworth Higginson. Three volumes were published between 1890 and 1896, and their popularity led to Mabel's lectures on Emily and her work.

In the novel, Margaret briefly refers to working at the Dell while Mabel transcribed Emily's poems. Margaret did this work (at Vinnie's instruction) in addition to her work at the Homestead. She received no compensation beyond her regular wages. I can only assume that she agreed to do it out of a personal desire to shepherd the poems into print. During this time she was eyewitness to the ongoing affair between Mabel and Austin, details of which she testified to in her deposition.

Margaret worked for the Dickinsons for thirteen years after Emily died, but it appears that she left Amherst for a year during that period. There's no documented evidence of her reasons for leaving or of where she went but I've imagined that she spent time visiting her brother on the West Coast.

In 1896 the relationship between Vinnie and Mabel soured to the point of litigation. At issue was a parcel of land Mabel claimed Austin had promised her. After his death in 1895, Vinnie had signed papers agreeing to the transaction, but later she asserted Mabel had tricked her into it. Vinnie brought a lawsuit and Mabel countersued. Margaret was deposed in May 1897 and her testimony revealed Austin and Mabel's affair, which resulted in the collapse of Mabel's case.

The events in the 1916 chapters are largely fictional. Beyond the fact that Margaret referred to the Homestead as "the dear old place," I have no documentation of the emotional impact the house's sale might have had on her, let alone any evidence that she actively opposed it. The house remained in the Parke family until 1965, when it was sold to the Trustees of Amherst College and used as faculty housing for several years. It is now a museum and is being painstakingly restored to appear as it did during Emily's lifetime.

Following Vinnie's death, Margaret ran her own boarding-house in Kelley Square for many years. She died in Amherst in 1924 and is buried in St. Mary's Cemetery in Northampton, Massachusetts, with her parents and brother.

Every novel is ultimately the author's story. In taking on Margaret's voice and perspective, I've expanded my understanding of the United States in a tumultuous time and deepened my awareness of those among us who are often overlooked. And, like my protagonist, I've completely fallen under Emily's spell, dazzled by her brilliant mind, astonishing talent, and transcendent spirit.

Acknowledgments

My wholehearted thanks to:

Susan Ramer, agent extraordinaire. Thank you for your tenacious interest in my work and long-term support of my writing career. Thanks for your diligence and business expertise, for never settling for mediocrity over excellence, for promptly answering my many questions, for helping me grow as a writer, and for so often nudging me in the right direction. Thanks especially for your directness and honesty, and the assurance that I can always rely on you to tell me the truth.

Margarite Landry, longtime friend, fellow fiction writer, and first reader. Thank you for your many writing insights, unflagging encouragement, and countless conversations over the years, and for so often gladdening my heart with your wonderful sense of humor.

Ina Anderson, poet, friend, and first reader. Thank you for your generous and warmhearted camaraderie and for your endless curiosity about this novel, which regularly revitalized my passion for the work.

Emma Wunsch, Andi Diehn, Tamar Schreibman, Susan Kaplan Carlton, Kimberly Kol, Becca Yuan, Sarah Dickenson Snyder, and Patricia Baird Greene, fellow writers in the Upper

Valley Fiction Collective. Thanks for your straightforward feedback, invigorating discussions, and supportive friendship.

Amanda Bergeron, editor and fellow native New Englander. Thank you for your contagious enthusiasm, warm encouragement, and gentle guidance throughout the process of bringing the dream of this novel to fruition.

Emily Osborne, art director. Thank you for the brilliantly imagined cover that so beautifully captures the soul of this novel.

Jane Wald, executive director of the Emily Dickinson Museum. Thank you for generously making time in your busy schedule to answer my questions, and for giving me a peek into the servants' quarters in the Dickinson Homestead.

And especially and always, thanks to Duane, my husband and soul mate. Sharing married life with a writer for more than fifty years is not for the fainthearted. Thank you for your astute insights, untiring patience, calming reassurance, and—most of all—for your unconditional love.

Emily's House

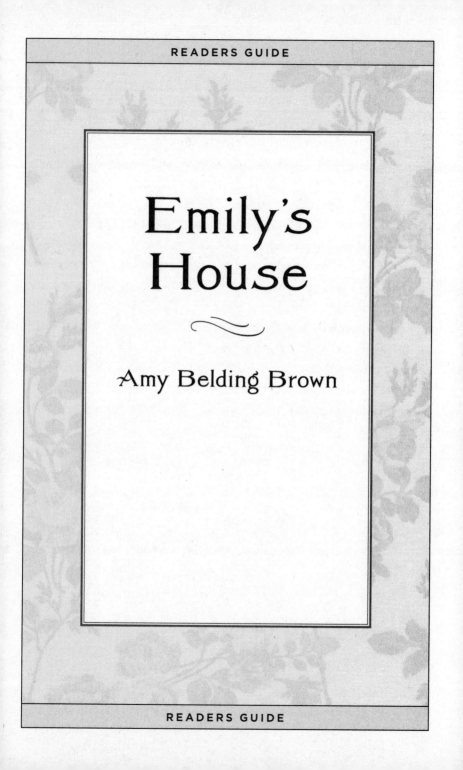

Amy Belding Brown

Further Historical Notes from Amy Belding Brown

My Take on Emily Dickinson

There are dozens of interpretations of Emily Dickinson, as evidenced in the many biographies and papers about her life. In popular culture, she's been portrayed as psychologically repressed and painfully shy, or—more recently—as boldly unconventional and even subversive. In her own day, she was labeled "the Myth of Amherst," and in my view, her personality and motivations remain frustratingly elusive. I have come to believe this mystery was one she intentionally constructed, compounded by her family's desire after her death to protect the family reputation through obfuscation and misdirection.

The Dickinsons were one of the most prestigious families in Amherst. Emily's father went to great lengths to shelter his family, particularly his eldest daughter. He regarded her as sickly and pulled her out of Mount Holyoke Seminary after she completed only one year. Yet, as a young woman, Emily was active in the town's social scene, attending parties, concerts, and festivals. At that time, the Dickinsons were living in a large home on North Pleasant Street, next to the cemetery that would eventually become her final resting place.

In 1855, the Dickinsons moved to the newly renovated Homestead on Main Street, a relocation that was an unwelcome change for both Emily and her mother. Emily's letters suggest that sometime in the next five or six years she may have suffered some personal adversity. Emily's biographies are filled with speculation about this crisis, proposing everything from rejection by a suitor to the onset of epilepsy. Whatever the reason, she became gradually more reclusive. There's no way to know for sure why she secluded herself or what prompted her strange habit of wearing white most of the time.

After her death, her family made vague references to an unnamed lover. Family members passed off her eccentric behavior as simply Emily being Emily. It's possible she suffered from panic attacks and agoraphobia. Or she might simply have been protecting her privacy to concentrate on her poetry. Similarly, she might have adopted wearing white because it somehow helped with her eye problems or just because she liked the way she felt wearing it.

Both her letters and actions suggest that Emily enjoyed posing as an eccentric. She seems to have meticulously curated the image she presented to friends and relatives, adjusting her words and behavior to her particular audience. Dickinson's poems are frequently cited, with slim supporting evidence, as a record of her personal experience. But Elizabeth Phillips, in her book *Persona and Performance*, suggests that Dickinson combined her extensive reading, personal observations, and brilliant imagination as frames of reference for her poetry. I'm inclined to agree.

The Dickinson-Todd Feud

I first learned about the feud between the Dickinson and Todd families when I started reading in-depth accounts of Emily Dickinson's life. I was surprised and a bit scandalized. Austin Dickinson's affair with Mabel Todd seemed like it belonged in a steamy romance novel rather than in a biography of America's greatest poet. Yet the more I researched, the more twists and turns the story took, creating a controversy between contentious camps that continues today. The crux of the dispute was control of the narrative of Emily Dickinson's life and literary legacy.

When the poems came into Vinnie's possession, she was determined to get them published. Knowing her sister-in-law's familiarity with Emily's work, she gave them to Sue Dickinson, but soon grew impatient with her progress. She then handed them to Mabel Todd, who knew the publishing world and was eager to help. Mabel edited the poems to conform to nineteenth-century conventions, changing punctuation, spelling, and even some words. During this period, Margaret temporarily replaced Mabel's maid, working part-time at the Dell, the large home Austin had bought and landscaped for Mabel. There Margaret witnessed not only Mabel's work on the poems but also her frequent assignations with Austin.

The first volumes of poems were critically and financially successful. Vinnie held the copyrights and received the majority share of royalties. According to Mabel, Austin, in an attempt to "make things a little more even" on her behalf, wanted to give Mabel a strip of the Dickinson meadow adjacent to the Dell. However, he never actually deeded the property to her.

When Austin died, Mabel responded by publicly acting the part of a grieving widow, behavior that not only offended Sue and her children but Vinnie as well. When Mabel pressed Vinnie to make good on Austin's wish, she refused. Mabel continued to pressure her, using work on the third volume of poetry as leverage. When the book was near completion, she asked Vinnie to deed her the strip of land as a gesture of gratitude. Vinnie verbally agreed to the transaction. But when Vinnie's business adviser learned of this, he warned her not to sign any papers without his knowledge. What happened next has been given conflicting interpretations, depending on which camp the writer is in.

Shortly before Mabel left with her husband on a trip to Japan, she and a Northampton lawyer visited Vinnie one evening at the Homestead. In Julie Dobrow's account in *After Emily*, Vinnie agreed to sign the papers but wanted to do so under cover of darkness to avoid inciting Sue's anger. She asked that Mabel bring a lawyer as a witness. But according to Lyndall Gordon, author of *Lives Like Loaded Guns*, Vinnie was tricked into signing the deed. Mabel brought the lawyer along without warning Vinnie, telling her he was interested in Emily's poetry. During a moment when Vinnie was showing off the family china, Mabel gave her the papers and secured her signature.

It was Margaret who overheard gossip at the post office about the deed transfer and told her mistress. Vinnie soon discovered what she hadn't read—the terms of the deed prohibited her niece and nephew from making claims on the land. Her adviser insisted she contest the deed.

In November 1896, Vinnie filed suit against the Todds. The next spring Margaret was questioned, and in her deposition, she revealed the true nature of Mabel's relationship with Austin. Though the deposition was never read in court, both parties were aware of how seriously it damaged the defense's case.

The trial opened on March 1, 1898. Vinnie was first on the witness stand, answering questions with composure and conviction. When it was Mabel's turn, she claimed she knew Emily well and that the poet had asked her to edit the poems. Under cross-examination, she was forced to admit that she had never seen nor spoken to Emily. Bit by bit Vinnie's lawyers shredded Mabel's defense.

The trial was closely followed in the press, with readers taking sides in a bitter divide. The *Hartford Courant* reported that "society circles are agog" and the proceedings were "likely to furnish gossip for afternoon tea in the Connecticut Valley for a long time to come." It was a prescient prediction, for the stories surrounding that trial are still sources of controversy.

In April, the judge delivered his verdict—the deed was void. The Todds appealed to the state Supreme Court, which upheld the lower court's verdict. After she lost the case, Mabel refused to have anything more to do with the Dickinsons. She wrote in her diary that Margaret was a liar and had been coached by Vinnie. Instead of returning the Dickinson papers, she locked them away in a chest, where they remained untouched for decades.

In 1950, Emily's heirs donated the family's large collection of manuscripts and furnishings to Harvard University. Six years later, Mabel Todd's daughter, Millicent, gave Todd's collection to Amherst College. In 1965, the college purchased the Homestead from the Parke family, and took ownership of the Evergreens in 2003. The two buildings now form the Emily Dickinson Museum.

But Emily Dickinson's estate remains divided to this day.

Questions for Discussion

1. Patrick Quinn plays a major role in Margaret's self-discovery as she begins to embrace her heritage but he also drives her away from her roots with some with his more radical ideas for Ireland. How would her life (and identity) be different if Patrick Quinn never knocked on the kitchen door? Would she have continued to seek out her Irish culture?

2. Though she tried not to let it show, why did Margaret care so much about the Dickinson family's opinion of her?

3. Put yourself in Margaret's shoes—would you have burned the poems? Do you think Margaret ever regretted sharing Emily's work, especially after Mabel's meddling in their publication was revealed?

4. Why is it so important to Margaret that she own and run a boardinghouse lodging Irish tenants?

5. As the Dickinsons' maid, Margaret witnesses the various romantic relationships that take place, including Emily's infatuation with Judge Lord and Austin's affair with Mabel, and Vinnie's fascination with everyone else's trysts. How did the Dickinsons' personal lives affect how Margaret viewed her own love life? Why do you think Margaret never married?

6. Before reading this novel, what did you know of Emily Dickinson's life? Did you learn anything new about her life, family, or poetry that struck you?

7. The title of this novel refers to the Dickinsons' beautiful Homestead, designated a National Historic Landmark in 1963 and recently restored by the Emily Dickinson Museum. What role does the Homestead play in the novel? How does physical space play into Emily and Margaret's connection?

8. When Tommy comes back to Amherst, Margaret and Mary are overjoyed to see their brother. What was Margaret's reaction when Tommy told her that his letter instructing her to stay in Amherst was the Squire's idea? Why did the Squire trick Margaret into staying with the Dickinson family instead of traveling West? Could you ever have forgiven him? What does Margaret mean by "life was inventing [her]"?

9. Mattie D., or Madame Bianchi, was left in the lurch by her husband, which forced her to sell the Homestead. When he ran off to Europe, she continued to send him money until she had nothing left. Margaret's initial reaction is to blame Mattie D. for the sale of the Homestead. What does this say about the position of women in the early twentieth century?

10. According to the Emily Dickinson Museum website, "Bianchi's will stipulated that, should [the inheritor or their family] ever choose not to live in the house, the Evergreens should be torn down rather than sold to another owner." Luckily, the property, like Emily's poems, was saved from this fate and now belongs to the Trustees of Amherst College as part of the Emily Dickinson Museum. Discuss possible reasons why the Dickinsons would insist on destroying their legacies. Pride? Sentimentality? Embarrassment? Why has someone intervened each time?

Recommended books for readers of *Emily's House*

Aífe Murray, *Maid as Muse: How Servants Changed Emily Dickinson's Life and Language* (Durham, NH: University of New Hampshire Press, 2009).
   This book is where I first met Margaret Maher, the protagonist of *Emily's House*. A fascinating and well-written survey of the people who worked for the Dickinson family in Amherst.

Cristanne Miller, ed., *Emily Dickinson's Poems as She Preserved Them* (Cambridge, MA: Belknap Press, 2016).
   Out of the many collections of Emily Dickinson's poems, this is my favorite. It's comprehensive while offering a wealth of information. Importantly, the poems are ordered as Emily herself arranged them in the booklets Margaret Maher hid in her trunk.

Jerome Charyn, *A Loaded Gun: Emily Dickinson for the 21st Century* (New York: Bellevue Literary Press, 2016).
   A new look at Emily Dickinson's mythology and some of the most interesting aspects of her life, including a section on Margaret Maher.

Martha Dickinson Bianchi, *Emily Dickinson Face to Face* (Boston: Houghton Mifflin Co., 1932).
   Martha Dickinson's biography of her famous aunt, which features vivid scenes, including the one in which Margaret Maher reveals that Emily asked her to burn the poems after her death.

Lyndall Gordon, *Lives Like Loaded Guns: Emily Dickinson and Her Family's Feuds* (New York: Penguin Books, 2010).
   A riveting biography of Emily Dickinson and her family, focusing on the second half of her life and the Dickinson-Todd drama that followed her death.

Margaret Lynch-Brennan, *The Irish Bridget: Irish Immigrant Women in Domestic Service in America, 1840–1930* (Syracuse, NY: Syracuse University Press, 2009).

   An overview of the experience of Irish women who emigrated to America to work as domestic servants in the nineteenth century, this book offers important insights into Margaret Maher's day-to-day life as Emily Dickinson's maid.

Marta McDowell, *Emily Dickinson's Gardening Life* (Portland, OR: Timber Press, 2019).

   A delightful introduction to the flowers and plants in Emily Dickinson's garden, presented with descriptions that bring to life her daily surroundings at the Homestead.

Paola Kaufmann, *The Sister: A Novel of Emily Dickinson* (New York: Rookery Press, 2007).

   Of the many treatments of Emily Dickinson in fiction, this little-known novel is my favorite. First published in Spanish as *La Hermana*, it's a beautifully crafted and well-researched book that offers an intimate view of the Dickinson family through Lavinia Dickinson's eyes.

About the Author

Amy Belding Brown is the author of historical novels including *USA Today* bestseller *Flight of the Sparrow* and *Mr. Emerson's Wife*. A New England history enthusiast, Amy was infused at an early age with the region's outlook and values. A graduate of Bates College in Lewiston, Maine, she received her MFA from Vermont College and now lives in rural Vermont with her husband, a UCC minister and spiritual director.

CONNECT ONLINE

AmyBeldingBrown.net